Readers love *Ash and Echoes* by AUGUST LI

Readers love *Iron and Ether*
by AUGUST LI

"I have to recommend this story if you love high fantasy, epic storylines, fantastic characters… and an ending that lets you know there is still more to come."
—MM Good Book Reviews

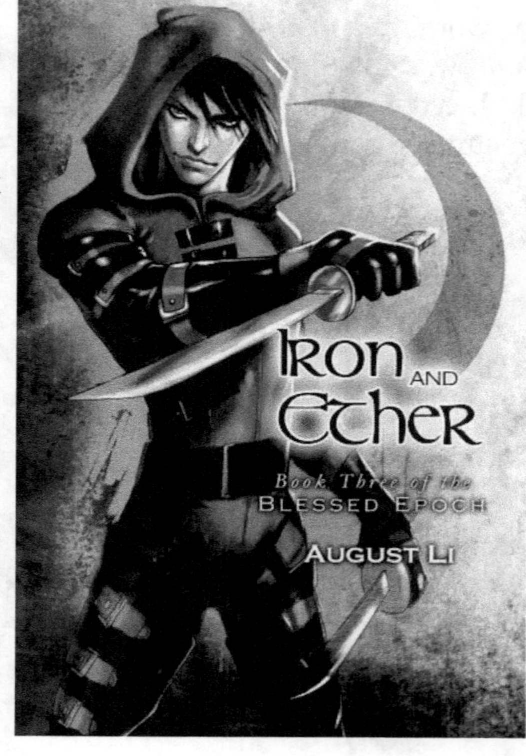

"Thanks, Augusta, for a heart-rending, intense, and uplifting experience."
—Rainbow Book Reviews

"*Iron and Ether* will appeal to those who love a richly detailed fantasy romance."

—Joyfully Reviewed

By AUGUST LI

BLESSED EPOCH
Ash and Echoes
Ice and Embers
Iron and Ether
Cairn and Covenant
Calling and Cull

Published by DSP PUBLICATIONS
www.dsppublications.com

Calling

AND

Cull

AUGUST LI

DSP PUBLICATIONS

Published by
DSP Publications

5032 Capital Circle SW, Suite 2, PMB# 279, Tallahassee, FL 32305-7886 USA
www.dsppublications.com

ISBN: 978-1-63477-432-1
Digital ISBN: 978-1-63477-433-8
Library of Congress Control Number: 2016902733
Published September 2016
v. 1.0

Printed in the Uni(∞) States of America

This paper meets the requirements of
ANSI/NISO Z39.48-1992 (Permanence of Paper).

When everything else crashes into the sea
and is washed away, there is still hope.
This book is dedicated to those who refuse to abandon
hope no matter how insurmountable the odds may seem.

Glossary

Abode of Shades—The realm of the Cast-Down, the unworthy dead, and all those rejected by the goddesses.

Amarzio, Amarzia—An Esperon term of endearment: "my greatest love." Male and female, respectively.

Arbek—A group of nomads wandering the deserts between Johmatran city-states. A unique culture with their own customs, they are revered craftspeople and do not share in the religion or culture of the city-states.

Bairn—The second-highest title of nobility in Selindria, after "valen."

Baska—An obscenity in a language dead to all but the Order of the Crimson Scythe.

Cast-Down—A term used to refer to those gods and goddesses disowned by the Thirteen because of their wickedness. Most pious Selindrians will not speak of them. In some rare cases, a person can be referred to as Cast-Down.

Emiri—An ethnic group, or possibly a completely different race of people, who arrived in Selindria about 150 years ago. Their name is derived from *Emir*, the word for the sea in their language. Emiri have no formal homeland and are expert mariners. Their culture and values are quite different from that of Selindrians, and this leads to many misunderstandings.

Eru—The Emiri word for "wind."

Espero—A large and wealthy island nation to the southeast of Selindria, best known for the high population of mages and the arcane university there.

Estrella Lake—A huge freshwater lake in the northernmost corner of

Selindria. Aside from providing most of the nation's water, it has a religious significance, is surrounded by shrines and temples, and is often visited by those on spiritual pilgrimages.

Everdale—A fertile valenny near the center of Selindria, which provides most of the kingdom's food, and sister province to Merryvale.

Eyrle—The third highest title of nobility in Selindria, after "bairn."

Fane—A legendary mage-emperor who ruled over a period of unimaginable peace and prosperity eons ago. Eventually he demanded his people worship him instead of the goddesses, and the ensuing war destroyed the known world. No one knows if Fane ever actually existed, but his story is told as a cautionary tale and given as the reason mages are forbidden to rule.

Farang phreet—The Arbek word for the winged and horned creatures living in the most remote corners of the desert. The Arbek consider these beings protectors, but they are as fickle as they are powerful.

Gaeltheon—A powerful nation to the east of Selindria, across the Kanda River, almost equal in size and wealth.

Kahlka—A specialized servant who satisfies the sexual needs of a Johmatran aristocrat. This prestigious position requires the kahlka to remain pure and untouched by anyone else.

Kanda River—An enormous river separating Gaeltheon and Selindria. The Kanda is fed by Estrella Lake and considered holy by association.

Kifi—permanent ink applied beneath the skin by Emiri seafarers.

Lapir Mountains—A huge, impassable mountain range marking the eastern border of Gaeltheon. No one has crossed them in centuries, and what lies on the other side is a subject of speculation.

Lockhaven—An ancient valenny, ruled by the L'Estrella family for as long as anyone can remember. Because it houses the sacred Estrella Lake, Lockhaven is highly respected throughout Selindria.

Meritage—The oldest and largest city in Selindria. Meritage is a port along the Kanda River, and while it is held by the Selindrian monarch, the territory around it is unstable and ruled by barbarians and warlords.

Merryvale—A fertile plain, sister province to Everdale.

Mir—An Emiri ship's captain.

Mu-bo—A spicy Emiri dish made from shellfish.

Muri-ku—A very potent Emiri beverage made from fermented sea plants.

Narxium—A tree producing a fatally poisonous sap. It grows only in the Forest of Elwyd.

Order of the Crimson Scythe—A legendary and unstoppable cult of assassins. Thalil is their patron. While many people doubt the existence of the Crimson Scythe, their symbol, the red crescent, is still the most feared icon in the land. The Crimson Scythe are considered almost supernatural. When they have marked someone for death, that person has no chance of escape.

Selindria—The most powerful kingdom in the known world.

Shagiri—The Emiri word for "death."

Starmont—The highest peak in Selindria, marking the northern edge of Estrella Lake. In the past, many Selindrians believed the goddesses resided atop Starmont, but that belief has been abandoned by all but the most superstitious.

Syrai—The Emiri word for "friend," used to express a wide variety of relationships from casual acquaintance to intimate partner.

Tam—The lowest title of nobility in Selindria as well as a common expression of respect, similar to "sir."

Thalil—A very powerful Cast-Down god associated with seduction, subterfuge, murder, and deceit. He is the patron god of assassins, particularly the Order of the Crimson Scythe. Thalil, usually portrayed as a beautiful youth, is also associated with male beauty and homoerotic love. The Thirteen Goddesses forbid his name from being spoken, and his worship is punishable by death. Thalil is known by many epithets, some of which are: He Who Stands Just Out of Sight, The One You See at the Last, The Whisper Heard Too Late, The Dark One, and The Invisible Blade.

The Thirteen, or the Thirteen Goddesses—The main and most important deities of Selindria and Gaeltheon. They have many sons and daughters, both benevolent and Cast-Down. They are sometimes referred to as the Sisters. Each goddess presides over a month, or moon, of the year.

Tsubik—The spiritual leader of an Arbek band, usually female and one of the few who can safely communicate with the farang phreet.

Valen—The highest title of nobility in Selindria, second only to the royal family. Valens rule large holds of land known as valennies.

Yu-me—The Emiri word for hope.

THE GODDESSES AND MONTHS

Both Selindria and Gaeltheon observe a thirteen-month lunar calendar. Each month, or moon, is presided over by one of the Thirteen Goddesses:

Fayelle, ruler of the first month—A virgin goddess of purity. While compassionate, she is a very demanding goddess who expects perfection from her devotees.

Sarmine, ruler of the second month—The goddess of romantic love and marriage. Most weddings take place during Sarmine's Moon.

Mother Goddess, ruler of the third month—The only goddess without a name, she is the matron of all living things. Her month is a time of devotion and celebration. The Mother Goddess is said to love all her creations, even the Cast-Down.

Myint, ruler of the fourth month—The goddess of warfare, battle, weaponsmiths, armorers, and martial arts. She is the patron goddess of all knights.

Diarana, ruler of the fifth month—The goddess of travel and transition. She is the patron of children coming of age. Certain worshippers of Diarana maintain that the goddess loves and protects men and women who favor the clothing of the opposite gender. This belief is not widely accepted.

Vestrafori, ruler of the sixth month—The goddess of truth and justice, protector of the blind and mute. Vestrafori's priestesses conduct all legal proceedings in Selindria and Gaeltheon, and their verdicts are absolute.

Laud, ruler of the seventh month—A mysterious goddess associated with fate, the passage of time, and abstract concepts. Her devotees live hermitic lives of deprivation and contemplation.

Jelsyn, ruler of the eighth month—The goddess of artisans and merchants. She adores handmade items, particularly woven cloth. Jelsyn is also said to protect the poor.

Berris, ruler of the ninth month—The goddess of farming, plenty, and the harvest. Her festival is one of the most joyous occasions of the year.

Ix, ruler of the tenth month—The goddess of the wilds and protector of forests and animals. Ix is well-known to favor those who follow instinct over reason. Ix is also associated with the moon.

Strella, ruler of the eleventh month—The goddess of the sun, stars, and weather, Strella is also a liaison between humans and the goddesses. She carries prayers to the goddesses and guides the worthy dead to their rest.

Illira, ruler of the twelfth month—The goddess of music, poetry, history, and communication. She is the patron of all storytellers and scholars.

Pherara, ruler of the thirteenth month—The goddess of magic and arcane scholarship, and patron goddess of Espero. Most people feel Pherara values only her mages and turns her back on those without the gift. She is not widely worshipped outside Espero.

Lesser Gods and Goddesses

Helwyn—A goddess of solitude and a patron of lonely and abandoned women.

Ilverus—A deity (usually depicted as male) associated with the knowledge of healing elixirs and potions.

Keltha—A daughter of the Mother Goddess, patroness of pregnancy, childbirth, and nursing.

Starmont
Lockhaven
Estrella Lake
Rosecairn
Lapir
Kahladreia
Barrier Bay
The Starlight Bridge
Windwake
Overdale
Mountains
Gaeltheon
Greenclif
Kanda River
Cirion
Johmatra
Selindria
Lelzard
Warden Plains
Meritage
Thulemore
Bay of Blossoms
The Revenant Coast
Alvara
Espero
The Twenty Nine
Pala Reapaza
The Dredges

Chapter One

OCTAVIAN ROSE understood the efficacy of illusion. By casting off his ceremonial golden armor and scarlet cape, the trappings of his station as Bairn of Rosecairn, and replacing them with scuffed leathers and matted furs, he could travel Selindria's roads without distraction, unnoticed and ignored by those he passed. If he had learned one thing, it was that people focused on the shell: the gilt encasing the man rather than the flesh, blood, and spirit pulsing beneath. Sad, in a way, but convenient for his current pursuits. Just as the fancy plate sometimes nudged others toward his influence, the garb of a pauper served him now. Without outward evidence of riches and influence, he would be disregarded—just another throwaway, displaced after a decade of war, traipsing the dusty thoroughfares of the kingdom. It saved him answering questions and explaining plans he preferred to keep to himself, things he couldn't quite articulate in his own mind yet. It had its place, and it allowed him to proceed unmolested along the Kanda River to the archipelago at its mouth, the region the crown called the South Coast.

Others knew it as the Twenty-Nine, or Twenty-Nine Pieces of Paradise. A desolate area spanning miles marked its border with the rest of the kingdom. The monarchy's respectable subjects gave it a wide berth, though Octavian wondered how much of that owed to exaggerated tales of the debauchery along the southern shores. The sun beat down, and Octavian soon cast off his bearskin cloak. His companion and partner, D'Aurelian, did the same, a sheen of sweat coating the Esperon mage's dark face. D'Aurelian used the gauzy blue sleeve of his tunic to mop his brow, and Octavian saw the exhaustion dragging at the corners of his eyes and mouth. They'd been on foot for weeks, ever since leaving the king's old fortress in central Selindria. They could've taken horses, but horses were a sign of wealth, and intimidating. The man Octavian sought to meet with was not one he wanted to intimidate.

"You look tense," D'Aurelian noted. "Do you have misgivings about this meeting that you haven't shared with me?"

Octavian looked ahead, focusing on the dusty brown road distorted by the heat lines shimmering up from the ground. By now, he had hoped to have a plan in place, practiced words to offer to their formidable would-be host. He turned to look at D'Aurelian, unburdening himself to the one person who wouldn't hold it against him. The one who wouldn't exploit a perceived weakness. "I'm afraid."

"Of what? It was your idea to come here, to uncover what truth we can."

"Maybe the truth is what I fear." Thirst and heat tickled Octavian's throat and roughened his voice. "It would be so much easier to believe in the peace King Garith has brokered. To believe it has a chance of lasting."

"Believing falsehoods doesn't make them come true," D'Aurelian argued gently. "And neither does ignoring them."

"That is the whole problem with this damned old world. People prefer to look at a beautiful façade instead of the truth behind it, to believe what they are told as long as it is something pleasant to their ears." Octavian closed his eyes for a moment that felt much too brief. "And the other problem is getting others to acknowledge it. Even if we chip away at the veneer, they remain blind to what stands beyond it. Because they do not want to see. Seeing means either doing something or admitting you're too afraid—or too complacent—to change what's wrong."

"I see two options, amarzio. We can seek solutions to these problems, or we can give up. I have known you for over ten years, and I do not think you want to give up. All you'll do if we return home now is torture yourself wondering. Though if that is what you prefer—"

"No." Octavian could smell the sea, feel the cool breeze coming off the waves he couldn't yet see. He took the salty air into his chest, held it, and let it out in a great gust. "We're close now. By nightfall, we'll have some idea what we're dealing with, or we'll be dead. I won't turn away from what's in front of my eyes."

IN HIS thirty-eight years as a mercenary leader, mage, and, against all odds and reason, eventually a titled noble, Octavian thought he had seen it all, but nothing prepared him for the sights that greeted him as he and D'Aurelian entered the Twenty-Nine. Their surroundings went from sunbaked and bleached to lush explosions of color so quickly Octavian wondered if they'd passed over the boundary of a spell. Perhaps they had. It would be well within the powers of the man who ruled these lands to conjure the vision that enveloped their senses.

The gray-green waters of the river widened out as they met a peacock blue sea dotted with white foam. There, the pigments mingled and swirled together like striations in polished marble. Green islands of various sizes checkered the surface of the water, edged in golden sand and connected by crooked bridges cobbled together from driftwood and rope. Tan houses decorated with swirls of bright paint, sea glass, shells, and mosaic lanterns hanging from the eaves stood clustered in no discernible pattern, flanked by copses of twisted trees and patches of brittle yellow grass. The chaotic beauty overwhelmed Octavian's perceptions as he tried to take in the details, catalog them in some way that made sense to his mind. Even the flowers, blooming wider than Octavian's open hand, moisture beading on fleshy petals, spoke of restrained decadence and sensuality. Beneath it all hummed a current of magic, but not the unruly and destructive sorcery he'd expected. The steady flow vibrating beneath his feet seeped into his legs, skipping over his skin in a light caress and inspiring a calm that made it hard to hold on to the caution he didn't dare abandon.

All around them, dark-skinned people, smaller of stature and finer of bone than Octavian's own, lounged in the surf, swam, fished, or napped on the shore in tangles of sand-colored limbs. Their hair, in vibrant shades of scarlet, gold, orange, and burgundy, hung around their graceful shoulders and svelte waists in matted ropes and braids adorned with ribbons and beads. Most of them wore little else, maybe a scrap of printed cloth around the hips or a few necklaces, but the majority went naked. A group of about half a dozen children crossed in front of them, chasing each other through the shallow pools dotting the path and splashing their legs. A boy of six or seven stopped, regarded them with wide marigold eyes, grinned, and offered Octavian a dried starfish before darting away.

D'Aurelian leaned in. "So these are the fearsome Emiri raiders? The notorious pirates the Selindrian nobles demand be driven from their lands? I have to say, they are much less threatening than I imagined. I haven't seen a single person carrying a weapon."

Octavian looked at the little red starfish on his palm, and then up at an adolescent girl sitting on the edge of rock, dangling her feet in the shoals and playing an atonal melody on a flute. "Appearances can be deceiving. These people are the bane of every coastal settlement in the kingdom."

"They're also much of the reason for our victories against the Johmatrans. The war would've lasted much longer without their superior nautical skills."

Octavian raked the sweaty hair out of his face, regretting the leather trousers and vest he'd chosen to wear. Though he'd once thought it impossible, he'd grown accustomed to the cold of the northern mountains. Pulling open the laces of his doublet, he said, "I wonder how many of those triumphs can be laid at the feet of their leader." He shook his head. "Or protector. It's difficult to guess what he would want to be called."

"We shall have to ask. Where is his residence?"

Octavian looked around. In the distance, dozens of ships with gaudily painted hulls and striped sails bobbed on the waves. If he hadn't seen them in battle, it would be hard to believe they comprised the most formidable seafaring force in the known world. "I'm not sure. Little is known about this valenny. Few but the Emiri call it home, and they're not quick to share their secrets with outsiders. We should find it with little trouble, though. I'm sure he has a fortress, and probably an impressive one."

"There's a great deal of magic here," D'Aurelian said, "and not all of it is his."

"I sensed that as well."

"Where could it be coming from? Why is the air so thick with enchantment when the rest of the world is starved for magic these days?"

"Another question for our host." Octavian licked over the salt crust on his lips. "If I'm not very much mistaken, Yarroway L'Estrella knows much about many things. He once said to me he would need allies in the coming days—other mages."

"I pray that means he'll be glad to see us. I shudder to imagine his reaction otherwise."

Octavian brushed his knuckles down D'Aurelian's dark cheek. If nothing else, they could be open with their affection here. The priestesses and nobles condemned the Emiri people as much for their preference for either gender and their regard of intimacy as just a fun pastime as for their piracy. "Yarrow is powerful, but we are not exactly helpless, especially not the two of us together. Besides, he might be mad, but he always seemed to me to possess a peculiar code of honor. He despises the aristocrats, the priestesses, and the Johmatrans. But regardless of the fancy titles in front of our names, we're mercenaries. Never doubt that polite society rates us only a small step above these Emiri. Yarrow will respect that. Now, let's find him. If I can count on nothing else, I'll wager my fortune he has wine."

"Let's find him quickly, then, and hope he's in a mood to be hospitable."

For the next several hours, they meandered between islands and over bridges, discovering majestic waterfalls and lagoons so perfect they seemed painted in a storybook. Under different circumstances, Octavian might be content to never leave, if everything he'd built hadn't been at stake. But as the sun started to melt and spread molten gold across the surface of the water, they were no closer to finding the fortress of the legendary mage. Octavian had expected to see a castle atop a cliff or sitting on a knoll surrounded by high walls, yet all the little houses, with their patterned curtains instead of doors or window glass, looked the same. They hadn't eaten since breakfast, and Octavian salivated as the scent of roasting fish reached him from the fires the Emiri were lighting along the beach.

"I'd hoped to avoid announcing our presence here, but we might need to ask for directions."

D'Aurelian looked at the nearest bonfire, glowing bright against the darkening sky, sending up clouds of sparks. Probably a dozen people had gathered around it. "These folk seem friendly enough."

D'Aurelian approached a willowy man standing at the edge of the firelight. The Emiri's gold hair and eyes contrasted sharply with his dark skin, the flames behind him gilding the edges of a lean but muscular form. A frayed strip of floral-printed cloth barely concealed his choicest parts, and he held a clay jug between his ribs and his upthrust hip. He spoke a few phrases in his melodic but indecipherable language, and D'Aurelian held up his hands.

"I regret that I don't speak your tongue. Do you know the common language of the kingdom, or perhaps Esperon?"

The Emiri man grinned. "My Esperon is not so good, but I can talk in the common language. I'm called Toumo. Will you drink with me?" He extended the jug, and before Octavian could warn his companion, D'Aurelian took it and knocked back a healthy swig. He handed it back to Toumo, sputtering.

"Your liquor is potent," he rasped out.

Toumo laughed and clapped D'Aurelian on the back the way one would a choking infant. "Muri-ku can be an acquired taste, at least for you land people and your delicate constitutions. You handled it well. What are you called by your mother and her syrai?"

"D'Aurelian."

Toumo draped an arm over D'Aurelian's shoulders. "Come, then, D'Aurelian. Food is cooking and there's plenty to drink. Join us. The mages of Espero are allies and always welcome in the Twenty-Nine."

Octavian went to stand a few paces behind D'Aurelian. His partner had things well in hand; there was no need for Octavian to assert himself. Once his ego might have demanded he make himself the focal point, but he'd learned to trust in his companions. He'd paid a high price for doubting them in the past, and he had greater faith in D'Aurelian than any other.

"Actually, I am hoping for some direction," D'Aurelian said. "My friend and I have come here with the hopes of meeting your valen… the one who watches over these islands. Yarroway L'Estrella."

Toumo's hospitable grin never faltered, but Octavian didn't miss the slant of his eyes or the way his spine stiffened as he pulled away. "And what do you want with Yarrow?"

D'Aurelian held his hands out to his sides and bowed slightly in the Esperon fashion. "My traveling companion and I were fortunate enough to meet him at King Agarick's old fortress in Selindria. He was kind enough to extend to us an invitation to his lands. We are here in acceptance of that offer and wish to pay our respects."

Toumo's golden gaze snapped to Octavian. "What is the name of your syrai?"

Octavian stepped forward and extended his hand. "Octavian Rose, of Rosecairn."

Toumo grasped his wrist and squeezed with what might have been a challenge. Octavian squeezed back, never looking away from the Emiri's eyes. "I can assure you we mean Yarrow no harm."

Toumo chuckled and tossed his head, the ornaments in his magnificent hair rattling softly. "Your name is known here, Octavian Rose. You are held in high regard, but Yarrow has little to fear from you or anyone else. Come, I will take you to his land home."

A dark-haired Emiri with large, pensive eyes joined them, and Toumo introduced him as Kin. Octavian and D'Aurelian followed them along the shore to a small raft. Toumo gestured for them to step aboard, and when they did, he maneuvered the little vessel around the islands until they reached a midsized one at the southern end of the archipelago. He moored the craft in the shallows, and the four men stepped into the knee-high water. Round lamps made of bits of colored glass hung on iron hooks and lined the sandy path up the hill, casting flecks of shifting tincture on the sand as Octavian and D'Aurelian followed the two Emiri toward the cluster of houses atop the knoll. It was quiet save for the waves cresting behind them and the soft whisper of the breeze through the high grass lining the trail. Octavian's muscles tensed as they stepped beneath an open arch and into a courtyard with a burbling fountain in the center.

Five of the modest brown structures typical of the islands stood in a star formation, with the tallest to the center. Walkways not unlike the rustic rope bridges connected the upper stories, and more colorful lanterns dangled from the boards, tossing scraps of wavering color across the sandy ground like confetti. Chimes hung from the eaves echoed erratically. A snuffling drew Octavian's attention, and he turned to see an older Emiri man atop a stack of barrels, passed out drunk and slumbering happily with a jug clutched to his chest.

D'Aurelian leaned in. "It's possible we've been deceived."

"Let's wait and see," Octavian whispered. Though this place resembled a tavern or brothel more than the fortress of a landed aristocrat, cousin to the king, Octavian sensed something tickling at the edges of his perception. The two of them stood next to the fountain while Toumo went to the curtain over the door of the main building and called out, "Syrai!"

He got no answer and called again. Voices and noise grew louder behind them—probably as the evening celebrations spread and the revelers drank more. Toumo shouted for his friend a third time, and finally the gauzy drape over the arched doorway rustled, and a man appeared, backlit by the golden illumination within the dwelling. Assuming this was some servant of Yarrow's, Octavian continued to wait. The man greeted Toumo and Kin with embraces and kisses, and then a flash of lightning blue from his eyes indicated his defensiveness—or his irritation. Clutching D'Aurelian's hand to pull him forward, Octavian hurried toward the door. He stood in front of Yarrow, who appeared cut from the darkness, save for the glow of his eyes and the long white ropes of his hair.

Octavian felt like someone had poured icy water down the back of his shirt, and he shuddered despite the heavy, wet heat as Yarrow's magic, with its sharp, crystalline edges and unfathomable depths, scraped against his own. He struggled against his instinct to back away and forced a smile. "Valen Yarroway. I am Octavian Rose, of Rosecairn. I hope my companion and I are not imposing by calling upon you at your home."

The tension dropped from Yarrow's posture, and the luminescence dimmed from his eyes, though they remained unnaturally blue and bright. His teeth flashed white in a genuine smile. "Haven't I told you to call me Yarrow, Octavian Rose? We don't stand on ceremony here in the Twenty-Nine. I'm glad you're here. I hoped you would come. You and your lover are most welcome." Yarrow held the curtain aside and indicated that they should enter.

Octavian didn't know what he'd expected to find inside the residence of the Valen of the South Coast, cousin to King Garith of Selindria and Gaeltheon, and irrefutably the most powerful magic user of the age, but it wasn't the… *mess* that greeted him in the foyer. During a decade of fighting the Johmatrans alongside the Emiri, Octavian had learned a little of their ways. The concept of ordering possessions, or even of valuing material goods, was as alien to them as restricting themselves to a single sexual partner or ten. They couldn't understand why anyone would bother. Yarrow appeared to have embraced their philosophy wholeheartedly. Chests, jugs, barrels, and bolts of cloth sat stacked against the walls. Books and scrolls covered the small tables and spilled over onto the floor, discarded clothing heaped among them. Some Emiri, two women and a man, sat cross-legged in a corner, playing a game with smooth round stones. Despite the chaos, Octavian couldn't ignore the wealth on display—coins and jewels overflowing from wooden crates, fabric so fine as to be metallic and see-through, art, armor, and weaponry worthy of the king piled like a peasant might pile turnips for the winter. Octavian had been a mercenary too long for all those shiny, expensive goods to escape his eyes.

"This way." Yarrow brushed aside a curtain of small shells with a soft clatter, and Octavian, D'Aurelian, Toumo, and Kin followed him down a corridor and into what looked like a dining hall. Tables— everything from finely carved Gaeltheonic pieces accentuated with bone and gold leaf, to boards propped on pieces of driftwood—were arranged in no order, many covered with more loot, scrolls, and dirty dishes.

Yarrow took a seat at a cleaner table, a simple wooden one flanked with long benches, and Octavian and D'Aurelian sat across from him while Kin threw some dried seaweed on the fire.

"Would you like something to eat or drink?" Yarrow asked.

Though Octavian wasn't at all sure of this man, his plans, intentions, or indeed the state of his faculties, he was hungry and thirsty. Besides, if Yarroway L'Estrella wanted to harm him, he would not have to resort to poison. Octavian nodded. "That would be nice. It's been a very long journey."

Yarrow stood and went to some shelves. Here, with dozens of candles burning and lanterns dangling from the rafters, Octavian was able to finally get a good look at him. Yarrow's disregard for what his noble kin and countrymen considered propriety was notorious. He wore only the billowy trousers native to Espero, though the material was much thinner and hid nothing of his slender legs and taut ass as he rooted through canisters and jugs. His white hair, arranged in knotted ropes and braids in the Emiri style, hung to his waist, decorated with ribbons, beads, and shells. The permanent ink the Emiri called paint, or kifi, accentuated the angles of his lean face and body. He seemed to have added more since Octavian had seen him last—blue lines and swirls reminiscent of the sea and the clouds covered much of his right side. But what struck Octavian most was that, after ten years of hard fighting, hunger, and hardship, Yarrow hadn't aged a day. He still appeared as a lad of around twenty years.

Yarrow returned to the table, some bowls and platters balanced precariously in his arms. As he arranged them, he said, "I'm afraid I'm not much of a cook. I usually eat whatever the others are roasting on the beach, when I remember to eat at all." He laughed. "But I have some of the dried fruit we take on sea voyages, and pickled fish. I think this bread will be all right." He picked up the dark loaf and sniffed it.

"Thank you. This is most gracious." D'Aurelian did a passable job of masking his surprise at his surroundings. Octavian, though, had known him a long time. He patted D'Aurelian's knee beneath the table.

Yarrow was on his feet again, hopping about the kitchen like a bird. If Octavian hadn't known better, he would have said Yarrow was nervous and trying to make a good impression of his hospitality. Octavian and D'Aurelian helped themselves as he dug through chests and cupboards. The bread, while hard, was edible. The fish was pungent, spicy, oily, and strange. But then, Octavian was very hungry.

When he returned to the table, Yarrow set down three fine crystal goblets and pulled the cork from a dusty green bottle. With a wink, he said, "This should make up for any shortcomings."

Octavian gratefully accepted the wine Yarrow served. When he sipped it, he tasted layers of elegant nuance: tart cherries, smoke, and leather, with a finish like the rain against the ironstone in the northern mountains. Octavian liked his wine, and he recognized quality. "An exquisite vintage, Yarrow. I'm surprised you offer it to acquaintances at a regular meal. This is worth saving."

Yarrow shrugged. "Emir will provide more. So, I'm anxious for news of what has transpired since I left my cousin's fortress. Did Garith go through with the peace treaty with the Johmatrans?"

"It's little surprise that he did," D'Aurelian said. "Everyone, nobles and priestesses included, supported the accord."

Yarrow slammed his own goblet down and precious burgundy liquid splashed the pages of the open book by his elbow. "Fool." His eyes flared like sunlight striking a mirror, making Octavian squint and recoil. Power rushed off him like a cold wind, raising the hair on the back of Octavian's neck. "Tell me. Do you support the truce with those monstrous barbarians?"

Before Octavian could choose diplomatic words that would slander neither his host nor his king, D'Aurelian spoke in a strong, clear voice. "I do not, tam. I cannot. The Johmatrans set upon my home island of Espero. They moved through the streets of our towns and cities, slaughtering everyone from farmers and bakers to infants in their baskets. And for what? Because they feel we have no right to wield magic? That it should belong to them alone? That's an excuse to cut down women washing clothes, or children cowering in cellars? They murdered my entire family, to distant cousins I had never met. And I do not believe they will stop. And I would have vengeance for the Esperon blood that flooded our shores."

Yarrow held his cup halfway to his parted lips. Though Octavian knew he had little chance of success, he gathered his own power in his belly and prepared to defend himself and his partner if the other mage snapped. Silence stretched as the three of them regarded each other. The two Emiri men moved to Octavian's back. Octavian slid his hand to the dagger at his hip. Sparks erupted and stung his fingertips where enchantment met steel.

After several moments, a wide smile split Yarrow's face, and he raised his goblet. The tension burst like a soap bubble. "Then we are of a like mind, me, my people here, and you. I cannot abide these Johmatran pigs keeping the Sea People in bondage. I will have no part of this truce, and I told my cousin as much. Emir help any Johmatran vessel that comes within shooting range of our ships, because they will get no mercy from us. Garith knows this."

Octavian huffed out a breath and took another deep drink of the other mage's very excellent wine. He doubted anyone in the kingdom had forgotten Yarrow's tirade at the treaty signing ceremony, or the way he had stormed from the king's hall with the insistence that his lands would have no part of the accord.

Yarrow turned and reached out to the dark-haired Emiri, Kin. "Syrai, what shall we drink tonight?" He put a hand to Kin's bare waist. "What would please you?"

"The ice wine is very good," Kin said in a soft, husky voice.

Yarrow clapped. "Excellent choice! I think there's some in my study, or if not there—"

A cacophony of several voices moving closer cut Yarrow off. He smiled as they grew louder. "It seems our celebration has grown. We'll need to break into the stores in the cellar. I'll help you fetch them, and we'll move our festivities to the courtyard."

Just as Yarrow stood, a group of Emiri men and women burst into the hall. "Yarrow, we have some unwanted guests." The woman who spoke sounded more like she was delivering news of a surprise feast.

Toumo beamed. "Our friends from the east can't seem to get enough. Is it possible they enjoy taking a beating?"

"Again?" Yarrow said with a wide grin. "I suppose we'll have to oblige them." Blinding blue light spilled from his eyes and from his shoulders in a semblance of wide, powerful wings. The air crackled and popped with magic, making Octavian's limbs tingle. Yarrow turned his head, his eyes leaving trails of light like falling stars, to look at them. "Will you fight with us as you once did?"

D'Aurelian was on his feet, red-gold light forking from his outstretched fingers. "I will. Gladly. I do not miss the war, but I find myself missing killing Johmatrans."

Octavian would have liked more time to consider where to place his allegiance. On one hand, Yarrow was powerful, and he might prevail against his cousin. But could he rival the resources of the crown? Despite everything, he was one man—yet one man with a seafaring force second to none. Could he stand against the combined forces of the monarchy and the priestesses? What if the Johmatrans threw in with the king? Would D'Aurelian's fellow Esperons take up arms against their old enemy? There were too many variables, and Octavian liked to weigh all possible outcomes. He'd come here to acquire information to allow him to do just that—choose the path that would benefit him and his people. Weigh who held the advantage. Discover the secrets Yarrow held that might tip the scales in one direction or the other, so Rosecairn, his legacy, could side with the victor. But Yarrow, bathed in cerulean light, his hand outstretched in camaraderie as a fellow mage, had forced Octavian's hand. Refusing would forfeit any access Octavian had to the knowledge Yarrow held.

He stood and drew his assassin's blade. "All right, Yarrow. Lead the way."

Chapter Two

OUTSIDE, A throng of fifty or more Emiri clogged the courtyard. They hadn't bothered to dress, and the lantern light glimmered over dark skin glistening with the evening's moisture, but they'd produced weapons— mostly small, curved swords—as if by magic. When Yarrow appeared, his ethereal wings stretched dozens of feet and shedding scraps of azure light, a great whoop rose from the crowd. Shouting and clanging their weapons, the group turned and ran down the hill. Their patron strolled calmly behind them, D'Aurelian by his side. Octavian followed a few paces behind.

What else could he do?

When they reached the water's edge, the Emiri continued unabated into the froth, and at the point where the sea became too deep, they arced their bodies and disappeared beneath the surface almost without a splash. Within minutes, they broke from the water and began climbing ropes to board the four ships moored about a half a mile from the beach. Though he had witnessed it during the war, the Emiri ability to move as easily through water as across land still astounded Octavian. Soon only he, D'Aurelian, and Yarrow remained on the sand.

"If you cannot swim, I'm sure I can find a dinghy," Yarrow said.

"Nonsense." D'Aurelian quickly shed his tunic and sandals, tossing them into a clump of grass behind him. "I'm Esperon. I was born with one foot in the ocean." In nothing but his loose trousers, he dove into the surf.

"Can you swim, Octavian Rose?" Yarrow asked.

"I can manage, but not well. It might take me time to reach your ships, but I assure you—"

Yarrow laughed. "No need to delay the fun."

Before Octavian could question or protest, Yarrow stepped behind him and wrapped his arms around Octavian's waist. His chest was hard against Octavian's back, and Octavian had a heartbeat to notice how stimulating the mingling of their magic felt before Yarrow beat his wings and they left the ground.

It felt less like flying and more like being flung, like an arrow shot from a bow. The humid air hit Octavian's face like a wall and whooshed loud in his ears as his toes skimmed the surface of the water. In a few blinks, they reached the hull of a ship, and a stroke of Yarrow's wings propelled them upward and over the rail, where they landed lightly on the deck. Octavian prided himself on staggering only slightly before regaining his balance.

The twenty or so Emiri on deck cheered Yarrow's arrival. Kin was at the helm, while a few others unfurled and adjusted the sails. The rest stood on the starboard side, weapons drawn, looking out over the sea.

Yarrow rested his hand against the back of Octavian's neck and met his eyes with a smile. "I'll enjoy fighting with you by my side."

"The honor is mine," Octavian said automatically, though in truth, he had no idea what he'd be expected to do. Looking around, he also realized D'Aurelian wasn't among this crew. He must've boarded one of the other three ships. This would be the first time in a decade they'd entered battle separately. It felt strange, like fighting with a sword he wasn't used to, but Octavian trusted in his partner's ability.

The swift little ship turned with ease. The sail snapped, catching the wind, as it headed southeast and toward the open sea. Try as they might, no one had been able to duplicate the Emiri ships' speed or maneuverability, and before long Octavian saw white sails in the distance, coming up fast. The four Emiri vessels surrounded the foreign ship, boxing it in. To Octavian, the other ship didn't look Johmatran in design, but then he hadn't kept up with the other nation's nautical developments. After the many beatings they'd received from the Emiri fleet, every nation was struggling to compete.

"Don't sink her if you can avoid it," Yarrow shouted. "I want to know what she's carrying. Fire off her bow, as a warning."

The sailors loaded some of the ceramic balls filled with explosive powder into a catapult bolted to the deck. Octavian had seen them used before—to devastating effect. Now, though, instead of filling the device, the sailors only placed about a half dozen of the spheres in the basket. They swiveled the catapult on its axle to aim it, lit the fuses, and fired. The smoking balls arced through the air with a whistle. One of them struck the enemy ship at the bow, near the waterline, exploding and shaking the vessel. The others landed in front of the ship, bursting and producing founts of seawater.

One of the other Emiri ships launched a volley of its own, and a few of the spheres struck near the stern, rocking the boat and almost pushing its portside toward the ocean's surface.

Yarrow chuckled. "Move in closer."

Kin's hands danced over the wooden pegs of the helm to turn his ship. The sails caught the wind, and the little boat skimmed swiftly over the surface of the water, easily intercepting the enemy ship and cutting it off as it tried to make a break through the narrow gap between the Emiri vessels.

Octavian didn't understand. "They're trying to retreat! They're clearly not a threat anymore."

An Emiri woman clapped him on the shoulder. "Don't worry, syrai. They won't give us the slip. They never do."

"But why?" Octavian looked around for Yarrow, and it took a moment before he located him, clinging to the rigging halfway up the mizzenmast. He shielded his eyes with his hand as if it would help him see, and he ignored Octavian's shouts. Off to his left, the woman hauled out what looked like a huge crossbow, steadied it against the rails, and fired a bolt with a heavy rope attached. Sailors on the other ships did the same, until the ropes extended outward like the spokes of a wheel, with the enemy vessel caught at the center. By now, they were close enough that Octavian could see the soldiers on that ship frantically trying to cut the ropes, shouting to each other as they readied weapons of their own. Octavian shook his head. The poor fools didn't want a fight. They hadn't come to attack the Twenty-Nine; they'd just been sailing around it. When they were threatened, they'd tried to run, but now they'd been backed into a corner. Trapped. And they didn't stand a chance.

This wasn't the Emiri defending their land. It was a raid, plain and simple.

Still, Octavian supposed Yarrow had warned the Johmatrans to avoid his lands, that they were not welcome. Surely the lure of trading at the many ports along Selindria's western coast had tempted them to take the chance, a decision they were certainly coming to regret. Octavian had no love for the Johmatrans, but these were likely simple men—merchants trying to make a living, the same as anyone.

Some of the Johmatran soldiers had made their way up the rigging and into the crow's nest. Octavian could just make them out if he squinted: small smudges a little darker than the dark sky, little patches that blocked stars brighter and more numerous than he'd ever seen. As the Emiri sailors moved across the ropes, climbing hand over hand, the Johmatrans fired arrows in an attempt to stop them.

A futile attempt.

Almost as soon as the arrows left the bows, Yarrow swung his arm toward them and erected a dome of shimmering, crystalline blue above the Emiri. When the arrows struck it, they conjured tiny blue sparks before disintegrating. The Johmatrans aimed at the mage, but Yarrow folded one of his wings in front of himself and deflected their shots. Flashes of red-gold on the opposite side of the enemy ship told Octavian D'Aurelian had adopted a similar strategy. It was an impressive sight, the bright, glasslike shields reflecting off the churning waters, flaring in a bright purple line along the seam. Octavian, unsure of what else to do, stood with the few sailors who'd stayed with the ship and watched. Soon he heard the clash of metal against metal, saw shadows moving in a jumble on the other deck, and knew the Emiri had reached the other ship—obviously planning to board and capture it.

With four ships to the Johmatrans' one, the Emiri had them greatly outnumbered. Yarrow dropped his barrier. He spread his wings and they extended almost the length of the ship. The light they spilled allowed Octavian to see the things nearby as if it had been midday, but erased his vision of what was happening across the water, forcing him to gauge by the shouts he heard. The Emiri sounded amused as they taunted the Johmatrans in their language. Interspersed with their cheers were cries and grunts of pain, the occasional splash of something, or someone, going overboard.

A pop and a screech sounded. The scent of burnt minerals reached Octavian, and he looked up as a trio of iron balls poked holes in the curtain of smoke. Reacting instinctively, Octavian lifted his hand, stopping the projectiles with little more than a thought. A flick of his wrist hurled them back the way they'd come, where one shattered the other ship's railing and the others tore through the main sheet. The Emiri around him cheered and patted his back. For a few moments, Octavian stood shocked, watching red and blue light strobe, illuminating tendrils and puffs of smoke, casting the fighting on the other deck in stark clarity for a few heartbeats before the darkness swallowed it again, making the people battling there seem to move in halting, jerky bursts.

From the time he'd realized he had the gift, Octavian acknowledged he'd been granted a mediocre talent at best. He'd studied and honed his talents, concentrating on what came easiest, healing, and using the rest to augment his combat abilities and give him an edge over his adversaries. But he'd never been able to accomplish anything like Yarrow was doing now, shooting miniature comets from his outstretched fingers, effortlessly knocking enemies off their feet. To cast, Octavian had to search the ether for the anemic veins of magic and concentrate to drain off enough energy for even simple spells. At least he always had before.

Now that he'd reached for it, the magic surrounded him, as plentiful as the ocean water or the smoky air, inescapable. It flooded into him with every breath he took, swirling in his chest and belly, pouring in through his skin, and making his fingers tingle. His teeth wiggled and his hair stood out from his head, the ends crackling with energy. It was intoxicating, the power swooshing through his veins, making him feel like he could lift the enemy ship as easily as he could pick up a stone and skip it across the water. Another volley of Yarrow's glowing spheres sailed over him, and Octavian wondered if he was feeding off the other mage. But that didn't coincide with anything he'd learned about the arcane over three decades. No mage produced magic; they could harness it, draw it inside, and transform it with their wills, but….

Octavian's ruminations were cut short by another round of projectiles headed their way. In Octavian's acute state, they seemed to creep across the sky as slowly as snow melting on the mountainsides back home. He raised his hand, and they stopped their downward arc, hanging eerily in the air. Then he directed them upward, high above the ships, where they exploded in riots of color.

"Well done," Yarrow called over to him. "Should we see what our efforts have gained us?"

The Emiri remaining on the ship hollered, and all but a few took to the ropes or dove into the sea to swim the short distance to the other vessel. Yarrow stretched his wings and glided to the deck, touching down lightly. Octavian climbed to balance on the railing, his mind alight with possibility. If he could lift the iron balls with his power, then he could lift his body… he could fly. As if echoing his desire, a gust of warm wind hit his back, and Octavian pushed up on his toes. He imagined wings sprouting from his shoulders, red and gold, but despite wading in what felt like an infinite pool of magic, he could not manifest them. Saving it as another puzzle for later, Octavian let the breeze bear him up and carry him across the strip of ocean to the other ship.

A few bodies littered the deck, and some blood smeared the polished wood, but the Emiri had captured most of the other crewmen and tied them in groups to the masts. Most of them looked like common sailors, sun-darkened men in simple trousers, wearing open vests or barechested. If any of them had carried weapons, they'd been removed. They looked afraid, huddled together and watching their attackers with darting eyes. While they possessed the lean muscle earned by a hard life at sea, they were clearly not warriors—

Nor were they Johmatran. None of them bore the decorative scarification of the lands beyond the mountain, and none of them wore face paint in the Johmatran way. All Johmatrans shaved their hair—men and women—but these sailors had long locks tied back with cords, braided, or swept up in topknots. They wore beards as expected of men in the kingdom. Since the war, facial hair had become almost a symbol of nationalism, with Selindrians in particular wearing it to demonstrate that they weren't Johmatran, Emiri, or Esperon.

Octavian turned to Yarrow. "Where is their mage?"

Yarrow looked at him with eyes like full blue moons that went dark for a moment when he blinked in confusion. "What mage?"

"Every Johmatran ship has a mage on board," Octavian said, stepping closer. Something bitter and sharp tickled at the edge of his mind no matter how hard he tried to ignore it. Around them, Emiri sailors emptied barrels and overturned crates, looking for booty. "Why did he or she not oppose us?"

One side of Yarrow's mouth quirked up, and he trailed his fingertips down Octavian's arm. "Would you oppose us? Maybe they're simply not as stupid as they look. Don't think on it. Come on. Let's go below deck. Amongst our people, spoils are shared equally. Let's see if we can't find something you'd like to keep for yourself."

Though all he really wanted were answers, Octavian followed Yarrow to a hatch and down a rope ladder into the smoky gloom of the ship's hold. The lanterns hung on the walls and rafters swayed with the motion of the boat, casting wavering patches of light and shadow that made Octavian dizzy. He pressed a hand to the curved wall.

Yarrow looked over his shoulder and smiled sympathetically. "Don't worry, syrai. You'll get your sea legs. Before you know it, it'll seem strange when the land doesn't shift underneath you."

"That's not…." Octavian closed his eyes for a moment, hoping his head would stop spinning. "I don't understand what's happened here."

In response, Yarrow just laughed and wound his way deeper into the bowels of the ship, some Emiri sailors following him. What they found when they entered the open cargo area at the stern tied Octavian's stomach in knots.

"Oh, no."

Six Defenders of the Thirteen, those knights who had sworn fealty to the goddesses and the priestesses who represented them, stood surrounding a stack of crates, their swords drawn, their shining bronze armor and lush purple capes a stark contrast to the sailors tethered on the deck above. Two terrible truths occurred to Octavian: one, these well-armed and well-trained men had done nothing to defend their comrades, and secondly, and worse….

"This is no Johmatran vessel invading your seas, Yarrow. It's a merchant ship, hired by the temples."

Yarrow grinned and winked. "Good luck tonight. Let's see what they've fought so hard to keep from us, shall we?"

Even though Octavian knew it would be prudent to hold his tongue, he couldn't resist. "Whatever it is clearly means more to them than the lives of the men they've been sailing beside."

A Defender with a thick blond beard took a step toward them. "These goods are meant for the Sisters at Fayelle's new temple. You'll have to kill me to take them, you heretical scum!"

Yarrow heaved out a theatrical sigh. "If you insist." He made no gesture, but the knight choked and seized, blood-specked froth spewing from his lips. In moments, he fell twitching to the floor, and then he went still.

The other Defenders shouted and moved to stand shoulder to shoulder in a defensive formation. Though he had doubts about what was happening here, Octavian had been a warrior too long not to react to a threat. He lifted his hand and the swords flew from the Defenders' grips, their points lodging in the wooden wall behind them. Undeterred, the five men balled their fists and widened their stances. A group of a dozen armed Emiri sailors gathered behind Octavian and Yarrow.

"These are our waters," Yarrow said in a bored way, as if reciting an often-repeated speech. "Anything on them or in them belongs to us."

"This land is part of the Blessed Kingdom of Selindria and Gaeltheon," a young knight with dark hair protested. "It belongs to High King Garith, the people, and the goddesses. You must let us make our delivery."

Octavian had not known Yarrow long, but he knew that was the wrong argument to make.

"I don't like being told what I must do," the other mage said, "never have."

"What is in these crates?" Octavian asked, moving to stand between Yarrow and the knights, still hoping to prevent a rift that could lead to bloodshed far beyond this skirmish.

"None of your business, heathen!" another of the Defenders shouted. "Who are you to stand in the way of temple affairs?"

Octavian lifted his empty hands. "I am Octavian Rose, Bairn of Rosecairn."

The knight snorted. "Mercenary scum."

"I am a noble." Octavian fought to keep his anger in check. Ten years of being belittled by those who thought their birth made them better was more than enough for him. "Granted a title by your king."

"We answer to a power far above, and far more permanent, than your fool king," said another of the knights.

"That's treason." Octavian shook his head.

"It is no affront compared to the one you're committing," the knight continued. "You dare to stand between the goddesses and what they desire?"

"I dare!" Yarrow drew a dagger from his belt and threw it, embedding it in the knight's throat and drawing a thick spurt of blood. "We do not recognize those thirteen whores here in the Twenty-Nine."

"How dare you." Another knight produced his own blade and plunged it toward Octavian's chest. With his years of practice, Octavian caught the man's wrist, twisted it, and broke the bone. His knife fell to the floor, and Octavian drove the heel of his hand into the man's nose with a sickening crunch. The man staggered backward, his hand lifting to catch the blood streaming down his face. Behind him, Emiri blades protruded like the spines of a sea urchin.

"Stand aside from those crates or be killed." Yarrow batted some cords of hair off his shoulder and crossed his arms over his chest.

Unarmed and outnumbered, the Defenders bowed their heads and offered their wrists to their captors. As the Emiri bound them and led them away, Yarrow gestured to the wooden boxes. "Friends, if you would have all this delivered to my home?"

"Ha!" the Emiri responded, moving to carry out his wishes.

Yarrow threw an arm across Octavian's shoulders. "A good night, syrai. Come back to the ship. We'll sail back to my house, and the celebration will last for days."

Octavian nodded, though the repercussions of this assailed his thoughts. Yarrow had no idea what he had done, and consciously or not, Octavian had participated. What would happen when that ship didn't make port, when the priestesses didn't receive their expected shipment? It wouldn't take a great scholar to deduce the probable cause. Even without proof, blame would almost certainly be laid at the feet of the Emiri, as it had since almost as soon as their sails had been spotted on the horizon. If this couldn't be salvaged, he and all of Rosecairn had made an enemy of not just the monarchy, but the priestesses as well.

The goddesses.

OCTAVIAN STOOD in Yarrow's courtyard, staring into his goblet of wine while the Emiri drummed, played flutes, and danced amid the flickering firelight. An Emiri woman came to stand in front of him, circling her hips to grind her crotch against his, her arms undulating over her head. Her pert nipples grazed Octavian's chest, and her blood-colored ropes of hair swayed behind her shoulders. She said something in her language, something suggestive, judging by the lilt of her voice, and Octavian shook his head. With a shrug, the woman pecked him on the lips and disappeared into the crowd of rippling bodies. Octavian sagged back against the wall. Octavian just hoped *someone* was sober enough to keep watch over their captives.

Toumo approached him, his lids heavy over his gold eyes and his cup swaying in his hand. His gaze traveled down Octavian's body and then back up. His tongue darted out and traced his upper lip, too slowly for the gesture to be subconscious. "Yarrow would like to talk to you inside, syrai."

Octavian nodded and followed Toumo through the curtain, into the tallest building, through the foyer, and up the stairs. Yarrow waited in a large room with a balcony open to the crescent moon hanging over the sea, tinting the waves with mauve and claret light. The gauzy curtains were pulled back, and the breeze off the ocean skipped through the large chamber, empty except for a bed draped in printed curtains, a desk, and some scrolls and wine bottles piled against the walls.

Yarrow sat on a rug at the center of the space, some candles in front of him struggling to stay lit against the wind, green glass bottles at his side. D'Aurelian, never comfortable among the kind of noise and chaos that filled the courtyard, sat nearby, his head down and his dark hair hanging in front of his face. A wine-haired Emiri knelt close to Yarrow. One of the wooden crates from the ship waited next to them, pried open, the lid propped against the side of the box.

"Join us." Yarrow patted the rug next to him. "I would very much like the opinion of another mage."

Those words did nothing to assuage the tugging and tearing at the edge of Octavian's thoughts, like a barbed hook had lodged there and couldn't be removed, doing more damage the more he pulled at it. He sat on the floor and scratched at the hair above his temple, as if he could physically excise whatever was burrowing into his mind. "What have you found?"

"See for yourself."

Octavian slid the crate closer. Inside, nestled among sawdust and wood shavings, were some broken bits of pottery, pieces of metal, and fragments of what might have been jewelry. It was tarnished almost beyond recognition, covered in green scales and white powder. Octavian chewed the corner of his lip. What could the temple priestesses want with this worthless junk? He continued digging, delving toward the faint hum making his fingertips tingle. Eventually he discovered a stone slab about the length of his forearm and twice as wide. It almost seemed alive, the energy flowing through it in steady beats mimicking a pulse. He drew it out, blew across it to remove the dust, and moved closer to the candles to examine the carvings he felt on the surface.

Few knew that Octavian had spent the years before he'd run away at eighteen as the son of a wealthy merchant and trader. His childhood had allowed him to study many things: religion, history, literature… art. He'd always loved art—he could draw tolerably himself—and he'd familiarized himself with styles of many periods and cultures, but he'd never seen anything like this.

The depictions were realistic, the proportions correct, if a little elongated, lending the figures a lanky elegance. There was little detail on their limbs—no shading or lines to indicate musculature—but their clothing and jewelry were rendered with elaborate patterns. Octavian couldn't imagine a carving tool precise enough to produce the almost lacelike designs. The tablet seemed to tell a story in pictures, similar to the most ancient Esperon relics, those made before the advent of written language. Most of them told of Pherara, the goddess of magic, raising the island of Espero from the sea and leading her mages there. This one….

A man sat on an intricate throne at the top of a set of stairs. A group of women—thirteen women—stood at his sides. Some held infants to their breasts. In the next panel, the man, an important figure judging by the detail of his jewelry and headdress, copulated with a woman with heavy breasts and wide hips. It was very graphic, leaving nothing to the imagination. It reminded Octavian of scrolls in the most expensive brothels, those illustrating for patrons the services available for purchase. Yet somehow, it lacked the crudity, the shame. It could have been a depiction of two people eating. Farther down, the woman squatted, giving birth. Despite the simplicity of the style, the infant boy was beautiful, a cunning expression on his face. The woman turned her back on the child, her face hidden in her hands as if crying. The father looked on with a neutral expression. Then the baby was a child, a crescent moon hovering between his outstretched hands… then a beautiful youth, the most beautiful youth, looking over his shoulder as he held a dripping knife with a twisting blade. Around him, masks of human agony hovered, misshapen faces trailed by wispy tails.

Octavian felt both intrigued and horrified, torn between wanting to clutch the tablet to his chest and throwing it against the wall and shattering it to dust. The source of his revulsion eluded him, though. Nothing pictured here was especially gruesome, yet it kindled in him a sense of dread, almost of panic. At the same time, it was… weirdly arousing. He traced his finger down the back of the young man with the blade, letting his nail catch in the grooves that formed his shape.

A chill emanated from him, moving up Octavian's hand and making his bones hurt. He pulled his fingers back and rubbed them against his trousers, trying to dispel the disconcerting numbness. "What am I looking at here?"

D'Aurelian reached for the carving but stopped before touching it. "There are things similar to this in the libraries back home, but the way it is drawn is very different, and I have never seen symbols like the ones along its edges. It's clearly an account of… something. The history of an influential ancient family, perhaps? I wonder where it was discovered. This is, by all accounts, a significant find."

Yarrow chuckled, and it sounded more ominous than amused. "Significant doesn't begin to scratch the surface of this. How much do you know of the scholarly expeditions that have been traveling to the Lapir Mountains and Johmatra?"

"Some," D'Aurelian said. "Everyone has heard of Mellinger's Tablet by now, with its account of the goddesses fighting evil beings threatening mankind. Artists sell supposed copies on the streets of every city. I have heard of other things being found, but it's hard to learn of any details."

Yarrow's eyes flashed and a thread of lightning blue outlined him. "That is because the bitch priestesses are doing everything in their power to suppress this knowledge! They don't want the people to know the truth!"

"What truth?" Octavian asked gingerly.

"These are things from Fane's world." Yarrow stroked the tablet with reverence. "Like Mellinger's Tablet, they tell the stories of his reign."

"What does this one tell?" The eyes of the carved youth drew Octavian's gaze, and though he didn't want to keep looking, he couldn't stop himself. He took a long drink of wine in a vain attempt to banish the prickly cold crawling up his back.

Yarrow looked up and met his gaze, his white teeth exposed in a feral smile. "This… this is the birth of Thalil, the Dark and Beautiful One. See here—Fane fathering him on the podgy whore the world has been tricked into calling the Mother Goddess. His birth. Her shame. And here is Thalil coming into his power, donning his symbol of the Crimson Scythe. The red crescent."

D'Aurelian shuddered. "You would… dare to claim that Th—that *he* is the offspring of the goddess?"

Yarrow pushed his lower lip out and canted his head. "I already knew of this. But now… now the world can know. Now we can start to chip away at the filthy lies our society has operated beneath for far too long. We were fortunate to find this. It's no surprise those idiot Defenders fought so hard to keep it from us. They would have certainly destroyed it, as they do anything that disagrees with the horseshit the temples are trying to force down everyone's throats."

Octavian picked up the closest bottle of wine and took another long pull. Goddesses. He had never been a religious man, but he'd never felt compelled to shit on an altar, either. Yarrow's words rang of paranoia. Octavian knew the world was brutal and indifferent—he just wasn't sure it operated under a vast conspiracy, thousands of years old. Still, he would need to tread carefully here, especially if Yarrow was as mad as he seemed. Like it or not, their fates were at least loosely tied together now.

"My friend, help me to understand. How can you be sure the people drawn here are Fane and the others? Can you read this language?"

Yarrow blew out a breath. "No, though I have been trying for a long time. But it all makes sense."

"How?" Octavian dared.

Yarrow shook his head and waved his hand at the tablet. "Look at it! It's all right there."

"Forgive me, but… I am lacking some insight you seem to possess. How do you know the priestesses are trying to keep these finds hidden? And how… what has given you the idea that… that Thalil is a child of the Mother Goddess? Please, I only want to understand."

Yarrow reached out and cupped Octavian's knee, but he turned his head to look out the window, where the moon balanced on the edge of the water, ready to slip behind the horizon. "Forgive me. I forget, you know? I forget how much most men cannot see, how short their memories are. I have been me… as I am… for so long I forget it's not the same for others." He met Octavian's gaze. "I know the priestesses are trying to suppress these findings because I was beside the Cast-Down assassin sent to kill Tam Mellinger and his company. I watched him strike that priestess down when she refused his payment. And I know about Thalil because I discovered a man who lived as Fane's apprentice and lover over ten thousand years ago. Nothing, *nothing* is as you have been told, Octavian Rose. Haven't you wondered why your magic is so much stronger here in the Twenty-Nine?"

"Yes…."

Yarrow clasped Octavian's hand, his grip strong enough to hurt. "If I could show you the truth, explain everything, what would you do?"

"I… it depends."

"Would you champion the truth?"

"I would champion what would most benefit the people of this world… the common people and not just the wealthy and titled. And I won't mince words here. My people, those in Rosecairn and the Esperon mages who have fought next to us, are my first priority."

That seemed to satisfy Yarrow and he relaxed the vise of his hand. "Then we can accomplish much together. Stay here with me, Octavian Rose, and I will dispel the illusions you have lived under. I'll clear those cobwebs from your eyes and show you things beyond anything you ever imagined. Will you do it?"

Again, Octavian would have liked time to ruminate, to weigh his options, but he stood on the edge of a cliff, and he could either dive off into the unknown or retreat to safety.

He had never hesitated to dive in the past, and he knew everything he had built, everything he hoped would outlive him, had been possible because of the risks he'd taken.

Octavian jumped. In the end, he could sacrifice many things for the good of others, but he could not live in ignorance, not when there were things to know. No matter the cost to him, or the world. Treasure he might have been able to walk away from, but knowledge, especially magical knowledge, lured him like a man dying of thirst to a pool of clear, cold water. And he had felt a hint of what it might mean to have wings.

He'd stepped across the line, then. Rosecairn would stand with Yarrow and the Twenty-Nine.

Chapter
Three

KING GARITH, High King of Selindria and Gaeltheon, Herald of the Blessed Epoch, stood before the double doors of his throne room in the fortress of Eirion-Vale, and all he wanted was to be back in his rustic cottage in the woods, where he and Sander could play at being commoners, where they could be men pursuing men's desires without the world's fate in their hands. The few weeks they'd spent there after the signing of the peace treaty with Johmatra had passed like a daydream on a summer afternoon. Garith felt like he'd just stretched out beneath the sun and closed his eyes for a moment before someone had come to rouse him and drag him back to his responsibilities. The dream he had almost slipped into still danced at the edges of his thoughts, and hands still reached out to pull him into a soft gambol with no prescribed steps, just swaying and the gentle brush of body against body, but now he had to be king. Thousands of people depended on him to make decisions that would determine the course of their lives.

Garith looked to Sander and nodded. Sander pushed the doors open and horns sounded as they entered. Light pierced the colored glass of the arched windows facing north, and both of them squinted as their eyes acclimated to it after the gloom of the hall. Wondering what fresh torment the Shades had spewed up to throw in his face, Garith plodded up the steps to his dais and sat down. The crowd he presided over had changed since the end of the war. Instead of knights, nobles, and advisors from his kingdom, the gallery now included priestesses from various sects, scholars who would inevitably argue against them, and ambassadors from Espero, who seemed to delight in scandalizing both parties with their attire and ideas.

And somehow Garith, a mortal man of thirty-four years, was expected to humor them all and make sure they got along. Lately he felt a hundred years older. At least when they'd been at war, they'd all been on the same side. He turned and looked over his shoulder at Sander, resplendent in his Royal Guard armor, his hair shining in copper curls beyond his helmet, his eyes the color of the open sea, and his fair skin still colored across his cheeks and nose, just as it had been when they were barely men. Later, they would ride out across the plains and find a hidden thicket where they could be alone. Garith held that picture in his mind as he faced the expectant eyes looking up at him, judging him. He could get through this, as long as he remembered that life still held things to enjoy. Even if the audience contained many more priestesses than usual.

Tam Vartanan used a cane to struggle to his feet, and then maneuvered his rotund body to the foot of the stairs. Any other man might have retired at his age—and goddesses knew Garith had offered him a generous stipend to find an estate by the sea—but Vartanan remained like a sore that wouldn't heal. He unfurled a scroll and cleared his throat. Weak as his voice was, it still managed to be condescending. "There are many orders of business to attend to after Your Majesty's… absence of the past few weeks. Without explanation, I might add. But we must carry on. Firstly, we must address the ironstone shipments arriving from Greyrclif. I have here a signed contract pledging one part in twenty-five to the crown, but auditors have uncovered discrepancies in the yields being delivered—"

"Stop!" An ample woman, maybe thirty-five, in sumptuous purple robes made her way up the aisle to stand next to Vartanan. Garith knew her well, unfortunately—Amosa Lammas—current head of the order of the Mother Goddess, and a woman always in search of something to rail against. Garith wanted to ask what she'd found to offend her this time. Maybe a puppy had looked at her the wrong way.

Instead, he said, "My lady, can we not address the court's concerns in order?"

"We cannot." The waddle beneath her chin swayed as she shrieked. "I'll not sit idle, twiddling my thumbs while you discuss cartloads of stone. Not when an egregious outrage has been committed against the goddesses!"

Garith resisted the urge to roll his eyes. "What is this offense?"

"My king," Vartanan interrupted, "the ironstone shipments—"

Garith raised his hand. "Are of the utmost importance, Tam Vartanan. You are a patient and reasonable man, a man who surely realizes half an hour will not affect the weight of that stone. Let us indulge those who are more… passionate."

Oblivious to the slight, Amosa Lammas shook her shoulders and smirked victoriously in Vartanan's direction. "Thank you, Your Majesty."

"We have much to address," Garith said. "Do not keep us in suspense."

Not even the soft chuckles from the other people on the benches cowed the priestess. "Your Majesty, I will be frank."

"Imagine that," Sander muttered, and Garith fought not to grin.

"Something needs to be done about your cousin in the South Coast. The man is not only an affront to the goddesses and all they represent, but he is now a threat to their servants—those of us who tend the temples!"

Garith had heard this before. "How so?"

Amosa motioned to a young knight, one garbed in the livery of the Defenders, and he rose from his bench to stand at her side. "Tell the king of your ordeal, Tam Brycelin."

The dark-haired young man bowed his head and would not meet Garith's eyes. "Your Majesty. I was part of a company, a group of Defenders assigned to guard a delivery to the temple of Fayelle. We hired a ship to transport our goods, and we laid out the safest route possible. There was no way we could avoid the South Coast completely, but we sailed as far from their shores as we could. We didn't want to offend them, but…. They set upon us, barricaded our ship with four of their own. Even outnumbered, we fought to protect the goods meant for the temple, but we didn't stand a chance. Our… items were seized, and those of us left alive were captured. I thank the goddesses I was lucky enough to escape. The tales of drunkenness amongst the Emiri are not exaggerated, or I might not have managed."

"This could have been a misunderstanding," Tam Vartanan said. "Likely the Emiri raiders did not know your intentions."

Tam Brycelin shook his head. "I wish that were the case. When our ship was boarded, we explained the situation. Yarroway L'Estrella was there, as was Octavian Rose. Each of them killed some of our men, and then they stole our cargo."

"This cannot go unpunished," Amosa wheezed. "It is an outright act of aggression by your cousin and his heathen band of pirates. The temples demand retribution… and accountability!"

A blue-robed priestess of Vestrafori rose from the pew and shook her fist. "It is past time for Yarroway L'Estrella to be removed as Valen of the South Coast. He and his raider minions must be driven from those lands so they can be settled by those loyal to the Thirteen… and the crown."

To Garith's surprise, Fleet Commander Bartoum Astir rose from his bench. "Begging your pardon, King Garith, but the Emiri fleet, under Yarrow, or with Yarrow, are responsible for our victory over Johmatra. They saved the lives of thousands of Selindrian sailors. If it wasn't for them and their ships, we'd all be shaving our heads and painting our faces. It's time we accepted them as part of this kingdom. Mark my words, we'll need them again."

A young Esperon mage, who had served as diplomat and translator during the peace talks, stood and smoothed back her blonde curls. Though she had facilitated the truce, Courtenay Jardine-Lamont clearly held no love for the Johmatrans—or the priestesses. "This man speaks the truth. It's only a matter of time before the Johmatrans rally their forces to strike at us again, and my home will be their first target. As a representative of the Council of Espero, I would rather have the support of the Twenty-Nine and its fleet than these indifferent priestesses. After all, the Emiri provided aid to our island before they were ordered to do so. Amazingly enough, they seemed to figure out that preventing Esperon children from being slaughtered was the right thing to do without being told by your temples. Espero is, therefore, inclined to stand with them."

"Heretic." A priestess of Laud, covered head to foot in cobwebby gray rags, rose and pointed a bony finger at Courtenay. "Harlot. You dare to stand there in your whore's garb and defend thieves and pirates? You dare to oppose the goddesses?"

Courtenay shook her head. "I will not stoop to defending the native dress of my country nor our position. Nor will I sink so low as to bend to personal attacks. In my experience, they are the last resort of those who have abandoned reason for fanaticism. Give a solid argument why the king should forsake four hundred ships for the sake of one, and I will be happy to listen."

"Let us not forget that the goddesses' mercy alone allowed us to triumph over our foes," Amosa huffed. "Only a great fool would dismiss them, or the many men who wield swords in their names."

"Is that a threat?" Sander demanded, his hand on the hilt of his own sword. The past decade had not dampened the protective streak that rose in him when he thought Garith was under attack.

"It is a statement of fact," the priestess said.

But Garith knew that over the years, since before the war, the temples had gathered warriors and armed them, claiming the need for defense of their holy orders. He also knew they now had the allegiance of almost as many soldiers as the monarchy, and it would take nothing more than a word from the priestesses to set the two forces against each other. If that happened, Garith wasn't sure his army could prevail. One way or another, he had to keep the peace. He owed his cousin Yarrow much—all of them did—but the people could not afford to be plunged into another war when they had barely recovered from the last one. He could not leave his kingdom splintered, vulnerable for their enemies to return and pick apart the pieces one by one. They had no chance unless they stood united.

"The goddesses will win this and any other battle we face!" the priestess of Vestrafori screeched.

"Reason and good sense win battles," Courtenay responded, "which leaves you woefully unarmed!"

"How dare you!" The priestess of Laud succumbed to a fit of coughing.

"Enough!" Sander banged his sword against his shield. "The king will speak, and all of you will be silent."

Not having prepared anything to say, Garith shot Sander a look over his shoulder. Sander's cheeks colored, and he pressed his lips together before whispering, "Sorry, Garith. But better you than them."

Garith stood. "We are not wild animals, and we will not behave as such in my hall. Sit down, all of you." They complied, though Courtenay held her chin defiantly high. Garith met her eyes and smiled. She smiled back, and an understanding passed between them. She would play along. "Now, then. If goods that were property of the temples were… lost, we will endeavor to replace them. What was this ship carrying?"

"Supplies to rebuild the temple of Fayelle, which was sacked by the barbarians before the war," Amosa said.

Garith didn't bother admonishing her use of "barbarians" since the promised delegate from Johmatra had yet to arrive at Eirion-Vale. Surely that would be an entirely new collection of miseries, but he would worry about it when he had to. "I will replace these supplies, gladly. What do the priestesses of Fayelle require? Food? Herbs for healing? Building materials? Name it, and we can put this unfortunate incident behind us."

"Your Majesty is most generous," Amosa said with a miniscule dip of her head. "But I'm afraid it is not that simple. Your cousin committed heresy by attacking our ship, and he must be punished. Furthermore, he and his… people will allow no temple to the goddesses to be built on their lands. This blasphemy cannot continue."

"So long as the Emiri provide ships when we need to fight, what does it matter?" Bartoum Astir said in a booming voice.

"It matters." The priestess of Vestrafori narrowed her eyes at the big sailor. "Let this heathen land carry on, and it will not be long before the goddesses drag the rest of the kingdom down to the Shades' along with it."

"Nonsense." Courtenay clenched her fists so hard her hands shook. "What do you base that on? We've been fighting alongside the Emiri for over ten years, and your goddesses have yet to make an appearance to slap our fingers. What, are your ghosts going to come down from the sky and take away our dessert all of the sudden? Over a single ship?"

"You will pay for your insolence," the priestess of Laud said.

Courtenay tossed her golden curls around her bare shoulders, planted her hands on her hips, and curled the corner of her lip. "Here I am."

"Enough." Garith's shoulder ached with steadily building tension. "What will satisfy you? Shall I order my cousin to pay retributions? Goddesses know he can afford it."

"Because his raiders roam the coasts and pillage any ship trying to make port with saleable goods," a nobleman near the back of the room shouted. "The temples are not the only ones suffering because Yarroway L'Estrella is being permitted to run amok. Those of us who hold lands bordering the sea are at our wit's end."

"Now, you cannot suggest that Yarrow is personally engaged in piracy or thievery," Garith said.

A woman dressed in heavy Selindrian gowns made from the most expensive Johmatran cloth rose from her seat, with some difficulty given the excessive layers of her clothing. Her beaded belts clattered. "Forgive me, Your Majesty, but it does not matter. If Yarroway cannot compel his people to abide by the laws of this kingdom—your laws—then he is not fit to rule. He should be replaced with someone who can keep the Emiri in line… or, better yet, drive them off."

"Oh, grand idea!" Bartoum Astir threw the scroll he held to the floor with disgust. "Let's toss away the finest seafaring force we've ever seen! Let's leave the Twenty-Nine, the gateway to the Kanda River and the heart of our lands, ripe for the Johmatrans to pluck!" He got to his feet and glared at the priestesses. "I've been to the lands beyond the mountains. I've seen how the people there live. Have you? No? Well, hear me now, my fine ladies. You would not want it! You wouldn't want it one bit, and I don't want it for my family or my people. So unless one of your goddesses appears before me and promises to stand straddling that river, I'll sleep better with a capable seafaring force holding it."

"How can you speak this way?" Amosa's shrill voice made Garith fear for the hall's colored windows. "You are no barbarian, tam! No Esperon mage! You're a Selindrian. Have the goddesses not been good to you and this land?"

"They didn't fight and bleed beside me and my men," Bartoum said. "Neither did you. The Emiri did. That's enough for me."

"Exactly." Courtenay crossed her arms as if that logic settled the matter.

"The people do not agree," the priestess of Vestrafori said in a warning tone. "They will not abide this."

"Neither will I." The noblewoman in the outlandish dress fluffed her skirts like a cat puffing up to intimidate another, and though it only made her look sillier, Garith knew she represented a mouthpiece for many others. "Powerful titled families are fed up with allowing our coasts to be ravaged by these heathens."

It surprised Garith how many people in the hall vocally agreed. "What would you have me do?" Too late, he realized he'd made a mistake. He'd catered to their demands. Trying to recover, he said, "I will hear counsel on this matter."

"Yarroway L'Estrella must be brought here to stand trial," Amosa said. Garith was really starting to despise the sound of her voice. "Those of us who serve the Sisters will settle for nothing less."

"Nor will those of us who hold the coastal lands, by virtue of our fathers' blood," said the gaudy noblewoman.

"He cannot be judged by these women alone." A flush soaked through Courtenay's deep tan. "They are not impartial. Espero should have a say, if Your Majesty wishes to continue our alliance."

"Will no one represent the men who have bled for these lands?" Bartoum waved his hand in the general direction of the coastline. "Does the service of generals and fleet commanders over these many trying years mean nothing?"

"Since when have commoners had a say?" The nobleman failed to look down his nose at the much taller fleet commander. "Judgment is passed by the priestesses of Vestrafori; it has always been so."

Bartoum snorted. "And when the soldiers and sailors decide they no longer want to die for you to enjoy that privilege? What will you do?"

"You overstep your station, tam!" The nobleman poked a ringed finger in Bartoum's direction. "Your words are approaching treason."

"You sail the ships against the enemy, then! You draw a blade and stand against wicked sorcery that can rot the flesh from your bones. You face death day after day for a pack of lace-bedecked dandies who won't appreciate it!"

Men and women rose from the benches and shouting voices filled the room. Faces reddened, and Garith thought he saw a hint of flames outlining Courtenay's fingers. Orange light reflected off her blue eyes, and her smile was feral.

Garith had had enough. What was wrong with these people? Why couldn't they make any attempt to work together? Goddesses, was their stupid pride and devotion to their ideals more important to them than their survival? Could they yield nothing? "Be quiet, all of you!" Garith stood and strode down a step, then another. The people in the hall quieted; they were not used to seeing him assert himself. They were used to him tying himself in knots to avoid conflict. No more. He was king. He'd united these lands and fought off an enemy his father could never have imagined. He had earned the right to be heard, not through his blood, but through his actions. "Sit down. I will not have this. I have heard counsel, but I am still king. This is what I will do, and

I will hear no further dispute. I shall summon my cousin here to present his side of this story. I will hear him, and then I will make a decision. I will make a decision based on the evidence presented, and I will not be intimidated. Not by the temples, not by Espero, and certainly not by the men who have pledged to serve this land. We will revisit this matter after Yarrow has pled his case. I'll hear no more on it now. Does anyone protest?"

There were murmurs, but no one openly defied him. Garith sat back down. "Tam Vartanan, let us speak of the ironstone shipments."

Agonizing hours later, the hall had finally emptied out. Only Garith, Sander, Vartanan, and Bartoum remained. Something had broken in Garith. When he'd taken the throne, married Cothryn, united Selindria and Gaeltheon, and ushered in what they had prematurely named the Blessed Epoch, he'd sworn he would not abuse his power. He did not want to be the tyrant his father had been. His duty, as he'd understood it, was to see his people thrive and live in prosperity. And he had tried. Goddesses knew he had tried. Today, he had finally seen that they had all been pushing him around like a game piece on a board. They'd exploited his intentions. No more. Everyone had his or her interests at heart, and he had to do the same.

"Your Majesty, I don't think it's necessary to mention that if your cousin Yarroway does not come here of his own accord, there's little we can do to compel him." Vartanan sounded uncharacteristically cowed.

"You don't think it's necessary, yet you feel the need to mention it." Garith was annoyed, angry that he'd let these people manipulate him for as long as he had.

"Things will become… increasingly unpleasant if he declines to show," Vartanan continued. "The priestesses command a formidable force."

"Yarrow will show," Garith said. "It's a simple matter of threatening his pride. If we imply that he is afraid of the priestesses, he won't be able to resist proving us wrong. My cousin is still a little boy at heart, trying to drive off the play-yard bullies. I can get him here."

"And then what?" Bartoum asked. "Your Majesty, we cannot sacrifice the Emiri ships. If Johmatra sees that weakness, they'll invade. The peace treaty will mean nothing without the might to back it up."

"And what will happen if Garith must choose between the support of the temples—and the army they have amassed—or Yarrow's forces? Who is the better bet? Who will win if it comes to fighting?" Sander shook his head.

"Yarrow, Octavian Rose, and likely Espero?" Vartanan said. "Combined with the monarchy's loyal forces, they would make an intimidating adversary."

Garith rubbed his forehead with his fingertips. When had the lines become so deeply etched in his skin? Only yesterday, it seemed he'd been a boy handed a game field to play with, men only pawns to advance his strategies. Since then, he'd seen them die, blood pouring from their lips as they called out for their wives and children. He'd held them tight to his chest as the light left their eyes, and he did not want any more deaths. "Yarrow, Rosecairn, and Espero. With our forces, we would prevail. Wouldn't we?"

"The priestesses have no boats," Bartoum said. "On land, they might oppose us, but on the sea, they won't stand a chance. They don't respect the sea, and it'll bite them in the ass, sure as the sun will rise."

"But the damage they could do on the land can't be dismissed," Sander said. "The land is where the wheat grows; it's where the hogs and cattle grow fat. It's where the apples and grapes are harvested. It's where the milk flows to be made into the butter and cheese. Without those things, ships and armies mean nothing. Sailors and soldiers cannot fight without food, and we all know the common people, those who produce that food, will follow what the priestesses say without question. I cannot imagine what it would take to lure them away from the temples' influence."

Garith shook his head. "Nothing we possess. This country cannot enter into another war. We will not survive it, I fear. How can the people be made to understand that? Do they not know peace will be to their benefit?"

"They have been conditioned to fear the wrath of the goddesses." Vartanan leaned heavily on his cane. "They fear it above all else. What can we threaten them with that can compare to an eternity in the Shades' Abode?"

Garith pressed the heels of his hands into his eyes, but it did little to lessen the pounding in his skull. "I don't want to win their allegiance through threats, and I don't want to believe that's the only motivation they can understand. My people are not dogs who will only obey through fear of being beaten. My people hold the blood of Gar the Undefeated in their veins. They do not need to cower before anyone. We should be standing together."

"Your idealism is… inspiring, Your Majesty," Vartanan said, "but it might not withstand the test of reality. Would you really ask your subjects to defy the will of the goddesses?"

"I… of course I wouldn't." Garith knew there was no other answer he could give. "It hardly matters if I imply the priestesses do not represent the will of the Thirteen so much as their own interests, and it hardly matters if I note that the city-states of Johmatra have thrived without either. No, that would be blasphemy, and I would not dare. It's of no consequence. It seems I must entice Yarrow to come to court. That is what the people and the priestesses want, so that is what I will do. Though I fear to do it. As should they. Nothing goes as expected where Yarrow is concerned, and Yarrow is not without powerful allies of his own. Those we will not name here."

"You've committed to this course of action now," Vartanan reminded Garith, as if he needed it. "You must summon him here to answer for the actions of his people. Backing down now will be seen as weakness, or worse, as condoning his actions."

"I'll say it again," Bartoum added, "we cannot lose that fleet, Your Majesty. If the Emiri abandon us, we'll have no chance if the Johmatrans strike against us. And your Selindrian sailors are right tired of watching their mates die. You will have to strike some sort of balance. I don't envy you the task."

Garith met the sailor's eyes. "And you? Where will you stand?"

"I'm loyal," Bartoum hurried to say.

"Please speak frankly," Garith said. "It will not leave this room. I swear it on my father's blood."

"I… would not lead my men into a battle with no chance of victory, Your Majesty. I would not ask them to throw their lives away to make a political statement. Couldn't look in the mirror if I did that. I'd rather step down as fleet commander and go back to captaining a free vessel."

"Many of the commanders of the land forces feel the same," Sander said. "No one wants to see any more bloodshed without necessity. We have lost too many lives."

"I can only hope my cousin will agree." Garith turned toward the window, suddenly starved for fresh air and the ride he wouldn't get to indulge in today. "I will write to Yarrow now. He values the lives of his Emiri. I can only hope I can appeal to him on that level. We will get the message to him as quickly as possible, and… and I suppose we can only go from there."

OCTAVIAN WAS glad to find Yarrow alone, sitting on a rock amid some tidal pools with his feet in the water. He took a seat on a nearby stone and watched the other mage staring into the sky. After the Emiri raid he'd participated in, Octavian had sat up many nights making plans, writing down various scenarios in his journal, trying to formulate a response to anything they might encounter. He had strategies devised to counter anything the king or priestesses might do, but his plans couldn't be complete, not with an unknown and unpredictable factor in the mix: Yarrow himself.

Most people were easy to figure out, even those who thought themselves too complex or special. Sometimes those people were the most transparent. With little variation, people's actions could be traced back to their simplest needs. Quests for wealth and power, political machinations, and military conquests were just ways to secure food, shelter, safety, and the opportunity to have sex. Now and then vengeance, cruelty, or even honor and compassion held a slight sway, but more often than not, baser things influenced behavior.

Except Yarrow.

Watching the mage, naked except for blue and gold cloth tied loosely around his waist, Octavian couldn't figure him out. He could have wealth if he wanted it, and he could have power. Octavian had never met a man who seemed so determined to thwart his own happiness, to forsake a smooth path to climb barefoot over jagged rocks. And for what gain?

Yarrow pointed out at the open ocean and spoke without looking at Octavian. "Do you see the way the sky is tinted red? A storm will be coming before long."

Octavian didn't doubt it. "Should we not make preparations, then? Plans for weathering it?"

"Hm."

"Is it wise to leave everything to chance?" Doing so went against everything in Octavian's nature.

"Things come and go," Yarrow said.

"They do, and speaking of, a message arrived from your cousin, the king."

Yarrow shifted to face Octavian and tucked his bony brown legs against his body. "I suppose it was to be expected."

Octavian tried not to let Yarrow's flippancy frustrate him; Yarrow was quick to anger and slow to release a grudge, and Octavian did not want him as an enemy. The king, at least, he could understand. "He wishes for you to come to his fortress and defend your actions. Have you given thought to how you'll do that, what you'll say?"

"It hardly matters."

"It does matter." Yarrow didn't seem to realize he wasn't the only one affected.

"Why? What can he do? He can't compel me."

"You'll refuse, then?"

"Oh no. This is an opportunity."

"To do what?" Octavian scarcely wanted to know.

"To tell the truth. To start to peel back the scale that has built up over the truth for so long. Will you come with me?"

Octavian considered. What did he have to gain by accompanying Yarrow? More than by staying behind? Yet again, Yarrow robbed him of the time he'd have liked to weigh his options, his blue eyes glowing brighter as the sun dropped into the sea. And again, Octavian decided anything was preferable to making an enemy of this man. "I am not a coward, and I won't shy away from explaining myself. Nor will I expect others to do it for me."

That seemed to please Yarrow, and he smiled. "I'm glad. I don't suppose the cold will bother you too much?"

"I—" Octavian thought Yarrow must be kidding. Was that really his concern? "I've grown used to it over the years in Rosecairn."

"I hate the cold. But ice and frost have always been easiest for me to control. Isn't that strange?"

"Perhaps it stems from a desire to master your fear," Octavian suggested.

Yarrow nodded. "Perhaps." He turned his attention back to the water, and Octavian knew any further prodding would be futile. If plans were to be made to avoid hostilities, he would need to make them himself.

"Yarrow has responded to your summons, Your Majesty." Tam Vartanan stood before the desk in Garith's library, holding a scroll. "He will come to Eirion-Vale."

Garith looked up from the trade contracts he'd been reviewing. "That was fast. But?"

"He has some conditions."

"Yes?"

"He will bring a contingent of his own people."

"Seems fair."

"He asks for representation from Espero."

"As we anticipated," Garith said. "We could hardly keep Courtenay Jardine-Lamont away from the proceedings."

"She is a force," Vartanan agreed. "Your cousin further demands, however, that the proceedings be held in a public space, away from the castle. He insists the common people from the town and countryside be invited to attend."

Garith sat up straighter, abandoning his papers. "Why would he do that? Yarrow is the very epitome of the ruling mage the peasants fear. He's as relatable as a lightning storm to them. What's he trying to do?"

"Who can say?"

Garith pushed the sliced ham, turnips, and beans around on the silver plate beside his right elbow. "Very well. We will hold the proceedings in the town square, though I worry this will not be to my cousin's liking. He… he's deluded. Maybe he will finally realize that."

"He asks that certain other parties be invited."

"Of course. I will request the presence of Duncan of Windwake. As for any others, Yarrow can ask them himself. Though I am sure they are already aware of the situation and have determined how it can most benefit them. Still, I will not invite certain people personally. It scarcely matters. I could hardly keep their eyes from anything that might transpire." Garith pushed his plate of food away, no longer hungry. He felt suddenly watched, and his gaze darted to the shadows clustering in the corners of the room, as if the mistakes of his past had gathered there to stare at him in judgment.

"Then I will tell him we agree to his terms?" Vartanan asked.

"Yes, though I don't dare to imagine where this will lead us."

Chapter Four

UNCLE SASHA said the thing wasn't to try to see in the dark, but to learn to see the dark. Most people only concerned themselves with what the darkness hid, and they never saw the darkness itself, the way it breathed and moved and lived, the way it could tell a person who knew how to look everything she needed to know. Others couldn't hear what the night and the shadows had to say, what they offered to share. Others didn't know how to listen, or to see. They didn't even know there was anything to look for.

But Marlythe Helwyn Purefroy had been practicing. She'd observed the way the dark gathered in the hallways of Windust Castle, the way it shifted and shimmied when the servants passed by, the way the forks of shadow slithered into the light the torches cast. She'd seen the way it hid and revealed the pale linen of the women's skirts as they carried out their tasks, the way it settled into the hollows of their haggard faces, below the eyes and beneath the lips and cheekbones. How it painted their skin could reveal their thoughts and feelings. In her bed at night, Marly watched the darkness dance with the moonlight and starlight across her ceiling—the way the shadows advanced and retreated, blending and separating from the silvery luminescence. By observing carefully, she had learned to intuit the movements of the clouds and the wind by the way the darkness moved in her room.

Tonight, the moon was an emaciated curl obscured by heavy clouds, like a pale dent left by a fingernail pressed into flesh. She knew because her own nails dented her palm as she folded her body over her knees to make herself small. Her Uncle Yarrow said a lot of things she couldn't follow and didn't understand about illusion and the purpose of appearances. One of the few things she'd gleaned from his meandering talk was that it mattered how things looked; people placed more stock in the façade than what was behind it. She wanted to appear as nothing, insignificant. Invisible. She'd begged Uncle Sasha to teach her how to appear out of nowhere as he sometimes did, and he had given her tips, but her mother did not approve of him. When he came to the castle, Marly's mother did everything in her power to keep them apart. Uncle Yarrow, too, even though he tried to bribe Mother with all sorts of fascinating gifts. Usually things from the sea. Sometimes flowers conjured from thin air. The blossoms, though perfect, always smelled like flint struck to build a fire.

The movements of the heavy clouds painted curving paths across the grass in front of the simple hut with the thatched roof. The smoke from the crooked chimney was white against the strip of indigo sky beneath the cloud cover. From the patch of ferns and bracken across the dirt road from the humble dwelling, Marly watched and listened to the darkness. Soon she heard the damp swish of feet coming through high grass, the sucking sound of boots pulling up from the mud. Uncle Sasha said when one couldn't see, it was easier to notice every noise. She had found it to be true. Soon columns of darkness tainted the grass. They grew denser and larger, the darkness coalescing and bunching in on itself just as she did, and Marly knew the ones she'd expected were approaching. She closed her fingers around the hilt of the sword at her hip, but she didn't pull it from its scabbard. Uncle Sasha had taught her not to make a sound, not to reveal her presence until she was ready to strike.

He said patience was the hardest thing to learn, especially for the young. He said it was easy to understand but difficult to practice.

He was right.

Goddesses, she could smell them. A scent like onions and greasy meat drowned out the sweet night perfume of rich, wet soil and plant life. It grew stronger as her quarry approached. Soon she saw them, three boys standing on the gravel trail, not even trying for subtlety. As Marly predicted they would, they made their way around the hut, toward the small, fenced-in enclosure out back. She waited until they disappeared around the corner, and then she stood and emerged from her cover, moving carefully, trying to avoid the rustle of the fronds. She'd been crouched in the patch of woods so long her back was stiff and her feet tingled, but now it was about to pay off.

Marly crept toward the boys, staying close to the small house and the shadows it cast. When she reached the back side, she pressed her body against the rough planks and watched. She knew where the boys would go and what they were planning to do, but she wanted to catch them in the act, preferably with enough evidence of their crime that no one could ignore what they'd been doing.

One of the boys was big—as tall and stout as a grown man, but a smaller one appeared to be the mastermind of this operation. He had curly hair that reached his shoulders, and the first hint of whiskers darkened his jawline. As he crossed the small field, the curly-haired boy kicked over a clay pot, shattering it and spilling dirt and herbs onto the grass. Marly pressed her lips together and gripped the hilt of her sword tighter.

The boys finally reached their destination: the henhouse. Since the Widow Wynnfred's eggs had started disappearing, she'd attempted to secure the door to the chicken coop with a length of coarse rope. The curly-haired boy pulled a small knife from his belt and sawed through it easily. The small door above a ramp that gave the hens access to the yard popped open when the cord was severed, and all three boys chuckled. The hens inside clucked softly at the interruption to their sleep, but they were docile old birds, and they barely protested as the boys raided their nests and put the spoils into a canvas sack. They made so much noise Marly couldn't believe no one noticed. It occurred to her that what the widow needed was a dog. Her old hound Ribbon woke up and growled every time a servant passed by Marly's door.

After the boys pilfered everything available, the big one slammed the chicken house door with a bang. The smallest one, maybe a brother of curly hair, slung the bag over his shoulder and spat on the ground.

This was it! Marly had been planning this night for weeks, and she was ready to defend the people of Windwake, just like her father. She stepped out of the shadows and held her sword out in front of her, blocking the boys' path to the gate that would lead them back to the dirt road. "Stop there, egg thieves."

The big boy jumped; his feet actually left the ground. The smallest one clutched the egg sack to his chest, and the curly-haired boy stepped in front of them both. His lips curved up at the corner—and his fingers were still curled around the hilt of his knife. Marly's heartbeat raced, but she fought hard not to show her apprehension. "You've no right to those eggs. They don't belong to you."

The curly-haired boy raised his fuzzy chin and took a step toward her, eyes narrowed. "Oh yeah? And what're you gonna do about it? Little bitch."

The others laughed like they appreciated his wit, but the pitch was high, nervous. They were at least a little bit worried.

That was good. Uncle Sasha said when people were scared, they made mistakes.

Marly kept her face neutral. Uncle Sasha said it was important not to let your enemy know what you were thinking. She knew things these idiots didn't. She could beat them. She pushed her shoulders back and stood up a little straighter. "I'm going to take you to Windust Castle to answer for what you have done."

The boy moved in until his chest was only inches from hers. He towered over her; the top of her head only reached his chin. But size wasn't everything. Marly looked up and met the boy's gaze. Held it. And while he was looking into her eyes, trying to stare her down and intimidate her, she lifted her leg and drove her knee into his groin.

He doubled over and fell to the ground, clutching his crotch, howling, and rolling from side to side. Her father's seneschal, Tam Allwynn, had taught Marly that move after she'd pestered him for moons to show her how to fight. Goddesses, she was glad she wasn't a boy. They certainly had a weak spot. Tam Allwynn hadn't exaggerated.

She leveled the point of her sword at the chest of the boy on the ground. Even in the moonlight, she could see how his face flushed. It was satisfying to watch his eyes puff up and shine with tears. Too late, she saw the littler brother drop the bag of eggs and launch himself toward her. Before she could move out of the way, he caught her around the waist and tackled her to the ground. The impact drove the breath from her chest. Her sword flew from her hand. The small boy straddled her and grabbed her wrists, pinning them to the ground. He was stronger than he looked, and not as much smaller than Marly as she'd estimated. Marly bucked and twisted, and when she couldn't throw him off, she drove her forehead into his. His momentary dizziness allowed her to roll out from beneath him and get back on her feet. Head ringing and vision blurred, she looked desperately for her weapon and caught the moonlight glinting off the edge of the blade—three feet from where she stood. She lunged to the left.

"Dyl, you stupid oaf!" the curly-haired boy squealed. "Stop her!"

A big, booted foot stamped down on Marly's blade just as she crouched to reach for the hilt. Instead of trying to pull it from under Dyl's weight, she curled her hand into a fist and drove it up between the big boy's splayed legs. It had worked once, after all. When he bent in half, hands wrapped around his belly, she lifted her arm and hit him hard in the side of the head with her fist. She'd never punched anything besides a burlap sack filled with straw, and pain shot through her knuckles when they connected with the bone of Dyl's cheek. He sprawled on his side in the wet grass and pulled his knees to his chest, his mouth open, moaning. The sounds he made reminded Marly of a calf being gelded.

Before she could pick up her sword, the smallest boy threw himself at her again, and both of them landed hard. Marly's cheek jammed up against her teeth; she tasted blood. She struggled with the boy, but neither of them gained the upper hand, and they remained on their sides, facing each other, trading blows and trying to grab each other's arms. Their legs twisted together, and Marly had almost succeeding in subduing the boy when his brother recovered and stumbled to his feet. He kicked Marly hard in the lower back, and it hurt like the Shades'. The big boy, Dyl, was also up, and he kicked her with a vengeance, his foot connecting with her chest, neck, and chin. Marly had to release the small boy's wrists to shield her head with her arms. Soon, all three of them stood over her, kicking savagely. She could do nothing but roll into a ball and hope they'd take their prize and run away. A boot heel struck her cheek. Another smashed into her lips, splitting them. Pain exploded across her back, then along her legs. She reached for an ankle and almost caught it, but then a foot came down on her fingers, driving them into the ground. It hurt so much she couldn't hold back her scream. The boys laughed.

Then there was a muffled grunt, the wet sound of a body landing in the churned-up mud. There was a swish, the crack of bone against bone. A shrill cry. Sobbing. The moist slap, slap, slap of feet striking mud—running away. The rickety sound of the gate slamming. Through it all, Marly saw only strips of shadow moving over her, flashes of moonlight interrupted by darkness. In almost less time than it took her to notice something happening, it was over and the night was quiet once again. Then gloved fingers curled around her hand. The leather was as soft as velvet against her skin. Slowly, Marly uncurled her body and looked up. A pale face framed by spikes of light yellow hair and shaded at the edges by a cowl looked down at her. Though the other girl did not smile, her expression was not unkind. She tugged at Marly's hand, and Marly stood on legs trembling with anxiety and anger.

"Are you all right?" the girl asked. She was taller than Marly, maybe five or six years older. With her senses acute and her pulse thrumming, it took a moment before Marly recognized her as Uncle Sasha's friend, Asphodel. They'd been at the castle a few times, and as hard as Marly's mother had fought against it, Marly had managed to watch them, even sneaking into their quarters to speak to Asphodel a few times. Asphodel was so pretty, with hair like gold and skin like marble. A face like a statue, never changing, frozen and perfect. Blue eyes impossible to read, hiding everything like jeweled screens. But she was nice; she'd always talked to Marly like an equal and without dismissing or humoring her like she was a child.

Marly's face throbbed, and she felt bruised from her neck to her ankles. But she stood up as straight as she could. She wasn't about to complain and look like a baby in front of Asphodel. Two of the boys— curly hair and the big one—lay unconscious on the grass. The little fellow was nowhere to be seen. Marly schooled her features, trying to mimic Asphodel's placid expression. "Thanks," she said, picking up the canvas bag full of eggs. "The poor old woman who lives here depends on these chickens to eat. She's lodged several complaints, but there's never been any proof. I'm sure my father would help her if he could, but there was a war on."

"I'm sure." Asphodel stood with her arms crossed over her chest, her black trousers and gray vest immaculate even after the skirmish. How had she managed to keep the hood of her cloak in place?

Marly ran her free hand through her long brown hair. It was caked with dirt and bits of grass, maybe with some blood, and her scalp was sore. The whole left side of her face felt tender; just grazing her cheek hurt, but she struggled not to show it. When she started to cross the paddock, pain shot up her thigh, and she saw her pants had ripped, and blood plastered the wool to her torn skin at the knee. Seeing the wound somehow made it hurt more. She ignored it, opened the gate, and left the bag of eggs on the old woman's porch. The night hadn't gone the way she'd imagined, but she doubted these fools would risk bothering the widow again. Slowly, feeling as battered as if she'd fallen off a mountain, Marly made her way to the narrow road. She startled when she sensed Asphodel behind her. The other girl had approached without a sound.

"You should get back to the castle," Asphodel said in a flat tone. "Your mother will absolutely disintegrate if she discovers you've snuck out… again."

Marly snorted. "I'll sneak in through the kitchens. She'll never know."

"Really?" Asphodel arched an eyebrow. Her brows were thin and defined, not thick and bushy like Marly's. "Did you not know she's had a scullery maid watching the kitchen door for you for six moons now?"

"I-I knew that," Marly hurried to say. "I'll go through the soldiers' barracks and up through the main hall."

"Good luck getting past Tam Elys," Asphodel said. "Your mother has him stationed for the sole purpose of reporting your comings and goings."

Marly was getting annoyed. By now, they'd moved about a half a mile through the tiny settlement to the north of the Windwake village. The castle loomed on the hill in the distance, black against the gray storm clouds tinged pink with the coming of dawn. Marly stopped and turned to face her rescuer. "What do you propose, then? I don't suppose you know a way into the castle that my mother isn't watching?"

Asphodel's face betrayed no emotion. "Of course I do."

Marly didn't like being outmatched. No matter how she tried, she couldn't keep the exasperation from her tone. "Well… what? Are you going to help me? Or does it satisfy you just to let me know you have knowledge that I don't?"

"What are you, Marly? Ten years old?"

Marly pulled herself up to her full height. "I'm almost twelve."

"That's good," Asphodel said. "You do as you like, and you have no fear. Yet you are not rash, and you have acquired at least some skill…. Marly, you lost your sword back there. Didn't you?"

"Shades! It took me forever to steal—uh, find a sword that no one wanted in the barracks. Can we go back for it?"

"No. It's almost daybreak. Your hopes of sneaking back inside the castle are already becoming slim. Starved, even. Can't you just ask your father for another weapon?"

Marly hung her head as she trudged up the widening road, dragging her feet through the gravel. "He'd probably give me one if it wasn't for my mother. But she forbids it. She wants to train me for marriage, to be a lady. Ugh. I liked that sword. I was getting used to it."

"Here." Asphodel reached beneath her cloak and drew a long dagger. She flipped it in her hand and presented it, hilt first, to Marly. It was almost as long as Marly's sword had been, but much lighter. Marly slashed and thrust it into the graying air.

"Nice! Thanks, Asphodel."

"You can call me Del. And please know it is not given lightly. You must practice and learn to use it as it deserves."

"Del. It's a good blade, but kind of small. It's only half the weight of that sword I had."

"The size of a weapon is far less important than one's skill at using it. And it never hurts for an enemy to underestimate you. Now, hide it underneath your vest. Just in case."

After close to an hour of walking, they reached the steep hill that led to the gates of Windust Castle. As they approached them, Del canted her head to the right, and Marly followed her along the high wall until they came to a small wooden door. Marly went up to it and tugged on the steel handle, but it didn't budge.

"Let me." Del knelt down and pulled a slender piece of metal from her glove. She inserted it into the keyhole beneath the handle, and in moments a soft click sounded and the door swung open.

"Can you teach me how to do that?" Visions of opening locked kitchen doors and absconding with sweets formed at the front of Marly's mind.

"Given enough time, anyone can learn." Del secreted the spindly piece of metal away near her wrist. "It is not magery. Just a skill. Now come."

They passed through the doorway and into a tiny courtyard, where square beds of herbs lined the gravel pathway and vegetables grew in neat rows.

"I thought you said we couldn't go in through the kitchens." Too late, Marly realized she sounded petulant, and she tried to make herself sound nonchalant before she spoke again. "Didn't you say there's a maid who'll tattle on us?"

Del stopped beneath a pear tree, and the light dribbling through its leaves speckled her skin and lit her eyes. She was so pretty, so immaculate, but she'd bested those three boys like it was nothing. The things Marly's mother preached about a girl not being alluring if she scrapped and fought rang falser than ever. Then Del smiled, a real smile that crinkled her eyes to crescents, and Marly sensed a tenuous connection between them. Del was helping her because she wanted to, because maybe they were friends.

"I haven't forgotten about your mother's spy," Del said. "That's why we're not going through the kitchens."

Without further explanation, she continued through the gardens, and Marly followed. Soon they reached a desolate semicircle of lawn where the grass reached their knees. Two rounded turrets secluded it from the rest of the grounds. Del pointed at an arched window shuttered with warped wooden slats about five feet above their heads.

"I never knew about this place," Marly said.

"That was your first mistake. Whenever you will be staying in a building, the first thing you should do is learn every possible entrance and exit."

Marly wanted to rebuke her. She didn't like being told what to do or reminded that others knew more than she did. But Del had proved she did know more, and if Marly checked her pride and listened, she might learn some of it. It was one of the things that separated men and women from children, and Marly was done being regarded as a child. "I'll remember that."

Del nodded once. "Good. It's likely to save your life. Now, up you go."

Marly wanted to ask how, but she wanted to impress Del more. Looking up, she assessed the grooves between the stones. They weren't so different from cracks and crevices she looked for when exploring the rocky cliffs around Windwake. She wedged her toes into the deepest groove and pushed with her leg. The strain awakened the bruises on her thigh, but she ignored them and concentrated on finding a handhold. When she did, she pulled herself up, bracing the soles of her feet on the wall for added leverage. Perspiration soaked her clothes and stung where her skin had broken open, but she concentrated on the next place to grip or step. And then the next. It took time, but eventually she swung her leg over the window's stone ledge and pushed the brittle shutters open with her elbow.

Del scaled the wall like a spider, and when she joined Marly inside the empty, dusty room, she wasn't even sweaty.

Marly went to the heavy door at the other end of the chamber and opened it with a strained creak. After poking her head out, she looked left and right. The hallway dead-ended on one side and wound to meet a small door on the other. Confident they wouldn't be discovered, Marly stepped out. "What's the point of something like this?"

Without so much as a shrug, Del said, "It's hard to say. Possibly it was forgotten as the castle was built up over the years. People tend to forget what isn't immediately useful to them, and that makes it useful to us."

"We see things differently." Marly nodded in understanding. "The darkness itself. The things others ignore. That they don't even know to look for."

To Marly's shock, Del looked genuinely surprised. "Yes. That's it exactly. You have to look at the things you're told to ignore. The things at the edges. You're perceptive. You must have stolen time with Sasha."

They moved toward the door. "Del, is Sasha your father?"

"No."

"It's all right if he is. I understand. I know children aren't always born to a husband and wife."

"He isn't, and you should leave it."

Del's tone froze Marly's blood, and she let the subject drop when she would normally have pried. Instead of pressing Del further, she opened the small door and looked beyond into a hallway she recognized. They were on the castle's third floor, which housed her bedroom along with those of the other members of the noble family. The nursery was just two doors down from the tapestry of the lake-wyrm. Her bedroom stood right around the curve in the corridor, past the alcove housing the statue of Ix. If she could reach it, her mother would never know she'd snuck out again.

They crossed over worn carpets Marly knew well: her blood still stained one of them from the time she'd insisted she could ride a spirited red filly, and another bore a hole from when a nurse had dropped a candle rushing to her brother, Boone's, room. Sunlight bisected their path as it streamed in through the castle's diamond-shaped windows. Uncle Sasha said the shadows were friends, protectors, and Marly rushed into their shelter, following the soft rustle of Del's black cloak. They reached the door to her bedroom….

And found her mother waiting in front of it, arms crossed over her freckled bosom. She didn't look angry so much as resigned and defeated, at least until she saw Marly's face. After sparing a moment to glare at Del, she knelt down to Marly's eye level, looking like she might be sick. "Goddesses, your poor little face. What in their name have you gotten into this time?"

Unsure whether to lie or try to placate Mother, Marly darted her eyes over to Del, who stood as the epitome of cool, unaffected perfection, as if removed from and above everything happening around her. Marly stood a little straighter and lifter her chin ever so slightly, attempting to emulate Del's calm, blank expression.

Her mother did not appreciate her bored impression. She gripped the front of Marly's torn and dirty vest, pulled her closer, and spoke through clenched teeth. "Don't. Don't you dare look to her as an example. You are not that kind of person, and you never will be. You are a lady, and a lady does not leave her bed in the dead of night and return in this state. Do I make myself clear?"

Marly considered. Del and Uncle Sasha would remain impassive, not gracing the question with a reply. Uncle Yarrow would rant against the injustice of the world in tangled loops only his logic could follow. Neither reaction seemed right, so Marly did what she knew her father would do. She shook her head. "I'm sorry I've upset you, Mother, but it was the right thing to do. A group of boys have been stealing eggs from the Widow Wynnfred, and there was no one else to stop them. Should an old woman be allowed to starve in Windwake?"

Her mother stood and grasped Marly's hand in a vise grip. It hurt, but the worst part was being dragged down the hall like a child in front of Del; it was absolutely mortifying, and Marly's cheeks burned, but she managed to hold back the tears stinging her eyes.

"Don't you try that righteous nonsense on me, young lady," Mother was saying. "I'm sick to my heart of hearing why everyone else needs saving while your own family is disgraced and ignored. Those who deserve your devotion above all others."

Del's voice was a calm monotone, almost soothing. "It is not right to project the resentment you feel toward your husband onto your daughter."

Marly's mother stopped and turned around. "How dare you. What do you know?"

"Only what is right in front of me and impossible to miss," Del said.

"Get out of this house," Mother hissed.

"I'll do so gladly, if the master of the house orders it," Del said. "He is the one who summoned us here, after all."

"Us?" Excitement buried the humiliation Marly had felt at her treatment. "Uncle Sasha is here?"

"Wonderful," Mother muttered, shaking her head. "Exactly what we need."

Marly gave a little hop. "He'll be with Father! We must go to Father!"

"We certainly shall," Mother said.

When they didn't find Father in his throne room, the formal dining room, or the kitchen, they descended the narrow stone stair into the barracks. Marly rolled her eyes. She would've checked there first. Father loved having breakfast with his men, hearing their tales from their posts around the bairny. He hated sitting alone at the long table in the hall with only the servants for companionship. As predicted, Marly's father, Duncan Purefroy, Bairn of Windwake, sat at a small round table, laughing along with a few of his infantrymen. He wore the battered old suit of armor he refused to replace no matter how much Mother nagged. Uncle Sasha leaned against an arch behind him, a lock of dark hair falling in front of one eye and the sole of one foot resting against the wall. The labyrinthine barracks, with their low, vaulted ceilings, smelled of metal, the oil the soldiers used on their leather, and the lanky, long-legged hounds resting along the walls. Marly loved it there. Finally, she tore her hand from her mother's clawlike grasp. "Daddy!"

His chair scraped along the stone as he pushed it out from the table and opened his arms. Marly jumped into his lap, threw her arms around his neck, and rubbed her face against his coarse whiskers. Her father was the handsomest man in the world, and everyone said she took after him. They said Marly would be "statuesque." She loved her father's scent: steel, leather, earth, and fresh air. She loved the way he laughed when he embraced her and bounced her on his knee like he had since she'd been old enough to stand. It sounded like the boom of a drum at one of the soldiers' ceremonies, and its honest happiness echoed in the small room.

"There's my girl," he said. "And what gives me the sense that you haven't been in your bed?"

"Your daughter snuck out again." Mother's voice dripped with challenge. "Duncan, I have tried everything I know to bring her into line. You'll have to discipline her. This cannot continue."

Marley's father shifted her on his lap so he could look into her eyes. "Is that true?"

"I would never lie to you, Daddy. It is true. But I had to do it! Boys have been stealing the Widow Wynnfred's eggs, and no one was doing anything about it. Somebody had to stop the arrogant little shits."

Uncle Sasha grinned, his black eyes glittering.

Mother stomped her foot. "Do you see why this cannot continue? She has the mouth of a foot soldier."

"Daddy, you said if something is wrong in the world, a good man can't stand by and do nothing."

"You are not a man!" Mother stamped again, quickly approaching a tantrum.

"What difference does it make what I have in my trousers?" Marly countered.

"It does make a difference!" Mother looked pleadingly at Father, but she only looked at him with any kindness when she wanted to get her way, so her expression felt like a mask to Marly. "This cannot continue, Duncan. Sisters, look at her face! That face is her future!"

Father mock punched Marly's swollen cheek. "Oh, let's not be dramatic. It's nothing but childhood scrapes. They'll heal soon enough."

"And if they scar?"

"And what if they do?" Father said.

Mother threw up her hands. "She is to be a queen! Do you think Garith's son wants a beat-up, scarred woman enthroned next to him?"

That Marly could not ignore. "You don't know Thaneyael. He's better than that."

"Only because he is not yet a man," Mother said. "When he is, he will expect a demure, cultured, and beautiful wife."

"He doesn't want a wife at all," Marly replied. "He told me so. He said when we're married, we don't have to do the married things.

He doesn't want to, and neither do I. I'll hunt and fight while he researches magic."

"Duncan, honestly," Mother huffed.

"Now, then, let me see those wounds." Father leaned in closer to Marley and whispered, "You did the right thing. I'm proud of you. Did you give them a good thrashing?"

"I… not really."

"Well, next time." He cleared his throat. "I doubt any of these injuries will leave a permanent mark, but we can always have Tam Fulgrig look them over. Or better yet, Yarrow."

"Yarrow?" Marly bounced on her father's knee. "Is he here too?"

"No, but we have been summoned to meet him at King Garith's fortress at Eirion-Vale."

Marly squealed. "When do we leave?"

"What is the purpose of this meeting?" Mother asked. "Forgive me if I doubt His Majesty wishes to honor that… him."

"There has been a bit of a misunderstanding between Yarrow and the priestesses," Father admitted.

"We should distance ourselves from it." Mother straightened and lifted her chin. "Why drag our names through the filth along with his? We fear the goddesses, and we obey the temples' rules. We should refuse to attend."

"I will hear what is to be said." Father's tone invited no argument.

"Then I beg you, do not take your daughter. Leave her the opportunity to claim innocence."

Uncle Sasha stepped forward. The way he smiled, an old woman would want to wrap him in a quilt and give him biscuits and a hot drink. "Would you deny your daughter the chance to spend time with her betrothed? If, as you claim, her only chance at a comfortable life lies in their marriage, should they not become familiar?"

Mother narrowed her eyes. "The goddesses will judge you, tam. They will toss your filthy soul into the blackest pit of the Shades' Abode."

Uncle Sasha arched one brow. "The last refuge of those who have no influence in this life—to threaten pain in an imagined next one."

"I cannot wait for the day when you learn you are wrong." Mother's voice oozed hatred, and Marly didn't understand why she was so angry. She loved going to court, and Father would make sure she had the nicest dress of any of the ladies. Still, Mother turned to her husband. "The goddesses will not turn a blind eye to your wrongs, either. How much will you sacrifice for these… men? Your daughter? Your family?"

"We are only going there to observe the proceedings," Father said. "Everything is going to be fine."

Mother shook her head. "I pray it will be so, but experience has shown me everything involving that heretical mage is the spark that ignites an inferno. I pray you're not leading us into a pit we won't be able to crawl out of."

Chapter Five

ALL OF those who had ascended to godhood, Thalil included, had constructed realms to their preferences, havens away from the eyes of the others. His was a place of pleasure, full of the things that brought him joy: images of himself, sumptuous furnishings of red velvet, firelight, fountains of blood, the bones of enemies, the souls from which he drew power, and, of course, the bodies of comely young men ready to do anything to please him. He'd conjured a Crimson Palace of shimmering dark stone and decked it with glimmering gems, reflective surfaces that would volley his countenance back to him as he passed by. Sinfully soft cushions filled it, and candles burned behind scarlet glass, casting everything in a rubicund glow that enhanced his many natural attributes and glowed along the lithe limbs of his hundreds of consorts. His aunt and sister, Ix, venerated as goddess of the wilds and the hunt, had built for herself a boundless forest, brimming with trees and waterfalls of unimaginable beauty and populated with infinite numbers of wily prey to pursue.

Only the abode of Pherara, goddess of magic and protector of mages, was different. She let the enchantment run rampant, giving it no direction, boxing it in to no channels to suit her or anyone else.

Thalil would not dirty his feet in the realms of any of his father's other wives, but he adored coming here. No matter what the masses believed, all of them had started out as mages, and stepping through the silvery crack in the wall of his own domain imparted a sensation of coming home.

His foot, bare except for the golden, ruby-studded chains that draped from his ankle to the ring around his big toe, met a surface as buoyant as tightly stretched canvas. It bounced back against his weight as he stepped forward. As soon as he entered, power tickled and crackled over his skin, awakening his senses in a way that was almost sexual. The magic crested and ebbed, flooding perceptions he couldn't label before withdrawing, only to crash over him in another all-consuming wave. Thalil shook his dark hair, the beaded strands hanging from the edges of his horned crown rattling softly. He could enjoy the power here, the way it swelled the tendrils of his own magic, but he couldn't let himself be swept away by its flow.

Almost as soon as the intent formed in Thalil's mind, the ground beneath him grew more solid; there was less bounce as he walked a few steps into Pherara's universe. A path formed, glimmering light separating the irregular stones. The raw arcane energy was responding to the will of a powerful caster. Pherara let the enchantment flow freely, but magic sought direction. Energy and thought wanted to become form, something palpable. To exist on the material sphere if only for a fleeting breath. It was the reason mortals drew pictures and wrote stories—to translate the intangible within them to something recognizable, something communicable to others. Here, though, no tools were needed. The magic reacted to the most fleeting of dreams. The briefest of desires.

Thalil couldn't imagine the nightmare this realm could become to a burdened soul, one for whom guilt and memories of horror lingered close to the surface of the mind. Luckily, he harbored no such regrets. His heart held only pride in himself and his accomplishments, alongside the desire to advance further and thus entertain himself.

As far as his eye could see, the magic flowed like water, tinted with hues as if reflecting colored light. Or, Thalil thought, it looked like liquid crystal, malleable rivers of diamond, forced to obey none of the laws of the mortal plane. The glittering clear substance surged around him, dripping upward to form something resembling trees before bubbles broke from the ends of branches and took the shapes of birds, butterflies, and floating flowers. Some of the masses drifted up into what passed for the sky, where they burned as suns for a moment before fizzling out or streaked like stars across the firmament. Even without direction, the magic seemed to want to mimic the fixed world most people inhabited. Thalil had always wondered about that.

But it was a puzzle for another time. Today, he had a goal in mind, and so he made his way through a glasslike forest. Wherever he stepped, the translucent stones turned the blackish red of old scabs, and crimson roses with thorns dripping blood sprung up around his feet, only to wither, lose their pigment, and sink back into the never-ending magical stream after he had passed.

Pherara reclined on an undulating mound. The magic became vaporous and flitted in little smoky trails around her thin, pale limbs, caressing her skin like lovers. Yet her face looked peaceful and contemplative rather than aroused. Unlike his father's other twelve wives, Pherara had never struck Thalil as a sexual being. Nothing about her slender body, draped in filmy silver material similar to the energy burbling around her, suggested fertility. She was cool and pure, but not in the prudish way of that awful bitch Fayelle. With Pherara, it was more a disinterested elegance, and one Thalil could appreciate.

At Thalil's approach, Pherara sat up, and the substance around her adjusted to cradle her posture. It became more solid and took the shape of an ornate silver throne studded with opals. Her covering transformed into a billowy, beaded gown that exposed only her shoulders and long neck. Jewelry sprung into being at her throat and wrists, mutable gems sparkling. Is that what she thought he would expect?

Thalil bowed; the beaded ornaments of his crown brushing against his skin. He looked up through the rich waves of hair framing his face and met her eyes without rising.

Pherara's seashell-pink lips turned up. For all her innocence—genuine or feigned—her gray eyes were shrewd. "Such formality, my brother. Or nephew. I scarcely know what to call you anymore, Thalil."

He straightened. "Does it honestly matter after all this time?"

She brushed a long lock of silver hair off her shoulder. A large gem had appeared at the center of her forehead, held in place by twisting platinum filaments inset with tiny diamonds. "I don't suppose it does," she answered. "What does matter enough to draw you from your Crimson Palace? I know how you appreciate the charms of the world you have made."

"All charms grow dull with time," he answered. "Everything loses its shine with enough wear."

"And the charms of your realm have grown dull? I find that difficult to believe, as they are so… numerous."

Thalil grinned. Even after ten thousand years, he could not help but be pleased by a nod to his splendor. "Even so, I always yearn for variety."

"And so you have come here?"

"Yes. I am planning a little excursion, and I hoped you might accompany me."

One of her gray eyebrows arched, and she leaned her elbows on her knees. "You should not presume, Thalil. I do not despise you as my sisters do, but that doesn't mean I do not know you. If you seek to trick me, you'll find it difficult."

"Why would I need or want to do that?" He reached out and fondled her chilled fingertips. "I only want the pleasure of your company. I ask nothing in return."

"Oh, and where are you planning to go?"

"To the mortal world."

"And why?"

He canted his head, not quite sure how to answer. "I have a sense that something significant is about to happen, and I want to witness it."

"And you want me to witness it."

"Yes, but nothing further. I swear on my father's blood I will not ask you to do anything in response to whatever we may see."

She was intrigued; he could tell by the way she gnawed at the corner of her lower lip. Funny how those mortal habits remained after so long. After a few moments of consideration, she rose and lifted her layered skirts to descend the slope of her hill. Where her beaded slipper touched down, long stalks covered in bell-shaped blooms sprung up. They jingled like chimes where the fabric of her garment brushed against them, the eerie sound echoing. She took the hand Thalil stretched out, and the two of them followed the pearlescent path that had appeared between the trees.

"Will we go unseen, or blend in amongst the mortals?" Thalil asked when they reached a marble archway.

"Let us go unseen," Pherara said. "I'm out of practice passing as a mortal, and I have no idea what clothing they wear now. Besides, you detest making yourself even a little less beautiful."

He chuckled, never one to deny his vanity. "We'll need to take care. There will be powerful mages present, as well as one who might be able to detect at least my presence."

Pherara made a soft sound too delicate to be called a snort. "You seem to know more about what we'll be witnessing than 'something significant.' Would you care to fill me in?"

"Where would be the fun in that?" Thalil gestured beneath the archway, and they stepped through the blinding white light when it flashed.

Marly twisted the lacy edge of the tablecloth in her hands. Despite silver dishes piled with cakes, biscuits, fruit, cheese, and even some of the spicy little candies from beyond the mountains, she was irritated. She sat in a large hall, the vaulted ceilings supported by a dozen columns on each side. The tall windows to her left offered a view of a flower garden, and sunlight streamed through, but it still felt like a prison.

For the hundredth time, Marly sighed theatrically. Finally, Prince Thane looked up from the tattered old book he was reading, and his bright blue eyes met Marly's. "Since you're just going to keep doing that until I ask you what's wrong, we might as well get it over with."

Marly wanted to be angry with him for being an arrogant jerk— and for being right—but her annoyance at their situation trumped all that. "Doesn't it bother you, being shut in here like babies in a nursery? We should be able to watch what's going to happen. We're the future rulers of this kingdom."

Thane grinned. He had full lips like a girl's, she'd always thought. It was one of the things she liked about her future husband's appearance. In most other aspects, she just thought he was strange. His eyes were the bluest blue she'd ever seen, bluer than the clearest summer sky. Glowy like candlelight shining through cobalt glass. They didn't match his dark olive skin. His black hair was shoulder length and shiny, which would've been all right if not for the white swath on the left, from his part at the center to just above his ear. It looked like an old person's hair, but Thane was just her age. They'd only been born a week apart. It was part of the reason everyone swore they were destined to form a union.

"Now you're concerned about our ruling the kingdom?" he asked. "Before, I've only ever heard you complain about it."

"Only because you'll get to do all the fun parts, like going to battle and chopping off the heads of your enemies. I'm supposed to stay here and put on dresses and have a bunch of babies."

The smile dropped from Thane's face. "We are not having babies. Do you know what we would have to do?"

Marly lifted her chin. "Of course I do." She had a vague idea, mostly gleaned from things she'd been able to weasel out of Uncle Yarrow, but she suspected Thane knew more.

Thane closed his book and stashed it in a pocket of the long black cloak he wore over his simple doublet and shirt. "We won't need to worry about it. We'll use my magic to become immortal, and my magic will provide everything the people need. We won't have to have battles or cut off anyone's head, unless…." He squinted like he had a sudden headache, and turned to look out the windows.

"Magic can't do all that." He was always showing off about having the gift, even though he was supposed to be keeping it a secret, since mages weren't allowed to rule.

He turned back to her. "Can't it?"

"No. Everyone knows that."

With a wink, he asked, "How badly do you want to find out what's going on in the village square?"

"Umm, a lot?"

Thane stood and placed his palms flat against the table. He closed his eyes, and a swirl of wind lifted his hair from his shoulders, accompanied by the faint scent of sun-warmed bricks.

Marly heard a distant thump and turned toward the sound. One of the ladies who'd been watching over them had crumpled in a heap beside the fireplace. Two others slumped on a bench, their heads on each other's shoulders and their embroidery forgotten on the floor. A maidservant who'd been cleaning the flue leaned against the wall, still clutching her brush.

"Whoa," Marly whispered. "Are they dead?"

Thane's eyes seemed even bluer than usual, if that was possible. "Do you want them to be?"

"What? No! I was mad at having nursemaids, but they're just doing their jobs. They don't deserve to die."

The way Thane chuckled made him sound somehow much older. And kind of scary. "Don't worry. They're only sleeping. You shouldn't underestimate magic."

Marly rolled her eyes. "Do you want to brag about how great you are, or do you want to get out of the castle before they wake up?"

"They won't wake up for at least an hour."

"Still," Marly said, exasperated, "we'll have to sneak past the guards. If you want to stay here and admire your big accomplishment, we'll miss whatever's happening in the village. Come *on*, Thane." She stood, grabbed him by the sleeve, and yanked him toward the door.

"There aren't many guards in the castle," Thane mumbled. "Most of them are down in the square."

Marly looked left and right as they entered the hall, but she didn't even see a servant. "That's a bad strategy." Still, she continued pulling Thane along. "If someone wanted to attack the castle, this would be their opportunity."

"Who in the world would attack Eirion-Vale?" Thane asked as they rounded a corner and hurried down a wide stone staircase.

"All sorts of people." Marly stopped to press her ear to a set of double doors. When she didn't hear anything, she pushed one open, and they stepped out into the cold, bright morning air. They'd come out on a narrow strip of grass—brown and covered in frost now—between the castle and its outer wall. Besides them, there was nothing here but a few ornamental bushes, so Marly felt safe continuing her argument. "The Johmatrans, for one. Emiri raiders."

"We have a peace treaty with the Johmatrans. And Emiri raiders never come this far inland. Besides, where in the Shades' are you going? The closest gate is to the left."

"Well there are Esperon rebels," Marly said. "Mad about the treaty. And I'm going right—toward the stables. The town is a few miles away, so we'll need a horse. Unless you plan to fly."

Thane stopped and looked longingly at the crystal-blue sky. "I wonder if I could. I often have dreams about men with wings."

"Just come on."

The castle had several stables within its walls, and Marly chose the one where the ladies' pleasure horses and children's ponies were housed. It was more likely to be empty than the soldiers' stables, and they would get a better mount than they would from where the carriage animals were kept. Though she would've adored riding a warhorse in all its armor, she chose a long-legged gray gelding and quickly saddled him up. She hoisted herself onto his back, a little hindered by the simple yellow dress Mother had insisted she wear, and Thane mounted up behind her. They trotted toward the nearest gate and found it open—but guarded by two bored-looking soldiers.

"Hold on!" Marly said. Thane wrapped his arm around her waist, and she dug her heels into the horse's ribs. She'd picked well. This horse was fast! By the time the two guards had gathered their wits enough to shout after them, they were a good way down the road. Marly reined the horse to a steady canter, and in less than half an hour, they reached the outskirts of the village.

They dismounted, and Marly took the gelding's reins, leading him into the woods to look for a safe, hidden place to tie him up. Behind her, Thane coughed and sputtered.

"What's your problem?"

"Your hair flew back in my face while we were riding," he said miserably. "I think it went down my throat."

"Well, I wanted to cut it all off, but my mother won't let me." She thought wistfully of Del's spiky blonde locks.

"It's your hair." Thane pulled a long strand out of his mouth. "Why is up to her?"

"She says ladies don't cut their hair." She secured the horse to the low-hanging branch of a thick tree. "She says no man wants a woman without long, beautiful hair."

"But a man doesn't have to want you. You're marrying me, and I couldn't care less if you shave it to the skin."

"When you're king, you should make a rule that all women can cut their hair and wear trousers, and no one can say anything against it. Not even mothers."

Thane shrugged. "I will if you want."

He was all right, her future husband. "Now put your hood up. We have to walk through the town, and everyone will recognize your weird white hair."

He did as she said, and they moved to the side of the street. Throngs of people filled the old town's winding lanes, and most of the shops were shut and shuttered. No one worked in the smithies or bakeries; everyone moved to join the huge crowd in the market square. Marly and Thane shouldered their way through until they could see into the square. At one end, an awning had been set up over a raised wooden platform. Thane's parents, the king and queen, sat at the center on chairs slightly larger than the others. Some nobles sat on either side of them, but Marly didn't see her father or mother. Not even in the angled wings where people sat four rows thick. A line of royal guards in their bronze and blue stood in front of the dais, halberds held stiffly at their sides. Another row of guards stood at the front of the crowd, keeping the common people back. Across a wide aisle stood a group of the warriors called Defenders of the Thirteen, the mirror image of the royal soldiers except for their colors and their livery.

Some of the people gathered to watch the proceedings murmured in soft conversation, but for an event this size, it was eerily quiet. Marly leaned close to Thane's ear. "This is weird. Do you have any idea what is supposed to happen?"

He shielded his mouth with the wide sleeve of his cloak and whispered, "Not much. I overheard my father and grandmother talking about the priestesses. They're angry, and Father isn't sure how to deal with them. Apparently they have a lot of soldiers—probably enough to challenge him openly."

"They seem to want to make a show of matching him. It almost looks like the two sides are ready to face off. What's got their knickers in a twist?"

Thane grinned. He loved it when anyone spoke against the temples. "It's something to do with Yarrow, my father's cousin. He's coming here to meet with them about something."

Marly nodded. "Father said Uncle Yarrow would be here. Uncle Sasha too. But I don't see either of them anywhere. And this looks like some kind of a trial. Why are there so many priestesses here? And if it is a trial, why would they hold it here in the market square? I wonder if—"

The atonal sound of a horn cut her off, and both of them stood on tiptoe to try to see what was happening. Someone announced, "Your Majesty, High King Garith of Selindria and Gaeltheon, Herald of the Blessed Epoch, Yarroway L'Estrella, Valen of the South Coast, has arrived."

"Allow him through," King Garith said.

"He is not alone, Your Majesty" came the reply.

The king waved his hand. Even through the gap she saw him from, Marly thought King Garith looked tired, strained. "Allow the valen and those accompanying him to enter."

A collective gasp rose. Marly took Thane's hand and wriggled through the crowd, dodging knees and dipping beneath elbows, until they stood just behind the line of royal soldiers. She couldn't believe what she saw.

Uncle Yarrow walked with two other men: one in gold-toned armor and a red cape, and another in a heavy blue cloak lined with fur. They led a group of probably a hundred people—all Emiri. Marly was thrilled; she'd never seen an Emiri up close, but she loved listening to Uncle Yarrow's tales of them and always thought she would like them very much. Though small, they were a pretty people, she thought. She loved the bright colors of their long ropes of hair and the way they decorated it with beads and shells, and she liked the markings on their dark skin. Best of all, she saw that maybe half of them were women, and they carried weapons just like the men. They even dressed the same, in patched leather trousers snug against their slender legs and tight vests that exposed their muscular arms. Of course, here in the cold, all of them wore layers of mismatched furs. Uncle Yarrow said the Emiri didn't like the cold.

So why were so many of them here?

Marly leaned in to see if Thane had any theories, but before she could speak, he clutched the sides of his head with both hands, whimpering. Tears rolled down his cheeks, and his cries were starting to draw the attention of those standing near them. Marly almost panicked. If they were found, they'd be dragged back to the castle and forced to miss everything.

"What's wrong with you?" she hissed.

"I… this almost feels familiar," he ground out between clenched teeth.

"What? What does?"

"It… it's my… I don't know. There's something here. Something's going to happen. Something… profound. We need to be ready."

"Are you hurt? In pain?" No matter how much she resented being forced to marry him, she liked Thane. Maybe she even loved him, just not with the kind of love where people wanted to get naked together. "Thane?"

He hugged himself, his long fingers wrapped around his shoulders. "I don't know if I can explain. I… feel like I woke up to something overwhelming. For a moment I felt something precious, something I'd lost, returned to me. I felt… like I was finally at the place where I was supposed to be."

Marly shook her head. Magic. It could make people soft in the mind, she'd heard. Still, she didn't want Thane to suffer, and she'd do all she could to comfort him. "And now?"

"Now… I don't know. It was just a flicker, like the way the world is bright and crisp when lightning flashes during a storm. It's dark again now, and all I know is that something is going to happen. Something that will matter."

Chapter Six

"Yarroway L'Estrella," Pherara said. "What is your interest in him?"

Thalil sauntered to the edge of the stage, where the main structure met the wing where the priestesses sat. He flopped down, let his legs dangle over the edge, and propped himself on his elbows to look up at her. His position made the lithe muscles of his stomach look fantastic. "It seems to me we should all be interested in him."

She sat down beside him and folded her hands in her lap. "Why do I get the sense you know far more than you are sharing?"

"Perhaps you're distrustful by nature." He winked. "It's a positive trait, if you want my opinion. Keeps one safe."

"That's an awful thing to say."

"Is it? My father trusted all of you, his wives, and look what became of him."

"Do you think that mage capable of taking Fane's place?"

Thalil looked at the mage in his tatty leathers, his tangled white hair hanging in cords down his back. He possessed a power Thalil couldn't quite place or understand, but…. "He has no designs on power—not political power, at least. He views it as a nuisance. Also, he's more than a little insane. Has been for a long time, I would wager. The things he suffered in his youth have left him broken in ways that I doubt will ever mend."

"What things? How do you know this?"

"I know because I bother to know," he said. "You and the others could easily do the same, if you did not think yourselves above taking an interest in the mortal world."

"That's twice you've insulted me."

"Is speaking the truth an affront to you? Perhaps you're more like your sisters than I thought."

"Three times."

Thalil smiled at her, at the way her pale cheeks pinked. "So, being compared with your sisters is also an insult. That's rather insightful of you. You do keep me guessing."

"The things they say about you are not wrong either," she countered. "You're a monster."

He tossed his hair and lifted his chin. "The difference between me and them is I know it. I have never denied—"

"What?" Pherara asked. "What is it?"

How could she not feel it? Thalil had come here to observe what Yarrow would do—it always made for a good show—and even possibly intervene. He hadn't expected the power he felt vibrating in his bones, filling his chest and belly, and singing through his blood. It was familiar—but impossible. Pherara's eyes widened and he knew she sensed it too.

"How can this be?" she breathed.

"It… it can't."

YARROW FACED his cousin, King Garith. The man had done everything Yarrow had asked, and Yarrow had a plan in place. He only needed to say a few words to see it through. So why did his limbs tremble and his guts threaten to fall out as he looked up at the platform?

I'm a great mage. I'm stronger than everyone here combined. I'm the only one who knows the truth. I can show them. I need to show them. The world can't keep operating on lies. My… my beloved deserves vindication at least. He calls to me across the centuries.

What would his creature say? It would say Garith reminded him of Agarick, the man who had shown Yarrow he had no power, had no control over what happened to him… what others did to him. It would mock him, but it would tell him he wasn't powerless. Not anymore.

He wasn't afraid. He wouldn't be afraid. Yet something wasn't right. The air was thick with magic, a compact, shrewd, and efficient enchantment Yarrow recognized. He had encountered it far beneath the ground in a cave beyond the Lapir Mountains. And there were other strong currents flowing over him, breaking, branching off, and meeting again to form streams of energy he couldn't ignore.

But he had to ignore them. He'd come here to sway mortal minds. He didn't know if he had less faith in them or himself, but he had to try.

"South Coast," Garith said with a tip of his head.

"We refer to our lands as the Twenty-Nine," Yarrow replied. "Though it makes little difference to us what outsiders choose to call our islands."

Garith's expression remained neutral. "Your islands are part of our kingdom, cousin."

"Are they?"

"Perhaps that is what we are here to determine," Garith said.

"And if we determine they are not? What will you do?" Yarrow crossed his arms over his chest. "You cannot take them from me."

When Garith shook his head and swiped his hand over his face, he reminded Yarrow of the childhood friend who'd raided wine cellars and swum naked in cold mountain streams alongside him. Garith had aged; the lines around his eyes and the corners of his mouth creased his dark skin. Streaks of gray glimmered in his dark hair. It conjured in Yarrow an indefinable sense of loss, of all of the possibilities of youth cut short. Things lost before they'd been allowed to begin. But he could not afford to be emotional. He had to stay focused.

"We have no designs on your territory." Garith sounded tired. "We only want to prevent another conflict. More fighting is something our people cannot afford. It is not something this world can afford."

"I don't even know what I am being accused of," Yarrow said. "But I am tired of being accused and sentenced to punishment by those who think they are worthy to judge. Is that you, cousin? My friend. Do you intend to condemn me to pain?"

Garith shook his head. "You know it is not like that."

"Then what is it like? What has been my crime? Why the need for this spectacle, Garith?"

"The priestesses say you raided one of their ships," the king said. "That your ships intercepted it as it made its way around the coast of your valenny. They say they were attacked without provocation. And let's not forget that you were the one who demanded this spectacle."

Yarrow took a deep breath and held it in his chest. When he started to feel dizzy, he released the air. They had to know, all of them. He had the evidence to convince them, or at least make them think. Finding the tablet had been a colossal stroke of luck, and he could not afford to waste it. And he had managed to arrange for an audience. "The priestesses of the temples are liars and thieves."

Yarrow waited for the collective gasp from the audience to subside and the murmurs to taper off. "They have been stealing the finds of scholars, hoping to suppress the truth. I, along with my people, simply made sure yet another discovery wouldn't be buried. This knowledge should be known. It is priceless, and it cannot be destroyed. The people have a right to it, to interpret it, the same as the keepers of the temples."

Metal scraped off to Yarrow's right, and he turned toward the sound as a pair of Defenders moved aside so a woman in heavy plum velvets could step into the aisle. She headed the order of the Mother Goddess; she'd taken over when Corbin had murdered her predecessor for not paying her debts to the Cast-Down. She had the round face, plump build, and nondescript light brown hair of a country wife, but Yarrow knew she was a viper.

Red-purple patches blotched her cheeks, and her thick fingers shook with rage as she pointed at Yarrow's chest. "You, tam, are a blasphemer and a heretic. Thank you for proving it before everyone gathered here. It is forbidden to speak against the goddesses as you have."

Murmurs of assent rose from the crowd, but Yarrow shouted over them. "I have said nothing against those you call goddesses. I could speak of them, and I will, but I was referring to you and those of your ilk. You—the priestesses—are thieves and liars. You are trying to deceive all these people"—he swept his hand to indicate the crowd— "to keep them from knowledge they should be able to interpret for themselves. To keep them under your thumb and falsely thinking they have need of you."

"You are the liar, you villain! On what basis do you slander us, whose only concern is for the people of this land? Whose only mission has ever been to lead them into the love and light of the Sisters."

Yarrow reached into his cloak and took out the tablet he'd found on the ship. He held it over his head. "This ancient carving was found in the possession of a group of Defenders. It is not the first such find you or your lackeys have endeavored to bury. Everyone here has heard of Mellinger's Tablet. Everyone knows what happened to the man who discovered it. The priestesses did not like what it had to say, and they're going to like this one even less."

He dropped his arm and held the slab close to his chest. It wouldn't surprise him if the brutes serving the temples tried to knock it from his hands and shatter it on the frozen ground. "This was made before Fane's fall. It shows the one who calls herself Mother Goddess giving birth to the very embodiment of darkness and deceit… Thalil." Yarrow paused, allowing for the inevitable horrified whispers. He opened his arms. "See for yourselves. Look at what is depicted here, what the priestesses do not want you to see. They are afraid of nothing more than the common people thinking for themselves, asking questions, and wondering why things are as they are and if it might be better if they were different."

The people shrunk from him, cowering, huddling together with their cloaks and furs clutched tight around them. Fear and disgust burned in their eyes. Yarrow should be used to such judgment, of being reviled, but it still hurt, and he felt very alone in the center of that throng. But just when he thought his grand gesture had failed, an old woman hobbled forward, her weight supported by a wizened stick. Her lined face lacked much expression as she looked the tablet over, and soon she motioned to others. One by one, they came forward to inspect the carving, and before long a queue had formed.

Yarrow looked over his shoulder and met the beady blue eyes of the priestess. "Will you stop them? Use your warriors to drive them back?" She couldn't; doing so would only prove him right.

She waved a fleshy hand in front of her face. "It is you who underestimates these people, you abomination. That is surely a forgery, and they will be able to see that. They will not fall victim to your lies. The goddesses will protect them from those who would spread corruption."

"Let me see it." A woman in Esperon dress beneath her suede cloak wove gracefully through the throng to stand at Yarrow's side. When her magic brushed against his, it felt hot but controlled, like smith's forge, ready to shape reality to her will. "I am Courtenay Jardine-Lamont. I have spent many years at the university in Pala Reapaza, but I was born in Lockhaven, and I love this land and its people. In Espero, I studied ancient languages and artifacts." She leaned in and ran her slender fingers over the grooves in the stone, but she quickly pulled her hand back, just like Octavian Rose had done. Then she looked up at the people who had formed a ring around Yarrow and herself. "I can communicate in every language spoken in this world, and I understand half a dozen that have been lost to time. This… is a version of a very old language, but in a dialect I have not seen before. Besides myself, there are only four other people who could recognize these symbols, let alone understand them…. Let alone be able to write them. It's unlikely that this is a forgery. Further examination at the university could determine its authenticity beyond a doubt, though. This is certainly worthy of study."

"I would be happy to entrust it to the learned mages of the university," Yarrow said. Around him, people muttered and whispered. From what he could tell, most of them agreed that the tablet should be examined. That was a surprise. It always astonished him when people exhibited wisdom. It amazed him that they'd be willing to fight, even in their own best interests. But there was a definite current of defiance moving through the crowd. Garith, meanwhile, simply leaned forward, his elbows on his knees, watching. Yarrow supposed there was a dash of wisdom in that.

Predictably, the priestess waded in to dam that current. "And now we're going to bow to the whim of the mages of Espero? Believe anything they say?"

"What reason would we have to lie?" Courtenay asked. "Espero has thrived for thousands of years on knowledge, not on keeping people ignorant and easier to control. What would we have to gain by swindling anyone? In case you have forgotten, we are your allies. We gave as much blood as anyone in the war. I fought, and I watched my friends die. Did you?"

The priestess struggled visibly to rein in her outrage. She couldn't win this argument, and she knew it. "Very well. Take it to the island. We have no doubt it will be proved false. That piece of rock is hardly the reason we are here, after all." She turned to address Garith. "We are here to discuss the crimes of Yarroway L'Estrella, and we have been assured Your Majesty will take them seriously. Finally."

Yarrow pressed the tablet into the hands of Courtenay Jardine-Lamont; he trusted her to keep it safe. She might have specialized in languages and artifacts, but he had fought alongside Esperons long enough to recognize the posture and stance of a combat-trained mage. And she was powerful. Nobody would take the tablet from her without a fight. He turned to the flushed face of the priestess. "What are my crimes?"

She shook her head. "Do you even need to ask? Your raiders terrorize the coasts, and you do nothing to stop them. You speak blasphemy against the goddesses, and you will permit no temple to be built in the lands you govern. The heinous practices and immorality of the people under your rule are notorious. You attacked a ship hired by the priestesses and killed our sacred Defenders. You are unnatural, a traitor, a pirate, and a thief. And on top of it all, you are a heretic endeavoring to spread your filth to the righteous people of this great kingdom."

Yarrow clenched and unclenched his fists. She was threatening him, and as always, his magic rose up in his defense. The urge to strike her down, level her and all her supporters, laugh while their corpses smoldered, was strong. But he couldn't. He had to sway the minds of the people. He was just about to explain why he had needed to take that ship, how it would benefit society in the long run, when Octavian Rose stepped up behind him and put a hand on his shoulder.

"Is there any proof of this supposed attack?" Octavian asked.

The priestess smiled smugly. "We have a witness. A man who was captured by the Emiri barbarians but managed to escape."

Octavian clasped his hands behind his back and paced back and forth. "So, the only evidence you can provide is the word of a single man… a man who would likely benefit greatly from delivering a story to your liking."

"Do you dare call me a liar?"

"I would never dare," Octavian continued. "I only wish to point out that interpretation of events can vary greatly from one individual to the next. I was also there when the tablet was discovered. The ship in question ran aground. I doubt you are aware that the islands of the Twenty-Nine are protected by a vast coral reef that spans much of the area beyond the mouth of the river. It is quite a hazard for the sailor who does not know to steer clear of it. By the time we reached the ship, most of the crew had abandoned her and gone in search of help. We found no Defenders on board. While searching for emergency supplies, we discovered the tablet. I did, in fact. I had no idea of its significance, but I have always been a lover of fine art, and I admired it. You can hardly fault me. After all, I'm a simple man. Just a mercenary granted his title by the benevolence of our esteemed ruler. I could hardly be expected to predict the implications of my actions."

"Lies!" the priestess shrieked. "What proof do you have?"

"Plenty," Octavian answered. "Many members of that ship's crew appreciated the aid we provided." He pointed at the people gathered behind them, though Yarrow had no idea any of the sailors had accompanied them. "Many of them found the islands to their liking and chose to stay. Should we hear their accounts?"

The priestess sputtered. "Ruffians seduced by the debauchery of those unholy lands. What good is their word?"

When he next spoke, Octavian addressed the crowd of artisans, shopkeepers, and laborers. "I have always found the common people of this kingdom honest and honorable, my lady. I find it unfortunate that you disagree."

That got the people's attention. Yarrow couldn't help grinning as their voices rose in protest. Octavian let them go for a few moments before speaking again. "So, we have the word of one man against the word of several. Or does the word of a Defender mean more than that of a common sailor, Your Majesty?"

Garith leaned forward in his chair. "No, it certainly doesn't, Bairn Octavian. Not to me."

"Then we can agree there is no basis for the accusations leveled against the Valen of South Coast."

Nodding thoughtfully, Garith said, "It seems we must absolve our cousin of this supposed crime."

The priestess gathered up her skirts and strode to the base of the dais, looking up at the king. "I am afraid that will not do, Your Majesty. We had hoped it would not come to this, but if you will not hold your cousin accountable for his actions, we will. The goddesses demand it. The nobles holding the lands along the seas demand it. And we will see it done. The temples will claim the southern lands, and they will fall under the rule of the priestesses. Houses of worship will be constructed, and those who oppose that will… no longer be welcome there." She turned to her soldiers. "In the name of the Thirteen Sisters, apprehend Yarroway L'Estrella."

Garith was on his feet. "You have no right to defy the orders of the crown!"

Defenders and royal guards drew weapons. The Emiri who'd volunteered to accompany Yarrow armed themselves and closed in around him.

No. He would not let this happen. He had seen too many Emiri dead in a war that was not theirs, their blood staining the water for people who considered them less than vermin. No more. Not one more. His limbs thrummed with magic begging to be unleashed as he pushed his way to the foot of the stage. His luminous blue wings broke from his shoulders, and he couldn't dispel them. They stretched a dozen feet on either side of him, making it easy for him to ascend to the platform and stand in front of his cousin. Sparks crackled along his fingertips, and the sky mirrored his mood, black clouds roiling in and turning the afternoon to twilight. Lightning flickered and pallid faces strobed, appearing and disappearing before him.

"You are all fools if you believe a single, poisonous word that falls from the diseased lips of these falsehearted, power-hungry bitches! We have bled for this kingdom! Died for it! I have surrendered those I loved to the sea, and for what? What? So you can continue living the lie forced on you by the representatives of these so-called goddesses? They're nothing but whores! Faithless whores! Betrayers of the one who gave them everything. My… my…." Yarrow covered his face with his hands, overwhelmed at the visions assailing his memory. Wide lips turning up at the corners, brown skin decorated with dried white clay, shrewd eyes full of more understanding than he'd thought the mortals capable….

"My beloved."

Yarrow dropped his hands and looked down into the eyes of his ancient love, the bold boy he'd tutored in magic thousands of years ago, the one who had surpassed him and ultimately defeated him. But now… now that spirit lived in the body of the prince… of his son. Desire, protectiveness, vengeance, and hate clashed within Yarrow, the edges of those broken pieces grinding together as he stared down at Thane. He loved him, but he had been betrayed. They'd been everything to each other, and now Thane was his son, sired in secret on Queen Cothryn. A mage who would rule. Like Fane. No, not *like* Fane….

Fane.

How had he not realized?

Darkness poured in at the edges of Yarrow's perception, blotting out the screeching priestesses and shouting peasants. He was in a cave, staring into a pool of water, bargaining for his only hope of controlling his own destiny.

You must take me out of this place, end my imprisonment, Fane had said.

How?

Carry me inside you.

Yarrow shook his head. *I cannot agree to that. I came all this way to free myself of one presence trying to control my mind and body. I will not accept another and find myself in the same trap.*

You misunderstand, Fane said. *I have no desire to look through your eyes or act through your hands. I will not whisper inside your head. There won't be enough left of me to do so even if I wished it. No, this whole aspect of me is twisted and flawed after my time here. I'm mad and delusional, but horribly sane enough to recognize it. All I ask is for you to carry a single spark of my most basic essence until I can come back. You will never even know it is there.*

You plan to come back? Yarrow asked.

I must. I will be needed. I need to show people a world without the need for gods or masters. A world where we can take full credit for our triumphs and accept responsibility for our errors. That is all I ever wanted. Help me, and I will help you. As I said, you will not notice my presence.

And then the queen, Garith's wife, had asked for Yarrow's seed. To produce a mage. A mage that would rule.

And now….

"My… my beloved." *My son.* Everything in Yarrow rebelled at the thought, and he clutched his stomach as his body reacted to the realization, forcing everything out. He bent in half as bile shot between his teeth, vomit splattering against the wood of the stage. He had to get away. Run. Save himself from this awful truth.

"Apprehend him!" the priestess squealed. It sounded garbled and far away as Yarrow mopped his chin with his sleeve. "He's mad. Mad and dangerous. We must take him into custody. The people must be protected."

"No." Fane—no, Thane—lifted a hand. A shimmering blue wall materialized between him and the priestess and her men, shielding the stage area. "I… I need to hear what he has to say." The boy turned and fixed his glowing gaze on Yarrow. It was so familiar. In those eyes,

Yarrow saw himself, and he saw the brilliant boy he—his creature—had loved with all its being. Loved enough to impart the secrets that would lead to his destruction. And to the Shades' with it all, he still loved him.

No. Yarrow gagged again. There was nothing left to come up. It all made sense in a cruel, sharp way, but how could he be expected to see his former lover's spirit shining out from behind the eyes of his son? Eyes so much like his own it was a wonder no one had figured out what he and the queen had orchestrated. He wished he could throw up again, purge himself of this impossible conflict, force it out of his being. The boy still looked up at him, though. He was confused, hurting. Yarrow couldn't allow that. Children shouldn't have to suffer. He forced himself to straighten his back.

"Tell me what you want to know."

Prince Thane looked at the priestesses gathered in a huddle behind their warriors. "They hurt me."

"Yes, they did. They took the knowledge you gave them and used it to betray you."

Thane grasped the hair above his temples and shook his head violently. "I don't understand! I'm eleven years old, but... but I *remember* it."

"It's me," Yarrow rasped out. "It's my fault."

"No... you... helped me. I had to get away from you, though. Be free. I.... Did I do a terrible thing?"

"Thane, come on. We have to get out of here." A girl in a filthy yellow dress grasped the prince by the elbow and attempted to pull him away. "We're going to get in so much trouble."

Thane smiled indulgently and stroked the cheek of Duncan's daughter. "No. No one is doing anything to us, Marly."

"But Thane—"

"No. Trust me. I won't let anything happen to you, my beloved."

Marly wrinkled her nose. "Gross. Don't call me that, you idiot."

Yarrow shook his head in an attempt to drive out the phantom images filling it. He knelt down and placed a hand on each of the children's shoulders. Thane's eyes volleyed his gaze back at him with their familiar azure glow, and Marly's were just like her father's: deep brownish green and gentle. Soothing. Solid. "You both need to get out of here," he said in as firm a voice as he could muster. "This is about to get ugly."

"I'll stand with you," Thane said.

"Me too." Marly's chin jutted out. "I wish I had a weapon, though. I should have brought Del's dagger."

"I… all right. Be careful." Yarrow could formulate no argument to send them away. Most people saw children as incompetent, unskilled… but he was so old a couple of decades barely meant anything….

Wasn't he?

He stood. Looking out over the crowd, he had no doubt a fight was brewing. Royal guards faced off against Defenders, and the common folk had separated into factions. Those nobles who had brought soldiers of their own stood on the side of their choosing, and Yarrow's Emiri held their weapons at the ready.

"We demand Yarroway L'Estrella," the red-faced priestess bellowed. "We will not leave here without him. Know this, High King Garith: any attempt to defend him will be seen as an act of aggression against our orders, the temples, and the goddesses themselves."

"Do nothing, Garith!" Yarrow shouted. "I do not need you."

Garith stood, his hand over the mostly ornamental sword at his hip. Led by Sander, his guards closed ranks around him. Everyone stood silent and frozen, like snow piled thick on the mountainside. One wrong move, a wrong word, a pebble tossed haphazardly, and it would become an avalanche. As if he understood this, Garith moved slowly, raising his left hand. He motioned, and his soldiers parted to allow him to walk to the edge of the stage. At the same time, the priestess approached, and the two of them stared at each other. Garith shook his head and spoke in a soft, cautious voice. "This situation can still be salvaged. It does not need to come to violence. More fighting is not what this kingdom needs. It needs to heal, not have its wounds ripped open again."

"Give us Yarroway L'Estrella," the priestess said. "Let us punish his sins, and let your people see they, and not your wicked cousin, are your priority. You cannot put one man above the interests of the rest of your subjects."

Garith never got to respond. Yarrow stepped in front of him. "I am not something to be given, a token prize that says my cousin acknowledges you and the threat of the army you have amassed. You cannot take me whether he wishes it or not. And even if you could, you cannot stop the truth from being known." As subtly as he could, Yarrow glanced around the square. His people, gathered behind Octavian and D'Aurelian, stood surrounded with royal guards on one side and Defenders on the other. Courtenay had edged her way to the dais, probably planning to try to protect the king. Yarrow felt the magic she had gathered and now held ready. Thane and Marly had been pushed behind a trio of guards, and Duncan had made his way to the corner of the platform, his eyes fixed on his daughter and the prince.

Yarrow met the priestess's eyes. He smiled wide, flashing his teeth, and shook his head. "There are too many holes. Places where it's worn away. Places where it's been punctured. And what do you expect? Nothing can hold that weight. The weight of all those lies. It's coming through now. Just a trickle, but you can't stop it. Try plugging the leaks, but you'll just run out of fingers."

"You're crazy," she said, her voice oozing false pity. Genuine pity might have made him angry. "What are you trying to say?"

"I am trying to say that I am going back to my islands. You know you cannot stop me. Stand out of my way."

"You expect the servants of the goddesses to surrender to you? To a piece of filth like you? No." She turned to her soldiers. "Take him. He deserves to rot in the deepest hole we can dig."

"Your Majesty?" Sander asked. "What will you have us do?"

"Nothing," Yarrow said without turning to look behind him. "Do nothing. Don't give them an excuse to declare open war on the crown." He looked over to meet Duncan's eyes. "Do nothing. Just… keep everyone safe. Please keep them safe."

Six Defenders, weapons drawn, moved to surround Yarrow. One of them raised a sword. Before he could lower it, his eyes rolled back, and his weapon dropped with a resounding clang as he crumpled forward, a dagger stuck in his neck just below the rim of his helmet. Everyone seemed petrified for a few pregnant moments, and then chaos broke loose, tearing through the calm. A Defender turned to the Emiri woman who'd thrown the knife and ran her through with such force her feet left the ground. Yarrow stared at her face as her eyes widened and a crimson arc of blood shot from her mouth.

"No!" he cried. "No! Do nothing!"

But it was too late. The other Emiri surged forward to avenge their comrade, and the Defenders met the attack. Metal clashed against metal, and bodies blurred in a frenzied tangle of plate and leather. Royal guards rushed into the mess, trying to pull the combatants apart, but in mere moments, they had no choice but to defend themselves against attacks from both sides. The nobles retreated as their hirelings joined the fray, and some of the common people ran while others picked up rocks to throw, or fought with their bare hands. Yarrow had no idea whose side they were on, but it didn't matter.

It didn't matter, because his people were dying. As he watched, a young man took a blow to the waist, and a Defender kicked him as he withdrew his blade. He fell facedown, blood pooling around him, and tried to drag himself to safety. His legs didn't seem to be working, and before he could make it more than a few feet, a guard stepped on his back, and he screamed. The Defender facing that guard shoved the young Emiri out of his way with his boot, and soon he was trampled beneath the fray, his flesh and bones crushed and broken.

Because of Yarrow. Because he had volunteered to accompany Yarrow.

"No!" Yarrow spread his wings and leapt from the platform. An azure claw extended from his arm, and he used it to pry the Defenders away from his people, swinging it from side to side and tossing them into the air as he went. He couldn't let any more Emiri die because they'd made the mistake of trusting him. Nobody else should have to die for not having the good sense to run from him and the tragedy he always caused.

Even when he thought he was doing the right thing.

He carved a path between the Defenders and his allies, but more soldiers had moved to the far end of the square, boxing them in. Worse yet, Yarrow couldn't just blast through them without risking harming his friends. Octavian had drawn a short sword and a dagger, and he slowly thinned the enemy ranks while D'Aurelian drove adversaries back with gouts of flame that burned bright against the gray winter sky.

Yarrow chanced a glance behind him. The stage stood empty; Sander had gotten the king out of harm's way. That was good. Had Duncan taken the children out of danger? Yarrow searched the jumble of bodies. He needed to know they were safe. The curiosity cost Yarrow, though. His wings cushioned the blow that fell across his back, but the force sent him staggering forward. Before he could regain his balance, the club or mace struck the back of his head, and the world disappeared in a cascade of black sparkles. His chest hit the ground hard, and his teeth pierced the tip of his tongue, drawing blood. Instinctively, Yarrow rolled to his back and crossed his arms over his face. His wings cocooned him against the armored boots pounding down next to him, but he couldn't seem to clear the wool from his head or force his vision to clarity. A heel connected with his rib, driving the breath from his chest. He lashed out with his magic but couldn't tell if he hit anything.

Dark shapes loomed over him. He was flat on his back with soldiers standing above him. He remembered what happened next, saw it in sharp lines, recalled it in his flesh, no matter how he tried to drive the recollections away. They wanted to hurt him. Hurt him and laugh at his tears. Say he wanted the pain, deserved it. For all his power, the familiar sensation of helplessness reduced him to a whimpering child.

Not this. He couldn't. His magic built within him, gaining momentum and power as it swirled inside, and only the vague thought of those depending on him stopped him from letting it spill forth in a torrent and obliterate everything for miles. Duncan was here somewhere, and Sasha. He couldn't hurt them, even if it meant—

A whip of white light cracked over Yarrow, cutting through the hovering forms, burning through their armor and flesh. They fell, cut in half above their hips, innards spilling out, stinking and steaming. When the brilliance subsided, Yarrow looked up to see his son, together with the most beautiful person he had ever beheld: a young man with dark hair, black eyes, and full, red lips. The stranger smiled, and almost before Yarrow could reconcile his existence with the hideousness around him, he had faded away. Thane reached out a hand, and Yarrow clasped it and stumbled to his feet.

Behind Thane, Marly picked up a small sword and swiped wildly at the enemy soldiers, her erratic movements keeping the Defenders back. Her clothing was torn and soaked with blood, one eye blackened and swollen shut. Yarrow looked for Duncan; these children had to get back to the castle, to safety. They shouldn't have to witness these horrors. But amid the tangle of bodies, Yarrow couldn't find his friend. Octavian, D'Aurelian, and a group of Emiri had cleared a path at the end of the square. Beyond the open space, their horses waited. To the left and right, guards and Defenders closed in. Another Emiri fell to her knees, her throat cut and hands clutching the gash. A scream of frustration tore from Yarrow's throat. He used his glowing limb to knock the Defenders away from Marly, and then he scooped her up in one arm and tossed her over his shoulder. With his other arm, he picked up Thane, ignoring the conflicting emotions their contact conjured. Then he closed his wings around them and ran.

Octavian and D'Aurelian followed, along with most of the Emiri. But too many would never leave the market square.

What had he done? Where would it lead? The priestesses would not let this pass, Yarrow knew. He had experienced moments in his life when the form and energy of the world seemed liquid, malleable. When fate seemed to have no designs on the course the future would take. When the materials that would shape what was to come could be manipulated by anyone. This was such a moment, he knew. He had those ingredients, but he didn't know what they would combine to form. No one did.

He had to save his son, Duncan's daughter, and as many of his people as he could. So he ran, knowing that in doing so, in doing nothing, he had decided the form the future would take. He could only wait for it to reveal itself.

Chapter Seven

EVERYTHING WITHIN Jorian rebelled at what he had to do, and every new day marked a struggle to continue. As he stood before the filigree door to his master's chambers, he closed his eyes and reminded himself he had volunteered for this assignment. He was doing a great service to Espero, with the possibility of finding some reparation for the Esperon blood wasted by the Johmatran heathens. And further, he had proved damned good at it. He ran a hand over the stubble on his scalp, his thick hair probably the least of what he had relinquished, yet still missed. As he had forced himself to do for almost five years, he pasted on a false smile and quietly opened a door that looked made from golden lace studded with tiny gems.

Jorian went to each of the three fireplaces and stoked the flames before adding more of the desiccated stalks harvested from the desert. He hated the cold that settled over the palace during the night, a dry cold that made his skin itch and his hair feel brittle. Having nothing to wear but gauzy crimson trousers and little gold slippers didn't help. But he was complaining, even if only in his mind. He couldn't afford to do that; there was always the danger that a hint of bitterness would show on his features. His master was very shrewd. As he had been taught before coming to this strange and savage land, Jorian cleared his mind. He permitted himself only thoughts relating to his tasks: heating water for tea, preparing the rough sponges to scrub his master's skin, warming the oil to rub on him afterward, and laying out his clothes for the morning. His master would need a new ensemble by the midday meal, because his garments would be soaked with blood....

Everything was ready. It was time to wake him. Jorian went to the massive bed, the mat covered by a dome of delicate gold wires to match the door. He pushed the red curtains apart and looked down at the sleeping form of the one he served, wondering, for the thousandth time, if his ruse would be easier if the man was as ugly and deformed as most of the potentates of the Johmatran city-states. It would be easier to detest him, but feigned reverence had carried Jorian to the esteemed place he held in this great household. And that reverence came, in large part, because his lord was beautiful. Jorian was hardly shallow, but he had to cling to any sliver of positivity he could find in this awful place.

The man was five years younger than Jorian's twenty-eight, and he was truly an anomaly among his kind. Centuries—no, millennia— of inbreeding among the ruling class, in an effort to maintain the purity of Fane's blood, had resulted in a long list of physical and mental disfigurements. It had become accepted, almost a mark of prosperity and power. Through the intelligence he'd memorized before embarking on this mission, Jorian knew his sovereign had been produced through the union of his mother—ruler of this city-state—and a powerful noble from far to the southeast. It wasn't unusual for reproduction to be viewed as mere breeding for favorable traits—the man's mother was even married to a man not his sire—but no one could have predicted the result.

Behmarsan Kahladryia Sala N'hahseen was physical perfection, with long, elegant limbs covered by golden brown skin. Ebony hair so shiny it looked perpetually wet covered his jacquard pillows and draped off the edge of the bed. His oval face achieved the ideal balance between angular and soft, and his full lips, the color of red clay, were parted slightly in sleep. His birth had prompted all sorts of prophecies and interpretations, but the general consensus was one of hope: a symbol of Fane's imminent return. It granted N'hahseen the adoration of the populace—as well as powerful enemies. As his personal and most valued servant, Jorian shared in both.

"Master," Jorian said softly. "Do you want to wake up?"

N'hahseen grumbled, stretched his arms over his head, and slowly opened his eyes. The right one was almost as black as his hair, while the left was white tinged with the faintest hint of blue—and it was blind. That, along with deafness in his left ear, were the only limitations he suffered as a result of his lineage. He considered a moment. "Yes, I will wake up."

Jorian peeled back the tissue-thin coverings in various hues of gold and crimson. Beneath them, N'hahseen was naked and partially erect. Jorian quickly looked away from the thin trail of dark hair on his belly and what waited beneath, hurrying to fetch N'hahseen's slippers so he could step into them. Then he draped a robe over his master's shoulders but left it open. He gestured toward the water, oil, and combs arranged on a low table next to the nearest hearth. "How can I be permitted to serve you first?" Jorian asked. "Shall I help you wash and dress? Or would you prefer to eat first? Perhaps you require the talents of one of your kahlka? Would you like me to fetch the one you would fancy?"

"No, no kahlka," N'hahseen said. He pulled his robe shut and tied a sloppy knot at the waist. "Sex might settle my nerves somewhat, but I find myself loath to have any of them intrude on my thoughts. I'm irritated at just the idea of dealing with them."

Though surprised, Jorian kept his features neutral. N'hahseen had thirty beautiful young men whose sole purpose was to satisfy his every physical desire. The Johmatrans considered sexual release necessary to health and contentment. "If you are tired of all your consorts, my lord, there is a long list of eager volunteers waiting to audition for a place in your retinue."

"I do not wish to consider it at the moment." N'hahseen looked at Jorian with an expression Jorian couldn't interpret, but that raised gooseflesh along his bare arms.

"Breakfast, then?" Jorian was only too happy to change the subject. Watching his master fulfill what the Johmatrans considered a basic necessity with sometimes three or more young men twisted his emotions into a tangled mass he was only too happy to sequester at the edge of his thoughts. He hoped to leave this place—and this man—behind before he ever had need to tug at the ends of those threads.

N'hahseen pressed a palm to his belly and tapped two fingers against his forehead—the Johmatran version of a shake of the head. "I don't think I'm hungry," he said in a soft voice that belied the nerves he tried to hide. "I am scheduled for ornamentation this morning, am I not?"

Jorian knew he didn't need to ask. He knew, had known and dreaded it for almost a moon now. Jorian had watched as his master's appetite had tapered off and his sleep had become fitful and infrequent.

Even as he told himself he felt no pity for the man, Jorian stepped closer and brushed a strand of hair out of N'hahseen's eyes. He moved his hand down and squeezed the tense muscles at the back of N'hahseen's neck, his only acknowledgment of his master's anxiety. "It is scheduled for today. Before the midday meal."

A press of his lips into a tight line was the only reaction N'hahseen offered, but Jorian noticed the way his spine straightened and his shoulders bunched up. He clasped the other man's hand, carefully unfurled the fingers N'hahseen had curled into a tight fist, and led him to a mat on the floor by the fire. When N'hahseen sat on his heels, Jorian knelt behind him and slid the robe from his shoulders. Swirling scars covered his shoulders, his arms to the elbows, and his back to below his shoulder blades. They were deep and lined with thick, white keloids, the contrast stark against his dark skin. Over the years, Jorian had learned not only to ignore the markings, but almost not to see them. Today, with the addition of more looming, though, he could neither look away nor dismiss the pain he had felt—pain like nothing he had imagined in his worst nightmares—when his own small scars had been added across his cheekbones and down the center of his chest so he could pass himself off as a native.

"Rahsari?" N'hahseen called Jorian by his faux-Johmatran name. "Is anything wrong?"

Jorian hurried to pick up the golden comb and start working out the knots in his master's long tresses. "Of course not, my lord. I was just going over your schedule in my mind to make sure you reach all of your obligations. Today will be busy, with the ornamentation and the dinner to honor the delegates tonight."

N'hahseen leaned into Jorian's touch. "Yes. The meeting of the delegates has occupied much of my attention lately. I wonder if the ornamentation could be scheduled for another day."

Finished combing, Jorian gathered N'hahseen's hair up and secured it at his crown with a jeweled clip. Using his fingertips, he rubbed circles across the miniature curls at N'hahseen's nape. "Your mother will not like that. She personally designed a schedule to ensure your ornamentations will be complete by your twenty-fifth birthday. It will mean six more sessions, in closer proximity than is usually advisable, but she seems certain it will amplify your magic to fantastic degrees."

"Yes, I know. Still, I would prefer not to attend the banquet tonight weak and distracted. Normally after a session, I drink Blue Oblivion and sleep until the pain becomes tolerable—usually for days."

Without thinking, Jorian brushed the pad of his finger over an especially deep mass of scars. The hum of magic moved through his hand and into the bones of his wrist, producing a twinge and ache that, inexplicably, was also pleasant. "I know you do. I...." *I watched you sleep, bleeding all over the sheets, whimpering. I made sure you at least took in water and held the pot while you pissed.*

But I do not pity you. You are still my enemy, and the blood of Esperon babies is on your hands. Your barbaric customs are no business of mine, and neither is your suffering.

"Rahsari?"

Jorian hurried to pick up a coarse sponge made from a carnivorous desert plant and soften its prickly tines with fragrant oil. As he lifted it to his master's skin, he couldn't still the trembling of his hand.

"Forgive me, my lord. I only meant to ask what I can do to ease your burdens. How can I help?"

N'hahseen turned to face Jorian and met his eyes. Not until he closed his fingers around Jorian's wrist did Jorian realize he still held the dripping sponge. He needed to get a hold of himself. There was no reason this should be affecting him so deeply. What did he care if this spoiled Johmatran prince wanted to stretch out and have his flesh carved up until he sobbed like a baby and expelled everything in his stomach? If he didn't want to do it, he should just refuse. Jorian had to maintain the persona he'd developed. Espero depended on him. His own life likely depended on his being convincing. As casually as he could, he set the sponge down and lowered his hand to his knee. N'hahseen never let go of his wrist.

With his free hand, N'hahseen stroked across the scars extending from Jorian's temple to the side of his nose. He cupped Jorian's cheek and asked, "Would you really help me?"

Letting out a jagged breath, Jorian closed his eyes so he wouldn't have to look at the hopeful, gentle expression in the other man's gaze. "Of course. It is my honor to serve you in any way I can. My honor and my pleasure."

"Any way you can."

Sheer curiosity finally compelled Jorian to open his eyes. He should have been horrified at how close their faces were, the tips of their noses almost touching. N'hahseen's hand on his face should have repulsed him. He wanted it to repulse him; this man was his enemy, the epitome of everything he detested.

When N'hahseen spoke, his breath tickled Jorian's lips. "You are invaluable to me. Sometimes I think you are the only person who sees me as a man. Even my mother views me as some sort of accessory, a symbol of her status and power. Would you… would you have interest in comforting me?"

Jorian sucked in a deep breath, but it didn't seem to fill his lungs. "Comfort? You… you have your kahlka for that."

N'hahseen traced Jorian's upper lip with his thumb. "Yes, and they are beautiful and talented. By I don't harbor any delusions that they care for me. Do you care for me?"

"Of course. But I am not worthy of what you're asking. I'm not trained… I…."

"I don't care." N'hahseen rose up on his knees and moved closer. He looked down at Jorian, and when he pulled the clip from his hair, it fell in satiny sheets to curtain both their faces. N'hahseen moved his hand beneath Jorian's chin to tilt Jorian's face upward. Without thinking, Jorian moved his hands to clasp the other man's waist just above his hips. Their lips brushed together.

For a few heartbeats, Jorian relished the contact, opening his lips to admit N'hahseen's eager tongue, arching his back to press his belly against the other man's firm, lean torso. It would be so easy to give in; his body craved this even if his mind found it repellent. But where would it lead? How would he justify it when he returned to Espero? Because he had to believe he would return to Espero, or none of this would be bearable. Would offering himself to N'hahseen benefit his mission, make him privy to more secrets to pass back to his homeland? Or would it reduce his value in N'hahseen's eyes? He could not allow himself to be seen as replaceable, and no one was more replaceable than the prince's throngs of concubines. Since coming to Johmatra, nothing had horrified Jorian more than his current realization that he now considered lovemaking in terms of political advantage rather than pleasure or connection with another person. Until that moment, he hadn't realized how much he had changed.

He also hadn't realized he'd stopped moving his lips, tongue, and hands, or that his face had twisted into a pained grimace until a wash of light told him N'hahseen had pulled away. He got to his feet and crossed his arms over his chest, looking down at Jorian through narrowed eyes. "I did not think you would find it such a hardship."

Jorian turned his gaze to his knees. The habit of shaking his head had been one of the hardest to abandon, and he almost slipped as he whispered, "No. It isn't that it's a hardship. It just… I shouldn't. It isn't allowed."

"I am the First Son of Kahladryia!" N'hahseen picked up a vase full of dried flowers and threw it against the wall behind his bed, where it shattered in a shower of blue and gold glass. He went to the crystal doors leading to his balcony and pounded his fists against them. "I am Fane's gift to this world!" He kicked over a small table. "It's allowed if I say it's allowed. Anything I want is allowed!"

Jorian stood. He wasn't completely unfamiliar with these tantrums, though he had never instigated one personally. "Everything you say is true, my lord. And I am sorry. I… I never expected to be honored with your attention in that way. I was confused."

N'hahseen's anger faded much faster than normal, and he pushed his hair out of his face. "You don't understand me as I thought you might. I don't want you to feel honored. I just want you to feel… I don't even know. It does not matter. I have many more important things to worry about. Still, you should know that I would never compel you, not through force, or through guilt, or…."

"I know." Jorian didn't understand the sick feeling in his belly when he should be feeling only relief. He wanted to say something else, but every word he knew eluded him.

N'hahseen retied his robe. "I think I'll go to the harem after all. I'll see to my ablutions there. Please clean up this room, and have my clothing laid out for me. Then ready yourself. I wish for you to accompany me to the ornamentation."

After N'hahseen left the room, Jorian flopped down on his bed, trying desperately to ignore the way it smelled of him. N'hahseen was a spoiled monster, though Jorian supposed it wasn't completely his fault. He'd been told by everyone around him he was god's gift since he had drawn his first breath. And still, no one knew him. Not really. And no one loved him beyond the portents he symbolized. What must it be like to be that alone?

And why did Jorian care? This man placed himself higher than everyone else in the world, felt himself worthy of owning an army of slaves and killing any mages not descended from Fane. He would likely kill Jorian if he knew Jorian possessed the gift. No, he wouldn't dirty his precious little hands; he'd have a hireling see to it. And Johmatran executions weren't fast or efficient. Sometimes they lasted for days.

Jorian rose from the bed and started gathering bits of broken glass. As he did, he reminded himself only a child went on such a rampage when he didn't get his own way. He forced every recollection of N'hahseen's kindness or the good times they'd shared from his mind. He hated him. He had to hate him, because if he cared for him at all, he wouldn't be able to withstand what he would witness in a few hours.

Chapter Eight

N'HAHSEEN LAY on a stone table, cream colored and shot through with veins of rosy gold. Furrows ran perpendicular to his body, for the purpose of collecting his blood and channeling it into the metal troughs sitting alongside the table. And they were full to flooding, dripping steadily and filling the room with a ferrous odor that almost gagged Jorian. He'd witnessed this ritual before, and it never got any easier. As he'd sat on a stool to N'hahseen's left, listening to the man go through the familiar cycle of stoic gasps, to whimpering, to screaming, to sobbing, he had again tried to understand and found he couldn't. Nothing—no amount of magic or power—was worth this. He had tried to understand the Johmatran culture, to resist judging it against his own, but as he looked at N'hahseen's ashen face and bluish lips, tears pouring from his eyes, he could form only one thought.

These people are monsters. They need to be stopped.

The woman who'd been working on N'hahseen's decorations lifted her tool, finally finished. It was less a knife and more a triangular scoop—long, sharp, and designed to carve out furrows of flesh. She flicked skin and blood onto the tiled floor and handed the implement off to a dead-eyed Emiri slave. By now, N'hahseen had exhausted himself crying, and only a weak grunt escaped him with every exhale. Jorian made sure he wouldn't be seen and grazed the back of N'hahseen's hand with his fingertips. He would be screaming again soon.

The woman returned to the table's edge, followed by a pair of slaves. One held a batch of white cloths, the other a black stone pitcher. After the skin artist blotted the blood from the left side of N'hahseen's chest, Jorian could finally see the design. A circle covered his skin from collarbone to nipple, with three smaller circles inside. Each ring contained about a dozen swirling symbols, and a starlike pattern stood at the center. Blood welled up in the cuts again, and the artist soaked it up before throwing the cloth to the floor. N'hahseen was breathing hard and looking barely conscious, his eyes rolled back and lids fluttering.

For the hundredth time in the last few hours, Jorian tried to convince himself he didn't feel sorry for him.

But then the woman took a small brush and dipped it into the pitcher held by the Emiri slave, and Jorian braced himself. They wanted these cuts to scar, and that meant irritating them. They couldn't be allowed to heal cleanly. The fluid in the pitcher—a mix of acidic citrus juice and leaves from a mildly poisonous plant—would assure they didn't. When the hard bristles scraped along the fresh cuts, N'hahseen's head lifted off the table, and he screamed until he had to stop to suck in air. As soon as he managed to fill his chest, he screamed again, and he didn't stop until the woman finished. By then, he'd broken his fingernails clawing at the table, and specks of foamy spittle coated his chin.

Jorian could do nothing but sit idle and pretend not to notice the other man's distress. N'hahseen was descended from Fane; he should be able to take it. As his servant, Jorian should be able to abide it.

Next the skin artist withdrew a small glass phial from the pocketed belt around her waist. It contained a mixture of ground minerals that would further impede the healing of the cuts. She sprinkled it over the design, and then she used the callused pad of her thumb to grind it into the raw edges. His throat too sore to scream anymore, N'hahseen covered his eyes with his forearm, sobbing and gagging. He'd already thrown up twice, and his stomach was empty, but his body still shook with dry heaves. Finally she bandaged the wounds with clean linen, and she poured a greenish elixir down N'hahseen's throat. Again Jorian wanted to shake his head. That potion would stimulate N'hahseen, keep him awake and give him the illusion of clarity, but it would do nothing to ease the shock to his system or negate the abuse his body had taken. Still, it woke him like a splash of icy water, and he sat up on the table, looking around as if he didn't recognize his surroundings. Jorian reached up and rested a hand on his shoulder. N'hahseen startled at first, but then he looked at Jorian and offered a weak smile.

"We're done for today," the woman said. A slave handed her a towel, and she wiped the blood from her hands and arms.

Jorian helped N'hahseen stand, steadying him with an arm around his waist when he swayed. N'hahseen wore only billowing beige trousers, but the blood had run down to stain them from the waistband almost to the knees. They would have to be thrown out. As Jorian helped him limp slowly out of the room, half a dozen slaves appeared to gather up bloody rags, wipe down the table, and scrub the floor on hands and knees.

Jorian led N'hahseen to a small alcove a little way down the hall. This part of the palace was made entirely from crystal, so it was bright with the late-morning light, the browns and greens of the grounds beyond abstract shapes on the clear, gemlike walls. After he'd helped N'hahseen sit on an upholstered bench hewn from the same sheer stone as the walls and floor, Jorian went to a burbling fountain and dipped a cloth in the pure water. N'hahseen gasped when Jorian pressed it to his belly to start removing the coagulating blood.

"Are you hurt?" Jorian drew his hand back. What a stupid question. Of course he was hurt; he was as pale and gray as a rainy winter morning, his eyes were unfocused, and his hands were shaking. This was ridiculous. Jorian might have specialized in old tomes back at the university, but every mage who studied there learned a few basic healing spells—spells he could not use unless he wanted to be executed. Jorian dropped to his knees and let his forehead fall to N'hahseen's thigh. The other man rested a cool, trembling hand on the shorn skin at the back of Jorian's head.

"Are you all right?"

"Me?" Jorian lifted his head, shocked. "I am not the one who went through all that. Why… why do you agree to it?"

N'hahseen stared absently at the crystal walls and continued stroking Jorian's head. "We must all do whatever we can to make the world pleasing to Fane. We must entice him to return to us, to bless us again with his magic. He needs to see his children carrying on his traditions, doing everything as he would. Then, one day, he will return, and no one will have to toil, or suffer, or… ah."

Jorian couldn't help thinking that if Fane abided this sort of torture, the world was better off without him. He knew he couldn't do much, but he would not do nothing. He stood and offered N'hahseen his arm. "You've traumatized your body, and you've lost a great deal of blood.

You need fruit juice, or something sweet. You need to be kept warm, and you need to rest. Let me help you back to your room."

"You seem to know a great deal about healing."

Jorian could barely think of his own safety, of what would happen if he was discovered. "I aim to be a good servant."

"You are." N'hahseen leaned heavily on Jorian as they walked. "I'm very cold."

A shock to the body would do that, Jorian knew. It could even kill a person despite nonfatal injuries. But he wouldn't let that happen. "Your suite is not far. I… I'll see that you're all right."

"I know. You're good to me, better than a servant is required to be. I… regret my actions this morning. You are not kahlka. You are not expected to service me that way. I know that common people choose partners based on mutual desire, on feelings of companionship, and that is what you must expect. I have tried to imagine it… being able to choose. But Fane's blood is just too precious. Otherwise, I might lay with a woman. To see what it would be like."

Jorian didn't anticipate the stab of jealousy. "You would prefer a woman?"

N'hahseen forced a laugh, the sound reminiscent of the vase breaking against his wall. "I don't know. I enjoy being with men, but I'm curious. But I cannot risk impregnating one until I find a suitable mother for my children. The blood must be kept pure. Have you ever been with one?"

"A woman? No, my lord, but not because of lack of opportunity. I prefer men."

"How do you know if you've never been able to compare?"

"I just know." Jorian opened the door to N'hahseen's chambers and guided him toward his bed. When he got N'hahseen situated on the edge of the mattress, he eased his fouled trousers down his legs and then helped him to lie down. He tucked the covers tight around N'hahseen to hold in the heat of his body. "I'll go to the kitchens and get you some juice."

"No, please stay. Please rest beside me."

"You must at least have some water." Jorian went to a table and poured some before pushing it into N'hahseen's hands.

"I'll drink it if you agree to lie down next to me."

Jorian almost shook his head. "You act like a child. Cutting off your own nose to spite your face."

"What an odd expression," N'hahseen remarked. "I've never heard it before."

Damn. Jorian needed to be more careful. "An old farmer's analogy. Something my father used to say."

"You were a farmer? You seem so… refined."

"I studied. Farmers are not inherently intellectually inferior, my lord."

"No, though they are not of Fane's blood."

"No, but they will not refuse water when they need it to stay alive." Jorian again pushed the cup at N'hahseen.

"A fair point." N'hahseen drank.

Jorian noticed a vial of milky blue liquid on the night table, probably placed there on orders of N'hahseen's mother. In the most remote parts of the desert, a species of winged serpents lived on the highest crags. They liked to eat their prey alive, and they possessed a venom so potent that their victims would think they floated on a cloud in paradise while they were devoured. Catching and milking them was a precarious business, and many died in the attempt. It was the reason Blue Oblivion was so precious. "Will you have something for the pain?"

"Not that." N'hahseen was already fading, his lids heavy over his eyes and the cup dangling from his fingers. "I must be alert for the dinner tonight."

Jorian was used to a society where leeway was given to those who were injured or didn't feel well, where such things were not held against them. But the dinner seemed important to N'hahseen, so he didn't argue.

"I just want you to rest next to me."

Jorian complied, though he slipped beneath the bedclothes without undressing. N'hahseen cuddled up next to him and rested his head on Jorian's chest. Jorian combed his fingers through his hair. Sweat and thrashing had it twisted up into knots again, but at least some warmth had returned to N'hahseen's skin. "I wish you'd take a drop or two of Blue Oblivion. It will wear off in a few hours."

"Why?"

"Because I don't like seeing you suffer."

N'hahseen brushed his fingers down Jorian's waist. "You… you're just good, aren't you? You don't benefit in station if I'm comfortable."

"Decent, human, is what I would call it." Jorian wondered if he'd said too much, expressed an opinion that would mark him as a foreigner.

"You have a fire in you." N'hahseen's words were slurred and sleepy. "Do you think you might have chosen me?"

"You don't know what you're asking." With the comfortable mat beneath him, the soft covers above, and N'hahseen's body curled pliantly around him, the exhaustion that followed a state of acuity dragged at Jorian, and he yawned.

"I mean, if you were a man, and I was a man… a shopkeeper or something…. If we saw each other at the market. Might you give me a chance?"

Jorian stroked his hair and gathered him closer. "It doesn't matter. You need to get some rest. I'll wake you later."

"It matters…." In moments, N'hahseen was asleep, and Jorian could finally relax.

THE LACK of light woke Jorian, and he sat up in a panic. He'd slept more deeply than he had since leaving Espero, and now the sun had set. He scrambled out of the bed and hurried to light the oil lamps around the room. Soon their flames reflected off the crystalline walls, brightening the space enough for him to see easily. Thank Pherara he'd laid out N'hahseen's clothing earlier that morning, before the ornamentation.

If they dressed quickly, they might make it to the dinner without embarrassing themselves.

Jorian shook N'hahseen's shoulder. "My lord, we'll need to hurry to be ready to meet with the delegates."

N'hahseen sat up too fast. The motion pulled at his wound and he pressed a hand to the bloody bandage. An impression of the symbols carved into his body stained the cloth. "No! We must make it."

"Forgive me for failing you."

"You haven't failed yet. Help me get into my clothes."

Jorian complied, dressing N'hahseen in a gauzy scarlet vest that reached the floor and extended in a train behind him. Three golden buckles held it in place but left his chest—and the bloody bandages—exposed. Not that anyone would hold that against him; if anything, the markings symbolized status and power. The delegates would likely envy the augmentation they would provide to N'hahseen's magic. Golden embroidery depicting the winged snakes native to the area adorned the edges of the garment, and gemstones sparkled along the edges of its stiff, high collar. Instead of his typical loose trousers, N'hahseen wore a snug pair of very short pants; they barely reached the tops of his thighs. Black boots of the softest leather hugged his calves to the knee but left his toes exposed. As N'hahseen put on his dozens of rings and bracelets, Jorian knelt down to brush gold leaf over his toenails. Then he slipped an elbow-length leather glove, embossed with the same swirling patterns as the boots and reminiscent of the scarification, over N'hahseen's right arm. He placed a bracelet of rubies as large as grapes at his wrist.

Over his left shoulder, Jorian placed a leather pauldron mimicking armor. Feathers as long as his arm extended from it, and rows of tiny red and gold beads dangled from the ends of the feathers, giving it the impression of a wing. Jorian secured the strap beneath N'hahseen's opposite arm. "I must do your makeup, my lord."

"We'll be late."

"You can hardly show up without it. Besides, your presence is a gift to them. Bestow it when you see fit." Jorian urged him to a stool, where candles reflected off angled mirrors to produce a bright light. He hurried to take out the little clay pots of pigment and sets of brushes. He actually liked doing this work.

"I suppose you're right. Being a few moments late will show them their opinions mean nothing to me. That I am above convention."

"Exactly. Close your eyes." Jorian surrounded N'hahseen's eyes and the bridge of his nose with a smudged crimson cloud. He applied a line of red to the center of his chin and lined his eyes in smoky black. After brushing gold dust over his lips, along his cheekbones, and over his brow bones, he declared the effect complete. "You look beautiful. Amazing."

"Let me put some on you."

Jorian took a deep breath and closed his eyes as the brushes moved over his skin, the touches teasing… intimate. He knew there was no greater way to show love for another's features than to enhance them with paint, to carefully consider them and how best to show them off. And N'hahseen took his time, even though the dinner was important to him….

"You're finished."

Looking in the mirror, Jorian saw his dark eyes outlined with sparkling bronze, a heavy line accentuating his upper eyelid and curving up at the corner. A series of small dots lined his lower lashes, and the rest of his face had been coated in soft, light powder, making his eyes look large and commanding. "You have lovely eyes," N'hahseen said, running his pinky finger across Jorian's lashes, making metallic flecks drizzle down. "I see so much in them: wisdom, empathy, passion. But it could be my imagination. I would like you to wear something of mine."

"My lord?"

N'hahseen had already gone to a chest, flung it open, and returned with a circlet of twisted golden wires. A diamond-shaped black stone sat at the middle, in the center of Jorian's forehead when N'hahseen put it on his head. The way it angled and curved brought even more attention to Jorian's eyes. "Do you want a wig?"

"Do you want me to wear a wig, my lord?"

"I don't care. You… you're beautiful no matter what. What I want is for you to return here with me, to these rooms, after the banquet. But I only want it if you do also."

"I…." Jorian's senses filled to bursting, inundated with the soft rasp of N'hahseen's voice, the reverent gentleness of his fingers on Jorian's neck, the subtle scent of his oils and cosmetics, and the musk of his skin beneath them. It made it impossible for Jorian to think, so he let the blood pulsing so insistently in his veins make the decision for him. "I don't know how I'll get through the dinner, in anticipation of what will happen when it ends."

N'hahseen smiled. "I would kiss you senseless if I wouldn't ruin all my hard work."

"Speaking of, I must still attend to your hair."

N'hahseen shook his head, his black tresses whipping around. "I'll leave it loose. Very decadent, don't you think?"

Everything about N'hahseen was decadent, and extravagant, and utterly sensual. "It will be interesting to see how that is received, my lord. Shall we make our grand entrance?"

"SAY WHAT you want about these Johmatrans, they certainly know how to dress." Thalil grinned as he leaned against the crystal wall.

Pherara shook her head. In her billowing silver gowns, she looked like a cloud that had sprouted a head and hands. "They certainly have a penchant for the outlandish. The young lord who just entered the dining hall looks like he could have raided your closet. There's something about his servant, though. A sort of restrained power."

"He's one of yours," Thalil said. "A mage of Espero positioned here as a spy."

"So I am here to watch over him?"

"You're here to enjoy yourself." Thalil waved his hand and Pherara's shapeless drapings transformed into a slinky gown, red, with thin strips of gathered cloth barely covering her small breasts. Her silver hair curled into ringlets held back by a band of black leather, with golden chains dangling in loops in front of her ears. A belt of golden disks cinched the dress at her waist, and it hung in thin strips between her legs, front and back, exposing her long legs and the crisscrossing straps of dark suede that covered them to her upper thighs. "Much better."

"What are you thinking!" Pherara grimaced as she looked down at her attire.

"Oh, forgive me." Thalil wiggled his fingers and a thick golden cord appeared around her neck. At the center, a ruby cut into a crescent moon hung down, edged in gold and with red beads dribbling into her cleavage like droplets of blood. "Now you look perfect."

"I won't be seduced by you as so many others have," Pherara said.

"I have no wish to seduce you. It's male bodies that stoke my fire. But you should know what it means to feel beautiful. Because you are. You have nothing to hide." He looked up through his fringe and met her gray eyes.

She blushed and turned her head away. "I feel ridiculous, Thalil."

He took her hand and caressed her fingers with his thumb. "You look anything but. We should find a mirror so that you can see."

She pulled her hand away. "I suspect we'll have more interesting events to watch."

Long tables of polished black stone, arranged in an L shape, took up half of the extensive room. On the plush red benches around them, potentates from several of the most powerful city-states reclined, drinking the wine poured by their servants or nibbling at the predinner snacks arranged on tiered golden platters. Thalil appreciated the aesthetic of the décor. The diners… less so. He had never denied being shallow, but on the other hand, his appreciation of beauty was wide and varied. But all he saw were the twisted limbs, distorted features, and sallow, papery skin that had resulted after centuries of inbreeding. By the way her lips turned down and a tiny crease appeared between her brows, Pherara was also disturbed by the sight.

"No amount of fine clothing or headdresses can conceal that," she said with a shake of her head. "It pains me to think they have done this to themselves in Fane's name. He believed in nothing if not comfort and freedom for every person." Her eyes wandered to the Emiri slaves standing against the back wall, emaciated, heads shorn to provide the vibrant hair for the Johmatrans' wigs.

Thalil couldn't miss the fondness in her voice. He dipped his head. "Yes. He ruled well because he didn't feel it was his right to rule. He never acted as though others owed him power."

"Will we speak of what happened in Eirion-Vale? If I am not much mistaken, Fane, or at least his magic, was present at that spectacle."

Thalil didn't wish to discuss it, not before he'd gleaned some information that would grant him an advantage. What had happened perplexed him, and that was a dangerous position to be in. For all her innocent charm, Pherara was as sharp as a dagger; Fane wouldn't have chosen her otherwise. "Did you love him? My father?"

She folded her hands in front of her waist and focused on the delicate chain mail gloves he'd conjured. Her pale eyelashes cast spiky shadows across her cheeks. "Of course I loved him. Not only was he the most brilliant mage the world has ever seen, he was truly a fair-minded person. He genuinely wanted his people to prosper when he could have easily been a tyrant. I have often wondered what the world would be like, if his vision hadn't been cut short. If...."

The mean, mischievous part of him tempted Thalil to remind her Fane had fallen at the hands of her and her sisters—out of nothing more than petty jealousy. But she already knew, and showing compassion would serve him better, bind her tighter to him and his purpose. "We were all very young in those days."

"Yes."

Thalil gently unwound her clutching fingers and pressed her palm to the skin over his heart. He met her eyes and held her gaze. "What beautiful children you would have made. Why did you never have sons and daughters with my father?"

Her silver eyes glimmered. "I was young, as you said. I was not interested in such things. I cared only for magic. Now…. It is one of the things I most regret."

Thalil was about to take a chance, and a large one. It could very well destroy all the careful groundwork he had laid with his only likely ally, but nothing profound came without risk. With his thumb, he brushed away the single tear winding down Pherara's cheek. "It is not too late."

"What do you mean?"

"Fane's blood is in me, as is his gift. Of all his children, I believe his magic is strongest in me."

Her expression softened, lips parting slightly. "You look very much like him…." Then her eyes narrowed. "But you are deceitful. What are you trying to do?"

"I'm only offering to give you what you… desire." He stepped closer to her until only a hair could've fit between their chests. He wasn't a tall man, and he'd never felt the need to alter his appearance, so they stood eye to eye. "Can you imagine what we could produce together? What would result from the combination of Fane's power with your own?" He brushed the thumb still wet with her tear across her lower lip. She opened her mouth a fraction of an inch wider. "I do it well. I would make it very enjoyable for you."

"I—what would you ask in return?"

"Only that we keep what we witnessed in Eirion-Vale to ourselves. At least until we glean a greater understanding of the situation. We might have been given an opportunity here, and we should not squander it… or let it be taken from us."

"An opportunity to do what?"

He was unsure how to answer, but luckily he didn't have to. A courtier announced the arrival of Behmarsan Kahladryia Sala N'hahseen—the beautiful young man with the long, disheveled hair and mismatched eyes. Thalil licked his lips and leaned in to watch as the prince of Kahladryia took his seat at his mother's left side. His servant— the Esperon spy—moved to stand dutifully behind him. Another very appealing young man, with elegant magic—every stroke and wash of enchantment purposeful and precise as a masterful painting—hid just below his scant attire and dark brown skin.

"The First Son of Kahladryia finally deigns to grace us with his presence," said a man a few seats away. It was impossible even for

Thalil to judge his age. Skin like wet tissue hung from his bones, and his stunted limbs curled close to his torso in a way that reminded Thalil of a turtle on its back. He had only three fingers on each hand, and his elaborate headdress couldn't conceal his misshapen, conical skull. Thalil shuddered as he waited to see what N'hahseen would do.

The prince ignored the man, selecting a few morsels to move to his plate. That was smart, Thalil thought, not to give the man the justification of a response. Silence fell over the diners as servants brought around the first course: strips of meat from a local tortoise, dried in the sun and slathered in a sauce made from a succulent plant. The strong reptilian odor made Thalil wrinkle his nose even as the guests happily dug in.

The man who'd spoken didn't seem pleased to be ignored. "Thyre thanks Kahladryia for her generous hospitality. The food and drink is excellent."

N'hahseen's mother, Hachraf, was a twisted thing, legless and with a single stringy arm. The golden collar she wore did as little to hide the bend of her long neck as the layers of Emiri hair and gold cord did to cover the warped shape of her head. Still, her eyes were shrewd, if rheumy. "And Thyre wishes to place a 'but' at the end of that generous proclamation. Even though anything preceding a but is rendered irrelevant, you might as well continue, as none of us are getting any younger."

The man representing Thyre cleared his throat. "We have a great deal to discuss. No one can deny that. A representative to the heathen king must be chosen. This ambassador must be sent soon, or we risk the peace we have established with the savages. We have already agreed that further conflict will not please Fane."

Thalil rolled his eyes. This could make for a dry debate of hours, and he'd much rather watch the troupe of dancers he'd passed in the hall.

To his surprise, N'hahseen rose from his bench. Its legs scraped loudly in the gravid quiet. He strode to the front of the tables, commandeering everyone's attention.

"There is no reason for any debate," N'hahseen said. Thalil admired his air of authority and nonchalance, even if it was feigned. "I will serve as our land's ambassador to Selindria and Gaeltheon."

"Kahladryia decides this without the agreement of her sister cities?" the representative from Thyre wheezed.

The prince waited for the murmurs from the other potentates to subside. "I decide it. I am the obvious choice: a model of physical perfection that will appeal to the heathens. I embody the proof that Fane favors our lands through sheer virtue of my existence. I am not only beautiful, but strong in my magic. Further, I want nothing more than to bring these savage kingdoms to the light of wisdom, to help them see what will be gained by facilitating Fane's return. I will go there not only to represent our interests, but to lead them onto the path that will benefit their people. Fane would want nothing less. He would want all the inhabitants of his world to share in the bounty of his return. I will see that the people of these nations are not left out. It is the purpose I was born to. Look at me. Fane made me to appeal to them, and I have no intention of failing our savior."

Without waiting for argument, the prince gathered the train of his robes and left the dining hall, his servant, who had clearly not expected his speech, scurrying after him.

"There's something about that young man," Pherara said.

Thalil grinned. "Yes, it's destiny. I have learned to identify it, and it hangs like a cloak around that man's shoulders. He's important… probably in ways he cannot even fathom yet."

"Let's follow him, see what he'll do next," Pherara suggested.

Thalil let her think it had been her idea. "If you want."

N'HAHSEEN WALKED beneath an archway and into a garden lit by rusty moonlight, the compact desert plants casting geometric shadows across the sandy ground and neatly arranged pebbled walks. Jorian hurried to follow. The prince stopped next to a fountain and rested his hand on its rim. His hair, makeup, and jewelry glimmered in the ruddy light, but his features expressed compunction alongside the elation of a child who'd stolen something and gotten away with it. Jorian supposed, in a sense, that was what he had done. "I'm sorry I didn't tell you." N'hahseen's blind eye contrasted sharply with the ruddy half-light, glimmering like a pearl among gravel. "I worried you'd try to talk me out of it. The lands to the west are, by all accounts, terrible places."

"Yet you insist on going there. Why? What are you hoping to accomplish?"

N'hahseen sat on the lip of the pool surrounding the fountain and trailed a graceful finger across the water's glassy surface. "It's as I said. I can help those poor people. Show them the way. Lead them from their barbaric customs. I know I can do it, and I… I want you to come with me."

Jorian's thoughts competed like people in a tavern shouting to be heard over each other. His life in the palace would be considerably more difficult without his position as N'hahseen's servant. And yet this was the place he needed to be to uncover secrets to report to Espero; he would find little of use at Garith's court. Yet the urge to go, if not home, then at least someplace familiar, with foods he was used to, customs he missed, and a philosophy he could at least understand, called to him insistently. But one voice thundered over the others. N'hahseen had no idea what he would be walking into. He'd be alone in a world he might not have the capacity to understand, and he would likely be in danger. "N'hahseen, you must realize that those people do not see themselves as barbaric. Quite the opposite. They see our ways as backward and wrong. They're not interested in changing."

"All the more reason for me to go! I can help them. Help them see what can come to them if they please Fane—no more toil, no disease, food so plentiful it falls from the trees, leisure for people to pursue art, literature, music… magic. The others do not care. They're only interested in the prosperity of their cities. That's not what Fane wants."

"And you're so sure you know his will?" Jorian sat down next to him and let their thighs brush.

"I… I'm his descendant. On both sides. For sixteen generations."

"N'hahseen, I don't know if you're ready for what you'll encounter in Selindria and Gaeltheon. They might not welcome your advice. You might be in danger."

N'hahseen reached over to clutch Jorian's hands. His palms were soft in the way that only a man who didn't even have to brush his own hair could achieve. "That's why I need you to come with me. You are the only person I believe cares about me and my survival. You're the one I can trust."

"Of course, my lord. Always." The words made Jorian's stomach somersault as if he'd poured poison between N'hahseen's plump lips, and he didn't understand. He'd given the expected response, done his job.

"Good. So you will agree to go?"

"The delegates have not decided. Further, we must consider—"

A female servant interrupted them. "N'hahseen, First Son of Kahladryia. Forgive me, master. Your mother requests your presence in her sitting room."

N'hahseen stood and smoothed his garments. "She will likely try to dissuade me. She enjoys having me around, showing me off like a trophy she keeps on a shelf. But in doing so, she's wasting what Fane has granted me. No matter what she says, you must not intervene. She can be very cruel."

"You need not worry," Jorian said. "I know my place. I will wait in the hall."

"No, you must come with me. I must negotiate for you to travel alongside me, and you are a servant of her household. She must be convinced to pay your wages while we are abroad."

"I'll accompany you even without my wages. I would not abandon you for something as trivial as coin." It was the right decision, Jorian told himself. The best thing for Espero.

"OH, HE'S good," Thalil whispered to Pherara. "I wish I had found him when he was a bit younger. He would be perfect for my order, the way he coats his lies in honey."

"Has it ever crossed your mind that he might be sincere?" she asked.

He pressed a hand to the dip of her lower back as they followed the two young men back inside the crystalline palace. "Of course it hasn't. No one is ever sincere."

Pherara shook her head. "Sometimes I wonder how you can continue to face life when your opinion of it is so woefully distorted."

He turned to her and arched a brow. "Is it? I would ask you to reserve your judgment."

N'hahseen's mother waited in an octagonal room where lacy slivers had been carved into the crystal walls to allow the moonlight to paint delicate patterns on the red tiled floor. Coals smoked in braziers, keeping the evening chill at bay. The matron of Kahladryia sat on a round cushion, propped up by pillows, her two Emiri slaves behind her. "N'hahseen. That was quite a spectacle at dinner."

"People will be talking about it for weeks. That should please you."

"And what is it you imagine they'll be saying, my son?"

N'hahseen pressed the heels of his hands together, his fanned fingers pointed in opposite directions. In Johmatra, it was a gesture that apologized for ignorance as well as bought time. "I suppose if they have any insight, they will observe that the Behmarsan family is passionately devoted to the ideals laid down by our esteemed ancestor. That we, that I am absolutely certain in the path we must follow to ensure his return."

"They might say those things," she answered. "Or they might talk of a spoiled brat, given every opportunity and luxury in life, and who, instead of learning humility, became an arrogant ass with no idea of his limitations."

N'hahseen stood straighter. "What limitations?"

"Not being able to recognize them is telling enough," she said. "You have been sheltered in the walls of this palace all your life. You have no experience with other cities, let alone what you'll find in the savage lands beyond the mountains. I fear you will be an embarrassment. How far do you imagine your beauty will carry you? The heathens are not looking for a kahlka. Or do you imagine you have more to offer?"

He balled his hands into fists. "Being pleasing to look at does not make me a whore. How can you say that about me? From the time I was old enough to understand my duty to Fane, my family, and this city, I have done everything asked of me to fulfill it. The evidence of my devotion is carved into my skin. Please, Mother. You must consent to let me go. I swear I will bring glory to our family name, to you. I can sway these foreigners to our way of thinking; I know it. I can make them see how they will benefit from following Fane's laws."

"And if you fail?"

"Would it be completely terrible of me to sway her mind… just a little?" Thalil asked.

"And if I say it is terrible, will that stop you?" Pherara asked.

"Please. Your counsel is valuable to me. Obviously I could have come here alone." Thalil sighed theatrically. "And if I had, I'd certainly be naked between those two young men right now."

"Such sacrifices you make, Thalil."

"Stop it. I'm serious. I'm curious to see what N'hahseen will do in Selindria. Aren't you?"

"Is satisfying our curiosity reason to interfere with the mortals?"

He snorted. "Mortals. We're hardly a different animal. After all, we are nothing but mortals who learned longevity. And is withholding our experience not worse?"

"Aren't you always saying they should rise or crash by their own devices? Doesn't your mage Yarroway extol the virtues of mortals taking responsibility for their own actions? He… I think he would have the goddesses gone, Thalil. If he could manage it."

"You are so certain he can't?"

"Is that why you reached out to me?" Pherara asked. "So we can band together to survive the cull? Your hands have already been in this. I should turn my back on you and refuse to acknowledge your existence."

"Do what you think you must." Thalil shrugged. "I will remain here and let the mortals' saga play out—without my influence."

"I admit I'm curious to see," she said. "Our desert prince is full of certainty, but he's very young."

"Yes. It'll be fascinating to see if youth and certainty will tip the odds in his favor or destroy him."

Both of them waited as N'hahseen and his mother stared at each other. Finally she dipped her head. "This could work to our advantage, if you truly believe you can accomplish it."

"She agreed too easily," Pherara said. "Did you—"

"I said I wouldn't," Thalil remarked.

"Then why?"

Thalil faced her and smiled. "Perhaps she is sincere in wanting her son to succeed. Isn't that what you would like to believe?"

Pherara scowled as Hachraf continued. "We have received intelligence that the heathen king's son is a mage—a powerful one. That must be… addressed by the great city-states of Fane. With your youth and inexperience, you won't be suspected. Your shortcomings can be used in our favor."

"What would you have me do?" N'hahseen asked.

"It depends. Bring him to our side, have him swear his allegiance to Fane, and put him on the throne. He is a child and should be easily manipulated. Through him, our family could potentially rule the heathen kingdoms. However, if that is impossible…."

"He cannot be allowed to oppose us," N'hahseen said.

"No. If what we have heard is true, a mage of his skill cannot be allowed to assume the throne. He would be too great a threat. A threat you will need to nullify."

"I understand," N'hahseen said. "No matter what, I will prepare the world for Fane's return."

"Then I will assure you are selected as ambassador," N'hahseen's mother said. "Though if you disappoint me, I will make you suffer. Now take your servant and get out of my sight. You should prepare to depart. Kahladryia's influence isn't to be dismissed."

"Mother." N'hahseen dipped his head before backing out the door.

As they followed, Thalil couldn't help but notice all of Pherara's attention focused on the Esperon spy. "Poor boy," she whispered. "He must be so conflicted. I can see the loyalty he feels toward his master; his anger when that awful woman belittled N'hahseen was palpable. I don't know how he controlled his magic. But his love for Espero must also be strong for him to come here, abandon his home, mark his skin...."

"Yes, he will have a difficult decision to make, and soon."

"I will help him if I can," Pherara said, lifting her chin.

"You'll appear to him?"

"I... fear that might only add to his confusion. But I will not let him come to harm."

Chapter Nine

JORIAN CLOSED and latched the door to N'hahseen's chambers, his thoughts racing. Over the years he had spent here, he'd worked to gain the trust of the First Son and acquire what secrets he could. So far, he'd amassed a collection of minor details, nothing to tip the scales in Espero's favor. Often he'd wished to learn something significant, something that would make a difference. Now he wished he had never heard the words N'hahseen's mother had said.

The prince of Selindria and Gaeltheon was a mage. If she knew that, it meant Johmatra had spies embedded in Garith's kingdoms. Garith needed to know that. Further, N'hahseen could not be allowed to bring the prince to the Johmatran way of thinking—the philosophy that only Fane's descendants deserved to wield magic, and all others should be killed. If faced with the combined might of Johmatra and Garith's forces, Espero would not stand a chance. But on the other hand, a mage ruling Selindria and Gaeltheon could be a staunch ally for the island, and one that would keep them safe. Together, they would have the forces to oppose Johmatra… or at least to make sure no Johmatran ever set foot on Esperon soil with the intention of murdering Esperon children. The idea that Garith's son might be killed…. No. The young prince was part Esperon, on his grandmother's side. If he had to sacrifice his own life, Jorian would not let that happen.

He hadn't realized he'd been facing the wall, staring at his reflection in the crystal without seeing it, until N'hahseen squeezed his shoulder. "Are you cross with me for not telling you I wanted to be named ambassador?"

Jorian ground his molars, as if by clenching his teeth he could prevent being torn apart by the conflicting feelings this man sparked and the love he felt for his people. Goddesses damn it, he hated Johmatra, hated it to his bones for the Esperon blood wasted for no reason, but he did not hate N'hahseen. N'hahseen had never known another way, another philosophy. Was he capable of changing beliefs so deeply ingrained? What might he do if confronted with an alternative? In the end, it was easiest to focus on the role he had played for so long and slip on the mantle of the dutiful servant. "I have no right to question you or your decisions, my lord."

N'hahseen sighed and unbuckled the strap securing his shoulder ornament. He let it fall to the floor before flinging his rings and bracelets onto a table. It was a symbolic gesture, and one Jorian couldn't ignore. The First Son of Kahladryia should not have to dress or undress himself. That was Jorian's duty.

N'hahseen stripped off his red robe and let it flutter down behind him. His bandages were soaked with blood; some had even run down and smeared over his ribs. "Our relationship, the nature of our association… I want it to change. When we get to the barbarian lands, we'll have no one but each other. That should worry me, but it doesn't. It doesn't because I know I can depend on you. I want you to feel you can depend on me as well. We will be the only civilized people in a vile and twisted place. We might have to do… extreme things. I do not want us to be as master and servant, but rather two crusaders toward what is right and true… toward bringing the world the peace of Fane's return."

"You do me far too much honor," Jorian said.

"No. I am not the inept fool my mother presumes. I like to think I can see what a man holds in his heart. I know I can trust you. I—" N'hahseen staggered, and Jorian hurried to help him sit down on the edge of his bed.

"You should not have pushed yourself so soon after an ornamentation, my lord. You need rest badly. You have lost a great deal of blood. Let me get you some water, and then I'll see to changing your dressings."

N'hahseen nodded weakly, and Jorian crossed the room to a waiting pitcher and set of goblets. After pouring water, he emptied a half a vial of Blue Oblivion into the cup. N'hahseen gulped it down, and in moments his eyelids started to flutter. Jorian urged him to lie down. Soon he was fast asleep, breathing heavily through parted lips, with his legs still hanging to the floor. Jorian sat down next to him and looked at his face—the smudged makeup over the pallid skin and eyes swollen with exhaustion and pain. His attention strayed lower, to where N'hahseen's belly rose and fell slowly with his breath. The First Son wasn't an especially muscular man; he was maybe even a little underweight. As Jorian hurried to pull the bedclothes over him and remove the temptation to keep staring, he wondered if N'hahseen might fill out a little if removed from the constant turmoil of the Kahladryian court. He deserved better. He deserved to get away from this awful place. Jorian only prayed he would be able to see that there was a better way to live when he reached Selindria.

Prayed.

He had not done that in a long time. Growing up, he had believed in Pherara, believed she loved and protected her mages. Yet she had not appeared to save even one Esperon baby from a Johmatran blade. No, it fell to people—to him—to make sure such atrocities never repeated. In a rare moment of indulgence, Jorian smoothed back N'hahseen's sweaty hair and pressed a kiss to his forehead. Then he hurried from the room and out into the hall. He couldn't spare the weeks it would take them to reach Gaeltheon, before informing the king of the threat against his son's life.

He had nothing on the Emiri who had come to these lands as spies. His courage, suffering, and commitment paled in comparison to theirs. When he reached the kitchens, he found his contact: an Emiri woman called Kori. Though her orange hair had been shaved, her gold eyes seemed to glow in the light of the fireplace she was tending. She stood and brushed the ashes from her rags when Jorian approached. He started to speak, but she raised a hand. "Let me make sure we are alone."

After inspecting the underground room's niches and alcoves, she returned. "What is it?"

"I have information that must reach High King Garith," Jorian said. "It cannot wait."

"That's possible," Kori said. "I'm putting a group of liberated slaves on a ship out of here in two days' time. I can send your message with one of them."

"Is that our only option?"

Kori knit her brows. "Do you doubt my people's ability, or their integrity?"

"Neither. My lack of faith rests on the king and his people. Will they listen to the word of an Emiri?"

"If they won't, do they deserve the knowledge we have fought so hard to acquire?"

"A fair point," Jorian said. "Tell them this: The Johmatrans have spies in Garith's court, and they plan to either recruit his son to their side or murder him. The prince will need protection."

Kori chuckled. "Well, he has it. The last I heard, the boy was in the company of Yarroway L'Estrella. I would truly like to see the Johmatrans attempt to harm him. I don't know what would be better, letting Yarrow deal with them himself or leaving them to the tender mercies of his syrai… those who are death incarnate."

Jorian shuddered and looked at the shadows gathering in the corners of the room. "That is good news, I suppose, but the king should still know what I have learned. The spies must be rooted out."

"And he will," Kori said. "I promise your message will be delivered."

"Thank you, my friend."

"I'm afraid it cannot come for free. There is something I will need you to do in return."

Jorian curled his fingers around his bare arms. He swore he'd been cold since the night he'd snuck into this city in the northern desert, but he had never felt the chill rattling his bones as it did now. "Go on."

Kori went back to the hearth and slid away a stone next to the flue. From the shallow, hidden compartment, she withdrew a ceramic ball the size of a melon, almost as big as her head. She stood and pushed it into Jorian's arms.

"One of the men who attended the dinner tonight is a notorious slave trader from the south. He is responsible for the deaths of thousands of my people, and the suffering of tens of thousands more. He is spending the night in this house, in the east wing, in chambers the third door down from the corner where the frog fountain stands. Do you know the way?"

"Yes…."

"Good. As a valued servant of this household, you have a freedom I cannot imagine. No one will question you if they pass you in the halls. Go to that room and place this explosive. It doesn't matter where. It'll take out most of the wing. After you light the fuse, run like the Shades your people fear so much are after you. You'll have a handful of moments before that whole part of the palace comes down."

"Are you sure about this?" Jorian asked, feeling like he'd be sick. "Don't you worry the Johmatrans will know the Emiri rebels were behind it?"

"Worry? I'm counting on it. It's time these pigs learned we are not beasts. Worst-case scenario, there's one less slaver. But best-case scenario, our people see we are not helpless, are not alone. It might inspire more of them to rise up. It might make their so-called masters think twice before killing or abusing more of us." She pressed a work-roughened palm to Jorian's cheek. "I am sorry I have to ask this of you. You seem to have a quiet spirit, like a gentle tide rolling in…. But I have no choice. I would never make it to the wing. The sweet sea knows I wish it could be by my hand."

"What…." Jorian's throat felt swollen; it was hard to swallow. "What if I can't?"

"Then you'll need to find another way to deliver your message to your land-bound king. I'm sorry. I know I'm coercing you, but if it means freedom for even one of my people, I have no choice. They must come first. No one else cares what happens to the Emiri."

"No, that isn't true." Jorian clutched the ball tight to his chest and pushed his shoulders back. "I might not be able to imagine your peoples' pain, but I understand what it's like to be forgotten. I would be honored to do this, but…."

"But? You cannot waver in this, Esperon."

"I have never killed. I dislike the idea of a life cut short by my hands."

Kori frowned, and she pressed her hand closer to Jorian's face until it almost hurt. "You do have a good spirit. You're kind, and I'm sorry you have to dampen your light. But the world has forced us. We cannot stand by and let things continue as they are. Can you do that? Can you let these atrocities go on when you have the opportunity to at least hinder them? Don't think of the monsters that will die. Think of the innocents who will live."

"I… I'll do it. I'll be happy to do it. It's about time I actually made a difference."

"You're a fine man," Kori said. "I'm proud to stand beside you. I know this isn't easy. There are always wonders and what-ifs."

Jorian shook his head as he ran his fingers along the grooved clay sphere. "No, I have no doubts. I have seen what these people are, what they are willing to do. Even to their own. I will accomplish this with a clear conscience. But… but how will I light the fuse?"

"Sweet Emir. You're a mage, aren't you?"

"I have pretended to be someone else for so long I almost forgot," Jorian said, more to himself.

"Well, son of Espero, it's time to remember. Do it for your people. There's a justice there, that the son of a whore should perish by Esperon magic."

"I… suppose I am glad we could help each other." Jorian met her eyes and forced a smile, but Kori did not return it.

"Of course. We have a common goal. Now get out of here before you make yourself suspect."

"Pherara watch over you."

"Emir will watch me, and I would want no more. The favor of your land gods costs."

Jorian tipped his head. "Better to trust in what we can do ourselves."

"Exactly." Kori finally smiled. "Now get out of here, Esperon. Emir will carry us to each other again, or she won't."

No one bothered Jorian as he moved through the quiet halls of the palace. He kept the explosive Kori had given him concealed in a stack of blankets he'd taken from a linen closet. He made his way easily to the rooms she had indicated and went inside. The door was not even locked; the Johmatrans were so secure in their safety, in their mastery over those beneath them, that they couldn't even conceive of anyone daring to do them harm.

Jorian couldn't help being pleased to prove them wrong, to shake the foundation of their superiority, especially when he saw that the twisted man slumbering so confidently in his large bed was the same one who'd jumped at the chance to berate N'hahseen during dinner.

The slave-trading bastard. Profiting off the suffering of others. Good riddance. Jorian placed the sphere against the foot of his bed, and then he called on his magic. It felt amazingly good to free his power after suppressing it for so long, like waking up and having a good stretch after a long sleep. The flames came easily to his fingertips, and the fuse crackled when he lit it. Then he ran.

He ran past curious servants in the corridors, past guards who called for him to stop. It didn't matter that doing so would incriminate him; all the witnesses would soon be dead. Jorian made his way to a garden that led from the palace down to the center of the city by way of a winding trail just as the building behind him exploded into a bright bloom. The impact sent him sprawling on his chest as flames stretched into the dark sky, clawing upward like grasping fingers. It resounded through Jorian's ears until he could hear nothing beyond the swishing pulse around him. People—other servants and some slaves—rushed past in a blur. Someone yanked Jorian to his feet, and he let himself be carried by the current, his senses dulled. Muted screams and distorted light poured out of the crumbling structure behind him. Black smoke roiled out, so solid and heavy Jorian swore he felt it pushing against his back. As he sprinted away with the others, guards ran toward the burning, collapsing building.

Pherara forgive him, Jorian could only feel relief that he'd gotten away, that he hadn't been suspected. Right now, he could worry about no life but his own, and he was happy to blend in to the cluster of household staff and slaves gathering where the east road wound in front of the palace. A bunch of them cowered below a nut tree, Jorian toward the center, coughing globs of darkened phlegm into the dusty soil.

The guards surrounded the group, weapons pointed as they looked them over. One man's eyes settled on Jorian, and he leaned in to whisper to his comrade. A spear pointed Jorian's way. "You. You look familiar. We have some questions."

Jorian couldn't answer questions. The blast still beat a steady rhythm in his skull. He couldn't take his chances, so he ran, pushing through the others until he broke through onto the street. There, he ran as fast as his legs could carry him, twisting and turning between buildings, always hoping the shouts of his pursuers would get farther away.

But they never did. No matter how many corners he dashed around or alleys he hid inside, Jorian couldn't get away from them. Pherara, he was going to die. He'd run; he couldn't now proclaim innocence. Besides, the Johmatrans wouldn't care. They'd string him up and entertain themselves for a week while they cut his fingers off one by one…. And that was the least of the torture he'd witnessed.

No, no, please, Pherara. Let me die.

Jorian sprinted around a small house and hid behind the only cover available—a stack of wood desiccated by the heat and aridity. It was like hiding behind a pile of bones. The group of guards edged closer, and all they would have to do was displace a few planks…. Jorian prayed. It felt pitiful, the absolute last resort, but he had no other plans. He knew what would happen to him if he was caught. And he would be caught. Nothing stood between him, the guards, and the rough stone wall but some splinters of wood. Jorian summoned his long-neglected magic. Better to fall in battle than beneath the torturer's blade. If he did one last thing in this world, he would show them that not only their chosen mages could wield the gift. At least there would be a few less of them to kill his countrymen.

As he rose from his shelter, a bright flash scorched Jorian's eyes. The silver flowed out into the darkness from the central burst, taking the shape of a winged woman. The world Jorian could perceive washed to white. He blinked, desperate for some perception. Slowly, outlines appeared against the bleached landscape: the edges of buildings, the mortar between the stones of the road. The bright shape hovered, not so much a light in the darkness as a force that drove it back, negated it. Swallowed it. Jorian ran in the direction she pointed, toward the edge of Kahladryia and the vast and savage desert beyond its walls.

Despite whatever intervention he'd been granted, guards still pursued Jorian, and their numbers grew as they were joined by soldiers from the small outposts around the city. Whatever had happened back there—Jorian's mind couldn't handle the implications in addition to everything else—had granted him maybe a mile's head start, probably less. He feared he'd made a terrible mistake as he propelled himself beyond the city wall and leapt over a section of crumbled stones. The change from the crowded and colorful city was instant. Flat nothingness surrounded him, tinged rust by the moon hovering over the horizon. Nothing broke the desert extending for hundreds of miles in every direction except the occasional leafless, twisted tree casting a stark shadow over the sand.

Out here, there was nowhere to go, nothing to use for cover. Even if Jorian escaped, he would be dead before the sun rose in the morning. He might manage to find water, but the cold or the desert's predators would make sure it did not matter.

Still, with the shouts of the guards and soldiers getting louder, what could he do? He ran, the sand sucking at his feet, slowing him down, while his breath froze in a cloud behind him. In moments his legs ached and his chest burned. Up ahead loomed a sort of ridge—the crest of one of the desert's malleable dunes, and beyond it Jorian could see a muted glow… if it wasn't a hallucination.

It was better than nothing, and Jorian pushed toward what at least marked a variation in the endless expanse. Out here, he couldn't even judge the progress of his pursuers by sound. The only noise was the high-pitched, distant screech of the wind.

As he reached the apex of the dune and started down the other side, stepping carefully and hoping not to fall while still moving as quickly as possible, he noticed a dark shape coming toward him from the gully at the bottom of the mound. It moved so quickly he couldn't discern any details until it skidded to a stop in from of him, kicking sand up into his face. A large lizard with red scales and black dots across its back blinked down at him with enormous yellow eyes. From its back, a man wrapped from head to foot in gauzy beige cloth reached out a hand. With the other, the stranger pulled the fabric away from his mouth. He spoke in a clipped, urgent tone, and if Jorian concentrated, he could pick out words that seemed to be close cousins to the dialect of Johmatran spoken in Kahladryia.

"—told me you were coming—save you—quick—come—"

Jorian's best guess was that the man would be an Emiri, one of Kori's people. But his features were too harsh and chiseled; he was a man like Jorian, and Jorian didn't know what that meant. His hesitation earned him another barked "Quick!"

He took the man's hand and was jerked onto the lizard's back. The man's strength surprised him; he'd lifted Jorian with one arm like he weighed no more than a ladies' lace napkin.

"Hold on."

Jorian obeyed, wrapping his arms around the man's waist and curling his fingers in his billowy garment. The lizard leapt over the desert's curves and dips so fast the wind slapped at Jorian's face. Before long, the worry of his pursuers catching up faded as quickly as the shallow footprints the creature left in the sand.

He had no idea who this man was or where he was taking him, but it had to be better than being caught by the Johmatrans.

At least he prayed it did.

Chapter
Ten

FINALLY FREE from another useless meeting of priestesses and aristocrats, King Garith made his way to the midday meal—and his real council, the one where he might hear some useful advice instead of people blatantly pandering to their own interests.

It was cold, with winter pouring down from the mountains, sapping more of the warmth and fertility from Eirion with each day, but he'd asked for lunch on a veranda overlooking the gardens. His wife, his mother, and Sander waited around a table, enclosed by a framework of woolen curtains. With braziers burning in the enclosure, it was as comfortable as the castle. And they would not be overheard. Garith had posted guards both he and Sander trusted at the foot of the one stairway leading to the balcony. After the final guest he'd requested attend, Courtenay Jardine-Lamont, arrived, and the servants placed several silver domes on the table, they could speak freely.

No one needed to ask what the topic of conversation would be— the entire kingdom had been speaking of a single incident for almost two weeks.

"I want to go after my son," Garith said. "I feel any inaction in this situation is a silent acceptance of my cousin's actions."

"His actions?" Courtenay looked up from her plate of untouched food. "Yarrow merely responded to a threat, and he got the children to safety."

"True enough," Garith's mother said. "But the priestesses will twist this to their advantage. If we don't act quickly, they'll convince the people we are happy with Yarrow's course of action."

"And are we not?" Courtenay asked. "He presented a finding, and from what I could see, it was authentic."

"The question we must ask is whether Thane should be a game piece in this squabble between my husband and the priestesses," Queen Cothryn said. "I say, he is but a child and should not have such responsibility thrust upon his shoulders. He is too young to understand the implications of his actions, and he needs to be brought home."

"I agree," Garith said. "I will retrieve him myself. I do not believe Yarrow meant any harm to the prince, but Yarrow's continued custody of him cannot yield anything favorable, even though the Bairn of Windwake's last missive reported Thane is well looked after."

"The priestesses, and their army of Defenders, will march on the Twenty-Nine," Sander said. "Will you prevent them?"

"Why should he?" Courtenay asked. "They'll be smacked down hard, between Yarrow's magic and the fleet he commands. If you ask me, they could do with a lesson in humility."

"I cannot disagree." Queen Cothryn, Garith's wife, folded her napkin delicately and draped it over her knee. "But what we must ask ourselves is how the crown will be perceived in this conflict. As a staunch supporter of his cousin, or as an advocate of the people suffering Emiri raids along the coasts. As a representative of the goddesses, or as a man who advocates the best solution for all mortals involved. My husband, the king, must choose the position from which he will fight. Whether it's the goddesses, the people, his soldiers, or something else, he must choose."

"I fear we won't be able to put it off much longer," Garith's mother said. "When the war with the Johmatrans finally ended, I had hope for at least a grudging peace between the temples and the crown, and I do not yet think that is impossible. But the priestesses will never make peace with Yarrow."

"Nor he with them," Courtenay added. Garith heard a hint of admiration in her voice, but she was enough of a diplomat to keep it subtle. "They will fight, and we cannot stop it. I still say we let them. It is no secret that the priestesses have long opposed you, Your Majesty, and I can see no reason not to let Yarrow at least weaken a dangerous enemy of yours."

"I fear the people will not let such a defeat stand," Garith's mother said. "A defeat at Yarrow's hands—at the hands of a culture they already misunderstand and mistrust—could place the common folk more firmly in the temples' corner. I doubt anything we can say or do will lure them away from the goddesses."

Courtenay drummed her fingers on the tabletop and looked off beyond the table. A slash of gray sky could be seen between the cleft in the curtains. Before speaking, she closed her eyes for a moment. When she opened them, she fixed them firmly on Garith. "I… I am a mage, and while not even a mage can predict the future, I sense… coming changes. The wind is blowing in a different direction. I sense it in the currents of energy moving through the trees and ground, through the air. Something is happening."

Garith felt a chill that had nothing to do with the coming winter. "What do you mean?"

"Magic flows where it will," she explained. "There are many theories as to where it comes from and why it is here, but the truth is no one really knows. In Espero, especially at the university, there are theories…. Some feel there is much less magic in the world than there once was. It's harder for mages to cast simple spells, and the great feats of legend are practically unheard of… with one exception."

"Yarrow."

"Yes, Your Majesty. There was magic present at his trial unlike anything I could have ever imagined."

"And you believe Yarrow has some insight into this… this drying up of the magic?"

Courtenay shook her head. "I would very much like to speak with him, at least. Furthermore, Your Majesty, the attitude of the people is changing. By now everyone has heard of Mellinger's Tablet, and word of this new discovery will spread."

"You truly believe these things have swayed them away from their goddesses?"

"If nothing else, they have them thinking. Wondering. Questioning, when before they accepted blindly. That is something, Your Majesty… and…."

"Please go on," Garith urged. "Nothing you say will be held against you."

"If the priestesses march on the Twenty-Nine and are defeated by Yarrow and the people they call heathens, without the intervention of their goddesses, what will that tell the people? That the goddesses do not care even for their chosen, that they're impotent, or… that they do not exist."

Garith resisted the urge to drop his face into his hands. How the world had changed in his short lifetime. When he had been a boy, no one, not even a mage of Espero, would dare to imply any of that. And Courtenay had said it outright… and she was not wrong. Part of Garith longed for the certainty of the goddesses in their paradise, the comfort gleaned from being able to believe everything happened according to their will. "Can I really stand by the wayside?"

"Perhaps," Sander said cautiously. "We all know this conflict won't last long. Not even the Johmatrans could take the Twenty-Nine."

"And what will we do if they ask for our assistance against Yarrow?" Cothryn asked.

Sander waved a hand. "We tell them we will not sacrifice the lives of our soldiers to a lost cause."

"That simple?" Garith wondered aloud. "Go against them openly?"

"And what will we do if they turn their ire on us?" his mother asked, dabbing at the corner of her lips with a napkin. "Yarrow's territory is small, defensible. We must protect an entire kingdom. Nor do we have the forces; our army was decimated and then some by the war. We would not be looking at an easy victory."

Garith's heart plummeted into his belly, and he pushed his plate away a few inches. "A conflict like that would tear these lands apart."

"And lands torn apart fighting amongst themselves would be ripe pickings for the Johmatrans. Do not doubt it," Sander said.

"So my choices, should they request aid, are to deny it and risk a civil war—and conquest by Johmatra—or to send my loyal men as fodder to be slaughtered. To toss their lives away in a political gesture."

"It might cost less lives in the end," his mother said.

"And I am to stand on the battlements, stand over these men and deliver some inspiring speech! Urge them to fight for the right while knowing not a single one of them will return to his family? How can I? How could anyone?"

"You are the king," his mother said.

Garith pressed his knuckles to his lips. Some king. A king sitting on a veranda taking advice from three women and his male lover—and still so unsure. So alone in the end. Whatever he decided, he would have to face himself. None of them understood, not even Sander. In the end, the blood of those men would be on his hands and his alone.

"Garith, forgive me," Sander said, "but we cannot treat this battle as if it will be the end of everything. Even if the priestesses are defeated, they might still go against us. They have bolstered their ranks for over ten years now. I cannot help but feel that it's coming. That a conflict with them is inevitable."

Garith looked into Sander's face, at the deep lines etched around his eyes and across his forehead, the streaks of steel in his copper-colored curls. It seemed like only yesterday they'd both been boys—beautiful and awkward and so certain everything would work out. He'd seen such possibilities in those days, such hope. It added to Garith's sense that time was slipping through his fingers, and he had as much chance of holding on as he had of closing his fingers around the wind. "And what does that mean?"

If they had been alone, Sander would have cupped Garith's chin. Though his wife and mother knew of and accepted their relationship, old traditions still held some sway. Still, Sander's eyes conveyed everything he couldn't express with his hands or his body, and they held on to Garith, held him up. "We need to know who will stand with us if… if the worst happens. We need to form alliances." Sander looked at Courtenay. "Where will Espero stand?"

"It's hard to predict," she said. "The council was split the last time I observed it. While Esperons are not as staunchly religious as the people of this kingdom, many still resent how long it took for His Majesty to intervene on our behalf against the Johmatrans. You must understand that our losses were catastrophic. Every person in Espero lost someone, and many lost entire families. Many feel at least some gratitude toward Yarrow and his Emiri for their aid, and it does not hurt Yarrow's cause that he is a mage, nor that many former slaves have made Espero their home and are willing to fight for her. Many of them are integrating well into our society. Hatred of the Emiri will not win the priestesses any votes with us. I'll be frank. It comes down to what each side can offer. Espero will do what is best for Espero. We are a moral people, but this is a question of survival, and we almost did not survive this last war."

Garith tipped his head. He couldn't blame Courtenay or the Esperons, but he couldn't count on their loyalty either, it seemed. "I appreciate your honesty, and I do not begrudge Espero protecting herself. It would be a tragedy if she were to fall."

"Octavian and Rosecairn seem to have thrown their lot in with Yarrow," Sander said. "It was a pretty bold statement he made, showing up here by Yarrow's side. And it's no small matter. Octavian commands the elite force I helped him create: the warriors and mages trained to fight together. They're formidable and fiercely loyal."

"So we have no one." Garith stared down at the grease coagulating on his meat, at the crust forming over his small pile of beans. He felt sick… sick and numb and lost. And so damned tired all he wanted to do was curl in his bed and pretend nothing existed beyond the edges of his mattress. Pretend someone else would take care of this mess, make it all go away.

"We have the loyal men sworn to the crown by every noble who holds land by your grace," Sander said, but even he didn't sound hopeful.

"And how many of those men will defect to the winning side?" Garith asked. "How many nobles will throw in with the priestesses under the guise of piety? We… I cannot win."

"No!" Cothryn smacked the tabletop, rattling the cutlery and shocking everyone. Garith's wife was shrewd and intelligent, and he always valued her counsel, but he had never seen aggression from her, had always admired her reserve. "No, we are not giving up. We're not handing our land or our people's welfare over to those power-hungry hags. Don't look at me like that, Sander! We all know what they are. Whatever you feel toward the goddesses, those women are mortal, and they are corrupt. We have a duty to keep corruption from this land, and we will. I know two things. One, my son is in the Twenty-Nine, and if war is coming to those shores, he will not be safe. I cannot accept that. I won't. I did not lay sick in bed for months while he grew inside me to lose him now. Two, Yarroway L'Estrella can combine his forces with ours, and no one will be able to stand against us. Not the priestesses, not even Johmatra. If Espero allies with us as well, we will be unstoppable. That is what must happen. Thane must be safe, and Yarrow must be coaxed to our side. Which means someone must go to the Twenty-Nine and see that it happens."

"I will go," Courtenay offered. "I'm trained in combat, and I can keep the prince safe. I can appeal to Yarrow as a fellow mage."

"No." Garith almost wished he could send her—he trusted in her integrity, but—"You must stay here. The ambassador from Johmatra will be arriving soon, and you are the only one who can speak the language. I desperately need you to act as guide and interpreter. Johmatra is dangerous and unpredictable, and we cannot afford to give them any excuse to break the treaty. Especially not now."

Courtenay bowed her head and stared into her lap. "Of course, Your Majesty."

"I will go," Garith said. "I will go with Sander."

"You cannot." Wrinkles creased his mother's dark forehead. "You are the king. Your enemies could use your absence against you, and further, you will be making a statement. It could be viewed as advocating your cousin's actions. A royal visit is no small matter. And if you are killed and Thane is not retrieved, you'll be leaving the throne without an heir. Can you imagine what the priestesses will do with that? It could mean the end of our family's sovereignty."

"No! I'm going after my son!" Garith stood so quickly his chair fell on its back, behind him. "This is the one concrete thing I can do, the one way I can make a difference, and I'm going to do it. And I'm going to convince my cousin to stand with this kingdom."

"You are not the person for this job," his mother said, in the calm, condescending way she'd told him he couldn't have another biscuit when he'd been a child.

But Garith was not a child. He was a king, and it was past time that meant something. "Then who is? Who is better than me?"

"I am." His mother stood much more gracefully than he had. "I am a mage not without skill, and Yarrow trusts me above all others. I will go to the Twenty-Nine."

"And I will accompany her." Cothryn rose from her chair and stood shoulder to shoulder with the former queen. "As much as you might wish to deny it, I am also a mage, and I can look after myself. I'll go with your mother, and we will secure my son and secure the alliance."

"I forbid it," Garith said. "No. I will not send my wife and mother on a task that is meant for me. I refuse to let the two of you face danger in my stead."

"Even if we've a better chance of success?" Cothryn glared at him through narrowed eyes. "Is your pride more important to you than my son's life? You witnessed what I endured to bear him!"

"You and my mother!" Garith was shouting and he couldn't seem to stop. "You can't be serious!"

"And why not? Because we don't have cocks between our legs? I'm sick to my spirit of being judged less by lack of a sad little flap of skin."

"And how will it reflect on me?" Garith continued. "That I must send two ladies to fight my battles? How will it make me look? Do you even care?"

"I care about my son and the future of this kingdom," Cothryn said between clenched teeth.

"Why do you say 'my son'? He is our son, and I am his father. It will be a disgrace for me not to go after him, to sit idle, listening to fools prattle on…. Goddesses damn it! He is my son!"

Cothryn arched a brow. "Is he? Is he, my lord? Or were you too busy dallying with Sander to do your duty as husband? Are you certain that's not something else I had to take into my own hands because you were inadequate?"

Garith's mother took her arm and said, "My dear, don't let your emotions get the better of you…."

The queen shook her head. She had aged remarkably well, so well Garith sometimes wondered if some spell had aided her. The few streaks of silver in her hair looked intentional, added for decoration. "No, I have lived with this secret, and I do not wish to live with it any longer. It's time he knew."

"Cothryn…." They loved each other; Garith knew it. The marriage had been arranged to unite the kingdoms of Selindria and Gaeltheon, but they had made it more, made it a partnership.

"I am more than a receptacle for your seed, Garith."

"I have always known that, always respected you. You… you…. Who?"

"Your cousin," Cothryn said.

Dizzy, Garith moved to collapse into his chair before he remembered it was overturned. He grasped the edge of the table just in time to avoid falling on his ass. "You…. What? Yarrow?"

"We wanted to put a mage on the throne," his mother said. "We felt it in the best interest of the people."

Garith let his outrage out in a growl as he swiped his arm across the tabletop. Silver, utensils, and crockery hit the floor, shattering, bouncing around. Courtenay stood and retreated as far as the curtains would allow. "How could you do this to me?"

"Do what, Garith?" Cothryn folded her arms over her chest, her calm infuriating. "I did my duty. I spread my legs for you, and I gave you a daughter. I smiled like a fool when you said you wanted to go riding with Sander. I did not deny you that comfort. But I needed to produce a mage. Do you imagine I lusted after your mad cousin, that I even enjoyed it? Grinding on top of him while he lay practically unconscious, waiting forever for him to squirt his seed into me so I could run to my chambers and wash? No, it was not something I did for pleasure."

"I… I imagined you enjoyed laying with me… at least a little."

"And I did." The look of pity on her face made Garith want to skewer her on a blade. "You're a good man. I've always known that. I merely did what I needed to do for this kingdom, this world. We…. The magic needs to be restored. The world needs the magic."

"And I… I'm just an intermediary? Some tool?"

"Garith…."

He swatted her hand away when she came around the table and reached for him. "To the Shades' with the mages and my traitorous cousin. And to the Shades' with you too!"

Cothryn planted her hands on her narrow hips. "You're being unreasonable. Unfair. Why is it acceptable for you to wrap your lips around Sander's cock every other evening but not for me to go to another's bed once? One time, in almost a decade and a half, Garith! And not even out of lust. I was doing it out of a sense of duty, to this kingdom and the future of its people!"

"Because I am not worthy of fathering the future ruler of this kingdom? I'm not, but Yarrow is? For the goddesses' sake—Yarrow? This… this is like if I found you wanting as a mother to my children and went out to fill the belly of every whore and mad beggar I could penetrate!" He couldn't stay on his feet. With the world crumbling around him, he had thought he had one solid piece to cling to: the love and loyalty of his family. Garith sat down on the fancy rug covering the cold stone and hugged his knees to his chest. When Cothryn raked her fingers through his hair, he shook his head but did nothing more to stop her. It didn't matter.

"I, uh… I must go and prepare for the arrival of the Johmatran ambassador," Courtenay said with a small bow. "He or she will expect things to be a certain way, and any deviation might be viewed as a slight."

Garith couldn't blame her for wanting to escape. He nodded, and Courtenay hurried back into the castle.

"We will prepare to depart for the Twenty-Nine," Garith's mother said.

"I… I have men… men I know are loyal…."

"Thank you, Sander," his mother said in an indulgent tone, "but that will not be necessary. We will be just fine."

Before they could depart, Garith said, "Mother."

She turned, and their gazes met.

"I'm sorry I was not born a mage, and I'm sorry you found me so wanting… so wanting as to not even be worthy of siring your grandchildren."

"You know I have never felt that way." She bent down to kiss the top of his head, but Garith took no comfort in the gesture as he once had. "You have been a great king, and I'm very proud of you. I am honored to call you my son."

"Just not a mage," he muttered.

His mother straightened and smoothed her skirts. "We all have our parts to play: you, the queen, your cousin. Remember, my role in history will not be remembered as especially glamorous. I'll be lucky to be mentioned. But still, I have played my role, as we all must, and no one more than Thane. In many ways, we are all merely the stones he will step on to ascend to his destiny."

With that, the women were gone. Garith had more he wanted to say, but leaving it for later—or never—was a fair trade for having a few moments alone with Sander, who plopped down on the floor behind him and wrapped his arms around Garith's waist, his chin in the crook of Garith's neck.

Garith reached up to squeeze his arm, the solid cords of muscle familiar and comforting—the one thing, the one person he could still trust with his life. "That couldn't have been easy for you, Sander…. The way she spoke about our private life…."

Sander huffed warm breath into Garith's hair. "Years ago, I made a choice. I chose to be with you, and I knew that it might not always be easy. It's been worth it, though. I wouldn't change a thing."

Garith relaxed his head against Sander's shoulder, secure in the sincerity of Sander's words. It was good to have something to be certain of, but—"I thought I was a good husband. I thought my wife was happy. I… I thought I was a good king. I've tried so hard."

Sander pressed a kiss to the apple of Garith's cheek. "You're a damned good king. And husband. And Cothryn knows it too. She just…." He shook his head. "Mages. Mages and women. Who can understand how they think? Maybe what they did was for the best. It's not something I like to think about. I'll stay with what I know, and it's this: I don't care who came into Cothryn's womb. Thane is your son. You raised him, taught him, loved him. That's what matters. What's more, he cannot be made a pawn in anyone's schemes. If he's to rule these lands, he needs to learn from you what that means. It's more a burden than a privilege, in the hands of a decent man. He'll need you to show him that. He had no hand in the circumstances of his conception."

"I know," Garith said, "and of course I still love him. I just thought… I thought I was good. A good husband and a good king. But Cothryn seems so angry."

"Not at you," Sander said. "At the world. At a world that dismisses her on account of what's between her legs. She's not wrong. It doesn't make much sense. We venerate all these goddesses, think they're so wise and wonderful, but we won't listen to our own women. Maybe that mage, Courtenay, is right. Maybe things do need to change."

"I'm having a hard time reconciling this," Garith admitted. "Yarrow…. We grew up together. His betrayal hurts more than my wife's."

"For all his power, Yarrow is damaged," Sander said. "He was probably easy to manipulate. Besides, it doesn't matter. It's done. Thane is here, and he is what he is. He… he's a mage. Will he even be permitted to rule?"

"My mother and wife seem to have a plan. And if they can get Yarrow, the Roses, and Espero behind them, who will say no?" Garith shook his head. "I don't envy my son. If this is what I must deal with, being herald of the Blessed Epoch, what will he face?"

"There's time." Sander kissed along Garith's jaw. "We're not ready to bow out yet, and this world still needs us. What do you say we leave your son the best possible world we can?"

When Garith smiled, the expression felt foreign to his muscles, he hadn't done it in so long. "That's all we can do. Just our best. I have to hold this kingdom together and keep it out of another conflict. I know that much, and I intend to spare these people more bloodshed."

Sander gripped Garith's shoulders and turned him so they could face each other. In Sander's blue-green eyes, Garith saw nothing but trust, confidence. "We can do this."

Their lips met and their mouths opened, tongues meeting eagerly, desperately, until Sander, panting, pulled back. "If the ladies are preparing to travel, that means we have your rooms to ourselves. Let's not waste that."

"No, let's not."

Garith took the hand Sander offered and let Sander help him to his feet. He backed Sander against the wall beside the door to the castle's interior, devouring Sander's lips and pressing their bodies together. He needed this, needed to forget about everything driving him into the ground, at least for a while. He took Sander's hand and dragged him inside. Sander slapped Garith's backside playfully, and they headed toward the hall and Garith's bedchamber.

Just a few hours… an afternoon…. A brief stretch where he could be a man, and then Garith would be a king. He'd be the best king he could, and, somehow or another, he would hold these lands together if he had to do it with nothing but his own bare hands.

Chapter Eleven

IT AMAZED Octavian how quickly the royal children of the Blessed Epoch had gone native. As he sat in one of Yarrow's cluttered chambers, he watched the prince and his betrothed, daughter of the Bairn of Windwake, frolicking in the courtyard fountain with the Emiri their age, naked as the day they were born. Imagining the reaction of the queen and the bairn's stuffy wife made Octavian grin. But it was only a symptom of how differently everything operated here in the Twenty-Nine.

He turned to D'Aurelian, who reclined across some rugs piled against the wall. "Do you like children?"

"I suppose they're necessary," D'Aurelian said.

Octavian reached over and skimmed his fingers over the back of D'Aurelian's hand. His skin was warm from the sun pouring in through the glassless windows, and it had grown darker in the few weeks they'd been here. "The climate here seems to suit you," Octavian observed. "You seem… rejuvenated. Your skin looks remarkable."

D'Aurelian turned on his side and reached up to stroke Octavian's cheekbone. "Yours is burnt. But you're right; it agrees with me. Reminds me of home, I suppose. I feel much more relaxed now I'm not always tensing my body against the cold. Then again, it could be the magic here. With every breath I take, I feel it filling me all the way to my toes. It's like I've been empty all my life but never realized before. But enough about that. Why don't you tell me what you're really trying to ask."

Octavian sighed and raked hair that was getting much too long out of his face. It was a little disconcerting that someone knew him well enough to practically read his thoughts, but mostly it was comforting, and in Octavian's case, quite convenient. He had so many ideas filling his head, like a pile of worms, and D'Aurelian had a rare talent for plucking up the one relevant to the moment. "What was it like for you, growing up?"

D'Aurelian looked out the bright windows. "It's one of those things, childhood. We only really see it in retrospect. Certain things seem so important. For me, it was doing well on tests, impressing my tutors, and understanding magic. A bad day at school, forgetting a book or something silly like that, was like the end of the world, but of course that was before I had any concept of people going without eating or being slaughtered without discernible cause. I was… so very fortunate. Blessed. But I couldn't see that until it was gone. I couldn't enjoy the prosperity I had at the time. Looking back, I can't help but wonder if I wasted those years. What about you?"

"I always wanted it over. I wanted to be a man so others would respect me, so I could decide the course of my life. I was always so sure I would stand out somehow, make a difference in the world."

D'Aurelian twisted his fingers between Octavian's, lifted Octavian's hand, and kissed his knuckles. "You've certainly done that."

"Have I?"

"Amarzio, you rose from being an unknown mercenary to one of the most powerful nobles in either of Garith's kingdoms. You created a haven of freedom and equality in a land where those things are very scarce. Unlike most aristocrats, you earned your position, and you are loved. You've created something revolutionary."

"I wonder if it will last… when I am gone. What will happen to Rosecairn then?"

D'Aurelian nipped the tip of Octavian's thumb and then held Octavian's hand against his chest. "Are you saying you want a baby?"

Octavian watched the bony brown bodies of the children, the way their wet tangles of hair reflected the light. He couldn't remember ever being that carefree, nothing more important to him than splashing a friend before she splashed him. He shook his head. "I don't feel drawn to fatherhood, not really. But how else can one be sure the things he built will last? If I had a son or daughter to take over at Rosecairn when I'm gone…."

"There are hundreds of children in Rosecairn who wouldn't be alive if not for you."

"And can we trust that one of them will step up when our time is past, continue our vision?"

D'Aurelian shook his head, a fond smile on his face. "Only you would hope to control things even beyond the grave. I suppose we must trust to fate that the world will continue without us. Fate and the goddesses."

Octavian blew air out his nose. "The goddesses? Those who would condemn men like you and me to an endless realm of shadow? How can we? How can we trust to beings who would forsake people based on whose naked bodies they prefer to touch at night? Who would judge them based on that rather than the changes they have made in the world. The good they've done. Or tried to do."

"You sound militant. Has Yarrow swayed you to his way?"

"He's made me think," Octavian admitted. "Made me wonder. That is a good thing. A man's mind should never be stagnant; his course should never be so certain that it verges on fanaticism, that no amount of evidence can sway him. Should it?"

"It never hurts to consider one's options," D'Aurelian said. "And a wise man always recognizes what might be swaying him."

"Do you think I am being swayed?"

D'Aurelian toyed with Octavian's fingers, stroking each of them in turn before wrapping his hand around Octavian's wrist. "I think you envision a glorious future, and I think, for you, that means the freedom to love. It means the opportunity for people to realize their potentials. Mages ruling and sharing their gifts. Everyone equal. It's… it's a lovely image. Something from an old story. But can it happen in this world? And what's more, is Yarrow the one to lead us into this wondrous future? I would advise introspection. I know you hold no love for the temples, but you must consider whether they're best abolished… or changed. Yarrow…. It seems to me that Yarrow can certainly tear down, but can he create? If we follow him, will we be left with nothing but a waste to try to build back up? Much will be lost, if it comes to that. Think of the story of Fane. He had grand aspirations, and when he fell, the rest of us had to start over."

"You equate Yarrow with Fane?"

"Not Yarrow," D'Aurelian said. "His son… I should say the prince, but how his parentage has escaped everyone I'll never understand. Thane is… singular. We're both mages. When a mage meets another, he feels his or her magic. Yours is ripe apples, roses with swollen petals. Yours is the sap that rises from the ground in the springtime and makes things grow. It's slow like that, and it's gentle and predictable. Yarrow's is a hailstorm, cold and brutal and indiscriminate."

Octavian understood. "Yours is sunlight on old parchment, flickering flames just waiting for a splash of oil. The smell of books. Candles burning in windows. Yours is home."

D'Aurelian rubbed the side of his face against Octavian's. "You're sweet, and that's what I always wanted my magic to be: quiet, steady, warm. I never wanted anything flashy. But the prince. But Thane… his is everything. It's the sunrise and the night, the ocean and the land. Soft comforts and explosions… all at once. I've never imagined anything like it. There is nothing his magic does not touch."

Beyond the windows, the young prince stood beneath the fount flowing from the fountain's upper basin. The water plastered his white-and-black hair to his small shoulders and chest. His future wife, her cheeks puffed out, spit a stream into his face, and he sputtered and swatted at her. Octavian knew Thane could've leveled the girl with his power, but despite his age, he had the wisdom not to. Still, the power was there, held like an inferno in his belly. He clearly saw what D'Aurelian had described; there were worlds and stars and skies inside that boy. Octavian didn't know what impressed—or scared—him more: that might or the ability to control it.

"We must find out more about this before we make a decision," Octavian said. "Do you think we'll be missed if we slip away?"

"I doubt it," D'Aurelian said. "Most of the Emiri are still sleeping off their hangovers, and Yarrow wandered off at first light, so drunk I was surprised he could walk."

"Good. There's strong magic running through this archipelago, and the root of it is below this house. There's something hidden here, and I want to know what it is."

"Let's go," D'Aurelian agreed.

Following the faint hum of energy in the floor, the vibrations he felt moving from his feet and up his legs, Octavian came to an arched door. It wasn't locked, so he swung it open and descended the sand-strewn stairs into an underground chamber. At the foot of the steps, the sea poured in, covering Octavian's legs almost to the knees, plastering his trousers to his skin. At the opposite end of the chamber, a door had been drawn against the wall—white chalk, scratchy and hesitant, forming an arch in the brown stone.

Octavian pressed his hands to the wet golden wall. Something he'd never fathomed waited on the other side, but no matter what spell he tried, he couldn't coax the sand and shells to subside. Every attempt met with violent resistance, like a knight's lance glancing off an opponent's shield, making him recoil.

"What is it you're hoping to find there?" The voice was smooth, and it blended with the swish of the waves lapping against the cavern wall. But it held none of the warmth of the southern seawater.

Octavian turned and peered into the shadows collecting at the far end of the hollow. Eyes appeared, and then white skin. A sallow face, pallid but well proportioned, beautiful, even. A black cloak covered everything else, and the face seemed to float in the darkness. This magic had a green and wormy feel—something that wriggled in deep and corrupted, something almost impossible to resist. Like death. Octavian shuddered, and he fanned the bright flame of enchantment in his own heart to drive back the oozing darkness. "Who are you?"

The man crossed the water almost without disturbing it; only the hem of his cloak formed ripples across the surface. A bitter herbal scent reached Octavian's nose when the two of them stood almost chest to chest. "I'm… I don't know if friend is the appropriate word. Yarrow asked me here."

"For what purpose?"

The man tilted his head to the side and long dark hair spilled over his shoulder. His eyelids drooped over eyes like onyx, and he tilted his plump lips up in a feigned smile. "Maybe it is not my place to say. Yarrow's trust is not an easy thing to earn."

Octavian waved his hand to indicate the drawn door. "Is this your magic?"

"Mine? Only in my wildest dreams."

"But you're a mage," D'Aurelian said, his presence at Octavian's shoulder a warm contrast to the psychic chill emanating from the stranger.

The man crossed his arms over his chest—or at least his one full arm. The other was missing from above the elbow, the stump wrapped in thin strips of cloth. After a few moments, he arched a brow. "Oh,

I'm sorry. Was that meant to be a question? Of course I'm a mage, as you well know."

"What is your name?" Octavian asked.

"Corbin, if you need a word to define me."

"I'm—"

"Octavian Rose. Of course I know."

"How?"

"I make it a priority to have…." He reached out and wound a tendril of Octavian's hair around his finger. "Intimate knowledge of things that might affect me."

Octavian resisted the urge to flinch away. This man—Corbin—unsettled him, but he'd lived long enough to know when he was being manipulated. So instead he leaned in, grasped Corbin's wrist, and let his fingertips dent the skin. "When you have intimate knowledge of me, you'll know it, friend."

Surprise registered in Corbin's dark eyes for a heartbeat before he schooled his features back to placid ennui. "I suppose I'll have to take you at your word, until I can judge based upon experience."

The movements of his lips and eyes, the seductive cadence of his speech stirred Octavian's blood, a set of deliberate actions designed to elicit a specific response. On anyone else, it would have worked, but Octavian realized…. "You're very good. Trained well. Crimson Scythe, yes?"

Corbin couldn't mask his shock as easily this time. He pulled his hand from Octavian's grasp, and it flitted instinctively to a dagger on his belt. It took him a few breaths to regain his composure, to lean back toward Octavian. "Would that frighten you?"

Octavian shrugged. "You wouldn't be my first."

"Few men can make such a claim while walking in the light of this world. This is a story I would like to hear."

"You know what I'd like?"

"I'd like to find out." Corbin's dark gaze flitted to D'Aurelian. "You could show me on him. I'm a quick study."

"No doubt," D'Aurelian mumbled.

Octavian leaned in to whisper in Corbin's ear. "I'd like to know what's beyond those markings, who made it, and why."

Corbin tossed his head, his face angled toward the glistening stalactites hanging from the ceiling. His laughter echoed through the cavern. "Oh, is that all you want? Such a simple request deserves a simple answer. What's beyond that door? Sand and water. Barnacles, maybe some shellfish and seaweed. Or… or maybe it's a whole different reality."

"What does that mean?" D'Aurelian asked.

"I barely understand it myself." Corbin shook his head.

"Well, can we go inside?" The proximity of answers, of knowledge, pulled at Octavian until it physically hurt to be separate from it.

Corbin winked. "Can you go to a place that doesn't exist, at least not in this world?"

"Can you?" Octavian countered. "Have you?"

"Oh yes."

"Then can you let us in?" D'Aurelian stepped closer, stretching his fingers toward the cool stone.

"I… can. But I will not. It isn't mine to share. It belongs to Yarrow, though belongs is not accurate. It… it is an extension of him, and only he can decide who shares in that."

"We should go find him," D'Aurelian said.

"No, we shouldn't." Corbin rubbed at his stump below his shoulder, as if it pained him. "Let him be alone. He needs it, and it isn't good to disturb him. What we should do is go back up into the house, see if there's anything edible, and talk. Get to know one another."

Games. It seemed Octavian could never escape them. He'd learned to play them at an early age in the home of his merchant father, to trade tidbits of information and pull others away at the last moment, like pieces on a board. It was a useful skill to practice at the royal court, among people who considered him mercenary scum because he hadn't been born with a title. They didn't know the advantage they gave him by underestimating him, and neither did this mage-assassin. If Octavian manipulated his pieces correctly, he could learn a great deal. Octavian turned and swept his arm toward the stairs. "Let's discover what there is to discover."

SAI'S STATUE stood on its isle, the western sun striking its right side and bouncing off the polished golden stone, making it glow. Yarrow staggered up the path lined in high brittle grass, his feet catching in the sand, making him trip. It took a great effort to reach the plinth upon which the figure stood, and Yarrow dropped to his knees, exhausted. It wasn't his body that was tired; his body could go on forever if need be. This was deeper—a weariness in the core of his being—an exhaustion of his spirit, if he believed in such things. His mind, a little over thirty years old, buckled under the millennia of the knowledge and experience forced into a compartment much too small to hold it. Some days, it took all the will he possessed to keep that vessel from shattering. But that was not what troubled him today.

Yarrow wrapped one arm around the statue's feet. His other hand kept the half-full jug of muri-ku clutched to his bare chest. He took another long swig, hoping it might be the one to drag him into blessed oblivion, but his flesh could endure more now, and it wasn't as easy to get drunk as it had once been. He rested his forehead on the statue's toes. "Sai, I'm sorry. For all the good it does. I'm sorry I destroyed you. I'm sorry."

It wasn't just me, a voice whispered.

"No." Yarrow's thighs trembled. He fell on his ass and tumbled sideways, rolling down the hill and splashing spirits all over himself until he came to rest on his back near the shore of the small island. The waves lapped at his feet as he looked up at the sun—two reddish orange discs overlapping at the edges, sending blurred and wavering streaks across the sky.

"Maybe it's a curse."

Yarrow flopped his head to the side, sand pressing into the corner of his mouth. Sai looked over at him with his bright orange eyes. "You real?" Yarrow muttered.

"What's real, syrai?" Sai asked with a gentle smile. "You perceive me, and I suppose that means I have something to offer you, even if my body and bones are scattered across Emir. Probably feeding the fishes by now, if there's anything left."

"Sai...." His flesh and bones looked supple and alive, the skin the color of wet sand, bright white where the sun hit the right angles, his muscles beneath it firm and graceful but relaxed. "Are you here to torment me?"

Sai pushed his crimson ropes of hair out of his face. "If I am, it's because you want it." He winked. "I always wanted to give you what you wanted."

"I know." Yarrow threw an arm over his eyes, but it did nothing to dull what he saw. If anything, his visions grew brighter, more real. He could see the ridges and swirls in the shells decorating Sai's hair.

"But maybe I'll finally provide what you need." Sai's face was uncharacteristically serious as he gripped Yarrow's chin.

"What do I need?"

"Answers." Sai pressed a finger between Yarrow's lips and traced the edges of his teeth.

"To what questions?"

"Those are up to you."

Yarrow rolled on top of Sai. Sai had been one of the greatest of his supporters, and Yarrow recognized every detail of the umber swirls of paint outlining his face, every crease that formed around his eyes when he smiled. "The world needs you. You should be in the world."

Sai pushed aside the white ropes of Yarrow's hair and pinned them behind his ear. "Maybe I am, in the influence I hold over you. Now, you want counsel? Ask."

Yarrow scrunched down so he could rest his face against the smooth, sea-scented skin of Sai's chest. Sai wrapped an arm around him, and Yarrow tried to ignore the idea that his mind was comforting itself, holding itself in a protective embrace. "You were with me on Hale's island. You know what the so-called goddesses are: powerful mages, trained by Fane, eager to betray him for their own benefit. And now… now they're taking more than their share of the world's magic. They're doing that, and they're making people blind and stupid, incapable of questioning their rules."

"So?" Sai pinched along the shell of Yarrow's ear. "Are things really so bad? There's still food and drink, sun and sea. Ships and people. Are they stopping the world from going on?"

"So… so it's all a lie. People should know. They shouldn't have to live under the fallacy."

"No, that's true," Sai said in his languorous Emiri drawl. "The question is: Does it have to be you, Yarrow? Do you have to be the one to tear the curtain down and expose everything behind it?"

"I think I'm the only one who can. I… I know it."

"And will the world be a better place if you pull back that sheet and show everyone the broken mess it's been hiding? Will their lives be happier?"

"I… I would want to know," Yarrow said.

"You do know, syrai. Has knowing brought you some kind of contentment that you lacked before?"

Yarrow blew out a long breath, fumbled for his jug, and found it empty. He let it fall from his hands and roll down the slope as he tried to find words Sai would understand, ignoring the fact that he was actually trying to make himself understand. "It's like… like being a child in a pretty room…. Soft fabrics, thick rugs, lace on the windows and pretty flowers painted on the walls. And as long as you do as you're told, follow your daily routine, somebody brings you meals and trinkets to play with. But the door is always locked. Maybe outside there's snow and ice, or a desert full of monsters and danger. Maybe out there, there's no one to guide you, but shouldn't you be allowed to look? To try to make your way?"

"Is it right to force the people who want to stay in the room to leave it?"

"How will we ever grow? How will the world change? When people acknowledge there's no one bringing their meals, they'll have to hunt. To come up with better ways of getting food. What's more, if they go hungry, they won't be able to shake their fists at that locked door. I just want them to have that choice."

"But you hate people, Yarrow. You think all of them are cruel and greedy and just waiting for their opportunity to cause you pain."

"But that could change. If there's no one looking out for us, won't we have to look out for each other?"

"It'll cost."

"I know," Yarrow whispered against Sai's warm, salty skin.

Sai wrapped his fingers around Yarrow's face, forcing Yarrow to look into his lantern eyes. "No, you don't. You've conjured me here to advise you, and the children of Emir have little skill at diplomacy. The truth is as clear as the patterns the waves carve into the sand, and it's this, my sweet syrai: if you do this thing, you must do it alone. If you try to pull others in, they'll be destroyed. There is… a precedent, you know."

"Yes," Yarrow choked out.

"If you drag others into the depths with you, you cannot pretend it wasn't intentional," Sai said. "If you want so much for others to take responsibility for what they cause, you must follow your own example."

Yarrow shook his head and buried his face against Sai's chest, shielding his eyes from light that seemed painfully brilliant. "I know."

"There is a choice." Sai stroked Yarrow's hair, traced the lines of Yarrow's face with his fingers.

"I don't see it."

"It's simple. Let go of it. Forget it. The world operates under a pretense? So what? Ignore it. Be Yarrow, and make Yarrow happy."

"What? Let the deception continue?"

"Exactly."

"And if I can't?" Yarrow asked. "If I can't sit by the wayside while the magic is usurped by these pretenders, while a few nobles get fat while everyone else suffers?"

"If you can't, then you have to pay, syrai. Everything is a trade, a balance. Emir teaches us that. The tide comes in and the tide goes out. But it always leaves something behind. It's not a good idea to ignore what Emir leaves scattered on the shore."

"No," Yarrow admitted. "I can ignore what has gone on in this world, or I can do something about it."

"Change the course of the currents?"

"Yes."

"It won't come for free, Yarrow. Is it worth it?"

"How can I not? People are living their lives according to lies. The system is broken, it's grinding them up and spitting them out...."

"But does it have to be you?"

"Who else?"

"You want so much to put the destiny of people in their own hands," Sai said. "You could do that. You could step back."

"Like I'm not a person?"

"You're not. Not anymore. Not really."

"No," Yarrow admitted.

"So is it even your place? What makes you worthy of choosing for them and not these goddesses? Are you sure you don't just want revenge? Vengeance against the whole world, and the chance to show them you're strong?"

Yarrow sat up and looked out across the water. The setting sun colored the sea with crimson and gold. The sand looked as smooth as glass in the diffuse light. There was no one beside him, and Yarrow dug up a handful of sand and let it fall in clumps from his fist, staring as it formed a jagged little hill and then crumbled under its own weight. Sai. Sai had been nothing but happiness and freedom, until Yarrow had stained him with his own tragedy, tainted him to the point where he could not continue. The same would happen to others close to him if he pursued the course he now set his feet upon. But could he turn away? Live in denial?

They… they had murdered his beloved. They had to pay.

Maybe it was vengeance, but it wasn't just vengeance.

People had to be free to set the course of their own destiny, whether it was glorious or abysmal. It had to rest on the shoulders of humanity.

Yarrow stood and brushed the sand from his billowy blue trousers. He couldn't let it go, couldn't let those pretenders and whores benefit from the ignorance of those they claimed to care for. No. He could never pretend it wasn't happening. But he also couldn't pretend it would come cheaply. It rested on his shoulders, and he would need to see it through. As much as it terrified him to stand alone, he would have to find the strength. He could handle many things, all kinds of pain and disappointment, but Yarrow couldn't abide seeing one more person he cared about destroyed by the realities only he understood. It would hurt to cut those ties, but he had no choice. Not if he truly loved them. And if he didn't work from love, he was no better than those power-hungry, cutthroat bitches who had killed his beloved. No. He was not doing this for himself, but he would do it by himself.

He wondered if it was time. Perhaps he could ask Sasha. With that thought in mind, and the desire to consult with Corbin and Octavian Rose, he strolled to the shore and waded out to the little rowboat that would carry him to his home island.

Chapter Twelve

ASPHODEL SAT on the railing of the third-floor balcony with her legs hanging down, watching the children play in the fountain. They'd been at it all day, and now only the colorful glass lanterns illuminated the courtyard. Del sensed a presence behind her, a subtle shift of the air currents, a miniscule warmth across the back of her neck where a body blocked the cooler air coming from inside the house. She thought she detected Sasha's scent, the peppery fragrance he seemed to have, but it might have been her imagination. With him, her emotions warped her perceptions, and nothing was more dangerous.

She shook her head but didn't look back at him. It wouldn't do for her to seek accolades for knowing he was there. "I can't understand what satisfaction these children get from spending the day running around in that water. What are they hoping to accomplish?"

"Nothing," he said. "It's something you must come to understand. Most people speak and act without thinking. They live for the moment and the pleasures they can take from it. They move their faces and bodies without regard for what they're showing the world, how their actions and expressions might be perceived. We, of course, must make others think we do the same. Our expressions might be deliberate, but they must appear accidental."

"It's made for a dull afternoon," she said.

Sasha leaned his elbows on the rail next to where she sat. "Your mission is to watch Duncan's daughter. Keep her safe."

Duncan's daughter. He did not use her name, and that was a way to avoid attachment. Del wondered if he did it on purpose, and then she felt foolish. Sasha did everything on purpose. She wondered what that meant for Marly.

"And I am." Del ran her fingers over the rows of tiny daggers at her hip. "If necessary, every person in the courtyard could be dead in the time it would take you to draw three breaths."

"And suppose I came here to ask you to do just that."

"Master?"

Sasha closed and opened his eyes slowly. "Do not call me that. And answer my question. If Thalil asked you to take the lives of those children, what would you do?"

It was a test. "I would obey Thalil, of course."

"And how would you feel about it?"

"I would feel nothing," she said, watching as Marly swung her feet over the lip of the fountain and landed in a sandy puddle. "Perhaps pride in a job well done."

When she turned to look at Sasha, his expression was blank, his eyes like portals into a starless sky. Her answers had been proper, but she almost sensed he was displeased. "Did I give you an unsatisfactory answer, Sasha?"

He blinked once. "Not unsatisfactory, but perhaps not honest. I would like you to think about it—really think about it. Imagine your blade going into Marly's flesh, opening her skin so the blood and fat poured out. Imagine her face: first surprise, then betrayal. Imagine watching the color leave her skin, her body doing all the foul things it would do at death, the ones others try to pretend don't happen. And then I want to know how you feel."

"What's the point of this?" Del fought not to let her irritation show in her face or voice. "Do you think I would fail the Dark and Beautiful One? Have I ever?"

"Do as I say." Sasha turned to head back into the house.

"Where will you be?"

He looked over his shoulder at her. "Yarrow has something he wishes to discuss with all of us. I suspect it will be… significant."

"I would like to be there."

"That's not my decision," Sasha said. "You were not invited."

"Perhaps I will… observe anyway."

"I had better not see you," he warned. "I had better detect no hint of your presence… because if I cannot, neither will anyone else."

She swore she saw a hint of a smile as he disappeared into the shadows. She was skilled, and he was proud of her. She knew it. He had taken an interest in her training and career that none of the other young assassins enjoyed. But he frustrated her. For all she wanted to be like him—Thalil's chosen, the one who had returned from the Crimson Palace—she didn't know how. He wouldn't tell her. She knew the usual order guidelines, but she didn't want to be the usual order agent. She wanted to be him, and no matter what she did, he would not help her. Maybe she wasn't as important to him as she assumed. And why had she assumed? Other than training her and taking her on some of his missions, Sasha hadn't shown her affection. In a way, he'd done her a favor; he could've easily feigned devotion and had her doing anything he said. His lack of manipulation showed respect. But that respect felt cold and hollow.

Feelings. Stupid weaknesses, the luxury of the children below, who were being collected by mothers, fathers, lovers of mothers and fathers, older siblings, friends…. The Emiri all lived together in huge extended families where only friendship and loyalty mattered. Del scoffed as children were wrapped in cloths, their hair rubbed dry, kisses sprinkled on their foreheads and noses. How claustrophobic, all those people worrying over you every minute, pandering to your insecurities…. Yes, it was weakness, and she wanted none of it.

She did not love Sasha, and she didn't want him to love her.

What she wanted was to learn Yarrow's plans. She might have a part to play in them, some benefit to receive. Or she might have to help put a stop to them. The mage was mad and dangerous. Maybe she would need to get Marly away from this place. Her safety was still Del's mission, until she was told otherwise.

Del hurried inside and down the hallway to the room she'd claimed. Being uninvited, she wasn't officially here, but with so many Emiri coming and going, it was easy to remain unnoticed, and Yarrow's compound of cobbled-together houses had plenty of forgotten spaces. Despite the heat, she slipped a dark cloak and hood on to hide the light color of her hair. After checking her weapons, she moved into the hallway and past some other unused rooms, empty aside from mismatched junk. Few people roamed the halls—most of the Emiri had already gone to the beach to light their fires and prepare for the night's festivities. Yarrow had no servants, as was obvious from the clutter. But the clutter made for plenty of places to hide, and Del found one on the first floor of the main house, not far from the kitchen. Any grand announcement from Yarrow would involve copious amounts of wine.

Over the next hour, a few Emiri came to retrieve bottles and jugs, but when Del followed them, she discovered only more waterside gatherings, and so she returned to her post. Soon full night had fallen, only a few candles pinpricking through the heavy dark in the kitchen, and she had yet to detect any hint of Sasha, Yarrow, Duncan, or any of the others who might be privy to the meeting. She was just about to give up and go check the places they'd be likely to gather, when she heard a soft thump followed by a muffled grunt. It came from the other side of the room, and whoever made it had been concealed for a while. Del had been watching for at least an hour, and with the exception of Sasha, there was no one here who could sneak past her. Not even Corbin, despite what he liked to believe. And she doubted Corbin would be hiding in a cupboard. Actually, he wouldn't have fit in this narrow compartment with the peeling blue paint.

Aware Yarrow had many enemies, Del took no chances. She drew a dagger as she threw open the double doors with her other hand. As soon as the doors opened, she had her blade against the throat of the person crouched inside, but she wasn't expecting the second person.

Her dagger grew so hot it blistered her palm through her leather glove, and she had no choice but to let it fall to the floor with a clatter. A force—hard and sudden as a boot to her ribs—blasted out of the cupboard, and she couldn't regain her balance before landing on her ass. As soon as she hit the floor, she had a dagger ready to throw at the shadowy forms huddled together. She'd almost loosed it when someone said her name in a harsh whisper.

"By the Shades! Marly? Who's in there with you?"

There was a soft whoosh and crackle, and then a wavering blue flame appeared over the hand of a scrawny boy—the prince Thane. Del pursed her lips to hide her annoyance. These two, likely here in search of treats to pilfer, might have cost her the chance to eavesdrop on the meeting. On the other hand, Marly's safety was her responsibility, and the girl should be in her room. There was absolutely no security in this place, and not even Del and Sasha could keep track of all those coming and going.

Del grabbed Marly by the front of her shirt and pulled her out. Everything looked distorted in the blue light. "Marly, what are you doing here? You're supposed to be in your room. What did you mean by coming here?"

Marly's lip jutted out, and her thick eyebrows bunched at the center. Del had hurt her feelings. After their encounter with the gang of boys back in Windwake, Marly probably considered Del an ally of some sort—maybe even a friend. In a heartbeat, Del decided not to shatter that illusion. Having Marly's trust would make it easier to convince Marly to do whatever Del wanted. She smiled and reached up to stroke Marly's hair, which stuck out every which way in jagged clumps.

"Oh… what have you done?"

Marly straightened her spine and raised her chin. "I've been wanting to cut my hair, and, well…. Mother's not here to stop me. And it's very hot."

"When did you do it?" Del asked.

"Just before we came down here. Thane helped me."

"What did he use, a rusty battle-ax?" Del muttered.

Marly's expression melted. "I told him to make it look like yours."

"It would have looked better if you'd let me use magic," the prince argued.

"Like I'm going to let you fling spells. At my head. Don't be stupid. Does it look really bad, Del?"

"No, it just needs some evening out. I can help you. Tomorrow. For now, the two of you should go back to your room."

"No," Marly said, "we can't. They're holding some big secret meeting, and we want to know what they're going to be talking about. We're worried about being sent home. We like it here. But of course my father said we couldn't be there, and even after I almost got Uncle Yarrow to say yes."

"Maybe it's none of your business." The last thing Del needed was to try to keep these two hidden while she observed the proceedings. It would be hard enough to keep herself unobserved. "Besides, do you even know where they are?"

"I can almost always find Yarrow," Thane said. "He leaves behind a trail of magic, like he's always performing a spell, even when he doesn't know it."

Del crossed her arms over her chest. "But?"

"He left the island, and I can't get a sense of him. It's unusual."

Del cursed mentally. Searching the cobbled-together houses created enough of a challenge, but if she had to search across twenty-nine islands, she had little chance of ever finding Yarrow and the others.

"I still know where they went," Marly said with a satisfied little smile.

"Where?" Del asked.

"I'll tell you if you promise to take us with you."

Del couldn't help being a little impressed. She weighed her options and decided she had a better chance with Marly's information than without. "All right."

Marly leaned in and whispered, her words tumbling in a torrent from her lips with her excitement. "Toumo and Kin were here a while ago picking up some casks. They said they were taking them to Yarrow at the feet of hope. Um… any idea where that might be?"

Grinning, Del said, "Haven't I told you I make it my business to be familiar with every detail about a place I'm staying? Come on. It isn't far. And by the Cast-Down, try to be quiet."

THE STATUE stood on its own little islet, slightly north of Yarrow's compound. It depicted one of the greatest heroes of the Johmatran War, a man who had sacrificed himself to prevent the enemy from reaching his home islands and who had been one of the first to risk rescuing Emiri slaves from Johmatra. For both reasons, a single character was inscribed upon the plinth where he stood: yu-me, the Emiri word for hope. Del could see why Yarrow might choose this place….

Except, apparently, he hadn't.

Many Emiri came here to pay their respects, often leaving seashells and baubles, or lighting candles and pouring their potent liquor on the ground. Flames flickered and glinted off bits of metal and some strewn coins, but there was nothing else here—nothing and nobody.

"A wasted trip, it looks like," Del said, disappointed.

"Why?" Thane asked.

She stared at him in disbelief. She'd been told by Sasha that the prince was highly intelligent, if a little strange. Could he not see what was in front of them? "Uh… because there's no one here?"

He walked to the edge of the firelight and moved his hands in figure eight patterns. "They're here. We're just not seeing what's really here, but a picture magic has painted in our minds."

"What do you mean?" Marly asked, hurrying to his side.

"Someone… I would say Yarrow, has replicated this place and put it like a screen in front of the real one. We're looking at the illusion he has woven, not what's really here."

"But how?" Marly knelt down and picked up a small round stone. She tossed it toward the statue, where it skipped across the sand, leaving a trail of divots in its wake. "I can touch it."

"You only think you can," Thane explained. "The spell has been crafted in such a way that it adjusts itself to outside influence. It's strong, but…."

"Can you tear it down?" Del asked.

Thane shrugged. "Perhaps. Probably. But I don't think it would be a good idea. Yarrow put this here to keep himself from the eyes and ears of others, and not us, I think. We could be doing him a great disservice by dispelling it completely."

"Then we're right back where we started." Del shook her head, trying to imagine what Sasha might do in this situation, but coming up blank. She'd been taught to fight magic users; creeping up and killing them before they knew you were there was invariably the best strategy. Barring that, she knew techniques to tire them out and wear down their power. But this was Yarrow, and it wasn't a fight.

"I think I can take us beyond the illusion," Thane said, "into the reality Yarrow has hidden behind this one."

"Will he be able to see us? Know we're there?" Marly asked.

Thane nodded. "Because we will be there. Right now, we're not."

"That won't be a problem." Del pointed to the heavy shadow behind the statue. "As long as you do exactly as I say. All of the candles are lit in front of the statue, and assuming that's where Yarrow and the others are gathered, the light will make it nearly impossible for them to see into the darkness beyond it. Let's get into place, crouch down behind the base of the statue. Then Thane can do… whatever. We'll need to be completely still. Even the smallest movement could make a sound that will give us away. Try to keep your breathing shallow."

They followed her instructions, and she nodded to Thane to do his thing. She expected something flashy, the scene in front of her burning away like acid thrown on cloth, the reality poking through the holes. She thought she'd feel something, a change in pressure or temperature, perhaps. A tingle over her skin. But Thane closed his eyes for a few moments and Yarrow, Sasha, Duncan, Octavian, D'Aurelian, Corbin, Kin, Toumo, and Zura were there, seated in a circle on the sand. It was as if she'd simply blinked and missed them before.

"I've asked all of you here because we all know there will be repercussions from what happened in Eirion-Vale." Yarrow looked around the circle, meeting each pair of eyes in turn.

"I agree that it's a wise idea to get ahead of this," Octavian responded. "It seems to me our first course of action should be to somehow infiltrate the ranks of the priestesses. Perhaps one of my young warriors could join the Defenders and gather intelligence for us that way."

"There's no need," Sasha said. "This has already been taken care of. Quite some time ago."

Del almost shook her head. Of course Sasha had seen to it; they'd be fools to think otherwise.

"Forgive me for being blunt, tam." D'Aurelian's features looked pinched. He was nervous, and rightly so. "But can the rest of us trust that your information will be shared? All of it, and not just the bits you choose? Frankly, we all know your people have little stake in any kind of political conflict. You can simply wait at the edges until it blows over. The rest of us do not have that luxury."

Del turned and waited for Sasha's answer. He looked so different from the rest of them, even in the common clothing of the islands: ebony and gold and so beautiful. The light from the candles didn't seem to stick to him or reflect off his skin and hair. No little specks of white glimmered from his eyes.

"I suppose you will have to trust me." Sasha's teeth flashed bright when he smiled.

"Seriously?" D'Aurelian lifted a hand and let it fall on his knee. Del couldn't determine the cause of his animosity toward her mentor, but she couldn't miss the obvious signs in D'Aurelian's body language and facial expressions. "I don't suspect it will offend you if I point out that you and your people are practically the embodiment of deceit."

"If we did not wish to help you, we would not be here." Corbin waved his spidery fingers dismissively. "As you so astutely observed, it would be a simple matter for us to learn of your plans with or without your participation."

Duncan raised a hand. "We'll get nowhere if we fight amongst ourselves. Our goal should be to smooth things over if we can, strike some sort of accord with the temples."

"That will mean handing me over to the priestesses," Yarrow said, picking up a stick and scratching designs into the sand.

"My sources confirm that," Sasha said. "They also believe the priestesses and their army of Defenders will march on the Twenty-Nine. We're unsure if they'll have the support of Garith's forces."

"It won't matter." Yarrow stabbed into the ground until he snapped his twig. "This place is for the Emiri, and no one is taking it from us. Sai died to protect it, and I won't let it be in vain."

"Our position is a defensible one," Octavian said. "The greater worry is what will happen as a result of the battle. Those of us who hold titles are likely to have them revoked. The temples will leave His Majesty with no choice. If I know the king at all, he's scrambling to prevent another war. He knows the people cannot weather another conflict so soon. I… do not wish to lose Rosecairn, or to abandon the people there who depend on my protection."

Duncan offered Octavian a strained smile, and the shadows deepened in the lines around his eyes. "I feel the same about Windwake. I never wanted to rule, and there's much about it I find distasteful, but I know my people are better off with me than they'd be with many others. I also have a family to think about, children I don't want to make into pariahs."

Beside Del, Marly fidgeted. Del could practically see the words trying to claw their way out of her throat, ready to tell her father not to worry about her, that she could take care of herself, and that they should do the right things no matter what. Del put a hand on Marly's shoulder. Though she could still feel the tension tightening the girl's muscles, Marly kept still and quiet.

"I… I do not want to cause pain to any of you." Yarrow's hair curtained his face as he hung his head. "No one else can suffer because of me."

Duncan rested a hand on his shoulder. "We will figure this out together. No one will suffer, and no one will be sacrificed. We'll find a way."

"There's only one way," Yarrow whispered. Del had to strain to hear him. "I have thought about this at great length. I'm still unsure of many things, but I cannot claim to despise lies while I perpetuate them myself. I have things I need to say, to all of you."

"Yarrow," Sasha said, "perhaps some things should remain unsaid. At least for now, until we work through our current troubles." He looked into the darkness beyond the statue, and Del was almost certain he knew she—they—were there. What else he knew, she couldn't begin to imagine.

"No." The mage's eyes flashed lightning blue. "No, because it is all connected. All of the world's problems stem from a single source. I have this knowledge, and if I have learned anything in this life, it's that hiding and speaking falsehoods robs me of those I care about. I cannot bear to let it happen again."

Both of the Emiri had been silent, but now Toumo said, "If you wish to speak, syrai, we will listen." Kin nodded his agreement.

"I will start at the beginning." Yarrow sounded resigned. His tone reminded Del of one who knew he could not avoid the assassin's blade and resolved to meet it with dignity. She preferred those marks to the ones who begged or blubbered. "Some of you know pieces of this story, but none of you know everything."

"Yarrow?" Duncan looked crestfallen.

"Please, just let me speak. Let me speak, and please know that if I kept secrets, I thought it was the right thing to do at the time. It was never because I doubted your loyalty.

"I was exiled at a young age. The king, Garith's father…. The reason is not important. I was young, alone, and afraid. If not for my magic, I have no doubt I would have been the victim of some predator or another before I made it a mile from home. I knew I needed power— power to protect myself. So I went in search of it. I… I didn't want to be hurt. Not ever again. Never again helpless. Along the way, I discovered something in the most remote reaches of the Lapir Mountains. I can only describe it as an entity of immense power. It had been stripped of its physical form, its essence locked away. I made a bargain with it. I would allow it to experience sensation through my body in exchange for the knowledge it promised to share with me. I bonded with it. I soon learned I had made a terrible mistake.

"My creature had monstrous appetites. It hurt the people I loved most to control me… and my control over it was slipping away. I had more and more trouble stopping it from taking over my body. I needed to be rid of it. I found some information in Espero. From there, I sailed with Sai to an uncharted island. We discovered it belonged to Hale, a once apprentice of Fane. I learned a great deal from him. He was present when the golden age of this world came to an end, and he told me why.

"Those the world knows as goddesses began as nothing more than Fane's wives, powerful mages in their own right who became nearly omnipotent under his tutelage. Later, I learned Fane had been a pupil of the creature that shared my body. He had… loved it after a fashion, and it him, so much as I was capable. But he betrayed it. He performed the spell that stripped its physical form. Since he knew it could not be killed, he had no other way to free himself of me… it. When he rose to his position as the emperor of legend, probably a thousand years later, his one great fear was others of its kind. His fear led to him making the biggest mistake of his life. He taught that spell to his thirteen wives and sent them to hunt down the rest of the creatures. When these women became jealous of the love Fane received from his people, they used that same magic against him."

While Del had been engrossed in the mage's tale, wondering if any of it was true and not the product of Yarrow's madness, Thane had crept up next to her without making a sound. With one hand, he clutched Marly's wrist. The other wrapped around a gaudy pendant he always seemed to wear. In the firelight, Del could see the tears spilling over his cheeks.

"Fewer mages are born each generation," Yarrow continued. "Those who are are much weaker. I learned the reason for this. The so-called goddesses are hoarding the world's magic, using it to maintain their lives and their false divinity. I… also found Fane, his essence, hidden in the mountain caves where his faithless wives struck him down. He made a bargain with me. He would help me with my creature if I carried him from that place. I had to agree. I had no other choice."

"Is he… within you still?" Octavian asked. "Is he the source of your great power?"

"No. That is, I don't know if he's still there. I never noticed his presence. But my power still comes from my creature, or, more accurately, from me."

"I thought you rid yourself of that awful thing," Duncan said.

"I… I was given a choice. I could destroy it, finally and fully, or I could bond with it completely. I was afraid, Duncan. Almost from as far back as I can remember, I have been afraid. Afraid that everyone I see will try to hurt me. Afraid I won't be able to stop them. Afraid that without my magic, I'll only ever be a victim. Afraid of being alone. I bonded with the creature. We are one being now."

"I cannot believe you kept this from me." Del could see the way Duncan's eyes sparkled even at a distance. "Did you think I would turn my back on you?"

"I wasn't sure," Yarrow answered in a broken whisper. "I would not have blamed you if you had. But as always, I was scared, and I was selfish."

"Oh my love." Duncan shook his head.

"I have more to say," Yarrow went on. "I… this will hurt some of you, but it's time I told the truth. On the night of Duncan's wedding, I was especially vulnerable. Raw and hurting inside like never before. I planned to drink myself into a stupor; it always worked before, at least temporarily. But my Aunt Den approached me. She and the queen wanted to put a mage on the throne. To that end, I… I laid with Queen Cothryn. Prince Thane is my son."

Duncan clapped a hand over his mouth and squeezed his eyes shut. Sasha nodded and muttered, "I suspected as much."

"I cannot ask you to forgive me," Yarrow said, looking at Duncan. "I did it out of spite, to get back at Garith for forcing you to marry that woman. But I am not sorry. I'm sure Thane is the balm this world needs—a mage-emperor. He can change things, fix them, or tear it all down and start over. But first I need to do my part."

"Goddesses!" Duncan drove his fist into the sand, his eyes red and shining. "What more? What more do you feel you need to do?"

Yarrow straightened and looked Duncan in the eye without flinching. Del didn't know if anything he said was true, but she admired his bravery, his conviction. "I need to make sure my son has access to the power he needs, power he and all mages have the right to share. I need to sweep away the filthy lies that have been festering in this world for far too long. This silly restriction against mages ruling that stems from the falsehood these women have spewed forth about Fane. And I need to avenge my beloved."

Duncan looked pale and horrified. "You intend to bring down the temples and the orders of the priestesses."

Yarrow shook his head. "They are only a symptom of a greater illness. I intend to bring down the so-called goddesses, those that betrayed my beloved and sentenced him to millennia of torment."

"So… you're saying the goddesses are actual physical beings?" Octavian asked.

Sasha looked up at him. "You doubted that?"

"I suppose I did. I always thought of them more as abstract concepts, something only the uneducated took literally. But then again, until the recent artifacts began appearing, I considered Fane nothing more than a cautionary tale. Do you have evidence of this?"

Yarrow nodded. "I have been in their presence. They tried to frighten me off. I faced the one who calls herself Mother Goddess atop Starmont. They are just mages. Mages of extraordinary power, but no more divine than any of us. And they certainly didn't create anything. My memory… it goes back a long way. Back to when people ran naked through the forests and slept on the ground like beasts. Back before any of them even conceived of using magic. They couldn't even understand using a bucket to collect water or sharpening a stick to hunt for meat back then. Fane was the first. And he learned it from me."

Everyone sat in stunned silence before D'Aurelian finally spoke. "What is it you imagine will happen, should you succeed?"

Yarrow looked up at the sky, where the stars were bright and clear with no city lights to compete with. "Magic will flood back into the world. In the tales, magic took care of everything: food, shelter, protection. People could focus on grander things than scraping by, merely surviving. But maybe what's more important is that people will finally acknowledge their own power. If their world flourishes, they can take the credit they deserve. If greed and pain continue to reign, they will have no one to blame but themselves. But I… I need help. I especially need the help of other mages. I have some things, things from Fane. Books and charts. But I cannot understand them."

"I knew you found something in that cavern," Corbin said.

Yarrow ignored him. "And there's magic I need to figure out. Fane taught his wives immortality, and I think that means the destruction of their physical forms won't be enough. I need to learn the spell to strip them down to their essences, the one they used against him. I'm close, but...."

"Am I alone in thinking this is madness?" Duncan asked. "Yarrow, you usually approach everything with such suspicion, yet you take the word of this Hale and whatever thing claimed to be Fane as absolute truth. Can you really start a war based on their claims? And why would you want a war? We've only just achieved peace. Can we not enjoy it? A quiet time in our lives, finally?"

"I don't wish for war." Yarrow's hair swayed as he shook his head. "Not if it can be avoided. I want to bring the truth to the people. Yes, I plan to destroy the so-called goddesses. I will hunt them down and finish them one by one. Then there will be no question of the validity of Hale's claims. The return of magic to the world will be all the evidence anyone needs."

"Are you sure?" Octavian asked. "History and the ways events can be interpreted are fickle things at best. How do you know you won't be painted as a villain, the same as Fane? Another arrogant mage who plunged the world into chaos chasing his own desires."

"The people draw great comfort from the goddesses," Duncan said. "Is it really fair to take that away from them?"

"It will make them take responsibility!" Yarrow said. "The goddesses are doing nothing for them. The war showed us that. Did the goddesses who claim to love and protect us appear even once? Did they save even one of their faithful from dying at the hands of the Johmatrans? It is all lies!"

"Might it not be better to let history run its course?" Sasha's silk-against-skin voice offered no clue to his personal feelings. "Every day, new evidence is coming to light about Fane's empire. If it's justice you're after—if there is any such thing—wouldn't it serve them right to be forgotten? To fade into obscurity as people shake off their need of them. Instead, you'll be giving them a grand end, an epic battle that will live on in stories." He reached over and cupped Yarrow's cheek. "You have done much more for the people of this world than you ever owed them. You trust them to see to their own best interests? Let them. Let them take these truths that are coming forth and interpret them. By your own admission, if they cannot or will not let go of their delusions in the face of evidence, then they don't deserve to break free."

"I agree," Duncan said. "It does not have to be you. You deserve some happiness."

"Yet"—Octavian stared dreamily out to sea—"magic returned to the world in full force. I would like to see that in my lifetime. And to be a part of it, to make some small contribution to fixing everything wrong with the world…. What a legacy that would be."

D'Aurelian nodded. "If history is clear on one thing, it's that great men and women are rarely the ones who wait around to see what will happen. We have a chance to influence how things turn out, and I for one would not shed any tears over the loss of the temples, especially as they are now: militant, aggressive, and grabbing for more and more power. The council in Espero isn't perfect and neither is the monarchy here, but I would prefer either of them to living under the rule of the temples. As for the goddesses… I don't know. I'm still struggling to accept much of this."

"I can attest to one thing, at least," Sasha said. "Thalil exists, and he has built for himself a realm somewhere beyond the reality of this world. I have been there."

"The goddesses have done the same," Yarrow said. "Again, it's just magic. Very difficult magic, but nothing that requires godhood. I have managed it myself, in a very small way."

Octavian's eyes widened. "The room in the cavern beneath your house."

"Yes. If I can expand it, it will give us and our allies a place to retreat where we cannot be touched. I would welcome your help, Octavian Rose."

"I'll consider it. It's a fascinating idea, even just academically, but I'll need to weigh it against what will be best for Rosecairn."

Del thought his decision would be a quick one. Octavian wouldn't be able to resist. He practically salivated at the idea of all that knowledge spread out before him. It was as plain in his eyes as the stars in the sky.

Corbin, though, looked even more ravenous. "I will help you, but I have a condition. If another of these creatures can be found, I want to bond with it. Of course, I'll use the power I receive to aid your cause."

"You really don't want to do that," Yarrow said.

"Oh, but I do."

Duncan stood and brushed the sand from his backside. He held a hand out to Yarrow and helped him to his feet. They stepped close, and Duncan rested his big hands on Yarrow's narrow hips. "I ask only this. Do nothing right now. Come back to the house and talk with me and Sasha. We should think about our future. All I have ever wanted is for it to be happy for you. Please don't do anything that will make that impossible. Not yet."

"All right." Yarrow waved his hand. Nothing looked any different, but Del knew his illusion had been dispelled. Each of the Emiri men said a few words to him in their language and pressed kisses to his cheeks before departing. The others followed, Corbin alone and Octavian and D'Aurelian engaged in passionate, if hushed, conversation.

Duncan still held on to Yarrow's waist, and Sasha put his hand on Yarrow's shoulder. "Shall we have something to eat? Watch the moon from the balcony in our room?"

"I would like that," Yarrow said. "Go on without me. I want to sit with Sai for a few moments."

"We'll meet you there." Sasha pressed a lingering kiss to Yarrow's lips and smoothed his hair back before joining Duncan on the narrow trail that wound down to the water.

Yarrow plopped back down on the ground. He seemed so lost in his own thoughts that Del had little worry they'd have trouble sneaking past him. But before she could point the children on the best path, Thane darted out of the shadows and ran to stand in front of Yarrow. Del barely grabbed Marly's shirtsleeve in time to prevent her from following.

After a sharp inhale, Yarrow said, "Be—what are you doing here?"

Thane touched the side of Yarrow's head in an oddly intimate and mature gesture. "I can help you with the magic you need. None of the others will be able to do it, but I believe I can. I would like to see these charts and papers, if you would be willing to show them to me. Together, we might finally make progress toward righting this wrong. It has been a long time coming."

Chapter Thirteen

Travel had proved anything but the exotic adventure N'hahseen had imagined. The ship had smelled of mold and men with no way to wash. It rained much of the time, forcing him to remain in quarters that, despite his escorts' best attempts at luxury, were so dank his bedclothes always felt clammy. The rocking of the vessel had him puking his innards into a silver basin much of the time, and before long, so did the rancid food even Kahladryian spice couldn't improve. Worst of all, it gave him too much time to think, to doubt himself and his abilities and contemplate what might happen if he failed. The line of people waiting to pick over his carcass would be long. His mother's husband, Wisam, who had always resented no one of his bloodline would rule the city-state, would be first in line, and his mother herself would not be far behind, seeking a way to twist his shortcomings to her advantage. He had no illusions about who he could call friends or allies. He'd had one, but the explosion on the night of the banquet had burned them away as surely as they'd destroyed a wing of his palace.

Rahsari had escaped after the attack. As was only prudent, N'hahseen wondered what had become of him. After all, he could reemerge as a threat, depending on who he truly worked for. As he lay on his soggy mattress watching the lanterns sway with the motion of the waves, he replayed in his mind every conversation he'd had with his servant, every word he could recall them exchanging. Had there been something he'd missed? Some indication of Rahsari's treachery? More importantly, what had he shared that his servant might use against him? Had he poked around the palace and found something incriminating before he'd murdered dozens of people and escaped into the desert? The last N'hahseen had heard, the guards had been unable to locate his former servant. Chances were good that Rahsari had perished in the desert, but N'hahseen would rest easier with some proof. His mother would upturn every grain of sand for a far smaller threat to herself. He wondered if he might find a trustworthy assassin in Gaeltheon. He'd heard peculiar tales of some so skilled the stories had to be exaggerations. Might one of them be able to deliver Rahsari alive? Because as much as he hated to admit it, even in the darkest corners of his own mind, N'hahseen wanted to know why. He wanted to know if anything they'd shared had been real.

The journey improved very little when they came ashore in Gaeltheon. N'hahseen was desperate for fresh air, but both his own guards and those provided by the barbarian king to escort them forbade him from riding. He would make too easy a target for an archer. So they stuffed him in a carriage that battered his bones as it bumped along the gouged roads. Through its windows, he observed a drab land of mud, snow, and tangles of gray trees. The little huts at the edges of the fields looked poorer than slaves' quarters. Fetid water collected in pits and drenched the hem of his cloak when he was permitted, under heavy guard, to see to his body's needs. Even magic couldn't keep his boots or socks dry for long.

The carriage jolted to a stop. After a brief knock, the door swung open, and one of his men bowed.

"What is it?" N'hahseen asked.

"We are nearly to King Garith's fortress of Eirion-Vale, First Son. Servants are available to see to your hair and makeup if you would like to freshen up before we arrive."

A gust of wind carried some fat flakes of snow into the carriage, where they melted as soon as they landed across N'hahseen's thigh. The air smelled of soil and the barbarians' animals—horses—but N'hahseen didn't care. He couldn't take being confined any longer; never in his life had his movements been so restricted. "No, that won't be necessary. Move out of my way. I'll walk the rest of the way to the palace."

"But the soldiers said it isn't safe!"

"Let them try to stop me, then. I am the First Son of Kahladryia, and I shall do as I please."

The servant looked like he'd been slapped, but he bent nearly in half and backed away. N'hahseen stepped out of the carriage, and his feet instantly sunk into the chilly muck. But the joy of stretching his muscles trumped any discomfort, and he made his way up the steep hill, silencing any protests with a glare. The weeks of inactivity showed in the way he panted by the time the palace became visible.

But palace was the wrong word. The only thing impressive about this place was its size; it rose higher than any building he had ever seen, though it was made all of gray stone, as dull as the landscape surrounding it. Only small slits that he supposed functioned as windows broke the monotony of the walls. What good was constructing a building to reach into the clouds if one couldn't enjoy the view? But it was clear: this was not a place of luxury, designed for study, dancing, and banquets. It wasn't a place for living, but a place for surviving. A place to cower during an attack. He reached up and tapped his fingers against his forehead. He had done the right thing by coming here. These people desperately needed Fane's blessing, and he could not imagine they wouldn't want to be a part of the glorious world of his return. Everyone, especially Fane's descendants, must do his part to ensure that return pleased Fane. This was the best way for N'hahseen to serve, and if it brought glory to Kahladryia, all the better.

A FEW hours ago, scouts had announced that the ambassador from Johmatra would be arriving soon. Courtenay awaited it with both impatience and dread. She'd been busy over the last couple of weeks, making sure every detail would please the representative the Johmatrans had chosen. Information had been scant, but she knew he was a man, young, and from the north. She had refreshed her knowledge of that region's dialect and customs, all while seeing he had suitable quarters—a suite of rooms on the second floor, so the unaccustomed height of the fortress's higher levels didn't disturb him; coached the kitchen staff on his meals—they wouldn't be able to provide lizard meat or fermented cacti, but she'd procured a variety of Johmatran seasonings; and hand-selected a dozen servants to attend him—those least likely to commit a misstep, and those guaranteed not to be assassins working for one of the many anti-Johmatran fringe groups.

Now only waiting remained. Pherara, she'd never trained for this. A linguist wasn't the same as a diplomat. But if she could prevent anything from going catastrophically wrong for a moon or so, the Johmatran would settle in. People adapted and shock waned to acceptance; at least it had for her when she'd left Selindria for Espero as a young girl. The Johmatrans couldn't be that different, could they?

Finally the gate to the outer wall opened, and Courtenay watched through the window as dozens of soldiers, several laden carts, and three carriages entered the courtyard. Servants poured out to unload cargo and lead horses off to the stables. She waited for the appearance of the extravagant litter that would carry the Johmatran potentate into the hall of the keep and wondered who would carry it. It had been agreed that the Johmatran representative was welcome to bring paid servants but not slaves, and Courtenay was glad. She didn't think she'd be able to keep a civil tongue otherwise. It would be hard enough with Esperon blood much too fresh in her mind.

The doors opened, and royal guards with their halberds held stiff marched inside, snow falling in clumps from their boots. They stepped to the sides, forming lines on either side of the door. She expected staff and advisors from Johmatra to follow, but they didn't. A single man in a heavy red cloak strode up the carpet toward where she stood with the king and his soldiers and staff, as well as dozens of nobles who'd wanted to witness the occasion and the servants they'd dragged with them—a group of almost forty people.

The man brushed his hood back to reveal long, ink-black hair, wet and glistening from the snow. He had the dark olive complexion typical to Johmatra and a well-proportioned face with sharp cheekbones and full lips. By the way he carried himself, Courtenay guessed he was important. As he came closer, she noticed his strange eyes—one the dark brown characteristic of his people and the other so pale blue it was almost white—accented by some smudged kohl and gold dust on the lashes. He was a tall man, but she could glean nothing else because of his heavy cloak.

He looked around the hall, his expression somewhere between fascination and horror. Then he focused on Courtenay's face, probably because she stood at the front of the group, ahead of even Garith, waiting to welcome their guest.

"I have heard the customs in the west are very different, so I will try not to be offended, but in my home, a guest who has traveled for weeks is afforded at least a greeting upon arrival."

Courtenay flinched. She'd still been expecting the litter. This was not a good impression to make to a person clearly valued by the Johmatran ambassador. She quickly took a few steps toward him and stretched her arms out to her sides. The many bracelets on her bare arms rattled. Exposing one's body was a sign of trust among the foreigners, however, and because they valued shows of wealth, she'd piled on all the jewelry she owned and borrowed some more from the king. But she would not fall to her knees; this man, no matter how important a servant, would have to learn to view her as his equal. She had no intention of kneeling even to the ambassador himself.

She answered him in his language. "Welcome to Eirion-Vale, home to His Majesty Garith, High King of Selindria and Gaeltheon, Bringer of the Blessed Epoch. Whom do I have the honor of addressing?"

He turned his palms up and slowly curled and uncurled his fists—a gesture of annoyance similar to rolling one's eyes and just as impolite. "I am Behmarsan Kahladryia Sala N'hahseen." Rather than bowing, he jerked his pointed chin upward. "I'd been led to understand my arrival here was expected. Am I incorrect in that as well?"

Courtenay struggled not to let her shock show on her face and to string together words that would appease this man, who was of a much higher rank than she'd expected.

But before she could speak, Garith strode forward with his hand extended. "It's… nice to meet you, and here at Eirion-Vale, be welcome, and happiness from me safe and arrived, you, Behmarsan."

Others might have been flattered that the most powerful man in the world had learned his language, however faltering and broken, but the ambassador narrowed his eyes and took a step back from the king's hand. The Johmatrans had very strict and complicated rules about personal space, particularly who was allowed to touch those who believed they were descended from Fane. And Garith had butchered his name, no matter how good his intentions. The king looked confused with his hand still sticking out as his gaze swept the hall, clearly looking for someone to rescue him.

Courtenay hurried to his side and leaned close to whisper to Garith. "If you wanted to learn Northern Johmatran, I wish you'd asked me, Your Majesty. It was an admirable attempt, but Johmatran names are arranged by surname, city-state, rank, and then first name. It would be proper to call him Kahladryia, his city, Sala, First Son, or N'hahseen, his given name. Although familial names are considered most important, they are almost never used. You also cannot touch him, he… I'll explain more later. May I speak to him?"

The king's cheeks darkened. "Of course. Please."

While they had spoken, N'hahseen had turned the right side of his head toward them and leaned in, so Courtenay was thankful he couldn't understand their language. She approached him but stopped several feet away, holding her arms out and leaving herself open and vulnerable. N'hahseen dropped his arms to his sides and lifted them a few inches from his hips. It was better than nothing, so Courtenay spoke.

"N'hahseen, First Son of Kahladryia, you must forgive our ignorance. We still have a great deal to learn about your culture. We are looking forward to learning, as I am sure you are looking forward to learning about us."

He drew his arms back to his body and his upper lip twitched.

"My name is Courtenay, and I am honored to be your guide and interpreter while you are here."

"You?" he asked. "Is this a joke?"

Courtenay felt her hands involuntarily curling into fists, and it took all her strength to straighten her fingers. "What do you mean?"

"You are an Esperon, are you not?"

"Yes."

"And a mage as well?"

"That's right," she said, fighting not to sneer.

N'hahseen looked around at the people slowly edging closer to watch the exchange. Finally his gaze settled back on Courtenay. "Is this a deliberate insult?"

"Unfortunately—for both of us it seems—I am the only one here who can speak your language. However, if my presence is offensive to you, I shall leave the castle, and you will be free to make sense of things on your own."

His eyes widened, and Courtenay cursed her temper. Who had thought it was a good idea to make her a diplomat? Worse, she could think of nothing to do but wait for his response.

"I… would rather not find myself in this strange and savage land with no guidance," he said. "It is far more horrible than I ever imagined."

"Then I shall try my best to fulfill that role." Courtenay's relief allowed her to release the tension in her shoulders. "Now, there will be a banquet held tonight in honor of your arrival, and you can be formally introduced to everyone then, if you wish. Or refreshments and introductions can be seen to now, if you would prefer."

"I have come a long way under horrendous conditions," N'hahseen said. "I would like to go to where I will be staying so I can wash and see to my needs."

"Very good. I would be happy to show you the way." She stretched her arm toward the side of the hall.

Followed by a dozen servants dragging heavy trunks, they made their way up the stairs and down a torchlit corridor to the suite of rooms Courtenay had chosen. In an attempt to mimic the crystalline walls of the Johmatran palaces, she'd hung mirrors on the walls and decorated with glass sculptures made by a revered artisan: *awrythe*, marl-cats, wyrms, and delicate flowers whose petals and leaves caught the light of the chandeliers. When they entered, N'hahseen cast his gaze around, unimpressed. He went and stood beside the huge bed she'd had draped in delicate cloth from his homeland as the servants deposited his items. When they departed, N'hahseen spun to face Courtenay, red staining the apples of his dark cheeks. "If your intention is to murder me and avenge your countrymen, you will not find it easy. Fane's blood is strong in me, and my magic is strong as a result."

She had already sensed that. Fire came easiest to Courtenay; her tutors had lovingly teased that it matched her personality. N'hahseen's was… changeable but solid, not quite like an air current or quite like stone, but some strange combination. It wasn't weather or a storm, but maybe the elements that summoned a storm: that elusive combination of forces that made things happen. Not a pebble dropped into a pond, but the ripples that resulted, tiny things leading to other tiny things that mingled to cause something profound. She had never experienced anything like it.

"And while you're at it, stop prodding at me. It's as offensive as if you were to put your hands on my skin."

"I… I did not realize you would know." Embarrassment heated her cheeks.

He snorted. "Of course."

Courtenay ground her teeth. She couldn't let her anger take over. Too much depended on this. Her tutor had warned against judging other cultures against her own, and she had to remember those words. Forcing a smile, she said, "I seek only peace between our lands, and to that end, I will do all I can to help you. Since we have just met, I know you have no reason to trust me. But I have little reason to trust you either. It is a choice I am making, to think the best of you, to believe you have the best interests of all of our people at heart."

She must have said something right because he relaxed his rigid posture and let his shoulders curl forward. His eyes held less hostility when he looked at her. "Yes, that's exactly what I want. What's best for all the people of this world."

"Good. Perhaps we can start again. I'm here to help you, and I will do my best in that endeavor."

"I… will attempt to be more gracious, but I must admit, the ways of your people make little sense to me."

"We will work together to change that, I hope. I would also like to understand more about Johmatra."

N'hahseen untied his cloak and let it fall to the floor. Beneath it, he had long limbs, thin but tight with muscle beneath his leather breaches, knee-length red tunic, and his ostentatious, fur-lined pauldrons held in place with heavy golden chains across his chest. He reached up and raked his fingers through his hair. "Why do you stare at me so?"

Courtenay felt heat in her cheeks. "I must admit you are not what I expected."

"Why? Because my body is whole and unblemished?"

"Well… yes. Is that not unusual amongst the aristocracy of your people?"

N'hahseen's lips curled, but the smile didn't reach his eyes. "It is. Most take it as a sign of Fane's favor, and others even see it as indicative of his return."

"Well… interesting." Courtenay could think of nothing else to say. "I'd be curious to hear more of your province and your family."

N'hahseen opened his mouth to answer, but closed it again as a trio of Johmatran servants entered the room with more luggage. After they left, he stepped closer to her and said, "We must be very careful what we discuss in front of the servants who accompanied me. Some of them might very well be spies. They could be working for another city-state, my mother, or her husband."

"You mean your father?"

"No."

After the awkward silence between them stretched a bit too far, Courtenay said, "You must be hungry and thirsty."

"No. I would like to take a bath."

"This way." She showed him to an alcove where a wooden tub had been filled with steaming water. Heated stones around and beneath it kept the water warm, and steps led over them. "Shall I call a servant to—"

"I'll be fine." N'hahseen unbuckled his pauldrons and shrugged them off. The rest of his clothing quickly followed, and Courtenay turned away—somewhat reluctantly—from his naked body.

Espero was a den of debauchery compared to the Selindrian countryside where she had grown up, but it had not taken her long to shake off her modesty and embrace the revealing clothes of the island. After all, it was hot and no place for woolen hose and heavy, multilayered gowns. At school, she had taken lovers, men and women whose friendship had grown into more: mutual pleasure, but nothing serious. She was not unfamiliar with the intimate details of bodies, but N'hahseen's total disregard surprised her. They were practically strangers.

Water splashed as he lowered himself into the tub, and a contented sigh followed. Courtenay continued to face the wall, acquainting herself with every detail of the mortar between the stones. As a scholar, she wanted a better look at the legendary Johmatran scarification she'd glimpsed on his back and shoulders. At least that was what she struggled to tell herself.

"I'll want kahlka, I should think," N'hahseen said.

"You'll want what?"

"Kahlka. To see to my sexual needs. Unless… I'm not expected to lay with you?"

The way he said it, like she'd handed him a platter of dung and called it dinner, made Courtenay spin around, all of her embarrassment forgotten. "You wouldn't know what to do with me, you—"

"I'm glad to see you find the notion as repulsive as I do," he said. "But do your people not have those trained to attend to these matters?"

Beyond the bizarre practices of breeding to preserve Fane's so-called bloodline, no one knew much of Johmatran sexual habits. "I take that to mean yours do?"

"Of course. I will require people to attend to me while I am here."

Courtenay hadn't planned for this, but she thought quickly. "All right. There's a brothel not far from here, in Crystal Springs, with a reputation of being one of the best in the kingdom. If you care to tell me your preferences, I'll arrange to have a suitable group of professionals sent here as soon as possible."

He slapped at the water and it sprayed up in his face, leaving him sputtering. "A… brothel? You mean whores?"

"Well, yes. What do you mean?"

He seemed to struggle to catch his breath before speaking. "I… they… kahlka are not whores! They have not been defiled by others, and are untouched by any but me. I will certainly not besmirch Fane's blood by letting my body touch a person who has been fucked by countless others, and for money. My kahlka train to pleasure me, and they are tested by a truth spell to insure they have not been fouled by the touch of others. Ugh. I would not risk dirtying myself."

"I'm afraid I don't know what to tell you," she answered, weirdly satisfied that he wouldn't be rolling any whores that night. "We don't do things that way here. I can get you a whore, but that's the best I can offer."

He sighed theatrically. "No, I cannot sully the precious lineage I carry. I suppose I will just have to suffer."

Courtenay rolled her eyes and resisted the temptation to laugh. "Well. I suppose I'll leave you on your own, then. In case you want to… spend some time by yourself."

"No, wait. I am apprehensive about tonight's dinner. I'm not sure what to expect, and I don't want to make a fool of myself. And…."

"Yes?"

"This water is growing cold. You… you're adept with fire, unless I am wrong."

"You need me to warm your bath? Me, no descendant of Fane and unworthy of wielding the gift? Will you strike me down if I cast a spell in your presence?"

He grinned, a real smile that made his mismatched eyes crinkle. "I could overlook it… just this once."

THE DINNER went as well as N'hahseen had expected. His translator, Courtenay, had advised him silence was the best course of action, and that listening could yield much information. He had found it to be true, especially considering the heathens didn't know he understood their language. But after his studies, combined with traveling with their sailors and soldiers, how could he not? It gave him much insight, and when the time came to leave, he was exhausted.

Courtenay waited for him outside the dining hall. "You look troubled."

N'hahseen hated that she was his only friend, this common-born woman unworthy of wielding Fane's magic, with her strange yellow hair and sky-colored eyes, in her billowy Esperon trousers that teased him with the gentle curve of her hips and exposed her toned belly. She wore a little blue gem there, just below her navel, and it glistened against her tanned skin. He shook himself, realizing he should answer her. "I am just tired. Not unexpected after my long journey."

As they walked to his chambers, he hoped for quiet, time with his thoughts, but she continued talking. "How did you find the dinner? The food?"

"It was… heavy. What was that thick white substance? And the oily yellow stuff?"

She laughed. "Cream and butter. They are appreciated here. Rich foods. By that I mean foods for the privileged. Do they not agree with you?"

"They have left a coating on my teeth."

"And that's all that's bothering you?"

He considered how much to share and how much to hold back. What did he have to fear from her, though? No blood of Fane's ran in her veins; back home, she would have been killed as soon as she manifested the gift. "Your people… I did not know they harbored so much hatred toward mine."

"Well, what do you expect? Your people killed Esperon infants just because they might someday possess magic…. Wait. How do you know that? I relayed nothing uncomplimentary to you?"

He raised his voice to imitate the whiny, nasal tone of one of the nobles, and he spoke in the common tongue of Garith's kingdom, though he had yet to get the accent right. "Look at him, painted like a whore. What kind of a man paints his face? I hope we'll not be expected to do this, because I will not. Unnatural baby killers, if you ask me. I think we should raze the whole…. What was the word? Shades' something? Raze the whole Shades' something to the ground. Damn them to the goddesses."

"I… oh." Courtenay looked at her sandals. "I did not know you understood our tongue. Though I can see why you kept it a secret. It was a wise move. I would have done the same."

N'hahseen tapped his forehead. "That man was not Esperon. His children were not killed by my people. And yet he hates me. Why? All I want, all I wanted when I accepted this mission, was to bring Fane's wisdom to these lands. You can all share in the paradise that will result upon his return, if you accept him."

Courtenay reached out and squeezed his shoulder. His instincts told him to recoil, but he liked the pressure of her fingers against his muscles; he knew it wasn't meant to despoil or exploit him, and it afforded some comfort, though he did not understand why. "N'hahseen, you must understand that the people here do not want to adhere to your philosophy. We have our own goddesses, and to us, Fane doesn't represent anything we want to aspire to."

"But I am here to change that. To see Fane's beneficence extends to these lands."

She moved her head from side to side—a negative response? "No, that is not what these people expect from you. They do not want to be led to a different philosophy… only to establish peace between our nations."

"Why?"

"So that no more people need to die!"

"So… so I am here as what? A symbol? A figurehead of some kind?"

"You expected something else?" she asked. Her fingers still dug into the meat of his arm.

N'hahseen looked up at the gray stones of the fortress, at the walls towering over him, glistening with the moisture of the evening. He sighed, and his breath came out in a frozen cloud. "I don't know how you live this way, so shut in. These thick walls between you and the sky. And… and the wine at dinner tonight was terrible." He forced out a chuckle.

To his initial horror, and then his curiosity, Courtenay stretched her arm across his back. "You like wine and fresh air, eh? I can help you on both counts. Come with me."

She led him to a balcony overlooking some kind of chaotic garden, with plants running rampant and twisting together where they met. Though it was hard to discern the paths between the unkempt shrubbery, it produced a pleasant herbal smell, and the crescent moon washed everything in silver. N'hahseen sat next to Courtenay on a stone bench, glad to have open space around him, glad for the breeze in his hair, even if it was wet and cold and smelled a bit like rotting leaves. Courtenay's body radiated warmth in comparison, and he leaned into it.

"I grew up not far from here," she said. "Well, relatively close, across the river in Lockhaven. On a vineyard. I thought my life would be tending grapes and making wine, but then… the gift."

"You wish it had not come to you?"

She did that odd thing the westerners did when confused or uncertain and shook her head from side to side. "No, I'm glad it came. I was just a farmer's daughter, so when I was kidnapped by a noble with a penchant for young girls, I couldn't depend on the nobility to rescue me. My fathers came, but I… I found I had the power to get myself out of danger. I killed those sick bastards, and I'm not sorry I did. The magic… I was sure it came from the goddesses. But you… you would slit my throat simply for being what I am."

"I'm… I'm sorry for what happened to you. That's horrifying, being left to protect yourself at such a young age."

"And would it have been different in Johmatra? Would one of your fine families have gone against a descendant of Fane and rushed to the aid of a fishmonger's daughter or a gardener's little girl? Or would you have considered me better off dead?"

Academically, it was an easy question. Kill the unworthy, please Fane, and facilitate his return so all could benefit. But sitting here, N'hahseen wondered: Would the world be better without Courtenay? "I… I do not know. We are taught these few deaths will benefit people, that the cost will be worth the price. Fane's return will mean no more toil, no more disease, no more death—"

"And I should be killed for this myth? Babies who might not even be mages should have their heads chopped off? Think about that: a crying infant's head chopped off while his mother is held back and forced to watch."

"I…." He shuddered. "No, it's disgusting."

"Then you disagree with the tenets of your people?"

"I… I have been taught it's worth it…."

"And do you believe that?"

"I don't know." Before, he had never imagined a specific face when he considered the culling of those unworthy of magic. They'd been anonymous in his mind. Now, a vision of this young woman, who had defended him even though she despised everything he stood for, with her throat cut and her blood running formed so sharply in his mind that he had to turn away. He couldn't bear to envision her bright eyes turning cloudy and cold.

Courtenay patted his shoulder. "My tutors at the university said the first step toward wisdom was admitting you did not know. You… I thought I would hate you, but you are not as bad as I anticipated. You have potential, at least."

He touched his forehead, strangely relieved though he shouldn't value her opinion. "I thought this place would be awful, and then they gave me you, an Esperon mage. A person guaranteed to hate me." He laughed. "And the wine is awful. How ever will I make do?"

"Well, try this." Courtenay pulled a canteen from the folds of her vest and unscrewed the cap.

N'hahseen arched a brow. "What if this is poison?"

She snorted. "I wouldn't need to sink so low. If I wanted you dead, I would use my magic. I've killed Johmatrans before. I fought in the war, and I'll wager you didn't."

"I… no. I wanted to, but everyone insisted I was too precious. I could have fought…."

She jabbed her elbow into his ribs. "Just drink."

He did, and…. Fane. He had never tasted such wine. Tart grape skins laced with floral sweetness, all underscored by a smoky, meaty sensation, with minerals and something like the sap of young trees on the finish. Traces of evergreen plants and tart winter berries lingered in his throat and sinuses. "Fane's glory, that's some wine."

Courtenay grabbed the skin and drank deeply. "Ah, Alain has not lost his touch. My fathers spoiled me, and now I compare all wine I taste to theirs. Predictably, I usually find it lacking."

N'hahseen could see why. "What are you trying to impart to me? Are you trying to prove common people, those without Fane's blood, have worth? That they can accomplish great things in his absence?"

"For fuck's sake." Courtenay drank again and passed the flask back to N'hahseen. "I'm trying to say drink, Your Worship. I'm not going to kill you, if that's what you're worried about. I'm sick of fighting. The war… the war was horrible. Made me wish I was back home trimming vines. But I wasn't, and now I can work for peace. If that's not why you're here, tell me now and I'll walk away. It's possible we'll never agree on specifics, but we might find some common ground if we're willing to try. I am."

N'hahseen drank. The wine really was excellent, and it gave him a moment to decide how to respond to this strange woman. Crass and refined at once… and such powerful magic. Her flames coaxed him like a moth, but he was nothing so delicate, and he would not make the mistake of trusting someone easily… not again. "I'm curious to see what can be accomplished here. The magic in these lands is… crippled, broken. As a mage, do you not notice it?"

"I have nothing to compare it to. Though at the university, my teachers had many theories as to why the world contains less magic than the stories claim it once held. It's a known fact that fewer mages are born every generation. Is it not so in Johmatra?"

He took another drink of wine and felt it tingle as it slid down into his belly and slowly spread its welcome numb warmth through his limbs. "Johmatra. Saying that makes you sound so uncouth. There really is no such thing. Johmatra is simply our word for 'land.' Imagine if I called your Selindria and Gaeltheon that. 'High Garith, King of Land.'" He chuckled. "We identify our lineage partly by our city-state, and the city of one's origin is very important."

"In Kahladryia, then."

"In Kahladryia, we have a reputation for magic that stretches back thousands of years, and we have continued to keep it strong by careful matches. Fane's descendants have always had more difficulty conceiving children than the common people, however. Most families are lucky to have a single offspring, and luckier still if he or she lives to reproduce. I don't know if it's because we have so many fewer mages, but the magic there has a steady rhythm, like a song I never noticed playing in the background until it was gone. It has a constant and dependable beat.

Here, it's like a battered instrument strummed by a drunkard: a few discordant notes now and then, and no way of knowing when or if more will be coming. It hurts my head."

"And you would say that's because we have displeased Fane?"

"Officially, yes, that would be the position of any of his descendants. But from what I have learned of Fane, how I have always understood him, he wouldn't do this. He loved magic. Sure, he might withhold it from the unworthy, but he wouldn't break or twist it, take away its beauty."

"Then what has, in your opinion?"

"I don't know. I don't even know how to investigate it, stuck here without others of learning to consult with."

"*I'm* a mage, you know. I have studied at great length in Espero."

He snorted. "Espero… that's—"

Courtenay stood and tossed the wineskin into his lap so hard he wondered if she meant to harm him in a very vulnerable place. "It's what? Nothing? Beneath you? Because we can't claim ties to a man who might have lived ten thousand years ago?"

He also stood and stepped close to her, looking down his nose into her blazing blue eyes. Courtenay was interesting, and she had some tolerable qualities, but he would not allow her to insult him, and certainly not to besmirch Fane. "You and your people know nothing! Look at the way you live: cowering in your dark citadels and scraping out a meager living! And you're content to continue! You don't even want to remedy your ignorance!"

"Our ignorance?" She squinted as if something he said had caused her physical pain. "And how do you suppose food makes its way to your table? Handed down from Fane himself? Right into your soft little hands? Do you suppose no one works in the fields to provide it?"

N'hahseen never remembered being so angered he felt compelled to physical violence, but there was something about this woman…. He grabbed her arms below the shoulders; they were hard with muscle and warm against his hands. "What do you think we are trying to end by coaxing Fane to return to this world? Do you think we don't see that life is short and cruel? Unlike you, we're trying to change that."

"Get your hands off me, and never lay them on me again, or I will show you what happened to that fat old bastard who wanted to rape me when I was eleven."

He dropped his hands and stepped back. "No… I would never… I didn't mean…."

She tugged at the hem of her short vest to straighten it. "I know you didn't. But you need to realize you are in a different world, and your ancestral claims will not go far here. Threaten or disrespect someone, and you might find you'd better be able to back it up."

He crossed his hands over his heart, a gesture of rejection. "I assure you I could do so quite capably."

Her eyebrows rose, and little sparks blinked among her chaotic curls, accompanied by the scent of flint. "We can test that theory any time you like."

He tapped his forehead. "No, this is not at all what I came here to do. I came because I thought I could help, show your people a better way. I still believe that. But this magic… it's like a dying animal struggling to drag itself to safety, and I don't know what to do with that."

Courtenay retrieved the canteen that had fallen to the ground during their altercation. Unfortunately, most of the wine had spilled out, and she sighed when she upended it and received only a few drops on her tongue. "Neither do I, but I suspect there's a mage who does: Yarroway L'Estrella. I would like very much to speak with him, but he would be no admirer of yours. He would likely kill you on sight, and before you argue, yes, he absolutely can."

N'hahseen sat back down on the bench. "Well, I'm not ready to die, so I suppose we should seek another source of information. Fane, a kahlka or two would take my mind off all of this for an hour or so."

With a grin, Courtenay reached into her trouser pocket and withdrew a book so small it fit into her palm. "Seems you need this more than I do."

"What is it?"

"A tale from Elvara. *Moonlight on Satin*."

"Tales of… men and women?"

She grinned. "Mostly."

He grinned back. "And what are you doing in possession of it?"

"I'm alone here too," she said. "But unlike you, I have the option to change that. I think I'll make my way to the tavern in the village. I'll have guards posted outside your quarters first, of course."

As she led him back to his rooms, N'hahseen considered what she proposed. It might take the edge off some of his anxiety, but he wondered if she would think about him doing it. If she did, he would be humiliated, but if she didn't he'd be disappointed. Worse yet, he would never know because he certainly couldn't ask.

Still, he thought as he closed his door and began undressing for bed, it was better than thinking about Courtenay in the tavern, or the horror of the broken magic and the fact that the only person who understood wanted to murder him.

Of course he knew of Yarroway L'Estrella; everyone who'd fought under the banner of any city-state did. He had planned to never cross paths with the hated Selindrian mage, and his plans would not change—not if he had any alternative.

Chapter Fourteen

THE SCHOLAR in Jorian enjoyed life in the desert among the nomadic Arbek people. He hadn't realized the strain he'd been under in the palace, always vigilant, always careful to say and do exactly the expected thing, until those pressures were relieved. Life here, while strange to him, was easy and slow. Using some of the jewelry he'd been wearing when he escaped, he'd had one of the tribesmen purchase him some paper and ink from the market. He'd spent the last several weeks writing and drawing the details of this unique culture so he could share it when he returned to Espero. Sketches of rounded tents, some with elaborate details, wagons with spiked wheels to move across the dunes, lizards curled up to sleep, and the friendly people he'd met in the camp now filled the sheets. He would need to acquire more paper, because he was in no hurry to leave. He could learn things here, and he was finally safe.

Today he accompanied a group of traders into the city. The gauzy cloth the Arbek wrapped around their bodies and faces for protection against the sun and sand saved him from being recognized, since he was still a wanted man. If the Kahladryians were good at one thing, it was holding a grudge.

Jorian and his group reached one of the city's northern gates around sunrise. The guards stationed there granted them entry, and they pulled their carts to a nearby market square. Jorian helped Joppa, the man who'd come to his aid the night of the explosion, and his sister, Jarratt, to erect a red-and-gold-striped canopy and hang some filigree lanterns along its front edge. They spread rugs on the ground and set up shelves. Wealthy and influential Kahladryians loved the delicate cloth the nomads wove and bought it by the bolt for clothing and draperies for their homes. The desert flowers also provided a sweet pollen, and other plants supplied saps and nectars that sold for high prices. And the Arbek tribes were the main source of Blue Oblivion, though the group Jorian traveled with didn't pursue the dangerous serpents for their venom. Jarratt had told him some families specialized in capturing and milking the deadly snakes, but hers was known for weaving. She and her brother spent most days under a scrap of cloth, sitting at their looms while they chatted and sipped tea made from cave mushrooms. They'd practiced since childhood to make the delicate patterns and designs, weaving the iridescent cloth so thin it was almost transparent, and Jorian couldn't assist them. He liked sitting with them, hearing their stories and learning their songs, and he was glad he could help them here at the market.

He finished setting out the clay jars of tear-tree sap and sat down on the rug next to Joppa. They shared some dried fruit and jerky as the city began to wake up. The slaves were always the first to leave their beds, and they moved through the streets with heavy loads on their backs. Servants followed, and finally the nobles in their extravagant ensembles.

Jarratt joined them, put some herbs into the end of a long pipe, conjured a small flame from her fingertips, and lit up. Those claiming descent from Fane overlooked the Arbek use of magic, probably because their magics were small, everyday things, and also because the presence of the Arbek meant they didn't need to venture into the dangerous desert themselves to procure the goods they wanted. Their beliefs could be conveniently swept aside when it benefitted them, but Jorian supposed most of the world operated the same way.

Jarratt offered him the pipe but he declined. The market started to fill with not only people, but the smell of food and the sounds of hawkers and musicians playing for spare coins. Jorian smiled. "I enjoy coming to the market. For all the years I spent in Kahladryia, I never ventured here until I met your tribe."

"Why is that?" Jarratt wore shimmery blue powder around her dark eyes; it matched the pattern of interlocking hexagons on her beige garments and represented something else the wealthy needed from the desert: minerals for cosmetics.

Jorian took the pipe after all. The smoking mix energized him, but it did odd things to his magic if he used too much, made his power harder to control. But today, minding the stall from sunup to sundown, he could use a little something. "I really never left the palace." A few of the crystal spires were visible in the distance. "It was like a city unto itself, with hundreds of servants overseeing various things. As N'hahseen's personal servant, my position was considered too important to do the shopping. After all, I might be touched by a common person or—imagine the scandal—even someone with magic. I couldn't risk spreading the corruption to the First Son when I did his makeup for dinner."

"It does not sound like you cared much for him." Joppa had pulled his coverings back over his mouth. The white cloth muffled his voice and looked striking against his dark skin.

Jorian shook his head; it felt good not to have to obsess over habitual gestures. "I did not care for any of them when I came here. I told you of the war they waged against my people. But N'hahseen…. He endeared himself to me, almost. True, he was pampered and did not even realize how much, and he was prone to going into fits of rage when he didn't get his way, but… I suppose I was very alone, and that made me see qualities in him that might have not been there."

Jarratt exhaled a long plume of smoke and patted Jorian's arm with her free hand. "The heart's first inclination is to kindness and generosity, and it is often the right reaction. Those whose eyes see goodness first lead blessed lives."

He smiled. "It certainly does my heart good to be amongst people who feel that way. In the palace, everyone worried about conspiracies and who they could trust. No affectionate feeling or kind deed came without a price, or at least a future expectation. Smiles and friendly words were things to mistrust. Tell me. How do your people think of the rulers of this city?"

She squinted into the brightening sun. "I suppose in a way we feel sorry for them, because they do not have the guidance or protection of the *farang phreet*. They feel sorry for us, because they think we would want to live as they do, in crystal palaces surrounded by gold and jewels. But we do not. For the most part, they leave us alone unless they want to buy our goods or need us to guide them to crystal formations in the desert, or between their walled cities. It works well enough."

"If you have not seen the market, why don't you go and explore?" Joppa suggested. "My sister and I can tend to things here."

Jorian remembered his desire for more ink and paper, and he still had a silver bracelet he could trade. Wandering the bazaar would give him much to write about over the quiet days to follow, while he sat with Joppa and Jarratt as they worked at their looms. "Thank you. I will not be gone long."

He made sure the ochre drapes he wore were wound tightly around his head and the lower part of his face, and then he closed the heavier cape over his shoulders and secured it with a pin made from a shard of clouded crystal. Some of the vigilance he had felt in the palace returned as he entered the crowd and let its flow carry him along; he felt like he needed to watch and listen to everything, that every person he passed could be a threat. But other Arbek from different tribes wandered the market, and no one seemed to notice him—not even the guards.

The plaza reminded him of the stalls that cropped up around festivals in Pala Reapaza, when the students were freed from their studies and spilled into the streets, eager to eat, drink, and squander their money. Well, there was much less drunkenness here. Jorian smiled wistfully, suddenly heartsick and longing for Espero: the grilled fish sold by the quayside, the strong red wine, the gardens perfected by centuries of magic, the way the stone smelled when heated by the sun… the friends he'd had, their quiet afternoons in the library and less quiet evenings in the taverns. Mostly he missed how things had been simple even though he hadn't seen it at the time. Why did things only seem valuable when they were absent?

A woman carrying a basket bumped against him, and Jorian realized he'd stopped in the street. He muttered an apology, careful to keep his voice soft since he couldn't quite mimic the Arbek accent, and then he moved to a stall where some pendants made from polished gems hung from pegs. Another stall sold feathered accessories, and the next flowers. Before long, Jorian found a vendor selling paper and ink and bought as much as he could afford.

As he made his way back toward Joppa and Jarratt's stand, taking his time and stopping to inspect other wares, he wandered into a circular garden with a large crystal statue of Fane at the center. He stood at the edge of the space as people gathered around it and began to sing. The melody was lilting and sad: a plea for Fane to return. Though N'hahseen and his family attended such ceremonies only on their holidays, Jorian knew many people performed these rituals several times a day. All of them wanted to draw Fane's notice and favor, if not for themselves, then for their children or grandchildren. When the song ended, people left sprigs of tiny desert flowers around the statue's base. Jorian found an unoccupied bench and sat down, thinking to use his new supplies to make a sketch of this monument and write a description of the ceremony and the meaning behind it.

On a nearby bench, a group of four women sat down and released their toddlers to chase each other around the statue. The women's shopping sat in baskets at their feet, and they were clearly tired from their errands. But then, if they'd been wealthy, they would have had servants or slaves to tend their children and lug their goods.

"I never thought it would happen in Kahladryia," one of them said. "Do you think things will change much?"

"Not for us," another answered. "It'll still be cooking and sweeping and changing diapers." The others laughed.

"But Hachraf was a strong leader, good for the city. And First Son N'hahseen was such a blessing on all of us. Many said Fane would certainly return when he ascended, and Kahladryia would be favored above all other cities. Now that will never happen."

Jorian's hand paused over his paper, his attention captured. They were discussing N'hahseen and his mother.

"The First Son won't inherit the city?"

"Not now. Hachraf's husband was not his father, and it's no secret he resented that fact. Now that he's killed his wife and taken over, the First Son will likely be exiled. If he returns from the heathen lands, he might even be assassinated himself."

"Watch what you say," one of the women scolded in a whisper. "Wisam is our leader now. You would not want to be overheard speaking against him, accusing him of murder."

"It's no secret. Hachraf found dead of poison only a few weeks after the First Son departed? Everyone knows he saw his chance to grab power and took it. I hear he's looking for a wife. He'll father a child as soon as he can, set his line up to inherit Kahladryia."

"I fear this will not please Fane," one of the women said, gazing up at the statue. "N'hahseen's birth was a clear sign of his favor. Such a beautiful young man. And now he'll die, and—"

"Enough. Let's gather up our brats and get to the baker's before the fresh bread is gone. Hey, you lot!"

Jorian waited until they'd been gone for several moments before he collected his things and hurried back to his friends.

THAT NIGHT, a nearly full moon washed the desert in pink. It was cold enough to numb Jorian's fingers, and the howl of the wind sounded mournful and almost human, but Jorian could no longer lie on his cot in the tent he shared with Joppa, Jarratt, and their elderly mother and pretend to sleep. Thoughts he'd managed to suppress since escaping the city bubbled to the surface to torment him, and he needed to move. Though the desert was dangerous, the Arbek used their magic to set up wards for at least a mile around their camp. He would be safe to pace for a while.

Near the outskirts of the settlement were the pens where the lizards were kept. Jorian approached the braided twig fence and looked inside at the three lizards curled up around the crystal enchanted to keep them warm. Joppa's red one, Kett, opened his eyes and blinked few times before going back to sleep. Jorian stood watching him for a long time, the bend of his body and the way his scales caught the light. The rattle of beads alerted Jorian to another's presence, and he pushed his annoyance away and turned around.

The leader of the tribe, Tsubik—Jorian still wasn't sure if it was a name or a title—stood a few feet away, leaning heavily on a walking stick. She had a face like a raisin, white hair arranged in two long braids, but very shrewd eyes. "You seem troubled, young man. What happened at the market today?"

He considered lying, but he had a profound feeling that she would know. "You and your people have been so good to me. You saved my life, and that's something I'll never be able to repay. But I think it's time I was leaving."

"Are you unhappy here?"

"No, I'm actually content here. I… It is a long story."

She pointed to a cluster of rocks rounded by centuries of blowing sand. "Then let us sit down. I'm very old, you know."

Jorian did as she asked, as she waved her hand to conjure a small fire to warm them. Then she leaned her elbows on her knees and focused her gaze on Jorian. Before long, he knew he wouldn't escape without providing an answer. So he told her everything: what had happened in

Espero, how he'd come to Johmatra to spy, what his time with N'hahseen had been like, his ties to the Emiri resistance, his role in the explosion, and finally what he had overheard at the bazaar.

"And so, as much as I think of him as my enemy, I… I feel like I should warn him. He's alone in a land he certainly doesn't understand, and now he might be in danger. I'm sure he thinks I betrayed him…."

"And you cannot bear that, can you?"

"I thought I could," he whispered. "I should be able to. His fate should be of no consequence to me. But…." The rest of what he wanted to say, he couldn't even articulate in his thoughts. He didn't want to. Changing direction, he said, "I came here to make a difference and protect my people. I'm no longer doing that, and I should go somewhere that I can."

"No, you cannot leave."

That surprised him. "You'll keep me here by force?"

"No, but the farang phreet came to me and told me of you. He felt there was something about you worth saving, and you cannot leave until you discover what that is. Ignoring the farang phreet will end in tragedy, not only for you but for our entire tribe."

Jorian wasn't sure he subscribed to that superstition, but he knew he would need assistance from the tribe to cross the desert and reach the shore, where he would hopefully find an Emiri ship to take him to Gaeltheon. Alone, he would never survive. "Well, can I just ask him what he wants from me?"

Her head drooped and she stared into the fire. "I feared that would be your request, and I cannot deny it."

"But?"

"It will be dangerous. The farang phreet who guards our tribe spends most of his time in an old crystal quarry several miles north of here. He is called Bensali. You will have to travel there alone, and if he is not pleased, he will almost certainly kill you."

"After going to so much trouble to save me?"

"The farang phreet can be… difficult to understand."

He nodded. He still had his magic, and it extended well beyond conjuring campfires. What other option did he have?

"Would he take this risk for you, this N'hahseen?"

"No," Jorian answered, "but that doesn't mean it's not the right thing to do. I will leave first thing in the morning."

With the aid of her stick, she got to her feet and put a gnarled hand on Jorian's shoulder. "Then prepare yourself, your mind as well as your body. Even after all you've endured, this will be unlike anything you've faced before."

Chapter Fifteen

By the time the sun was overhead, sand coated the strip of exposed skin around Jorian's eyes. His legs ached from trudging across the dunes, and though his throat was parched, he'd already drunk half of his water supply and would need the rest for the journey back to camp. Jarratt had warned him that it was easy to get turned around in the desert, and one could find himself walking in endless circles when he thought he was moving forward. He'd devised a technique: shoot a ball of magic ahead of him, one that left a shimmering trail on the sand, walk until he reached the end, and shoot another. But even if he avoided losing his way—and dying of dehydration or freezing to death when it got dark—he could easily fall victim to one of the desert's many predators. That thought encouraged him to walk a little faster.

The wind picked up as afternoon wore on, sand stinging Jorian's eyes. He didn't feel like he could take another step and was starting to think he'd made a grave mistake, when he saw some crystalline spikes poking out of the sand, almost as if they lined a trail. Nothing else had broken the monotony of the desert in hours, and that alone made them a welcome sight. Jorian hurried forward. By the time he reached the crystals, which towered several feet over his head, he could also see a steep cliff in the distance, extending for miles on either side. A trail wound up the side, crystal that might have once been cut into stairs, now eroded and covered with sand. It sparkled where an occasional crystal deposit poked out of the ground.

Jorian saw movement near the base of the ancient staircase: two lizards of a species he didn't recognize, dull black with red and orange frills on their necks and long red spikes down their backs. Snarling and snapping, they fought over whatever prey they'd brought down, and as Jorian crept closer, trying to stay hidden behind the crystal spires, he saw blood glistening on their maws. He crouched lower, hoping to go unnoticed until they finished their meal and moved on.

One of the lizards turned in his direction. A forked tongue the color of rotten meat shot out between rows of sharp teeth, and the creature bent its legs, lowering its belly to the ground. Its spiked tail lifted behind it and flicked from side to side, reminding Jorian of a cat… a cat preparing to pounce. He tensed and dropped a little lower, but it was too late. The lizard had caught his scent, and it was coming his way—fast.

For some reason, it was easy to gather magic here. Jorian had discovered that during his time with the nomads, and he'd wondered if magic—something he'd always considered infinite—could really be depleted by too many users. He had no time to contemplate it now as he let the power gather in his belly. When the lizard reared on its hind legs a few feet from him, he extended his hand and hit it in the belly with a blunt force. It flipped, landing on its back and skidding in the sand, but it quickly recovered and crouched for another attack. He'd need something more lethal than the basic self-defense magic he'd learned at university, and he'd need it soon.

The lizard lowered its head and snapped at his ankle. Jorian stumbled backward, narrowly avoiding teeth that were likely poisonous. Survival instinct took over, and he waved his hand toward the crystal pillar. A sliver broke off and hung in the air until he gestured toward the creature. Then it embedded in its back. The lizard let out a high-pitched squeal, but it kept coming. Jorian's next attack lodged another piece of crystal in its tail, but it didn't even slow down. It used its front leg to swipe at him, knocking him on his back and driving the wind from his chest. As it launched itself at him, foam dripping from its jaw, he rolled onto his back and scrambled to his feet. The lizard came back around and bit at his arm, but he recoiled, and its teeth succeeded only in tearing away the fabric of his sleeve.

By now, the other lizard had abandoned its small meal in favor of the larger feast Jorian presented. It moved more cautiously than the first, but Jorian knew that would change as soon as one of them wounded him. He'd observed enough of the wildlife in this place to know that at first blood, they would converge. If that happened, he'd have no chance. Panic shot through him as he wondered if they'd eat him alive, tearing meat from his bones while he was still conscious enough to experience it. He looked frantically around for an escape, cover, something. But he'd seen these creatures move, and he knew he couldn't outrun them. Sensing the dull hum of the crystals around him—and those covered by the sand—he attempted a last, desperate maneuver to save himself.

When the lizard leapt, he directed all of his power into the ground, tugging at the mineral spine. Glitter danced across his vision, and numbness spread up from his feet, threatening to collapse him. With a hoarse cry, he released the last of his power, and that piece of crystal broke through the sand and skewered the beast through its belly and out its back, lifting it off the ground. Blood poured from the wound, and the lizard's legs convulsed before it finally fell still. The effort cost, though, leaving Jorian so dizzy he had to grasp one of the columns to stay upright. The other lizard appeared as a blurry black smudge as it ran toward him. Consciousness drained from Jorian's body, the sparkling darkness reducing his vision to a tunnel. No matter how much magic this place held, he couldn't draw upon any more. He grasped the carved bone dagger Joppa had given him.

The lizard slashed at him with its claws, and Jorian slashed back. He had no training in nonmagical combat, and he could barely see or stay on his feet. One of the creature's strikes caught him at the waist, and pain seared across his stomach as it ripped his flesh. He brought his blade down with all the strength he could muster, and he thought it hit the thing, felt resistance as his knife met its thick hide. It made a gurgling, hissing sound as it backed away a few feet. Then it sprang again.

Jorian was knocked back, the lizard's front feet pinning him to the ground. Its drool burned where it dripped against his face, and he screamed, kicking and twisting to try to free himself. It roared in response and bit, sinking its teeth into his arm. He screamed again, slashing wildly with the dagger, hitting the lizard's neck and coating himself in its blood. It bit again, catching him in the side of the neck and producing a gush of blood that almost stole what little remained of his lucidity. He knew he had one last chance, and it was a slim one. Focusing, trying to stave off both panic and the unconsciousness that drew him with such allure, Jorian plunged his weapon into the beast's throat just below its jaw. With the last of his strength, he pulled down, cutting through the tough scales and revealing the vulnerable red meat beneath. Blood and innards spilled into his face and he sputtered, gagging, but the creature reeled and fell to its side.

Dead.

Jorian looked up at the sky, where the sunset pinked the edges of the wispy clouds and a few stars glimmered. He remembered lying on the university's lawn in Pala Reapaza, watching the stars and talking about spells, magical theories. Tests and tutors who annoyed him. Around him, friends. Even lovers. Wine. Shellfish stew. The pain was distant now; he felt numb and very, very tired. He thought of N'hahseen, the way he had looked when Jorian had painted his face before their last feast together. The gold dust on his toenails. Why hadn't he said yes?

Would N'hahseen ever know that Jorian had died for him? He wouldn't, and that hurt more than the wounds or the poison he could feel boiling through his veins. Jorian wanted him to know, and not so he'd venerate Jorian in some way, but so he'd know that the world contained a man who would do that—die for him. But he'd always think of Jorian as a traitor.

Jorian had tried. He'd planned to do so much good, but here he was, dying full of nothing but regret.

Time lost meaning as flashes from his life returned to Jorian's mind out of sequence. Breathing was harder now, not really worth the effort, not really worth fighting to get the air into his chest. *I didn't really matter....*

A voice cut through the haze dragging Jorian toward warmth and darkness, toward blessed oblivion. "Nice work on the first one. The second one... not so much."

A dark form towered over him, backlit by the flaming orange and magenta of the sky. And... it had wings stretching out a dozen feet on either side of it. The shape knelt down, and Jorian felt pressure on his arm and his neck. Tingling heat surrounded him, like being dipped into bubbling water. The pain flared white-hot for a moment, tearing a cry from his throat, and then it subsided. Jorian slowly sat up, his surroundings clarifying around him. He patted his body. His blood-soaked clothing clung to his skin, cold now that night had fallen, but he no longer bled. The gashes the creature had torn in his flesh had closed. Even the poison seemed gone. He turned to the dark form with the wings that eclipsed the moon.

It—he—chuckled. "Not much of a fighter, are you?"

"No, I'm… I was… a student. I worked in a library."

"Yes, I know."

"You do? Who…? Bensali?"

"Not as dumb as you looked fighting those beasts, then. And what do you want with me?"

Jorian's head spun. He'd been dead, or nearly so, and now he wasn't. He needed time to acclimate, to think, but his savior cleared his throat. "I…. Can we have some light? So I can see you?"

"A fine choice." The man waved his hand, and floating white lights appeared in a ring around them, giving Jorian his first real look at his rescuer. He was a man, or at least he resembled one. But he was tall, probably almost seven feet if he stood upright. And the wings hadn't been Jorian's deathbed hallucination; they stretched from his shoulders, as wide as a house on either side, inky, iridescent, and reflecting the arcane light. His fingers and toes were long and tipped in dark claws. Horns, thick and ridged, followed the curve of his head before flaring out in sharp points at the ends. His face was squarish and appealing, but his eyes were solid black. Nothing but loose trousers and a few belts of engraved metal medallions and colored gems covered his impressive musculature. And the magic… It burbled within him like a volcano ready to erupt.

"What are you?"

"The desert wanderers call my kind farang phreet. Fire and air."

"Yes, but what does that mean? Where did you come from?"

"And why should I tell you?"

"You wanted me here," Jorian argued. "You sent Joppa to rescue me from the Kahladryian guards. I must have some value to you."

Bensali licked his lips with a long, liver-colored tongue. "I could think of many things to do with you. I did not expect you to be so beautiful."

Jorian shuddered, though whether with fear or something else, he couldn't be sure. "Tell me what you are."

"I will tell you, but then you must agree to do something for me."

"What?"

"A favor."

"I can't agree until I know what it is, can I?" Jorian protested. "No matter what you seem to think, I am not a fool."

Bensali canted his head, perhaps in surprise. "No, it seems not. Isn't that refreshing? I will give you something, and I would like you to take it to the others."

"What others?"

"The other mages, those in the west."

"Ah. I had hoped to go that way, find… someone. Will it hurt me, this thing?"

"No."

"Then… then I agree. Tell me what you are. I am well educated, but I have never seen mention of a… a being such as yourself."

Bensali chuckled and sat cross-legged in the sand. "My kind are well-known to the desert tribes, though of course they don't understand the full story. What do you know of the world before Fane and the goddesses?"

"The same as anyone, I suppose."

Bensali winked. "Which means nothing. No one alive, except my kind, remember the world before, a world ruled over by beings of immeasurable power. They held sovereignty and struck down entire civilizations on a whim."

"And you are one of these… people?"

"No. I and the others like me are the result of the first race's interest in the mortal females. You can undoubtedly see our appeal to them when compared with males of their own kind, stupid, stinking brutes wrapped in matted furs and smeared with dung. Word of my fathers spread amongst the women, and they formed cults to meet with them in desolate places. I understand those were good times for everyone involved, and I am the result of one such union."

"What happened to the ones who fathered your kind?"

"A mortal mage rose to power, a man with abilities we never anticipated. Within a few hundred years, his influence and empire spread across the world. He trained his wives to hunt down my ancestors, and their children could do nothing but hide."

"Are you talking about Fane?"

Bensali dipped his head. "He took that name eventually, yes."

"Fane hunted down your kind?"

"Yes."

"So… do you want me to see that he does not return?" Jorian asked. "Because you're afraid he'll finish what he started?"

Bensali laughed. "No. He has been gone ten thousand years. He does not worry me. Your race is nowhere near to attaining the power, or the wisdom, it held in those days. You're like infants to us, mewling until you get attention and shitting your drawers."

"Then… what?"

"Here." Bensali waved his hand over the ground, and five smooth, round stones appeared between them. "I want you to work this out."

With a trembling finger extended, Jorian exposed each of the stones to a small amount of magic. The first felt heavy even though he didn't attempt to lift it, while the second felt light, ready to float away. The third seemed made of liquid, shifting and changing shape at his slightest prodding. The fourth blistered his fingertip, and the fifth froze it. When he stoppered the flow of magic, the stones returned to normal. No one would ever guess they held any mystery. "What am I to do with these?"

"Make them whole."

"How?"

The feathers of Bensali's wings rippled as he laughed again. "If I knew that, I would not need you."

"So… so I can go? The tribe wanted me to get your permission. Is it granted?"

"It is. Unless you would rather return to my cave on the cliffside. We could learn a great deal about each other. If you would share with me, I would share with you. I could make you a powerful sorcerer. You could take Kahladryia for yourself, if you wanted it."

"I don't want Kahladryia."

Bensali leaned in and spoke with breath smelling of burnt minerals. "What do you want?"

"Security for Espero. It's all I've ever wanted."

"That's a bit dull."

"Maybe, but I would like to go back to my library, read and organize books without the threat of barbarians killing my people. If that isn't grandiose enough for you, pick someone else to deliver your pebbles."

Bensali held up his hands. "No. I believe you are the one I need, the one the world needs. Take the stones and relay my blessings to the Tsubik. I will continue to protect her tribe. Then go, but remember this: sometimes things need to be torn down to build something better. It isn't always possible to repair things. Some of them need to be started over. I'll see you next time, Jorian."

"What makes you think I'll come back this way?"

Bensali only smiled. Eventually, Jorian stood and turned to leave. The walk back to camp would be long; he'd be lucky to make it by morning. He'd gone a few steps when he heard the flutter or wings behind him and felt a warm, heavy hand on his shoulder, pointed claws grazing his skin. "Take this. Show it to the snow-haired mage."

It was a dagger, clear as glass but with veins of blue and red running through it, pulsing as if pumping blood. It felt both hot and cold against Jorian's palm. He tucked it into his belt and nodded. "I should thank you. I would be dead if you had not intervened."

"You'll make it up to me," Bensali said with a wink.

A WEEK later, his good-byes said, Jorian stood on a dock on the northeastern coast on Johmatra. No ships here could fly the striped sails of the Emiri, or paint their vessels' hulls in the distinct colors of the Sea People, but friends could be found when one knew what to look for.

After spending most of the day observing the harbor, Jorian chose a ship to approach. Her captain was a younger man. Life at sea had tanned his skin, but he'd probably originally come from northern Selindria or Gaeltheon, with his light brown hair and neatly trimmed beard. Jorian had seen some coins discreetly changing hands while the captain's eyes carefully scanned the area, and he even thought he saw a few Emiri moving about on the deck, careful to stay camouflaged by the cargo and rigging.

Confident this ship's captain was at least a smuggler, Jorian approached him. Impressed by his success with the farang phreet, Jorian's friends in the tribe had given him some valuable items—mostly cloth and clear crystals—with which to secure his passage.

When Jorian walked across the gangplank, the captain smiled even though his eyes held suspicion. "Good morning to you, friend. It isn't often we see an Arbek nomad here along the coast. Have you come wishing to trade?"

"I do have goods to offer," Jorian said, holding up the large sack he carried. "But my… situation is a little more complicated than that. Is there a place we can speak privately?"

Nodding once, the captain led Jorian up some steps and into a cabin on a higher deck. There, he sat down on a small cot and indicated Jorian should take one across from him. "So, what exactly is it you're hoping I can do for you?"

Though he didn't suppose he looked much different from the nomads, Jorian unwound the wrappings from his head and face. "I am not technically a nomad."

"Not technically?" The captain arched a brow.

"Not at all," Jorian admitted. "I come from the island of Espero."

"A long way from home."

"Yes, and very desperate to get back, or rather, to Gaeltheon."

"Why?"

"I committed crimes against the ruling family of Kahladryia."

"Maybe," the captain mumbled. "Or maybe you're working for them, testing my loyalty. You could be one of their agents, let your hair grow in and ready to drag me off to be tortured as soon as I agree to help a so-called enemy."

"Believe me, I understand your suspicion. It's necessary for survival in this place. Yet…." Jorian met the captain's eyes and spoke the secret motto of the Emiri resistance: "When everything else crashes into the sea and is washed away, there is still hope."

"That there is… syrai." The captain extended his hand and Jorian shook it.

"And if you need further proof that I'm not spying for the Johmatrans…." Jorian conjured some fish made of blue light. They rose to the ceiling and slowly circled the cabin before they faded away.

"Excellent." The captain clapped Jorian on the shoulder. "A mage is always useful, especially since there are… vulnerable individuals on board. Can I count on you to fight to defend them if it comes to that?"

"I will give my life defending them if I must." Jorian meant it.

"Then welcome aboard the *Unchained Wind*. I'll get you at least as far as the islands of the Twenty-Nine."

Chapter Sixteen

THUD. THUD. Thud.

N'hahseen pulled the pillow over his head and recalled how much more pleasant his mornings had been when it had been Rahsari waking him rather than that disagreeable woman. Groaning, he peeked out from under the pillow at the slit of a window near his bed. Fane's favor, it wasn't even fully daylight.... But that didn't stop the knocking from coming louder and faster.

"Rise and shine, Your Worship!"

"By Fane's fingernails, Courtenay! I'm coming."

"Well come faster. We have a busy day."

He pulled on a snug pair of leggings and combed his fingers through his hair before opening the door. Was it too much to hope she'd brought breakfast? Of course it was. She stood there in a gauzy blue shirt, slit to her navel and held together by little golden chains. And of course those damned pants, the ones he could see right through, that only the beaded sash hanging between her legs saved from being completely obscene. She smiled wide as if to mock his exhaustion, but then her eyes traveled down his bare chest and the smile faded. "You're not even dressed."

"No, and nor have I bathed, or dressed my hair, or applied my makeup. I'm unaccustomed to doing these things on my own, and the servants you provided are practically useless."

"The world is a cruel and merciless place, Your Worship," she said as she pushed past him. He'd almost gotten used to her entering his chambers without permission… almost.

But he was in a foul mood this morning. He'd learned the prince his mother wanted him to manipulate wasn't at Eirion-Vale; he was in the islands at the mouth of the river, with Yarroway L'Estrella, the powerful mage who despised N'hahseen's people. Essentially out of reach. He was also used to having sex most mornings and often again before bed, and now he'd gone weeks with nothing but his own hand to relieve his frustrations. He'd been noticing the men around the castle: the knights and guards, the stablehands and blacksmiths, even some of the servants. He'd also noticed the women, though he couldn't see much of them beneath their heavy, shapeless gowns, and he couldn't understand why they would wear such unflattering garments. Well, except for Courtenay. Still, it didn't stop him from imagining their bodies when he was alone at night. A recurring fantasy had plagued him, a detailed vision of having both a man and a woman in his bed. Yet again, he'd woken up hard, and even his irritation couldn't fully wilt his erection.

"Your Worship? You look like you're dreaming with your eyes open."

"Would you stop calling me that? Do you think I'm stupid? I know you're making fun of me."

When she lowered her eyes, he regretted his outburst. "I admit I am," she said. "But it isn't meant to be mean or hurtful. You know? It's just teasing."

"It's not something I'm used to. I'm used to being addressed with the reverence I deserve. Do I need to remind you—again—that I am the First Son of Kahladryia and can trace my lineage directly back to Fane? You should not make me the butt of a joke."

She shook her head—a confusing gesture that could mean a number of things. "It's… it's actually a form of affection. When I was at school, my classmates called me River Whiskers."

"What? Why?"

She had her hair pulled back in a knot today and held in place by a wire cage, but she pulled a strand free and twisted it around her finger. "River whiskers are curly rushes. Guess where they grow."

He held up a hand and slowly closed his fist, but she ignored the indication of annoyance and continued. "They're bright yellow. No one native to Espero has yellow hair, and most of them don't have these curls. They were teasing me about my hair, but not saying my hair was bad… not really saying there was anything wrong with me, just that I had this feature that set me apart. Do you understand?"

He was imagining her with all that chaotic hair shorn away, her face coated in white-gold powder, except around her eyes, which would be painted pink to match her lips. His gaze wandered down her body, where a few golden hairs grew above her navel. The sash hid the rest, but he wondered if Esperon women didn't shave… at all.

"N'hahseen?"

"I understand some of what you are saying, but I would appreciate it if you would not call me that name."

"All right."

"I… thank you. I'll have a bath now."

"I'm afraid there isn't time." She went to an armoire that held some of his clothes, selected a black tunic and red leather vest with matching gauntlets, and tossed them at him. "The king is expecting us at council very soon."

"I haven't even eaten."

"We'll stop by the kitchen on our way to the meeting, but something tells me this is going to be important. We won't want to miss it."

Back home, he might have insisted. If he'd been denied his daily ablutions and a leisurely breakfast, he might have shouted, thrown things. Back home it would have worked. Here, he'd only be proving Courtenay's theory that he was a spoiled brat, incapable of accepting even the smallest deviation from the expected. With a dramatic sigh, he went into the alcove that held his tub and dressed. Then he combed the tangles from his hair and applied crimson powder around his eyes and painted a black line down the center of his face. Even among these barbarians, he wouldn't completely abandon civility; he was meant to set an example for them, after all. There was always time to create beauty around oneself.

After stopping by the kitchens for some bread coated in that oily butter—which he ate while walking—N'hahseen followed Courtenay to the king's library. Inside, the king sat at the head of a long table, next to his personal guard, Lysander. Along the sides sat some nobles and advisors, as well as some of the women who led sects of the barbarian religion. Courtenay took a chair near the foot of the table, and N'hahseen sat down next to her. No one even pulled out his chair.

An older man—N'hahseen thought he was called Vartanan— shuffled some papers much more noisily than necessary. Then, as if he needed to draw even more attention to himself, he cleared his throat. "We have several vital matters to attend to this morning, Your Majesty."

An ample woman in purple chimed in before the king could respond, shocking N'hahseen. If someone had shown that disrespect to his mother, she would have been publicly executed. "One of these issues is clearly of more concern than the others, King Garith. And now that the esteemed ambassadors from Espero and Johmatra have decided to grace us with their presence, I'm sure we can all agree that it needs to be addressed immediately."

"Indeed we can," Lysander said, standing. "The security of this castle and the royal family has been compromised. The king's life could be in danger, and if there's something that trumps that, I would like to hear it." He focused his sharp gaze on the priestess in purple, as if daring her to disagree. "Good. It's been brought to my attention that we have a spy in our midst. The Johmatrans learned very quickly of the events that occurred at the… the so-called trial of Yarroway L'Estrella. As these things happened in public, that in itself is not especially troubling. What's more worrisome is the speed that this information traveled to Johmatra. We are likely dealing with not just a single spy, but an efficient network."

"I trust this information came from a reliable source?" Vartanan said, one of his bushy white eyebrows lifting.

Lysander looked at N'hahseen a little apprehensively. "It came from an Emiri ship's captain, one who travels between Johmatra and the islands of the Twenty-Nine… delivering former slaves to freedom. This is not a practice condoned by His Majesty," he hurried to add.

"We are aware of this practice," N'hahseen said. "Do not worry yourself. We apprehend many more of these criminals than escape us."

"So we are honestly trusting the word of an Emiri? A pirate?" wheezed a skeletal woman in gray rags.

"She was only relaying the message," Lysander said. "The information itself came from an Esperon agent stationed in Kahladryia. He has been working undercover there for many years, I'm told. And before you ask, I cannot imagine what Espero would gain by alerting us to this threat."

N'hahseen ground his teeth. Rahsari was more treacherous than he'd ever imagined—and an Esperon. Though Rahsari had escaped after he'd murdered several dignitaries, N'hahseen should still pass this information to his mother. There was a spy in their house, which meant there could be others. He said nothing. He wouldn't rely on Garith or Courtenay—who he did not trust—to deliver the message. He would go through his own channels.

"This is not something we can dismiss, no matter the source," Garith said. "We must figure out a way to discover the identity of these spies."

"The obvious answer is to ask our esteemed guest." The woman in purple waved a fleshy hand, heavy with rings, at N'hahseen.

N'hahseen smacked the table, making everyone flinch. "Do you dare to imply I am involved in this nonsense?"

"Are you not from Kahladryia? The same city where this information was discovered?"

"Do not pester me with questions you already know the answers to. Accuse me if you dare, but do not be surprised when I answer." N'hahseen's magic hummed in his veins, making the fine hair on his arms stand up. To his shock, he sensed the controlled burn of Courtenay's power next to him.

"Are you threatening me?" She looked delighted. "Your Majesty, will you allow threats against a servant of the Mother Goddess?"

"I heard no threat, nor do I believe this is a matter that affects the temples in any way. Let us speak more of it later," the king said. "It is an internal matter."

"Then on to the reason we are really here." The plump priestess stood and smoothed the layers of cloth that made her look like a handkerchief dropped over a wine glass. It confused N'hahseen that anyone would put so much effort into dressing while leaving her skin bare and blotchy, her hair dully and frizzy. She took a long scroll from a wooden box on the floor and handed it to Vartanan, who handed it to the king. "Your Majesty, this is a formal request for royal aid against Yarroway L'Estrella and the criminal faction he harbors in South Coast. It has been signed by the heads of twelve orders of the goddesses, as well as the heads of forty-three noble families who hold coastal lands."

"Twelve," Courtenay noted. "The Order of Pherara didn't sign."

"Thus showing their loyalty lies with their fellow mage over the king," said the third priestess, a woman in blue robes.

"Espero's treaties and allegiances are with the king, not with the temples," Courtenay said.

"No matter." The woman in purple offered them a smug smile. "This is not a favor we are asking; it is a demand we make to right wrongs committed against us. Denial of this reasonable request will be seen as an act of hostility committed against the temples by the crown. It will force us to withdraw our support of this monarch… and possibly even take steps to install someone more suitable."

Garith stared at the parchment unrolled in front of him, his hands flat on the table and his face pale except for the streaks of angry red across his cheekbones. He spoke without looking up. "I will discuss this matter with my generals and military council."

"We will expect an answer by tomorrow evening," the priestess said.

Then, to N'hahseen's shock, she produced another scroll and handed it to him. Courtenay took it and broke the seal. "I will translate."

"There is no need," the priestess said. "It is an appeal—to an ally—for nautical aid against a common enemy. We are asking for Johmatran ships to help in our assault against South Coast. I'm sure we can come to terms that will be… lucrative to both of us."

N'hahseen could almost feel Courtenay vibrating with fury as she fought to keep her words from erupting from her mouth. He knew exactly what she would say, and he agreed with much of it. "As my fellow ambassador from Espero noted, we have no treaty with your religious cults. It's no exaggeration to say the very existence of them is supremely distasteful to most of my people. I cannot fathom on what grounds you beseech our assistance."

"Ambassador N'hahseen." She mispronounced his name on purpose: Now-sheen. "Surely you can see the advantage to removing a man who is hostile to your nation, who goes out of his way to sabotage your ships. It seems to me many in your land would benefit from trade routes being opened up and made safe. Is it not your purpose as their representative to work toward their best interests?"

He understood perfectly; she'd go behind his back, make him look incompetent to his mother and the rulers of the other city-states. Promises of the coin that could be earned through sea trade would go a long way toward making many of those rulers overlook the heresy the temples represented. He could play this game. He'd been playing it since he was old enough to understand language, but his best move would be to make these women think he didn't know what he was doing.

"That is an excellent point, and one I had not considered. This is my first diplomatic assignment, after all. I will write to my mother and the heads of the other city-states affiliated with ours. I'm confident that, when I explain the profit, they will be eager to help."

"We can ask for no more." The priestess's cheeks plumped with her smile. "Now we wait only on the word of the king, but we are confident the ruler of our kingdoms will show at least an equal commitment to peace and the welfare of his subjects as the ambassador from Johmatra."

King Garith's pallor acquired a greenish tint. "Leave me. You will have your answer."

The three priestesses, looking self-righteous with their noses in the air, filed out, followed by the rest of the advisors. Courtenay tapped N'hahseen on the shoulder and canted her head toward the door. "We should speak in private," she said in his language.

"Yes, and preferably over a real meal," he answered. "One with lots of wine."

"Let's go to my quarters," she said.

COURTENAY'S ROOM was small and simple compared to N'hahseen's suite: just a narrow bed, a chest of drawers, and a washbasin between four stone walls. There wasn't even a table or a chair, so they sat on her bed with the platter the servants had delivered between them.

"The food here is so bland," N'hahseen complained as he cut off a piece of roast meat. "I wish you could taste the feasts my cooks made for banquets back home."

She looked up from stacking slices of cheese on little pieces of bread and topping them with some sort of pickled vegetable. She grinned, her eyes sparkling. "So you'd like to show me Kahladryia? Take me there for some reason other than to be killed?"

He found himself very eager to change the subject. "So what do you think the king will do?"

Courtenay shook her head. "He'll have to aid the priestesses. They've given him no choice. If he refuses, it'll lead to a civil war between the temples and the monarchy. These lands cannot take another war so soon, and Garith knows that. I only hope Yarrow will see that it's an obligatory gesture. If he decides to become his cousin's enemy, it might be worse."

"It does make sense for my people to aid the temples. Yarroway L'Estrella has been a thorn in our side since before the war. The theft of our slaves isn't the small matter I made it out to be…." He tried to think of some way to bring the prince into the conversation without arousing her suspicion. "Isn't the king's son with Yarrow in his islands? Will he not be in danger?"

"I wouldn't want to be in Garith's place," she said.

"What will you tell Espero?"

"That… that isn't something I'm comfortable sharing with you, N'hahseen. If I tell you, you are obligated to pass it to your people, and my people still see your people as enemies. I cannot give them any advantage over Espero."

"And do you see me as an enemy?"

"I think you…. We're just too different. There are things we will never agree on. I do try to understand you, but some things—killing mages and slavery—will always be beyond my grasp, I'm afraid."

"Your people's reluctance to entice Fane to rebuild his paradise will always be beyond mine."

They finished their meal in silence, and Courtenay opened some wine. "No glasses, I'm afraid. I don't usually entertain here." She forced a laugh.

"Give it here." He drank from the bottle. "There is something I would like to understand, if you feel safe sharing the information. What is the source of the animosity between Espero and the priestesses? Are you not all followers of the same religion?"

"It's a complicated religion," she said, taking the wine back. "There are thirteen primary goddesses and dozens of minor deities descended from them. Most people worship them all, observe their holidays. Pherara is our goddess of magic, and it's widely held that she doesn't much care for anyone but her mages. The rules the temples enforce are much more relaxed in Espero, too. We don't care much who people have sex with, for one thing."

"But Espero needs her alliance with Garith, does she not? Or… or would you prefer to pursue an alliance with Yarrow? Do you see him as the more likely victor?"

She shook her head but grinned. The rich red wine had already stained her lips. "Nice try, N'hahseen. But I will say this: the world is changing, especially the world of magic. I think Yarrow knows a great deal about it, and I would very much like to speak with him."

This could be his way to the prince. "Why don't you?"

"Because I'm here representing Espero. That means being at court, doing what Garith asks." She tipped the bottle up and finished the wine. "More?"

"As if I would refuse anything so fine." She uncorked another bottle, and they continued drinking. "Speaking… not as a representative of Kahladryia, I would also like to learn more about what's happening to the magic."

Courtenay perked up. "If you asked to go, Garith couldn't refuse. His alliance with Jo—with your people is fragile. He'll cater to you."

"But won't Yarrow kill me?"

"He won't like you, that's for sure." She took another deep drink from the bottle. "Ah, Alain's pure fierrine. I've been all over the world, and nothing comes close to it."

"Are you…." The wine softened his thoughts, made it harder to remember the words in her language. "Homesick?"

She laughed and flopped back on her pillows. "Yes, but not for Espero. I grew up across the river, on a vineyard. It was the most beautiful place, the grapes stretching out as far as you could see, growing fat in the sun. And in autumn, everything smelled of leaves, fresh-cut hay, and wine. There was a hill at the center where you could see all the way to the mountains. I used to sit there with Alain when I was a girl, if I was scared or confused. I've never felt that… that safe, or at home, anywhere since."

"Why did you leave?"

"Mostly because I didn't want to be a wife or a mother. In Selindria, the only way for a woman to hold any power is to join the priesthood. I didn't want to do that. I wanted people to value me for what I can do, not for what I have between my legs. Espero offered that."

He stretched out beside her, their heads touching on the pillows. "I also miss home."

"Isn't it a desert?"

"Yes, and to you that means desolation, but the truth is very different. There's a beauty to the sand dunes, and when it rains in the spring, they erupt with flowers in every color, so dense the wind catches the petals and they carpet the ground. There are huge formations of crystal, and when the sun hits them the right way, they spray rainbows. Little gullies winding through the stones, ending in pools surrounded succulent plants and small trees. Rushes." He touched her hair.

"Then why did you leave? You had everything there. You didn't have to look elsewhere to be valued."

"I wanted to help; I really did. I do. I want all people to benefit from Fane's return, to share in the wonderful world he will create." He drank carefully to avoid the wine spilling down his chin.

"But what do you want?" She rolled to her side and looked into his eyes.

"I've just said."

"You said what you want for the world, what you're taught you should want. But what do you want for yourself?"

"I…." Her lashes were golden in the firelight and cast shadows across her flushed cheeks that reminded him of the shadows the desert plants painted on the sand. Her wine-stained lips were plump and wet, just the tiniest bit parted. He leaned over her and kissed her.

For a few wonderful moments, she kissed him back, but then she pushed him away.

"I… I'm sorry," he sputtered. "Your wine is very strong, and I'm used to regular sex. It's been hard to adjust to doing without it."

Her nostrils flared. "Oh, so when presented with any compatible body, you couldn't hold back? Well that makes it all right, then."

He didn't understand which part made her angry.

She pointed to the door. "I think you should go, N'hahseen."

"I didn't mean to make it sound like a last resort. I'm very picky when selecting my kahlka—"

"I am not one of your whores, and I never will be. If you ever touch me again, I will burn your face off. Are we understood?"

He went to the door and crossed his arms. "That's not what your body was saying when you opened your lips for my tongue. I bet you would love for me to put a child of Fane's blood in your belly. Who wouldn't? That would grant you the power you obviously seek."

A gout of flame shot past his head, scorching the stones beside him and making his hair smoke and stink before he patted it out.

"Get out of here, N'hahseen. We should forget this ever happened, and more than that, we should forget words that were said in haste."

He could only nod and retreat into the hall.

IN HIS quarters, N'hahseen found a young man sweeping ashes from the flue. He recognized the short black hair and olive skin, and he quickly cast a ward around the room that would alert him if anyone came too close, and then he sat down in a chair and crossed his legs. "I was wondering when we would speak again."

The young man brushed his hands together to shake off the ash as he stood. "I must take every precaution, First Son."

"Of course. But you also have good instincts, Reshe. I require your services."

"What can I do?"

"I need to get a message to my mother. It is too dangerous to write it down, so you must remember and pass it along to your network."

"Easily accomplished, First Son."

"Tell her my servant Rahsari was an Esperon spy. There may be others in our house. She would also do well to look amongst the slaves. One of them delivered intelligence here to the heathen king. Also, I will be sending a proposal by formal channels suggesting an alliance with the priestesses against Yarroway L'Estrella. She and the other households are, of course, free to choose, but I think agreeing to this alliance would be a mistake… I will learn more when I travel with my translator to South Coast. We must be very careful to throw in with the victors. So far, I think that could be Yarrow. An alliance with him could lead to our conquering Selindria and Gaeltheon. Especially if I procure the assistance of the mage prince. Tell her I am close to doing so. Of course, the formal documents will need to urge an alliance with the priestesses, to avoid raising their suspicions."

"A lot to remember, First Son," Reshe said.

"Too much?"

"No. It will be seen to, rest assured."

"Good. Now go. I wish to be alone."

"First Son."

"And Reshe, watch yourself. The king knows there are spies in the castle."

RESHE WALKED down the hallway with his little bucket and brush. Behind him, a redheaded girl carried a basket of clean linen. He turned a corner and proceeded down the steps toward the kitchens and the cellars beyond. It surprised him when she followed. Why would she be taking clean laundry that way? When he got far enough ahead of her that he wouldn't be seen, he pulled out the small dagger he kept hidden in his boot. He heard the shuffle of her skirts coming down the stairs, and he turned.

But it was too late. Almost faster than his eyes could track, she pulled a long blade from the basket, dropped it, leapt over, and cut his throat. He never got a chance to scream as she leaned in and whispered, "Go to Thalil."

Chapter Seventeen

SASHA WALKED through the courtyard, past the children playing in the fountain. He noticed Del perched on one of the second-story railings, watching. As he went through the house and down the stairs to the watery cavern beneath, he thought about what he had said to her, and the more he considered it, the more he realized it had been a question he'd been trying to ask himself.

What Yarrow intended to do was madness. Sasha didn't think the others believed he could accomplish it, but Sasha knew he could, and that was the problem. Yarrow had once told Sasha he would burn the world down for him, and Sasha had wondered at that—wondered at loving someone more than the whole rest of the world put together. It forced him to admit he did not feel quite the same. He loved Yarrow in ways he'd thought himself incapable, loved him more than his own life… but more than the world?

From what Sasha understood, Fane's battle against the goddesses had scorched the world to a cinder, destroyed it to the point that it took people thousands of years to crawl out from beneath the devastation and even consider rebuilding, thousands more until it resembled anything like civilization. Could he allow something like that to happen again for the love of one man? The irony did not escape him; he had killed a lot of people. Just not all of them.

If Yarrow needed to be stopped—if it was even possible—he had the best chance of accomplishing it. But could he? Once, it would have been easy. Now….

Sasha paused outside the barrier to Yarrow's constructed reality and rested his hand on the stone. The magic made his fingers tingle and hum, and it pulled at a place near the base of his spine. Yarrow had enchanted it so those he chose could pass through, and Sasha did. It felt like moving through electrified porridge for less than the space of a heartbeat before he emerged on the other side.

It was an average-sized room, round, the ceiling held up by smooth columns. Everything glistened as if coated with frost, though it wasn't cold. In the center, blue flames crackled in a brazier, and some furniture, benches, tables, and desks, stood around it. It could have been an elegant study except for what waited beyond its edges: nothing. It was dark, but not like the night sky was dark. The sky existed; it was something. This… wasn't. It was emptiness broken only by occasional wisps of prismatic vapor. Yarrow had tried to explain it to him, describing it as something like raw material, but Sasha found the comparison lacking. Even the rawest material was something. Even light and air were something. This wasn't.

All of their mages were here, even the young prince. They'd been working for weeks, spending most of their time crouched over the things Yarrow said had come from Fane, experimenting with the spells Yarrow wanted to learn. Duncan was also here, looking tired and pale. But young. At almost fifty, Duncan looked thirty, and a young thirty—maybe younger than he had when Sasha had first met him. Sasha knew Yarrow was responsible, that Yarrow had been siphoning life energy from their enemies before every battle to preserve their lover's vitality. He saw no need to tell Duncan. It would only disturb Duncan, and he was disturbed enough already by what was going on. But he still sought to persuade Yarrow against it, and Sasha didn't have the heart to tell him they were well past that point now, that the time to return anything to a semblance of what it had been had passed.

"I have news," Sasha said. "The priestesses have gathered their forces, and they have procured aid from Garith. A force of at least a few thousand will be marching on the Twenty-Nine."

"That isn't good," Octavian said.

"No," Sasha agreed, "but it could be worse. They had also planned to request aid from Johmatra. If we'd been boxed in by forces coming down from the north and ships at the mouth of the river, we'd find ourselves in a much tougher position. Fortunately, those letters will never reach Johmatra. Nor will any information coming out of Eirion-Vale."

Duncan shook his head. "We must make plans to fortify the northern border, then. That's where we're weakest, where we don't have the advantage of our seafaring force."

"You don't have to do this." Yarrow looked up from the charts and papers in front of him. "I know it will cost you your title. I will understand if you take your daughter and return to Windwake."

Duncan opened his mouth to speak, but he simply shook his head. He'd given up, then. Accepted what would happen as inevitable. That worried Sasha.

"There might not be a kingdom when all of this is over." D'Aurelian sounded resigned. "The repercussions will extend far beyond this battle. The priestesses will not give up, and it remains to be seen who will stand with them… and who will stand with us."

"Us." Duncan rubbed his eyes with his thumb and finger. "Why are they trying to tear the world apart?"

"It is all they know," Yarrow said in a raised voice. "They had excellent teachers!"

"And are we any better if we tear everything down for our own gain?"

Sasha had heard the circular arguments many times. They got all of them nowhere. He stood next to Duncan and put a hand on his shoulder. "The temples and their Defenders are invading. That we cannot change. Let us prepare for that conflict and worry about the rest when we've dealt with it."

Duncan nodded. "Agreed, though I won't give up hope that peace can be achieved."

"I've figured it out," Thane said from the desk where he sat. "I've finally figured out the writing. It's directions to… something hidden." He pulled the ancient chart in front of him and traced his finger along the eastern coast. "The… it's different now. The land has changed. It…." He held his hands over the map and the land masses shifted and rearranged themselves. "It was more like this."

No one asked how he knew.

"I think the chart is leading here, to a place in the north of Johmatra."

"But what is it leading to?" Corbin leaned over the prince's shoulder.

Thane smiled, just the tiniest curl of his lips, but it made him seem somehow dangerous. "Well, if I was Fane…."

Sasha shuddered for maybe the first time in his life.

"If I was Fane, I would not keep all my power where others could get to it. I would have a plan in place in case I was defeated, things in place for my return."

"But wouldn't they have been found by now?" Octavian asked.

Thane shook his head. "No, because I would not hide them in this world. I would make my own. What we will find in this area is likely only the doorway." He held up the carved jewel Yarrow had also found in the cavern with the books and maps. "This could be a key of some kind."

"All that power…." Corbin breathed.

"And the chance to find out what Fane really intended," D'Aurelian added.

"Beloved would have left something for us… for himself." Yarrow's eyes glowed. "Something we can use against the goddesses."

"Yes." Thane reached up and touched his arm, and Yarrow slapped a hand over his mouth and recoiled. "Yes, this treachery was not… it could not have been completely unexpected."

"Yarrow, have you considered what will happen to the world if the goddesses are gone?" Duncan asked, as he had done dozens of times already.

Yarrow's answer was also the same. "It will be as intended. The magic was never meant to be hoarded by so few."

"But could it not… I don't know. Uncreate? If those who created it are truly defeated?"

"I have told you those bitches didn't create a damned thing!" Yarrow answered.

"So you say, placing your absolute trust in those who claim it," Duncan countered. "But how do you explain it? Where did it all come from? How is the world here?"

Yarrow laughed and swept his hand across the room. "I created this little world. It was an enormous feat, and I'm still very new at it. But what if I could attain the knowledge to create a world in such detail, so vast in scope, that my creations began to live independently of me? What if they developed a will of their own? Would that not be the pinnacle of achievement? What if we're just some spell, designed to adapt and evolve and carry on?"

"What if it is all chaos?" Corbin said. "Some monumental accident?"

Duncan smiled sadly. "It is with both pride and despair that as a father I have watched something I had a hand in making, something brought blank and helpless into the world, grow into something I never expected."

"And yet you let go." Regret and pride both tinged Octavian's voice. "It's how I feel about Rosecairn. It… isn't truly mine anymore, and no matter how it might sting, I must let it become."

"But you still care for it," Duncan said. "I believe the goddesses still care for us."

"Where are they, then?" Yarrow's wings flared, an eye-scorching flash of blue, before disappearing.

Sasha stepped between them. "This is all interesting, academically, but it's best left for another time. We have preparations to make."

"I will stay here and keep working." Thane looked around and smiled. "I like this place."

"Your mother and father would not want you cooped up here." Duncan smiled at the boy. "You need sun and fresh air. Something to eat. I know my daughter would be very glad of your company."

As if he went from wise and ancient back to a boy of eleven in the time it took him to blink, Thane nodded and got up from the desk. Duncan put a hand on the boy's shoulder and led him from the cavern.

"Duncan will be upset if you don't at least try to eat something," Sasha said to Yarrow. When Yarrow waved him off, he added, "You have put him in a difficult position already. Do something small to please him, or at least take a small worry off his shoulders."

"I… all right. I could have wine, at least. Perhaps I should learn how to conjure it from nothing."

"That's a skill I'd like to learn," Octavian said as he passed Yarrow on his way out.

Corbin followed, and soon Sasha and Yarrow were alone. Yarrow slumped onto a bench and pulled at his hair. He looked up at Sasha with glowing eyes. "What's wrong with me?"

"Yarrow?"

"I… I can't stand him, Sasha. I can't stand being around my… my son. I look at him, and I see that boy who came to my caves in search of knowledge. I see those days… those things. I cannot get them out of my mind, and it makes me want to throw up."

"You believe he is Fane."

Yarrow screwed his eyes shut and pressed the heels of his hands to his temples. "I know he is. Of course I do not think of him as I once did, but he is still Beloved, and it's… it's horrifying, Sasha. Ha. You know, once my solution would have been to just go, go off on the road, to the quiet, wild places, me, you, and Duncan. Sleep out and ignore the world. Hide. But, but there are no places left to hide. I miss that. I want to go traveling."

"You could still leave all of this," Sasha said.

"No. Thane needs me, and the world needs him. I… I can't look away. I know what's what, and I can't pretend I don't."

It was pointless to argue. Illusion had its place sometimes, Sasha thought. After all, the world held few people capable of staring at its horrors directly without having their minds and spirits torn to shreds. Most of them learned early on to cover their faces with a gauzy veil, to look at life through a curtain that softened the edges of things and blocked out the shadows that gathered beyond their vision. It allowed them to view life through a pastel-colored, printed screen and pretend the things it hid didn't exist.

Sasha did not hold this against them anymore than he would begrudge a person opening an umbrella against a cold, cutting rain. He'd seen what had happened to Yarrow when the world tore that veil from his eyes, leaving him with no barrier between him and seeing all the pain man could imagine at once, a thousand images of despair flashing in his mind at every moment.

Yarrow was surrounded with howling phantoms, and he had no wool to shove in his ears. No matter how much he drank or how much power he gathered, Yarrow could not temper the brilliance or the noise. Even if he found a way, it was too late. He'd seen, he'd heard, and he couldn't forget.

Sasha had been assailed by the searing brightness and cacophony for so long that he'd grown used to it, in the way one could build up a tolerance to poison: slowly, methodically, and at the cost of great pain. For him, the poison trickled into his eyes and ears as harmless as water now. He could look at the world with his eyes unshrouded, and he could do it without suffering, because suffering had become commonplace, and he could not spare the energy to acknowledge it when he knew he could do nothing to change it. Others survived by shielding their vision;

he survived by staring into the fire for so long he no longer noticed how it scorched his eyes.

It was not so for his companion, and Sasha knew of only one way to free Yarrow from his pain.

"I wish I could help you."

"I don't know if anyone can help me," Yarrow said. "That's not an insult against you."

"I know." Sasha wrapped his arms around Yarrow's waist and pulled him close. He was so broken Sasha could almost feel the jagged bits poking into his flesh. "But don't say it to Duncan. It will hurt him."

"I know. That is what I want to avoid. Hurting anyone else. You might not believe me, but after all the bad decisions I have made, the series of mistakes my life has been, this is something I'm certain of. Have you not ever wanted to kill just because someone damned deserved it?"

Sasha brushed his hand over the coarse tangles of Yarrow's hair. "Yes. But we should go before Duncan comes looking for us."

THEY RECEIVED a surprise when they reached Yarrow's untidy kitchen, and one Sasha didn't appreciate. There, surrounded by a group of Emiri, stood Garith's mother and the queen. Both of them smiled sweetly, their hair tied back and dust from the road clinging to their simple dresses, but Sasha had realized long ago that they were worthy adversaries, as clever and calculating as members of his order.

"Aunt Den," Yarrow said, hugging her. "What are you doing here?"

She held his cheeks in her hands and looked at him with a mixture of sadness and pride. "Well, my favorite nephew is here, as is my grandson. And the future of the kingdom will be decided on these shores. I intend to be a part of that."

"Thane is the result of many years of planning," Queen Cothryn said.

Yarrow smiled tiredly. "You really have no idea."

"I am here to assure my son's safety and see that he inherits a kingdom he can nurture into something truly great."

"Yes, yes I agree," Yarrow said.

"But just what kingdom is that?" Sasha leaned against the doorjamb, tense and ready to act but careful to project a posture of relaxation. "There are currently as many possibilities as there are people with their eyes on the throne, whether to sit there themselves or control it from behind the scenes."

"The kingdom will need the support of the temples to be strong," Cothryn said.

"Or the elimination of them," Yarrow replied.

"No, that's impossible."

"Not as impossible as you think. Come sit down. You must be hungry, and I have much I need to share with you."

Part of Sasha wished Yarrow would keep his secrets, but his mage had never been subtle. For a time, Sasha had considered killing Garith's mother, as it was clear she held much influence over her son. But now that might work in their advantage. If she advised Garith to side with Yarrow against the priestesses, he would likely do it. Their combined forces, along with Espero if they could manage it, would be a match for the Defenders. Religion and politics would never erase the need for Sasha's people, but the idea of a world free from the confines of the temples interested him. If he was not mistaken, seeing the goddesses brought low would please Thalil.

And if the queen and the former queen didn't adhere to his ideas, it wouldn't be a problem to eliminate them later. Now, their arrival carried potential. Maybe the destruction of the temples would pacify Yarrow and, combined with undisputed rule of his islands, allow him to abandon his campaign against the goddesses.

Sasha did not want to think of the alternative unless no other option remained.

Chapter Eighteen

JORIAN WAS glad to get off the ship, and glad of the heat, bright sunlight, and delicious salt air. All were welcome after years spent in the chilly desert. His hair was coming in, and he raked his fingers through the spiky clumps as he turned his face toward the sky and took a deep breath. If he'd been poetic, he might've said it all tasted like freedom. Weeks at sea had put some muscle on him and given him a chance to practice magic again. He felt confident he could handle himself, even in what was a notorious, if fairly new, seaport off a southeastern island of the Twenty-Nine.

Slowly, the former slaves edged toward the dinghies that would carry them to their new home. A large group of native Emiri waited to welcome them. Jorian squinted. He couldn't be sure, but he thought he saw some of his own people in the group as well. When he waded through the warm water and came ashore, he recognized one of the people and smiled. Yarrow had been at the university with Jorian for a brief time, and Jorian had had a fierce adolescent crush on him. Though it seemed silly in retrospect, Yarrow's leaving had broken his heart. Things had been simpler then, but Jorian would be glad to see Yarrow again. He'd done more for Espero and the Emiri than anyone during the war, and Jorian wanted to thank him.

Some flat stones made a crooked stair up a hillock topped with windswept grass. Dozens of people were gathered there, and as Jorian approached, they broke into two groups: Yarrow and the Emiri facing off against a tall man in a cloak too heavy for the weather and a woman in Esperon clothing.

"I do not want him here," Yarrow shouted, magic crackling around him like lightning. "Leave now and just be grateful I do not kill you where you stand."

"Please listen to reason," the woman said. "We have come a long way at great personal risk. At least hear what we have to say. It could be we can help each other."

"I neither want nor need help from a slave-trading, baby-killing piece of filth. I won't permit him to stay here so he can watch me and report back to his masters."

The man in the hood loosed a vile curse in Johmatran. "I have no master but Fane himself. Though you do not deserve it, I have come here to spread his wisdom to you, to help you heal the sorry state of magic in this land."

Yarrow threw his head back and laughed maniacally until he was gasping for breath. "You know less than nothing about Fane! He would despise what you're doing in his name. It would sicken him!"

"And how do you know? Common-born and soiling yourself amongst the sea vermin."

Jorian hurried forward, pushing his way through the Emiri watching the argument, as a huge wing ripped from Yarrow's back, glasslike, blue, and reflecting the sunlight. A claw extended from his hand, and he swiped at the other man with talons like spears. It almost reached him when it bounced off an invisible barrier, making Yarrow stumble backward. In the brief respite, Jorian ran to get between the two groups.

"Stop, please! Yarrow, stop. I know this man!"

"J-Jorian?" Yarrow's magic fizzled out like a snuffed candle with his obvious confusion. "What are you doing here?"

He was about to explain when he was seized around the waist and tackled to the sand, the breath driven from his chest. N'hahseen rolled to get on top of him, and his fists rained blows on Jorian's face, shoulders, and chest. Jorian brought his arms up to protect himself and kicked his legs to try to get free.

"Murderer! Traitor! Fane curse you! I trusted you!"

"Stop!" the woman shouted. "N'hahseen, what in the Shades'?"

The punches quit coming, and then the weight lifted off Jorian's body. He sat up and gingerly touched his face. His lip was split, and he'd have at least one black eye. Yarrow extended a hand to help him to his feet, and he faced N'hahseen, who was held back by the woman and two Emiri.

"What, traitor?" N'hahseen snarled. "What do you want to say? That you never meant to do it? That you had no choice?" He spat on the ground. "Say whatever you want, bastard whoreson pig. I'll never again believe the bile that spews from your mouth. I'll kill you!"

Yarrow stood close to Jorian. "What's going on?"

"I knew him," Jorian struggled to say through an aching, swollen jaw. "I was a servant in his household… or rather, I pretended to be. I was spying for Espero."

"You became a spy?" Yarrow smiled and clapped him on the shoulder as if Jorian had told him he'd gotten married or received a promotion at the library. "Impressive."

"It wasn't, not really. It wasn't something I did for accolades, but after what was done to the university, I had to do something. I wasn't very good at it."

"Bastard! You blew up half of my palace! I bet you're sorry you did not kill me. You will be sorry!"

"No. No, N'hahseen. I would not have killed you."

"Only destroyed my family, then?"

Jorian didn't know anymore. He shook his head. "I would not have hurt you. I came here to find you because there's something you must know."

N'hahseen stopped struggling. "What?"

"Your mother is dead. Assassinated by her husband. He has nullified your claim to Kahladryia. If you return there, you will be killed. That's what I came to tell you, because I do not want you to be killed."

Panting, N'hahseen resumed his efforts to free himself. "You're lying!"

Jorian supposed he couldn't be surprised by the suspicion, but it still stung. "No. I wish I was."

"How can I believe anything you say? Why should I? You lied to me for years."

"I'm not lying now. I went into the city and learned what happened firsthand."

"I still don't believe you. It doesn't make any sense. He wouldn't dare. My people… they treasure me. I don't know what you're trying to do, Ra—*Jorian*, but you'll find me harder to deceive than before."

Jorian swore in Esperon, frustrated. "What do you imagine I would stand to gain? I escaped Kahladryia. Why would I come here instead of returning to Espero if not to warn you? Your mother is dead. The city-state is under the rule of her husband, and he plans to hold it—even if he has to kill you."

N'hahseen slumped, and when those holding him let him go, he fell to his knees in the sand. "Kahladryia… lost to me. That… that son of a whore! He will not get away with this! Kahladryia is meant to be mine."

Without thinking, Jorian hurried to his side and put a hand on his shoulder. "I'm sorry. I couldn't let you stumble into a trap. You can't go back."

"Fane's ass I can't. I will have my city."

"How? You cannot take it back by yourself."

"I will find a way."

"Well you can do it away from here," Yarrow said. "Get him out of my sight."

"Wait," Jorian said. "I learned many things in the desert. I would like to discuss them with you. All of you."

"Fine," Yarrow motioned to some of the Emiri. "Take him to my land home and find him a room, please, my friends. Do not permit him to leave it, and keep him under guard. We might find a use for him."

THAT NIGHT, Jorian had dinner on the beach outside Yarrow's house. They sat on blankets and roasted fish over a fire. N'hahseen attended, but he sulked at the edge of the firelight with the woman, Courtenay. Jorian supposed it was better than him flying into a rage. But N'hahseen was no fool. He might think the world revolved around him, but he knew the others here did not. He must also know he was outmatched. Jorian wondered what had compelled him to come here at all.

Jorian was speaking with a beautiful dark-skinned man: Sasha. "I lost myself a little, spying. I could never respond to anything with authentic emotion; I always had to think about what would be expected, what would give me the results or information I needed. I've found it a hard habit to shake off."

"So you don't plan to go back to it?" Sasha asked.

"I don't know. I guess I was good at it, though a lot of it felt like getting lucky."

"It does, sometimes. If you're interested in continuing, we should speak another time."

Jorian sipped cautiously from the big jug one of the Emiri—Zura—passed him. "Maybe. Who knows what state the world will be in when all of this is over."

"Perhaps we'll have no more need of spies," said Duncan.

Sasha shook his head. "No, that will never happen. People's natures will not change."

N'hahseen spoke for the first time that evening. "They very well might, when Fane is convinced to return. They'll have no need to swindle, kill, and steal for survival. All of their needs will be met."

"You don't know anything," Yarrow said.

"And you do?" N'hahseen looked at the other mage over the fire.

"Yes," Yarrow met his gaze and the two stared at each other for a moment. "I have the answers to everything you puzzle over. Why the magic is weakening, why there are fewer mages born with each generation. And it isn't because of us 'unworthy' mages using the power."

"Then why?"

"Why would I tell you?" Yarrow drank from the Emiri liquor, deeply and without even sputtering. "Let me ask you this: Why do you believe Fane left this world?"

"Because his people became corrupt," N'hahseen said. "Because they would no longer follow his just and necessary laws."

Yarrow snorted.

"Do we not want the same things?" N'hahseen persisted. "A world without suffering or toil, free of hunger and disease? Where people aren't so busy trying to survive, and where art, music, literature, and healing can flourish?"

"And this is accomplished by putting babies to the sword?" D'Aurelian asked.

"It… I have been taught it is a fair price to pay for the rewards we might one day receive." Though he sounded certain, N'hahseen wouldn't look at D'Aurelian.

Courtenay put a hand on his knee. Though she was a mage and an Esperon, the two of them seemed close. That surprised Jorian, and he wondered if he had given N'hahseen too little credit when he'd been certain of his execution. "But one must always question what he has been taught, decide for himself. We are taught the goddesses will protect us, but this war has shown us that is simply not true. We were on our own."

"As it should be," Yarrow said.

"Yet the people draw comfort from the goddesses," Duncan argued gently. "They teach us to strive for our best, for compassion, peace, and understanding."

"And can we not work toward those ideals on our own?" Octavian took the jug and drank almost as effortlessly as Yarrow, though he mopped his lips with the back of his hand before he continued. "Does any decent person really need to be told to help the weak and feed the hungry?" He set down the liquor, reached into D'Aurelian's lap, and took his hand. "And how do you explain their restrictions against two men loving each other? Or two women?"

"Perhaps the answer is reform, not destruction," Though he seemed devout, Duncan's voice was gentle. "Perhaps it is we mortals who have twisted what the goddesses once stood for."

"No," Yarrow said. "No, the world is broken, and they are the ones who broke it. But mortals will piece it back together."

Jorian looked up to see N'hahseen watching him intently, his dark eyes reflecting the firelight. "Wait. Men laying with men, women with women, is considered wrong here?"

"I take it it is not so in Johmatra," Octavian said.

"It is not so in Espero," Courtenay added. "Not really. The tenets exist, of course, but no one cares enough to enforce them. Many mages live with partners of the same gender all their lives, never marrying. It does not stop them from holding important positions or gaining respect in our society. I suppose we regard it as nobody else's business."

One of the Emiri, Toumo, spoke. "And will you also justify the Johmatrans keeping my people in bondage, shaving their heads, beating, and killing them?"

When N'hahseen answered, much of his bluster was gone. He seemed cowed, less sure of everything. "It is what we are taught, that because of our supremacy, we deserve dominion over the lower creatures. Would anyone advocate freeing oxen from plowing the fields? Letting them run loose?"

Toumo stood and drew a knife. Jorian also stood, his magic held ready. "I'm not an animal, you fuck. My syrai who died keeping you from this place weren't animals. I never thought I would see the day we welcomed your kind here. Emir swallow you and wash your bones to every shore." He tossed his knife on the ground and stomped away. The other Emiri soon joined him, followed by Yarrow.

After the silence stretched into discomfort, Jorian sat down next to N'hahseen. "Will you tolerate my presence?"

"What choice do I have? I am practically a prisoner here, and reviled by everyone it seems."

"I did not ask if you had a choice," Jorian said. "I offered you one. If you cannot stand me, if my presence disgusts you, tell me and I will go."

N'hahseen hesitated. "No, stay. I'm confused, lost. I always trusted in what I was taught and told, and now I'm starting to see that much of it might not be true."

"A hard lesson for all of us," Courtenay said. "But it's a choice: cling to what we want to believe, despite evidence to the contrary, or make up our own minds. The latter is much harder than the former."

"I don't know if I can doubt Fane wants to look out for us." N'hahseen tapped his fingers against his forehead. "I don't know if I can bear the implications of that."

"Truth cannot be abandoned because it is unpleasant." Jorian did something he had never dared before and put a hand on N'hahseen's shoulder. For a pregnant moment, Jorian felt sure he'd be admonished, but N'hahseen ignored him. From the corner of his eye, he watched Duncan and Sasha get up and leave, their heads tilted together in hushed conversation. Octavian and D'Aurelian moved closer, bringing the jug of spirits with them.

"Tell me again about the entity you met in the desert," Octavian urged.

Jorian repeated his story, and he pulled the five smooth stones from the pouch at his belt.

"It makes sense," D'Aurelian said. "Yarrow has told you the tale of his time in the Lapir Mountains?"

"Yes." From their expressions, Jorian realized N'hahseen and Courtenay didn't share that information. "But what does it mean? I have spent hours staring at these rocks, casting spells on them, but I have learned nothing."

A boy wearing nothing but a scrap of cloth around his waist and a necklace made of seashells skidded to a halt in the sand. Jorian had been surprised to learn he was the prince of Selindria and Gaeltheon, the heir to the throne. "They need to be brought into balance," the boy said. He waved his hand and the stones levitated off the ground, rotating slowly. They converged, and light flashed as they joined for a moment before breaking apart. "I cannot make it hold."

"What does that mean?" Octavian asked. "What will make them hold?"

"I don't know yet." Prince Thane's eyes looked glazed as he stared at the stones.

"Thane! Get over here!" a girl called. "You said this tower on our sandcastle would hold, but it's crumbling to pieces!"

"I'll use magic to make it stay!" He grinned at them before running away.

"I think the temples assuming more power will be bad for Espero," D'Aurelian said. "I still have some influence there. Jorian, after the bravery you've shown, surely they will listen to your advice."

"And what advice would that be?" Jorian wondered how much his fellow Esperon would say in front of N'hahseen.

"If it comes to war, Espero should side with Yarrow."

"Against the temples?"

"Yes. They are no friends to us."

Jorian could see the wisdom in that. "But if the Defenders are defeated here, it will send a clear message to the people. They'll see their goddesses did not come to the aid of even the most faithful."

"It could aid us, or it could cause a backlash." Octavian's fingers fidgeted as he spoke. "We must get word to Espero. You, Courtenay, and D'Aurelian can convince them. They have to be ready."

"Ready for what?" Jorian asked.

Octavian looked up, and the firelight glimmered in his eyes. "Don't you know?"

"I want to hear it said."

Octavian nodded. "Very well, you deserve as much. We plan to put Prince Thane—a mage—on the throne. The priestesses will oppose us. That will likely mean war, against them and possibly against the crown. We are ready to take that step. Will you stand with us?"

N'hahseen leaned forward slightly; Jorian wouldn't have caught the movement if they hadn't been sitting so close. He turned his head so his right ear faced those speaking—something he did to hear better.

Jorian looked out to sea, at the whitecaps glowing against the dark sky. Somewhere beyond that expanse of water was home, and he wanted to protect it. He wanted a world where people could spend their lives combing through old books, learning things, without the fear of being oppressed or killed. And he had sensed Yarrow's power. "I will."

Octavian dipped his head and smiled. "Good. We will speak soon." He took D'Aurelian's hand and walked down the beach. Soon everything but their footprints disappeared.

"You're a mage," N'hahseen said softly.

"Yes." Jorian picked up a seashell and began digging the sand out of it with his thumbnail.

"You kept that from me as well."

"What choice did I have?"

"Did you think I would have turned you over?" N'hahseen asked.

"Wouldn't you?"

He tapped his fingers against his forehead. "Did you not know you meant something to me? I… the world does not fit so easily into the boxes I imagined."

"It certainly doesn't," Courtenay said. "But people resist boxes, don't they? So few of us are one thing completely. It's all too complex to define."

Jorian nodded, only because he didn't want to be rude and make her think he wasn't paying attention. But his focus was on N'hahseen, the waves the sea air had formed in his hair, his face bare of makeup, a little stubble along his jaw. He reached out and held his hand an inch from N'hahseen's cheek, silently asking permission. When N'hahseen leaned his face into Jorian's palm, something broke loose in Jorian's chest and he almost wept. "I missed you," he whispered in Johmatran.

N'hahseen looked up and met his gaze. "I hated you."

"And now?"

"Now I am trying to understand. And I do, some of it at least. I… I would fight for my homeland as you fought for yours. I can appreciate the risks you took. You owed me no loyalty. You did not know me."

"I know you now."

N'hahseen reached over and tried to take Courtenay's hand, but she pulled it out of his reach. "I was so shut away. It's easy to accept things when one cannot see the proof that they're wrong. I still believe in Fane, but the rest of it… I don't know. I will need to think. It's been a long day, and a long moon. Many moons. I am tired, and my thoughts are jumbled. But I know this: Kahladryia is my birthright, and one way or another, I will take her back. Will you help me?"

"It depends what you intend to do with her," Jorian said. "I will serve the interests of Espero."

"It's good to really know you, Rahsari."

"Jorian."

"Jorian. Well, good to meet you. I suppose now I will decide if I can ever trust you."

"On that note," Courtenay said, "you should be aware that the queen and the king's mother are here in the Twenty-Nine. They claim to be here to protect the prince, but Sasha, at least, thinks otherwise. We haven't shared our plans with them."

"I understand," Jorian said. "I truly hope we're making the right decision… that Yarrow can accomplish what he says."

"Do you believe that?" Pherara asked.

Thalil stood knee-deep in the warm waves, bare except for a black satin loincloth fringed in red gems. The goddess of magic, in her filmy silver gown, rivaled the moon. She was beautiful, but he wondered how much he could trust her. "Do I think one powerful alliance can defeat another and roust control? It's certainly happened before."

She lifted her skirts and stepped delicately into the water, her light reflecting off the surface. "I'm asking if you think Yarrow can defeat the others. He is certainly powerful, but he's so scattered. Is all that strength going to do any good if he cannot focus it?"

"You have doubts, or you wouldn't be asking."

"Perhaps," she admitted. "I assume you will just let it happen."

He laughed. "I'll pour wine and watch the show. I have nothing but contempt for your sisters."

"Don't you worry he'll come after you?"

"No. I've already made sure that won't happen."

"How?"

"You know," Thalil said, "I bet he would spare you too. He sees you differently from the others, and he loves magic very much. You might consider doing something for him, putting him in your debt a bit."

"Like what?"

He rubbed his chin, pretending to consider. "You could teach him the spell he needs to erase physical forms and trap essences."

Her silver eyes widened. "You think I should hand him the very weapon he can use to destroy us?"

Thalil waved his hand. "It will be of little consequence in the end. His son will teach him the spell, if it's even necessary. Yarrow knows it already, but it's buried. It will come to him when he needs it, or when he wants it badly enough. Then he'll remember. After all, it's *his* magic."

"It was… it is Fane's magic," Pherara said.

"Yes, but he learned it from someone."

"You don't make any sense."

"I will." Thalil winked.

"Then tell me what you think about the boy, the prince. Am I alone in thinking—"

He pressed a finger to her lips. "Even here, we could be overheard. Will you come to my realm?"

"As much as it disturbs me, I will come there this once. I also have news to share, news I cannot risk anyone knowing I repeated."

He stepped closer to her. "Oh? Intriguing. I take it the others have plans of their own."

"They do, and it could change everything. None of this might matter… after. Besides, you made an offer to me, and I think I'd like to take you up on it."

"Indeed? It would truly be my pleasure. But remember, it was offered as trade, not a gift. Are you willing to pay?"

"I am."

He waved his hand and split the air in front of them like swollen skin. Together, they stepped into the red light that spilled out.

Chapter Nineteen

THE BATTLE would be the easy part, Duncan thought as he stood beneath the flap of the tent and looked out to the east. Even though they'd set their command center at the top of a hill, he could see only sand, sea grass, and the occasional stone poking up from them. Few Emiri made homes here in the northernmost part of Yarrow's lands, so there weren't any houses. He couldn't see the army that would invade sometime soon—maybe as early as tomorrow morning—but he knew they were there. Both Sasha's people and Emiri farther up river had reported a force of around three thousand Defenders, many of whom were fresh and untrained. The temples' militia had seen a small spike in recruits after what had happened in Eirion-Vale.

But then, men and women had been making their way to the Twenty-Nine too. Some of them came because of the tales of debauchery, drinking, and sex, but others believed in Yarrow's message and sought to live outside the control of the priestesses. Many of them were camped nearby, and tomorrow Duncan would be leading them into battle.

Against his own people… for a cause he wasn't sure he stood behind.

But he needed to push those thoughts away and be a soldier. He needed to think in numbers and strategies rather than philosophical abstracts. If he didn't, those trusting him to lead them wouldn't make it home. He turned and went back inside the tent.

Sasha lay on a cot in the corner, his ankle across his bent knee and one of his daggers twirling between his fingers. D'Aurelian sat on a stool in front of a table, looking tired, while Octavian shuffled papers and maps around, moving with frustrated, manic energy. Duncan didn't think

Octavian had slept for the last two nights, and he'd drawn and redrawn all the maps as well as made pages of notes, diagrams, and scribbles that made little sense. Rocks and shells held them in place in a ring around the main map. Propped nearby was a small mirror, something he'd devised back in Rosecairn that would allow them to communicate with Yarrow and the others who'd remained in the south. Duncan didn't really understand how it worked, but he couldn't deny it would be useful. They would be able to alert their forces if any aspect of the battle changed or went unexpectedly. It would provide a huge advantage. Not that they were likely to need it.

"I just can't figure out what they're playing at." Octavian took a few gulps of wine from a bottle. "It doesn't make any sense."

"You're driving yourself crazy," D'Aurelian chided gently.

"I'm missing something." Octavian paced around the table a few times, readjusting papers and maps, picking them up and slapping them back down. "They have around two thousand men here, south of Eirion on the Dairden Plains. And the royal soldiers coming down from Eirion itself—a small force."

"The smallest Garith could get away with," Sasha said without looking away from the steel flashing between his fingers. "He didn't want to send any of his men. He knows it's a lost cause, but the priestesses blackmailed him."

"He's doing all he can to keep the peace." Duncan knew it was the truth. "Garith is a good man and a good king. If he's agreed to this, it's only because he thinks a war between the crown and the temples would be worse. It sickens me to think we're opposing him."

"We're not alone," Sasha said. "His own wife and mother are opposing him. They're planning to fight beside Yarrow."

"Because they believe Yarrow is their best chance of getting Thane on the throne," Octavian said. "Unless I'm wrong, that is something they've been planning for a very long time."

Sasha sat up and looked at Octavian. "You're not wrong at all."

"But what I don't understand is why they're attacking with such a small force." Octavian picked up a quill and tapped the tip against his opposite palm. "We outnumber them three to one, at least. And we've had time to prepare, and we have the advantage of knowing the lay of the land. And we have mages. Ships. They're handing us an easy victory. Why? What am I missing?"

"It's hard to believe the Defenders are that inept," D'Aurelian said.

"Yes, it is." Duncan agreed. "Many of those men left the knighthood to join with the priestesses. You're right; they should know better. And that's saying nothing of Lysander and Garith's commanders."

"Could Garith be playing against them? Teaching them a lesson for forcing his hand?" D'Aurelian asked.

Duncan shook his head. "I have known Garith a long time. He is unlike most others of his station. He rarely plays those petty games, and never with the lives of his own men. Perhaps their intelligence is just bad. The Twenty-Nine is insular, and outsiders stand out here."

"There's more. I'm sure of it." Octavian returned to pacing. "That Johmatran, N'hahseen, was at Eirion-Vale. Could his hand be in this?"

"How would it benefit him to see Garith and the temples defeated?" Few besides Duncan would've heard Sasha's shrouded doubts. "He'd be smarter to weaken Yarrow's forces; they're the greater threat, especially with Octavian's mercenaries coming down from Rosecairn to flank the Defenders."

"Now, now." Octavian grinned. "My people aren't mercenaries any longer. They're proper knights and soldiers of my bairny."

"They won't be after tomorrow," Sasha said.

"They will." Duncan had to believe things could still be salvaged. There had to be hope when good men only wanted to do the right thing. "Garith will see reason. He has to. We'll sit down and figure this out. We all want peace."

"I'm not sure the temples do," D'Aurelian said. "They want power—control of the kingdom if they can get it. They're widening the cracks between people loyal to the throne, people terrified of another Fane in Yarrow, and people starting to question the lies they've told. They're splitting the kingdom apart, and they don't care."

Duncan hated that he couldn't dispute that. "But a thrashing here will cost them followers. People will see that they don't have the goddesses' favor after all."

"Or people will be scared." Sasha stood and moved closer, making Duncan feel warm and shivery at the same time. "Scared of magic, scared of the Esperons and their strange ways, of the Emiri and their stranger ones. Scared people are dangerous. Fear makes people do things in desperation. I will go look around. Perhaps we're missing something after all."

"I'd rather you stayed," Duncan said. He didn't think he could bear being alone with his doubts. "We'll know soon enough. For tonight, we should all try to get some rest. There's no such thing as a simple battle, and we need to be ready."

DUNCAN HAD always trusted and believed in the goddesses. But by the Shades, he had to wonder why goddesses so vehemently opposed to men making love would create a man with a mouth like Sasha's. Even though they'd lain together twice and Duncan was sated and spent, he couldn't resist Sasha's mouth, especially as it was now, red and swollen from kissing, from being wrapped around Duncan's cock, his lips lax and slightly parted. Sasha lay on his back, his arms folded beneath his head. Duncan, propped on his elbow, traced Sasha's lips with his fingers, leaning down to taste them and draw them between his teeth, into his mouth. Each time, Sasha smiled slightly, and it thrilled Duncan to know Sasha didn't realize he was doing it, wasn't doing it on purpose or for effect.

Duncan rested his head on Sasha's chest. Sasha's body was like a bowstring drawn taut, with him stretched out beneath Duncan. Lethal power held ready. But Duncan wasn't afraid of him, hadn't been for a long time.

Sasha wrapped an arm around Duncan and threaded his fingers in Duncan's hair. "It all seems bigger, now."

"What?" Duncan didn't want to say much, didn't want to shatter this oddly intimate moment. Sasha rarely voiced his concerns. He seldom saw a point in it. Instead, he identified the problem and discerned the most effective solution.

"The implications," Sasha said. "When we first met, I was assigned to kill Garith. I defied those orders because I didn't want to lose Yarrow, didn't want to lose you. It was such a monumental decision. I thought it would define my life. But Garith was only a man. It hardly mattered."

"It did," Duncan said. "He has been a good king, wise and generous."

Sasha sighed. "His mother has been pulling his strings the whole time."

"I think you underestimate him."

"I never underestimate anyone. But what I mean to say is that back then it seemed so important, who would sit on Selindria's throne, who was responsible for the plot against the royal family. But it was typical, the everyday machinations of the privileged. We've moved beyond that now. Now we're in the realm of gods, and our actions could preserve or destroy the world. History would not have likely been impacted much if someone other than Garith had ascended to the throne. But it's different now." He hesitated, his finger tracing the shell of Duncan's ear. "I wonder if we are on the right side."

"Not something that's concerned you before," Duncan noted.

Sasha trailed a hand down Duncan's neck, over his ribs, and along the sensitive places at his waist. "Well, no one is paying me now, are they? Some compensation goes a long way toward assuaging one's conscience."

Duncan nuzzled in closer, let his lips graze Sasha's nipple. He moved his hands over Sasha's lithe belly, through the drying come around his navel. "I'll need more convincing that you have a conscience, but as for compensation...."

Sasha's neck twisted as Duncan palmed his cock. "You don't have any coin. You're a traitor."

"Something else, then." Duncan shifted so his forearms supported him on either side of Sasha's torso. He drew Sasha's nipple into his mouth and bit it gently. Then he kissed down Sasha's belly, smearing the stickiness there over his lips and tongue until he reached the emerging stubble at Sasha's groin.

"Go on," Sasha panted. "Let me see what you're offering."

Duncan smiled and then took Sasha into his mouth.

THE SOLDIERS rose before dawn. Once, Duncan would have said the men, but that wasn't true anymore. Among the Emiri, women fought as well and as bravely. Many of the Esperon mages who'd fought alongside him—died next to the soldiers under his command—had been women. And why shouldn't they fight for what they believed in and defend the homes they loved? Early on, many had doubted their ability, but by the war's conclusion, few held to those delusions. Women had perished. They'd saved lives and decided victories. Many owed their time in the light of the world to the women who fought beside them, and such debts were not easily forgotten.

Now, Duncan just saw people: holding torches, waiting in formation, sweating beneath leather, chain mail, and steel, wondering what the dawn would bring. Whispering nervously because it was all they could do until something happened. Sharing stories with people they might never meet again. Thinking of home and loved ones and wondering if they'd see either again. And it was his responsibility to make sure as many of them as possible had that opportunity. He couldn't think about anything else until that duty was done.

The horns sounded, eerie and discordant in the coastal night. Duncan raised a distance glass to survey the field below. They'd scrounged up a few horses; the animal didn't thrive in the Twenty-Nine with nothing to eat but fish. Only Duncan, Octavian, and D'Aurelian had claimed mounts. Sasha had declined, and Duncan knew he could move faster on his own. The invading army was coming. The first rays of the rising sun glinted off their armor as they ran toward their adversaries. Duncan didn't see any long-range weaponry or siege equipment. The priestesses' men were going to be slaughtered, and he felt guilty for being relieved.

He had to see them as enemies. He had to make himself see the battle as his people or theirs leaving alive.

The first wave of enemy soldiers hit the traps Duncan's people had buried around their perimeter. Zura had modified the exploding boulders they launched from the ships, equipped them with pressure plates, and instructed they should be buried in the ground. They did what he had predicted to devastating effect. The traps exploded columns of sand. People shouted and bodies flew, torn apart by the explosions, limbs going everywhere. Those behind them leapt over and pushed through the carnage. Though Duncan would have ordered his soldiers to do the same, it made him profoundly sad.

What a world.

Zura's devices succeeded in thinning the enemy's ranks, and after they'd run about another half a mile, they hit the wards Octavian and D'Aurelian had put in place. Silvery blue flames flashed when they crossed those magical lines, and their legs began to disintegrate, sparkling as they turned to dust and left people cut in half and pulling themselves forward with their arms as their comrades trampled their backs. A few broke through, but the Emiri made short work of them.

"Excellent," Octavian said, though he didn't sound much more pleased than Duncan.

The scenario repeated—people blown up, their bodies scattered across the shore, people collapsed by spells, the rest cut to ribbons by those defending the Twenty-Nine. Just when Duncan thought it would be an easy, if costly and bloody, victory, something else appeared on the battlefield.

The enemy ranks parted, and something shining like a star moved between them. Duncan dropped his distance glass; his eyes couldn't handle the radiance.

"What in Pherara's name is that?" D'Aurelian shouted to be heard over the increasing volume of the battle below. The screams grew louder, higher in pitch—screams of terror rather than battle cries.

Duncan soon saw why. Whatever the thing was that was making his eyes stream and an ache pound in his skull was slaughtering through the ranks—an arc of crimson light rending bodies in half, mostly his soldiers who stood defending the base of the hill, but some on the other side as well. Duncan could see the blood from where he sat, see the bodies piling two and three thick. He could smell the death wafting on the breeze.

Octavian acted as Duncan sat in shock. He shouted to the archers they'd positioned at key spots around the perimeter, and soon a rain of arrows fell. They struck down a fair number of enemies—soldiers who had clearly not been trained to take advantage of the shields they carried—but they didn't touch whatever stood in that blinding pillar of light.

"Catapults!" Octavian yelled, raising a long dagger over his head. People scrambled to load the exploding boulders into the baskets of the efficient machines Zura had designed. They fired, but not only did the boulders not touch the shining center of the enemy army, the ricocheted off some sort of barrier it formed, flying back into Duncan's people and carving holes in his lines. The frontline fighters rushed forward and crowded together to form a wall with their shields, but one swipe of light brushed them aside as if they were flies.

Duncan had to do something. Without thinking much, he dug his heels into the ribs of his mount, and the bay mare stumbled down the sandy hill. Sasha called out behind him, but he had to put a stop to this, or if he couldn't, to try to get as many of his people to safety as possible. It was worse than he ever imagined when he reached the flat land: blood soaking the sand, bodies in heaps, injured people moaning as they tried to stumble or drag themselves away. The archers still tried to hold back the tide, but they might as well have been firing into the sun. Duncan urged the horse to canter almost to the enemy lines, and he couldn't believe what he saw when he got there.

A woman in golden armor, twice as tall as those around her, strode through, swinging a mace that shed red and golden sparks. Though her helmet covered her face, her red eyes glowed behind the slits, and her red hair tumbled around her shoulders. The armor was archaic—plate above a simple white tunic, her legs covered only by the greaves reaching to her knees. Gauntlets protected her forearms, but the rest was bare to the shoulders. Emiri archers fired on her, but the arrows bounced off of both armor and flesh, harmless as a spring rain hitting stone. She moved within a circle of rippling red light, and everywhere she stepped, the sand melted into glass. Even her own soldiers liquefied where her aura touched them. The stench of burning flesh was strong, and Duncan coughed out clouds of black smoke.

Duncan knew her. He had revered her since he'd been a nervous boy, unsure if he was worthy of the knighthood. He remembered praying at her statue when he'd taken beatings from the older boys, when he thought he should just run home and take care of his family's cows. She'd given him the strength to persevere, the faith that he could do some good in the world: Myint, the battle goddess, patroness of soldiers. Even as he stood here staring at the impossible, he remembered the prayer he whispered into his pillow every night. He spurred his horse farther, but when the mare came within a few hundred yards of the goddess's ring of light, she bucked so hard Duncan couldn't control her. He landed on his back in the sand, gasping for air. As soon as he could draw his sword, he advanced. The goddess kept coming, trampling over her troops, grinding them into puddles of spilled blood and crushed bone. Duncan stood in her path, raising his shield with the Windwake eagle emblazoned across it. Heat that felt like it boiled his skin hit his face like a wall. He thought his lungs had burned to powder when he breathed it in, but he managed to yell to his people, order them to get to safety.

Everyone retreated, backing off to the sides. The healthy helped the injured, those with shields protected them as best they could, and the archers tried to cover their escape. Soon they were scrambling up the hills, and Duncan stood alone, facing the goddess, feeling smaller than he ever had in his life.

He held his sword and shield out to his sides. "We are your people," he cried. "Please, revered goddess of war. Please stand down and let peace prevail. Is not the goal of all war to foster peace?"

Myint halted, and her glowing ember eyes met Duncan's. His knees shook and his legs felt like jelly. With all his strength, he resisted the urge to curl in a ball at her feet and whimper. He never imagined being in the presence of one of the goddesses would feel this way.

"Please," he repeated. "The people of these lands do not need more fighting. We are all on the same side, all your creations. We are looking to you to show us the right way."

She paused, seeming to consider. When she spoke, her voice was like thousands of swords striking shields mingled with the cries of the dying. Duncan felt it move up his spine, turning his guts to liquid. "Will you surrender these lands? Yield them to those who serve my temples?"

He forced himself to look at her face even though tears streamed down his cheeks. "It is not my land to surrender. I just don't want to see any more needless slaughter. I know the goddesses are good, and now others can see you are merciful as well."

"We will not be blasphemed. Bring us the arrogant mage who claims these lands so we can punish him as he deserves."

Duncan shook his head. "That I will not do."

"Then you and everyone else will pay the price for defying us. All of you will die."

Duncan tightened his grip on his sword as he looked right and left, trying to think of some way to spare all these people even if he couldn't save himself. "Most of these people are barely grown! I beg you to let them live! This is not what the goddesses should be to the people! They should stand for hope, for—"

Before he could dodge the blow, she hit him with the back of a hand the size of a battle-ax. He flew back and bounced along the ground, screaming as bones snapped in his chest, back, arms, and legs. His vision faded in and out as sand and sky tumbled around in no discernable order, and the clash of weapons and screams sounded farther away than they could possibly be. Duncan tried to sit up, hoping there was still some chance to save at least some of the people who had followed him into this battle, but he quickly realized his arms and legs were too shattered. He dropped his head to the ground and looked up. Funny how the sky could be so clear and blue while something so awful happened. There were even some white birds lazily riding the air currents, oblivious to the carnage below them. He laughed, and blood bubbled up between his lips.

Boots landed near his head, but he couldn't care much. A metallic chime followed, high and clear, and then a dark patch flitted off to Duncan's left. Sasha—he could tell by the whispery movements. Sasha leaned down and touched Duncan's forehead with his gloved hand. "Thalil. What did you do? Why did you do this?"

"I…." Duncan wanted to tell Sasha that he'd had to try, that lives had depended on him, but it hurt too much, and his head was too fuzzy to find the words. He was a soldier; it was always going to end this way. He hoped Sasha would understand, somehow.

"Move. Let me see." That was Octavian. "I'm a fair healer. Let me see if I can save him."

"You should… our soldiers…."

"Try not to talk. Save your energy." Octavian looked sad, and Duncan sensed it wasn't for him, at least not all of it. There were so many sources of sorrow in the world.

"G-Godddesses, I hoped to leave it better… even a little."

"Baska!" Sasha said. "That thing is cutting through our ranks. It'll move toward the river, and south. We're going to lose the Twenty-Nine. I have to stop it."

Duncan managed to grab his wrist. "No!" Even Sasha didn't stand a chance. "Yarrow—" He wanted to tell them the goddess was going after Yarrow, that they had to keep him away, but a coughing spell cut him off.

"Yes, we need to tell Yarrow," D'Aurelian said. "I'll get back to the command tent and use the signaling mirror."

"I'll do what I can here." Octavian leaned over Duncan again. "This… it's not as bad as I thought it would be. Goddesses, I don't even think anything's broken, and I'm not sensing internal damage."

How could that be? Duncan knew that blow should have killed him. He'd felt his bones snapping, his body tearing apart inside. But now, when he tried to reach out for Sasha, he found it easier and less painful.

"That's rather miraculous, isn't it?" Sasha said, his voice small and scared in a way Duncan had never imagined he'd hear.

Octavian nodded. "If I didn't know better, I'd say there's some kind of magic working in him. I think… it's siphoning stray bits of magic—and little scraps of life—in order to regenerate his flesh. I've never seen anything like it, but it's working quite effectively. I should be able to help it along, and then he'll be stable enough to get him to safety."

"Do it, Octavian," Sasha said. "Please hurry."

"BABYSITTING DUTY," N'hahseen grumbled, looking over his shoulder at the cobbled-together complex of houses. "I've never been so humiliated. Why would they station the most powerful mage here to look after children and old people who cannot fight?"

"Maybe you should be thanking them," Courtenay replied. "They're likely saving your life. Fighting in battles isn't as easy as you seem to think. It isn't like the battles you read about in history books. It's messy and awful, and people with much more experience than your none get killed."

"I'm trained to fight," he argued.

"Well then perhaps they just don't trust you. You might be the star at the center of the sky back home, but I tried to warn you that you wouldn't be seen that way here. If you want these people to trust and respect you, give them a reason. Do your job well here today."

N'hahseen hung his head. Jorian had imagined this moment over the years he'd spent in the palace and Kahladryia, and he'd always thought it would be glorious to see N'hahseen knocked down to everyone else's level, to seem him swallow a bitter dose of reality. But N'hahseen just looked like a confused child who couldn't understand why people didn't want to be his friend, and it was only sad.

"Besides, this is an important job," Jorian said. "We're not only protecting the prince but most of the children on the islands. We're at a crucial point to receive information from the queen at the mouth of the river and relay it to Yarrow if necessary."

N'hahseen grunted. "I'm not a child who can be pacified with exaggerations, but I suppose I should thank you for trying to soothe my feelings."

"Old habits die hard, I suppose," Jorian said.

N'hahseen looked around again. "No one's ever expected much from me, and I guess I can't assume that will change overnight. I will do my best here."

Courtenay nodded and smiled, looking at N'hahseen in a way Jorian couldn't decipher. It made his stomach hurt.

Just then, as if to save him from inspecting his thoughts too closely, the mirror Octavian had provided flickered to life, and symbols flashed across its surface. Courtenay had a way with languages, and she'd proved most adept at memorizing Octavian's invented one. A crease formed between her brows as her eyes darted back and forth, following the glyphs that rose like bubbles coming up through murky water.

"It's from the queen," she said. "It's… disjointed, erratic. Saying the same thing over and over: 'Broken through blockade. Down from Spearpointe Bay. Maybe a hundred.' Then it repeats. Wait! She says, 'Send help immediately…. Can't hold…. Yarrow….'

"There's another! This one is from D'Aurelian, and it's much more articulate: 'Northern lines decimated. They have summoned a goddess. No hope. Will lose all forces and the perimeter. Send Yarrow, or the islands will fall.'

"Fuck!" She swiped a trembling hand across the mirror to send her replies. "Ships broken through our southern defenses, and something else through the northern lines. I wonder what D'Aurelian meant by a goddess."

"It doesn't matter," Jorian said. "They both need Yarrow, and there's only one of him. We need to get to him. I'll go."

"I should go," N'hahseen said. "I'm more powerful."

Jorian touched his cheek. "Yarrow will take it better from me. Stay here and protect the children."

"Be careful," Courtenay said, concern clear in her blue eyes.

"I was a spy, remember?" Jorian forced a smile. "I'm good at sneaking." Then he hugged Courtenay and whispered into her hair, "Watch out for him. I know he's a smug pain in the ass, but he knows nothing of the world. Don't let him get killed."

She nodded. "All right, then. I understand."

As Jorian ran for the trail leading down the hill, he heard N'hahseen say, "If we work together, we can strengthen the wards around this place." Jorian smiled. That was not something he ever thought he'd live to hear: Kahladryia's First Son offer to work with an Esperon mage.

At the water's edge, Jorian motioned to an Emiri with a raft. He used his magic and they quickly made it to the large island at the center of the archipelago. Jorian ran the mile or so from the shore to the dead volcano that was probably the highest point in the territory. No Emiri patrolled the area, and at the top of the peak Jorian could see a faint blue glimmer that had to be the other mage. He yelled Yarrow's name but got no response. It would take him hours to climb to the summit, if the twisted vines growing over the surface would even hold his weight. In desperation, he raised his arm and shot three balls of flame into the air, as high as he could manage. Maybe if Yarrow couldn't see them, he would at least sense the magic and come down to investigate. Jorian hoped so; they were under attack from both ends of the river, and every moment counted. Every moment cost lives.

A few moments later, Yarrow landed at the base of the mound, his massive wings stirring up a curtain of sand. "Jorian? What are you doing here?"

"Bad news." Jorian huffed and bent down to clasp his knees, still out of breath from running and worry. "Ships have broken through the blockade at the mouth of the river. I think they were hidden in Spearpointe Bay. They're giving our armada a hard time. They could use your help."

"Those clever bitches," Yarrow said. "We've been scouting the coasts for months, checking every cove and inlet in case they'd hidden ships. We never imagined they'd stash them that far away. No matter. I'll blow them out of the water. Do you want to come with me?"

"No, that is, that isn't all. Our people in the north are also under attack and taking extremely heavy losses. D'Aurelian said they'd summoned a goddess. I don't know what he meant by that, but they also need help urgently."

Yarrow looked to the north and squinted as if he could see what was happening miles away. "Those rotten whores. I thought I felt something festering, but I assumed it was only the priestesses and those stooges serving them. I should have known. They're trying to take everything from me again, and if they can't do that, they'll take one thing I love or the other."

"Yarrow?"

"Don't you see?" Blue light poured out of Yarrow's eyes in hazy trails that hung in the air like wisps of fog, and his wings glowed so bright Jorian had to look away. "If I defend the ships, I'll lose Sasha and Duncan. I'll lose my chance to fight the bitch, and they'll be able to lord the victory over my head. But if I go north, I lose my people, my land, maybe even my son. I swore to protect the Emiri, but I can't save them both. How can I save both of them?"

Jorian still had questions, and he wanted to help Yarrow, but he didn't understand much of what Yarrow was shouting about, and he couldn't deny being afraid of Yarrow just then. The power flowing out of him was unlike any magic Jorian had ever experienced. His every instinct told him to run, but he balled his hands into fists and held his ground. "Tell me what I can do."

"Nothing. It has to be me, and they knew that, of course. Me to decide, and me to suffer afterwards. Because I can't not suffer; they've seen to that. They… they've outwitted me."

Yarrow stood looking to the north, his posture almost serene, for so long Jorian tried to think of something to say to remind him of the situation and urge him to do something. Before he could, Yarrow threw his head back and laughed. "Or not! Or not, you treacherous bitches!" He laughed until he had to gasp for air, and then he pushed off with his feet and glided back up to the summit of the volcano, leaving Jorian mute with shock and with no idea what had happened or what he should do next.

"Get back to the mirror!" Yarrow yelled. "Signal Aunt Den and see that our ships retreat!"

Chapter
Twenty

MARLY COULD hear the explosions to the south, distant and muffled like a storm coming in from far away, but from her room on the second floor, where she'd been sequestered along with Thane and some of the Emiri children, she could see only the blue sky and the sun glinting off the water in the distance. Still, she didn't leave the window, as if by staring hard enough she might find some clue about what was going on. She had always thought being in the middle of a battle would be exciting—it always was in the stories—but instead she felt sick and so tense her whole body hurt. She wanted the people she cared about to come back and for it all to be over.

Thane touched her shoulder and she turned around to face him. If he was worried, it didn't show on his placid face or in his still blue eyes. She wanted to hit him—no, that wasn't right. She wanted to hit something, though, let out the tension coiling inside her before it tore her apart. "We should be doing something!" she said through gritted teeth. "I can't stand this!"

"I agree," Thane said softly, maybe so the others wouldn't hear, maybe for some other strange reason only he understood. "I feel almost a compulsion to fight in this battle."

She leaned in. "Let's get out of here, then."

"Where would we go? We cannot just show up at the edge of a battlefield. We'd be dragged back here before we got within a mile of the lines. If we're going out there, I want to be able to do some good."

"I might be able to help you," said an Emiri boy with pale yellow hair and eyes like autumn moons. He was a few years older than they were, and he'd just started getting his paint done: a diamond shape at the center of his forehead, surrounded by delicate swirls that looked like waves cresting. Marly thought his name was Yei, and she took his hand and pulled him into a corner. Thane and another Emiri boy followed, and the four of them huddled together conspiratorially. "I have a ship. She isn't large, but she's fast and she steers like a dream. I know there's fighting near the mouth of the river. If we can get to my boat, I can get us there."

Thane looked in that direction, eerily calm and taking plenty of time before he spoke. "Good. I can use my magic to assist, and even if I can't, we can find injured people and get them to safety. I'm sure we can do something, at least."

"Better than staying here," Marly said.

"Good." Yei squeezed his full lips into a thin line. "I've lost my mother and many of my syrai to these land people, and now they want to take my home. If I can do anything to stop them, I want to try."

"How will we get out of here?" Marly darted her gaze around the room.

Yei canted his head toward the window. "Are you any good at climbing? We're only one floor up, and there are some vines to hold on to."

"We'll make it," Thane said, "but what about the others?"

"There are only children in here," said the other boy—Szu, Marly thought. "By the time they find anyone to tell, they won't find us. We were born to these islands, and we know how to get around without getting caught, if we want to."

Yei nodded and climbed out the window. The two Emiri boys skittered down the side of the building with spiderlike speed, and Marly made it almost as quickly. Thane took a little longer and held tight to the vines, and by the time he reached the ground, he'd scraped his knuckles and one knee bloody. But he didn't complain—he'd never been entitled like that, even though he was a prince—and they looked out across the courtyard. Two adults stood blocking the path that led down the hill, a blonde woman and a lanky man with black hair, but they had their backs to the houses and hadn't noticed the escape. Yei jutted his chin toward the corner of the building, and they jogged around back and down a bank covered in brittle yellow grass, to a muddy rivulet that oozed around some big, round stones. Marly and Thane followed the Emiri as they jumped along them and finally reached some deeper pools separated only by narrow paths, some covered in gravel and others strewn with bleached board to make it easier to cross the soupy sand. Beyond that, a bridge covered with a lattice of woven vines led to another narrow spit of land, another bridge, and finally, the river.

They'd almost reached the first bridge when Del appeared—really just appeared, like a shadow brushing across the ground when a cloud crosses the sun. Even though she just stood there, arms relaxed at her sides, Marly knew they were in trouble, and she stopped so fast Thane bumped against her back.

"What are you doing?" Del asked.

Marly stood straight and looked Del in the eye because Del wouldn't respect stammering or hesitation. Del would also know if she lied, so she didn't try. "We want to do what we can to help. To protect this place and save people if we can."

Del smiled, but it wasn't condescending. "That's admirable, but the best thing all of you can do is go back to Yarrow's house and stay safe. Those who are fighting don't need to have to worry about you too."

"But we can help!" Marly protested. Del could stop them if she wanted to; she had to be convinced.

"I'm sorry, Marly, but this isn't a game. It isn't like stopping village boys stealing eggs. These people are professional soldiers, and they won't just beat you up. They'll kill you. I can't let that happen."

As Marly tried to formulate some argument to sway Del, Thane stepped in front of her. As the two of them stared each other down, Marly thought Del looked uncertain, maybe even scared. "This is my fight," Thane finally said. "I have waited a very long time."

"I'm not even going to try to figure what that means," Del said. "I'm taking all of you back to the house."

Behind her, on the river, a ship came up, towing another with a broken mast and a huge, charred hole in her hull. Emiri shouted back and forth, and people on the shore rushed to haul in dinghies carrying the injured. In the distance, more sails appeared, all of them fighting against the current to move north, toward the shelter of the islands.

Yei shielded his eyes with his hand. "They're retreating. Why are they retreating? Who could've attacked us? No enemy ships have been seen for weeks."

"Del, we have to help!" Marly had to make her understand. "At least with people who are hurt, to get them to safety."

"No."

"Yes," Thane said. "I can make you go to sleep, but I would rather not leave you here vulnerable. I will, though. I… have to do this."

After a few moments filled with shouting and distant explosions, Del dipped her head slightly. "Then I'll come with you. We'll take your ship along the coast for a short distance and see if we can pick up any injured. Then we're coming back." She met Thane's gaze. "And if you think you can stop that from happening, Your Highness, I'm afraid you'll be disappointed. Magic is a great gift to have, but it isn't the only form of power."

"Let's go." Yei pointed. "My boat is tethered only about a half a mile from here."

All of them ran along the shore, spurred by the sight of burned and bloody Emiri lying on the banks and the bitter stench of the smoke wafting up from the mouth of the river. The vessel was indeed small, with only a single mast at the center, but once they were on board, Yei and Szu quickly maneuvered her to the center of the river and guided her between all the ships coming in the opposite direction. The wind changed so suddenly the sails snapped taut, chilled and coming from the north, letting them skim along the water's surface like a leaf. Yei stood at the helm while Szu manned the rigging.

"What are you doing?" Del shouted. "Get to the shore and drop anchor. We're too close to the fighting."

"No," Yei said. "I'm not turning back. My people need help. They're getting slaughtered down there, our ships smashed to pieces. The eru are taking me to them, and that must mean something. If you don't like it, jump overboard and swim home. You can't hurt us, because you don't know how to sail my boat."

They headed into thicker smoke and choppier water. All the while, they passed Emiri ships going the other way. Explosions, bright orange in the gloom, bloomed like flowers, and soon they came close enough Marly could feel their echoes moving through her insides. Next to her, Del had a dagger in each hand. Thane stood at the bow, his hands on the railing and his hair blowing out behind him. Marly wanted to pull him away from there, where he looked so small and vulnerable, and make him crouch down next to the shellfish cages piled in the center of the deck.

Everything opened up, and she knew they'd reached the mouth of the river. The mineral taste of the exploding boulders coated her teeth and bit into the back of throat like beestings. More enemy ships than she could count—more than she could see through the oily smoke—waited on the open ocean, and she was scared.

Her father had once told her courage didn't mean never being afraid; it meant pushing through your fear when others depended on you. She imagined him out there fighting, his armor more gold and shiny in her mind than it had ever been in reality, jumping in front of injured soldiers and cutting down the enemies threatening them, saving their lives, and them looking up at him with gratitude and adoration. She didn't expect the adoration part, didn't even want it. She just wanted to be a person that others could depend on, like her father. One who made a difference. Though the fear roiled hot and bitter in her belly and a cold, greasy sheen covered her face, she choked it down and went to stand beside Thane, draping her hand over his and staring unflinching into the disjointed flashes of fire, smoke, and ships.

"What should we do?" she asked him in the strongest voice she could muster.

"I have no doubt we'll know what it is when it's time to do it."

No, Yarrow thought. *No, no, no. They aren't taking anything else. My childhood, my syrai. Rini and Sai. My beloved. My damned body. Stuck in that filthy, frozen water, starved for a scrap of sensation. No more. I won't give this world even another shred of me.*

He stood on the summit of the volcano and a grin curled his lips as he thought back. It had been a long time, but his fingers recalled how it had felt to sink into warm flesh. His skin remembered the satisfying slick of fresh blood. He remembered flying—really flying, looking down on a world in miniature, full of tiny people with tiny little lives, people he could knock down like a child's figurines with a single swipe of his hand. He remembered other things, more recent: men laughing while he sobbed until he gagged on his tears, his mother turning her back as he walked away with all his possessions in a leather satchel, being alone and unsure whether to be angry or afraid. Angry had been better. Angry had been better than being used, hurt. Angry had tired him out, though, his rage burning through all his fuel too quickly, leaving him full of nothing but ash and fumes. Empty. For a while, he'd thought he could let it go.

But they wanted to take everything from him. Take and take and take, until he was even less than he'd been when he was trapped in that mountain pool, even less than he'd been curled naked and retching in his uncle's fortress. He saw what they wanted to do, and he remembered his anger.

Mostly, though, he remembered magic. All of them—Octavian Rose, D'Aurelian, Corbin, and especially Thane—had theories on what he needed to do, how he could realize the spells he needed. Thane's made the most sense, and as they spoke in Yarrow's tiny sanctuary, things started to correlate in his mind. He hadn't needed new knowledge; he'd just needed to see how the things he already understood connected to each other. Lately he'd been dreaming of a silvery woman. He always met her on the beach, under the moon, and they talked about magic. When he woke, he could never remember the words, only the abstract ideas, the pieces he needed to fit together.

Now, he remembered his own magic. He'd been the first to teach it to the mortals, and he'd also been a boy who understood it for as long as he could remember, knew it like a cherished friend. It had been his companion even before the anger greeted him. As he stood, those two pieces edged closer and closer to fitting together, locking into place, soldering together at the seams.

Yarrow waited as long as he could to give his ships time to retreat up the river, but he wouldn't give the so-called goddesses any more than he had to: not one more life, not one more moment of existence in a world where they'd already stayed long past their time. He spread his arms and looked south, letting his tongue slide between his lips to taste the electricity and power crackling on the air. It sparked along the edges of his teeth, filling his mouth with a metallic, mineral flavor. In his mind, using some sense no one had yet named, he perceived all the things that combined to make… being. The magic moving in shimmering curlicues through the air, the water, the baked, black stone under his feet. It would be easy….

There was a brief moment, just a flicker of recognition, where he knew it would cost.

But what choice did he have?

He didn't need to move his hands or utter a word to conjure the storm, small but powerful, distilled like muri-ku, just north of the mouth of the river. Dark clouds pulled together like iron filings to a magnet, shot through with veins of blue lightning that forked down and shimmied along the surface of the water. Wind raged beneath, scooping up sheets of river and sea, dipping so deep they laid the sand and soil beneath bare and froze the spume into lacy white peaks. The tempest ripped its way south, churning up foam and pelting everything beneath it with rain like nails, and then piercing shards of ice. It pulled a crest of water in its wake, and when it reached the enemy ships around the Twenty-Nine, it smashed many of them to splinters and dragged others under. It mowed a path through them, capsizing those along its edges.

Yarrow directed it back around in a loop, around again and again until it caught up the remaining ships. They circled, smashing together in a funnel of frothy water. Then he waved his hand, less because it was necessary and more because it was satisfying, that decisive motion, and the storm raced out to sea, taking everything with it.

Yarrow turned and leapt into the air, spreading his arms and letting his wings snag on an updraft. Without putting much thought into it, he made himself lighter, shifted the balance of his essence more toward air, toward heat. After that, a few beats of his wings propelled him higher, and angling them back pushed him forward, letting him cut through the air like a spear.

Any joy he might have found in finally being able to fly was washed away as quickly as the ships in his storm by what came into focus as he spiraled toward the ground. Blood soaked the sand and ran in rivers between the rock formations, thickening into rancid sludge. Bodies lay scattered like matchsticks, frail and broken, discarded as if they were nothing. He remembered orchestrating similar scenes, but these were his people. No one took what was his. It didn't take him long to find the one who needed to pay.

He somersaulted in the air, tucked his wings to his body, and dropped to his feet in front of the so-called goddess Myint. A tail of blue light followed him, and those who'd retreated and cowered on the surrounding hills shouted and pointed. It was right they should regard him with awe; this world had been his long before their kind had appeared. This pretender did not deserve the same, and she was going to find out very soon—along with the rest of the world.

Yarrow's feet slid along the seared glass the goddess's heat had produced, and he spread his wings to slow himself. She stopped her trudge inland, and they stood regarding each other. It grew very quiet, the sky a mix of bright and hot to the north and churning black and icy sparkles at Yarrow's back. The air crinkled and folded against itself where the edges met, sparks fizzling. It was like night and day stood side by side, and for a moment, Yarrow knew he waited on the edge of a precipice, and if he moved his toe even another inch forward, he would plummet and there would be no going back—not for him and not for the world. He took that step, as he had been called to do since the idea first whispered in his mind.

Myint opened her mouth, probably ready to berate him, but for once, Yarrow had no desire to shout or rail against her. He reached out with the blue-light claw at the end of his arm and swiped at her thighs. The bare skin there sizzled and split, stripes of ruddy light flashing before it knit back together. The goddess raised her massive weapon over her head and brought it down. Though he could have dodged the attack, retreated, Yarrow stood his ground and caught the blow against his crossed wings. It glanced off their edges with a screech, and Myint's foot moved behind her to stabilize her body against the recoil. Her eyes widened in surprise, and Yarrow smirked. She swung again, in an arc this time, splinters of red light netting over her weapon. Again Yarrow blocked, deflecting with his left wing. He dug his claws into the glass, webbing it with cracks, to avoid being knocked to the side.

Though the goddess towered over Yarrow, they proved evenly matched, and they traded hits and parries back and forth, neither of them landing a decisive strike. Yarrow itched, almost salivated to rip into whatever passed as her flesh, to see her broken and bleeding at his feet. At the same time, he wanted to prolong it, was enjoying the push and pull of their dance. And, he noticed, she was slowing down, tiring, and he wasn't. He reached out with his talons and snagged her ankle, pulling her leg out from under her. Her ass smacked the ground, tremors moving out from the source of the impact. She loosed a roar that made thunder seem like the soft rattle of wind in the grass, and rocks bounced against the ground.

Myint's eyes flared, spilling a crimson glow and a dry heat that tightened the skin of Yarrow's face and made his eyeballs itch. It formed an aura around her, slowly expanding out into a dome that burned so hot it not only scorched the ground black and melted the rocks, it reduced them to a fine dust, and then to nothing. It scalded away the air, leaving behind cutting vapors that hurt when Yarrow breathed them in. Still, he knew it wouldn't destroy him.

And he could deal with pain—another old and familiar friend.

The people huddled on the hills weren't as fortunate. They gasped and tried to cover their heads with their arms, but holes burned into their clothing until it smoked and fell away, and then patches of skin burbled, steamed and oozed, revealing the wet red beneath.

Yarrow considered countering with a brittle wind like he'd conjured to push the enemy ships out to sea. He'd always been good with cold, and frost tickled and tingled along his fingertips, sparkling white mist forming around his hands. He sent some of the chilled air to relieve those nearest to the goddess's corona, but the rest of the heat he simply took, pulling it out of the air, out of the furnace within the sprawled behemoth. If he squinted, let his eyes unfocus a little, he could see the tributaries of energy she drew on, sucking the magic from them like a bloated spider in the center of a web. One by one, he tugged at the threads, pulling them to himself and knotting them off, taking away the source of her power—

Or most of it.

When the goddess got to her feet, she'd lost stature and only stood a little taller than Yarrow. Her hair had lost much of its luster, and her skin looked dry, dull, and even sagged around her neck and below her chin. Sinew that had seemed carved from marble now hung from her bones like canvas left too long in the sun. If Yarrow had needed any more proof that these so-called deities subsisted off stolen magic, he had it now. Even a few moments cut off from the arcane flow had diminished her….

But it hadn't destroyed her. With her mace, she sliced the space in front of her, opening a gash in reality. It pulled at Yarrow, but unlike the wind that had sucked the ships out to sea, it didn't move his hair or his clothing, and it didn't disturb the dust or ash eddying in little cones over the flat plain their battle had carved out. Instead, it pulled at his being, his essence. Slowly, he was being unmade—a granule, a particle at a time being obliterated—not destroyed, but expunged from existence. Destruction left something behind: ashes after a fire, echoes of screams after dying. This would leave nothing, nothing but his essence, his mind crying out to experience any scrap of the world.

He knew this spell. He'd felt the effects of it for millennia, trapped in that oily pool in the mountain cavern. More than that, he knew the spell because it had been his spell. He had taught it to his first beloved, and Fane had passed it along to this monster. Until now, he didn't remember how he had done it. Thane and Corbin had had ideas, and the silvery phantom in his dreams had seemed to know it in theory if not in practice, but Yarrow still had not been able to understand, to perform the magic. He'd had the pieces laid out in front of him but had been unable to make them into a whole. Now everything they said slipped into place, but more than that, he remembered.

This was his magic. No way in the Shades' Abode would he have it used against him. Not again.

He waved his hand and easily sutured Myint's wound in the world. Then he used a glassy claw to open one of his own. He smiled and ran his tongue across teeth that felt much longer and sharper than they had when he had woken up that morning. Still it was familiar, and it pleased him, as did the way Myint's mouth went round with horror. She lashed out, first with the mace she held and then with whatever remnants of magic she could scavenge, but soon there was not enough of her left to affect the physical plane. She didn't become visibly smaller, just dimmer, less, until nothing remained but a rusty, eellike smear twisting through the air like a panicked animal, knowing the world was still there and wondering why it couldn't see, hear, touch, or taste it. Her breastplate, somehow unaffected, fell to the ground with an echo that seemed to chime over the landscape for miles. What was left of the goddess twisted toward it, as if it could anchor her to the physical world, but he pushed it away with the side of his foot, condemning her to something worse than oblivion. Yarrow knew that phantom world of smudged shadows, and a trembling in his spine made his wings shiver.

"Someone bring me water!" he called, holding his hands on either side of the writhing daub. "Water!"

Everyone stared. Some bold souls crept closer, but only by a few feet. Novice foot soldiers and seasoned warriors alike clung to each other like frightened children, all of them pale and many of them shaking. No one dared to approach until an Emiri girl, maybe sixteen years old, tiptoed up to Yarrow, stopped several feet away, and held out a battered metal canteen. Taking it in one hand, Yarrow unscrewed the cap with his teeth and funneled the remains of Myint inside. Then he sealed it and attached it to his belt.

"Monster! Bastard!" One of the young Defenders ran toward Yarrow, his sword drawn.

Yarrow reached out, not with his ethereal claw but with his own small hand, and crushed that soldier's windpipe, burying his nails behind the ridged tube. Blood spurted between the young knight's lips and sheeted over Yarrow's arm as he pulled the windpipe through the skin, then crushed it. He tossed the twitching body away and raised his hand to his face, smearing the hot blood across his mouth and over his cheeks. He had missed this. He wanted more of it, and he looked at the group of enemies in their bronze armor and purple capes. They were all soft flesh and easy to tear under their fancy metal shells, and his nostrils flared as he caught the mingled aromas of their blood and their fear. He took a step toward them, but two familiar faces stepped between him and his prey.

"Yarrow?" Duncan's voice quavered, and he couldn't hide the horror in his eyes. Suddenly the blood felt like a mask tightening around Yarrow's face as a cold truth took hold of his guts and twisted. He had forgotten about Duncan and Sasha. In his thrill at finally facing his old enemy, he had dismissed the one thing he lived for, the reason he had wanted to fight to begin with, the men who had allowed him to believe the world wasn't totally lost.

And they could have been hurt, or….

"I… I must return to the southern island, make sure our people, the ships that retreated from the storm… I need to make sure everyone made it back." He scrubbed at his face with the back of his hand and tried to hide behind his long hair. "I'm sure there will be a celebration."

"Yarrow, what about these men?" Octavian Rose waved his dagger at the Defenders and their soldiers and squires.

"Let them go," Yarrow said, turning away. "Let them go back to their temples and spread the word that I'm coming to tear them down. If they're too foolish to take that opportunity, kill them."

He scooped up the breastplate, pushed off with his feet, and winged his way toward the clouds slowly dispersing over the mouth of the river.

Chapter Twenty-One

MARLY KNEW she needed to reach the undulating gray light, but it seemed so far above her that no matter how hard she kicked and paddled her arms, it didn't get any closer. Her chest burned like nothing she'd ever felt, and she was pretty sure not all of the shimmery orbs around her were bubbles. They were growing thicker, swarming what little vision she had in the dark water. Soon they'd drag her under and she'd sink to the bottom of the ocean. Nearing panic, she clawed with her hands as if she'd find something solid to grasp and use to haul herself to the surface. Frustrated, she screamed before she realized she shouldn't, and a stream of misshapen silver bubbles wobbled from her mouth as salty water rushed in.

Just when she thought she couldn't manage another feeble flick of her foot, her head broke the surface. She hacked up spume and sucked in air. The waves buoyed her up and down, and even at the pinnacle of her ascent, all she saw was gray-green water pitted with the fat raindrops that continued to fall. Their impact hurt her skin, cold and stinging, but the storm had settled since it had come up behind their ship and tossed it, end over end, out to sea. Marly remembered trying to cling to a rope as ocean and sky flipped around her so fast she couldn't distinguish them. Then there'd been darkness…. She must have come to underwater.

The rain moved in serpentine sheets, as loud as gravel on glass where it struck the surface of the sea. It took a while for Marly to realize it shouldn't be so cold and that her hands and feet had gone numb.

Oddly, she was very tired. The temptation to close her eyes for a few moments was almost impossible to resist, and it was growing easier to ignore that part of her mind that said that would be a bad idea. "It's important to stay awake," she said, trying to convince herself. She could barely hear her own voice over the fury of the storm and the roar of the waves.

Something like a log floated by, and Marly fought through the tide to reach it, realizing when she did that it was a pole, part of a ship, the end splintered to sharp points. She flung her chest over it and let the waves rock her up and down, grateful for the chance to stop the motion of her aching legs. The rhythm was soothing, and she wanted so badly to go to sleep, but she knew if she did, she would never see her friends or family again. She had to find some way to get back to them, but… not yet. She needed a few minutes before she could think about what to do. All she could do at the moment was hang off the piece of debris.

Other scraps of wood and bits of cloth churned around her, surfacing before being washed back under. Absently she watched them sinking and bubbling back up like pieces of vegetables in a stewpot. The comparison made her suddenly very hungry, and she wondered if she'd ever eat again, and she almost started sobbing. Then something caught her attention, something that wasn't wood or cloth, something that bent and moved as the water tossed it around—pliant, not like the bits of the ship.

A body.

Part of Marly recoiled at the thought of being in the same water as a corpse, and her first instinct was to try to swim away from it, but she knew she couldn't. She was alive, and that person might be too. Luckily it bobbed off in a direction where the waves helped carry her, rather than making her struggle against them. She didn't think she had the strength left to do that. It still sapped her energy to cross the few dozen feet.

Soon she could see a skinny brown arm and a head covered in tangles of dark hair. The head rolled back and forth, and Marly felt sure the person must be dead. She'd never seen or touched a dead body and she didn't want to now. But she paddled closer anyway, because she needed to be sure.

"Oh goddesses," she gasped. With one arm wrapped tightly around the pole, she reached out with the other and grasped for the body. Her first few attempts, the waves pulled it away as if taunting her on purpose, but on her third try, she snagged a handful of snarled hair—black striped with white.

She strained to flip Thane over so she could rest his chest over the pole. She didn't think he was dead; his eyes were closed, and she knew people didn't close their eyes when they died. Someone had told her that, though right now she couldn't remember who. He also seemed warm, but with the lack of feeling in her hands, she couldn't swear to it. It might've been her imagination, because she really didn't want to be alone.

Thane kept slipping down, threatening to disappear below the water, so Marly moved behind him and pressed her chest against his back to keep him in place. She positioned the side of his head on the smooth wood, and then she draped her arms over his. His legs brushed against hers, limp as seaweed, but he was definitely warm. She was sure of it.

Marly didn't know how long they hung there, carried up the swells of the waves before sliding back down. Everything was gray: gray streaks of rain against a gray sky, gray sea crisscrossed with churning gray foam. She pressed her cheek against the smooth skin of Thane's bare back and closed her eyes, waking sometime later with a violent jerk.

"M-Mar…." Thane's eyelids fluttered and he lifted his head a few inches before giving up and letting it droop back down onto the pole.

"Yeah." Her throat felt scored, like she'd packed it with all the salt in the sea, but she was close enough to his ear she imagined he heard her.

"What happened?"

"Don't know. It happened fast."

"What do we do?"

She squeezed her eyes shut as those tears of despair threatened again. "I don't know."

More time passed. The rain tapered off but the clouds didn't thin. "Thane, I don't think I can hold on anymore. Do you think it hurts to die?"

"Yes."

"I'm scared." It wasn't anything she'd ever have admitted before—especially not to him—but she didn't suppose it would matter in the next few moments.

"I won't let us die." Thane's voice was a susurrus, like the drizzle on the water. Something rattled in his chest, and he coughed.

Marly just hugged him, the solidity of his bones a small comfort in a universe of liquid. Maybe she could hold on a little longer.

A while later, he lifted his head. "I see something."

Marly had been distracting herself by biting at a flap of skin on her dried lips. She squinted into the mist that had finally replaced the rain. Maybe there was something warm—orange—glimmering off to their left, but she didn't trust herself to believe it. But after staring for a while, the flicker grew larger. It separated and swayed, like….

"Lanterns? On a ship?" Her heart started beating so hard it must've been all but stopped before. "Hey! Hey, help us! Over here!"

Both of them yelled until their voices were gone.

"We have to get its attention," Marly rasped out.

With a grunt, Thane braced one elbow on the pole and dredged his other arm out of the water. Shaking, he reached over his head and shot three blue sparks into the air. They hung there, bright and beautiful, before fading away and leaving the world looking even darker than it had before.

Things happened in sharp bursts after that, snippets Marly observed in the seconds she forced her eyes open before they closed again. A splash. A dark man with a rope around his waist and strong arms and warm skin. Water washing across the deck of a ship. A scratchy blanket. Drinking something that burned her throat and scorched a trail down to her belly. She thought she saw Del and Yei, as well as a young man in a purple cape. Maybe they were dreams. With a pang, she realized the other Emiri boy wasn't with them, and then she curled into a ball and fell asleep with her head on Thane's shoulder.

"How?" Garith whispered, pressing his balled fists together in an unsuccessful attempt to stop his hands from shaking.

"Your Majesty?" The young Defender charged with delivering the message sounded scared, his voice as soft as if they stood in a temple instead of Garith's library.

"How?" Garith shouted, slamming his palms down on the table.

"It… it was a storm, Your Majesty. The prince, along with the Bairn of Windwake's daughter, were on board an Emiri ship. We do not know how they got there or why. Apparently they sailed to the mouth of the river, and a storm blew down from the north. They were washed out to sea or destroyed, along with all the rest of the ships the temples hired."

"And how did a storm that powerful spring up so suddenly?" Garith continued.

"It could only have been magic, Your Majesty."

"Then it was Yarrow," Garith muttered, staring down at the papers scattered in front of him.

"Most likely, Your Majesty."

"Get out of here," Garith knew he shouldn't vent his anger on this young man, who had done nothing to cause it besides follow an order to deliver news, but he didn't care. "Get out!"

The soldier bowed awkwardly, turned on his heels, and hurried from the room. Garith dropped back into his chair and cradled his head in his hands. Sander stepped over to him and rested a hand on the back of Garith's neck, gingerly, as if his touch might not be welcome. Garith stared down at his knees, at threads pulled loose from his red woolen pants along the inseam. It took a long time of replaying the words in his mind before he could even entertain the idea that he'd actually heard them, that this was really happening. Then he couldn't turn them off, and they repeated in his head, scraping at the backs of his eyes and the inside of his chest like shattered glass.

The prince was lost in the Battle of the Twenty-Nine.

…lost….

Prince Thane… lost….

He's dead, Your Majesty….

…lost… dead….

Garith threw his head back and screamed, the sound expelled out of the deepest parts of him. His chest cramped when he sucked in air, and then he turned in his seat and wrapped his arms around Sander's waist. He burrowed his face into the thick, soft shirt Sander wore and twisted his fingers in the cloth, clawing at it as if he could find a grip on something to pull himself out of this black place. The pain wiped every other sensation from him, every other thought from his mind, and he held on to Sander and sobbed.

By the time he lifted his head, the afternoon had gone and purple evening light crept in through the leaded glass windows. It was dark and chilly with no candles or fires lit, but Garith could see the books on the shelves and the maps and portraits on the walls between them.

Crying had purged him somehow, and everything was sharp and clear: especially his certainty about what needed to happen next.

He stood and stroked his knuckles down Sander's cheek, over warm, stubbled skin, tight with dried tears. He combed his fingers through Sander's hair and kissed his forehead to thank him for being someone he could trust to rip himself open in front of, to spread his heart and his guts and his spirit out for without worrying they'd be exploited. Sander said nothing and Garith knew he never would.

"Is the priestess Amorosa still in the castle?"

"She insisted on staying," Sander replied in a coarse voice.

"Find a servant for me, please. Have her brought here. Have as many of my advisors and generals brought here as possible."

Sander moved his hands up Garith's back and pulled their chests together, sheltering Garith in his arms, protecting him as he had always done. "It'll wait until tomorrow."

Garith shook his head. "It won't. It's waited too long already. If I hadn't waited, if I done what I knew deep down needed to be done, maybe my son...."

"Garith...." Sander hesitated, and his warm breath rustled the air over Garith's ear. "What happened.... Getting some rest tonight and looking at all this tomorrow, or even next week, it won't change what happened."

"I know. Please do as I ask, Sander. Please."

Sander nodded once and pulled away. When the latch of the door clicked softly behind him, Garith found kindling and flint and went about building fires in the inglenooks.

About half an hour later, he sat at the head of the table as he'd done so many times before. He'd sat here and wondered and worried about what to do, about how to be a good king and take care of his people. He'd put himself and his desires last while puzzling over how to protect everyone else. And now he finally knew.

"Yarroway L'Estrella is out of control," he said. "I did not realize until... until today the damage he is doing to this kingdom and my subjects. I was blinded by my love for him and my gratitude for his service, and I could not recognize what he has become."

"I'm sorry it took this tragedy to change that, Your Majesty," Amorosa said, failing to suppress the triumph in her tone.

Garith didn't care. Let her gloat; it didn't matter. Not only was he beyond hoping to ever find happiness in life, but he was beyond caring what others thought. All that remained was necessity, keeping his kingdom whole. Like it or not, he'd been called to fulfill that role, and now he would. "He can no longer be allowed to run rampant."

"A wise decision," Amorosa continued. "And of course, all of the resources of the temples to the goddesses will be at your disposal in this holy endeavor. We should draft a formal alliance."

"Yarrow is still my family," Garith said, "and I do not want to see any more blood in my lifetime. I will offer him exile. I will demand he take his Emiri and leave this kingdom. Then we will reclaim those lands, as was intended when I took the throne and married… Cothryn." His voice shook as unbidden memories of how happy he had been with his wife in the early days came into his mind unbidden. How her eyes shined when she presented him with their daughter, Denna Borea, and then with Thane…. They had been so full of hope back then that Garith didn't think it could ever run dry. "I will redistribute those lands to people loyal to me, people who will rule them according to the laws of this land. We'll finally be able to establish trade, to the benefit of all."

"Some of those lands should also go to the temples," Amorosa said. "We have suffered as much as anyone."

"Let's not get ahead of ourselves." Vartanan produced ink and a quill from somewhere on his person. "We have many details to iron out before we can move forward. What of Octavian Rose? The Bairn of Windwake?"

"More importantly, what if Yarrow doesn't go quietly?" Sander asked.

"And are we really willing to lose our seafaring force?" Captain Bartoum interjected. "I have said all along—"

Garith held up a hand. "These forces have never been ours. They are Yarrow's, and they will turn against us in a heartbeat if he asks them to. We are sitting in a room with a dangerous serpent coiled in the corner and calling it a house pet. It's time to cut the head off it, once and for all. The Emiri will be no threat if they have no sanctuary."

"How will we fight on so many fronts if we must split our resources between the South Coast and Windwake and Rosecairn in the north?" one of the knights asked.

"With the support of the temples, and more importantly, the Thirteen Goddesses, behind us, we will prevail in this." The priestess got to her feet, grandstanding to make a speech. "This kingdom has become corrupt, and it falls to all of us here to purge that corruption. It is time we cull the debauched and unfaithful from our shores, cull them wherever we find them, them and those who would harbor or ally with them. If these lands are to be truly blessed, we must regain the favor of the goddesses. I say, let the great culling begin."

DUNCAN SAT looking out to sea, watching the Emiri patrol the shore, looking for lost comrades or anything that might have washed up. He should have been crying or screaming at the sky, maybe at Yarrow. But he just felt empty inside, numb. And besides, Yarrow had been right about the priestesses, the goddesses… all of it.

But he'd never thought it would cost him his little girl.

Even after two weeks, a film of despair lay over the Twenty-Nine that the sharp sunlight couldn't pierce. The Emiri had collected their dead and sailed out to the open ocean to return them to the bosom of their mother, and the drinking hadn't stopped since, but it lacked the usual merriment. They'd lost people during the war, but throughout it all, this place stood sacred. Having their friends and families slaughtered here was a whole new level of violation. And it hadn't even come at the hands of Johmatra.

Their own people… their own goddesses.

Duncan looked down at the insides of his forearms, at the pale lines scarred into his skin by all the battles he'd fought over the years. All the times he lifted his sword to spill men's blood because he thought he was doing the right thing, because he thought he could carve out a better world with his sword.

Once, when he pressed his arms together, Marly fit perfectly in the space between his hands and his elbows.

The tears finally fell when he squeezed his eyes shut, but he couldn't close out the memories. He wouldn't want to.

After a while, Yarrow and Sasha came down to the shore and waited a respectful few feet behind Duncan, as if not to intrude on his grief. Duncan stood and faced them. He wasn't ashamed of his tears, at the pain he felt as he mourned his daughter. It would have been easy to blame Yarrow for all of it—he had conjured the storm—but Duncan wouldn't let himself do that either. Yarrow had done what he thought best to protect his people, and he'd had no way of knowing Marly and Thane would be there. He took each of their hands and pulled them close, so together they stood in a line, watching the sun's slow slide into the sea.

"Do you wish to talk?" Sasha asked.

Duncan squeezed his hand. Sasha had little use for talk—at least honest talk not meant to manipulate others or wheedle information out of them—but he would do his best if he thought he could help Duncan. "I don't know what I can say," Duncan answered. "I miss her. There's a hole that can never be filled. All my life, I have watched men die. I became accepting of death, maybe too accepting. But this should not have happened. They were too young. They should have had the rest of their lives ahead of them. Maybe they could have made a difference. I… I failed. Everything I have done has been to better the world, to change it. But it changed me, made me a killer, and for what? It's all been a lie."

He expected Yarrow to rail against the goddesses, or maybe against himself—to lament ever dragging Duncan into all this. Instead, he moved in front of Duncan and folded Duncan in his arms, holding him tight as if giving Duncan permission to stop being strong. With everything Yarrow had been through, Duncan endeavored to provide him with stability, to be a pillar Yarrow could always find steady. But he couldn't right now, and Yarrow's body against his, his stillness and silence, told Duncan it was all right.

He let himself cry, let his body hitch with sobs he muffled against the salty skin of Yarrow's neck while Sasha embraced him and leaned his forehead against Duncan's back. Once, he would have said that together, they could face anything, but now he didn't know.

"I believed it," Duncan mumbled. "I believed there was a design to the world, that the force behind everything was goodness. I had to. The alternative… that there's no rhyme or reason beyond the strong exploiting the weak… it's just too horrible. But that's all it is. That's all it is. How can we hope for anything, knowing that?"

Sasha didn't answer. He didn't have to. Duncan knew his philosophy: that death was the only guarantee, and even ruthlessness and talent merely delayed its inevitable victory, that believing in anything beyond one's own skills was foolishness.

Maybe he had been right all along.

"There is always hope," Yarrow said, his lips brushing against the shell of Duncan's ear. "If we cannot find it in the world, we must make it for ourselves. Otherwise, we can only give up, stop trying. Will we stop trying?"

They both lifted their heads, and Duncan looked into Yarrow's bleached eyes, physical proof of how the world had literally burned away much of what had been Yarrow. Duncan touched the ink on his cheek, traced it with his fingertip. "No. We… I won't stop trying. If… if the goddesses cannot be depended upon to care for their people, then people will need someone else to care for them."

Yarrow nodded. "They'll need Thane, and your daughter."

"Yarrow." Sasha's tone held a mild warning.

"Thane…. My feelings for him are a tangle, a mess of pain and love and all sorts of other things twisted up like seaweed… pierced through with hooks and knotted up around debris… so much debris…." Yarrow shook his head and swiped at a tear running down the side of his nose. "But we're connected, across the centuries, through magic… I would know if he was dead. I don't believe he is gone."

Duncan resisted grasping at that thread of hope dangling in front of him, but he couldn't douse the little spark it ignited in his chest. He wondered if he should contradict Yarrow, push him into a world of reality and adulthood he'd never been prepared to inhabit. But what good would it do?

"I assigned Asphodel to keep Marly safe. If she lives, she'll continue in that duty." The hope coming from Sasha was surreal; he didn't believe in sparing their feelings. His honesty had always seemed to Duncan the most concrete proof of his love. It left Duncan unsure of what to say or do.

"How will we proceed?" he eventually asked.

"Despite our losses, we cannot wallow in misery," Sasha said. "Garith has declared a formal alliance with the priestesses. He wants Yarrow and the Emiri gone, and he's also set his sights on reclaiming Windwake and Rosecairn."

"I cannot believe my cousin would do this," Yarrow said.

"He must think it is the only way to avoid war," Duncan said.

"And let's face it," Sasha added, "Yarrow is easier to blame than an entire religion. But his motives hardly matter. The combination of his forces and the temples' Defenders is not one we can likely stand against. Even I… I do not have enough assassins for every soldier."

"Where does he expect the Emiri to go?" Yarrow broke out of their huddle and kicked a piece of driftwood into the waves. "This is the only home these people have! I-I'll fight!"

"We're too outnumbered," Duncan said. "We wouldn't stand a chance."

"My magic—"

"Cannot be everywhere," Duncan gently interrupted. "The previous battle showed us that, if nothing else."

"So we just wait for him to drive us out?"

"We should speak to the others," Sasha said. "With Courtenay and Jorian's help, perhaps we can gain aid from Espero."

"They'd be fools to oppose a force like that." The spark of hope Duncan had felt was fizzling fast, unable to compete with the deluge of what they still faced. "The mages are hardly fools."

"We need people," Sasha said. "It is that simple. To face an army, we need an army of our own. If we cannot gather one, we either relinquish these islands or die on them."

Chapter
Twenty-Two

WHEN HE'D decided to come west, N'hahseen had two goals in mind: to bring the heathen people to Fane's fold and ensure the prince wouldn't become an enemy—one way or another. But when Jorian had delivered the news of his stepfather's betrayal, his desire to reclaim Kahladryia surpassed everything else. It was his birthright, and he would have it returned.

To that end, he sat in Yarrow's courtyard and let the others argue over what to do about King Garith's declaration. He listened as the suggestions became more and more absurd, yet he didn't interrupt, because he wanted them desperate. After the loss of the prince, he felt lucky Yarrow hadn't incinerated him. If it hadn't been for Courtenay, whom the other mage seemed to trust, Yarrow would never have believed N'hahseen hadn't let the children get away intentionally. The others had accepted his version of events, but his position remained precarious. He would have to tread lightly.

"I don't know what else to say." Octavian paced back and forth in front of the long table piled with shellfish and more kinds of alcohol than N'hahseen had known existed. "My people can hold Rosecairn, but getting any of my troops south to help with the defense of the Twenty-Nine is absolutely impossible. They'll be killed along the way, and I'm not willing to risk that."

"And if I empty Windwake of her knights—assuming they'll even come—the bairny will quickly be lost." The big soldier, Duncan, looked wan. The loss of his daughter had hit him hard.

Though torches lined the courtyard and dozens of candles burned behind colorful lanterns made from shards of glass, Sasha always seemed hidden in shadow. There was a matte quality to his skin, hair, and eyes that N'hahseen knew could only be a magic, and though it was a magic he shuddered to investigate too closely, it intrigued him all the same. Sasha was powerful in ways he didn't understand yet, and N'hahseen wanted him as an ally. But of all of them, Sasha was most likely to see through any attempts at flattery or manipulation. That much was obvious to N'hahseen.

Sasha also knew things, another skill that could benefit N'hahseen's interests. "Duncan, your wife has already petitioned the king to annul your marriage and leave her and your son as the ruling family. With Maury Damasca, her uncle, in her corner, Garith will not be able to refuse. It'll require her to marry again, but she's likely to choose a man who will be easy to control. Though I have heard rumors Wyeth Ashlinn is interested in the position. That will give the temples control of Windwake. I don't have to tell you what will happen if he puts a son into her. Boone is sickly, and now he's the son of a traitor."

"We have to remove him from the throne, or both kingdoms will be under the control of the priestesses in a generation," Octavian said.

"Or make him see reason," Garith's mother, Denna Corina, an Esperon mage, said. "Garith is grieving, and he's obviously not thinking clearly. The queen and I must return to him, help him make sense of this. My son is a good man, too good, perhaps. He can be easily influenced, and I won't let those women bring them under their control."

Queen Cothryn's eyes were red and her skin pale. She held an embroidered shawl tightly around her shoulders despite the heat of the evening. "What does any of this matter? What does it matter now that my son…. Where are we without Thane? Our plan was to put him on the throne. I… I don't know if anything I say will persuade Garith to try for another son with me. He could even remarry. The priestesses are hardly in a position to deny him anything he asks for."

Denna Corinna sat up straighter. "Our cause is not lost; we cannot let it be lost. We have come too far. We'll go home and tell Garith you were pregnant before you left. It can take a moon or more for a woman to be certain."

The queen scrubbed at her eyes with the heels of her hands. "But I wasn't pregnant. I'm not pregnant. I—"

Denna Corina put a hand on Cothryn's shoulder. "There are plenty of powerful mages here. Powerful *male* mages."

N'hahseen didn't understand the outrage and arguments that broke out at that suggestion. Back home, male mages competed fiercely for the honor of siring a child on a prestigious female mage. He also didn't understand the importance of that child being a son, but many of these people's ideas were strange to him. For now, he would watch and listen, determine where each of them fell, so that later he could agree with those he wanted to win to his side. If the opportunity arose, he would offer himself up as a father for the queen's child. It would certainly be a foothold toward Kahladryian power in the west. But sexual relationships seemed so nuanced here, he knew he'd be rejected if he didn't step carefully.

So he watched.

Duncan seemed horrified by the idea, despite the fact that he had two male lovers and children with a wife he seemed to despise. Octavian appeared intrigued, much to his partner's confusion. The quiet mage, the one who smelled of death and poison, drank his wine as if the whole debate was beneath him. Jorian looked uncomfortable—N'hahseen suspected the talk of women's bodies and their reproductive abilities made him fidget—and Courtenay put an arm across the whimpering queen's shoulders in what he assumed was a sisterly gesture of comfort.

Sasha only watched.

Finally Yarrow stood, a little unsteady with drink, and ended what had devolved into a shouting match. "Thane will rule this kingdom. Don't talk about him like he is gone. I know he's alive, and he'll return. Our task is to make the world receptive to his rule, and to do that, we need to make sure these lands don't fall under the oppression of the damned priestesses of the thirteen…." He smiled wide and a soft glow surrounded him, like the night worms that ate from the cacti in the deserts. "The *twelve* pretender goddesses."

"For that we need men," D'Aurelian said. "We cannot face an army without an army of our own."

The arguments gained momentum again, everyone repeating what had already been said and getting absolutely nowhere. It was time for N'hahseen to make his move.

He stood and held his arm out wide, almost parallel to the ground. "Forgive me if I am being presumptuous. I know that these are not my lands and this is not my war. Still, I have a suggestion if all of you honorable people would be willing to listen."

Only the tinkling of the fountain and the distant crash of the waves broke the silence, so he continued. "You need allies, people to stand against a king who has made himself your enemy. Or, if nothing else, the numbers behind you to compel him to listen to your side. I think I can help… in exchange for your help, of course.

"My mother's disgusting excuse for a husband stole Kahladryia out from under me almost as soon as I set foot on a ship to come here, to further the causes of friendship and peace. I am alone, but if I were to regain my birthright, I would not be. If I could take possession of Kahladryia, I would be in a good position to help you. The warriors of my land are second to none, and having them on your side would certainly give Garith pause."

"Espero might be more willing to throw in with you if it didn't seem so much like joining the losing side," Courtenay said.

"The council will not be eager to fall under the rule of the priestesses," Jorian agreed. "But right now, we need Garith and his knights to protect us from Johmatra. If that were to change…. Well, if that were to change, it might change many minds."

Just when N'hahseen thought things were leaning his way, Yarrow swatted a ceramic platter off the table, and it shattered against the side of the fountain. "No. No, absolutely not. How can any of you suggest this? How can you consider it? You want me to ally with slave traders and baby killers? I would rather cut off my own arms and legs and flail like a beached fish on the sand. I won't! I won't ask my people to stand next to those who torture and oppress their kind. In fact, when I'm done with the temples and the whore priestesses and bitch goddesses, I'll raze the entire east to the ground and put Emiri in every palace that still stands. Maybe I'll make them slaves, let them see how it feels! Honestly, to do this in the name of my beloved. He would be beyond disgusted—"

His rant might have continued, the arcane power around him building like a sandstorm, but Sasha stood. N'hahseen would've had to be dead not to notice the way Sasha moved, like a shadow encroaching with the sundown, as he stepped around the table and took hold of Yarrow's shoulders. "Excuse us for a moment," Sasha said with a voice like velvet catching against goose-pimpled skin.

He pulled Yarrow around the side of the main house while N'hahseen squirmed on his bench, his cock hard. How in Fane's name did these people go without having sex? This debate was important, and he needed to convince them to help him reclaim Kahladryia, and yet he couldn't keep his gaze from the crease between Courtenay's breasts, the way the ends of her hair seemed collected there, damp with sweat and stuck to her skin…. And Jorian, with his hair growing in…. It framed his face and accentuated his high cheekbones, intense dark eyes, and those lips N'hahseen had fallen asleep imagining more times than he wanted to admit. He should be thinking of Kahladryia, of Fane's glory, but all he wanted was a body against his, skin against his skin. He missed being touched, and he wanted to be touched by a person who didn't consider it work.

Yarrow returned, cowed, his tangled hair hanging in his face. "I apologize for being so hasty in my judgment of Johmatra. It's true that we need soldiers, and I am willing to listen to your proposal."

"It's simple," N'hahseen said. "Help me reclaim Kahladryia and I'll help you in your war against the king and the temples. Kahladryia is powerful; at least seven city-states will be honor-bound to follow her, should it come to war."

"Seven?" Duncan asked. "I don't mean to diminish your offer, Tam N'hahseen, but is that significant when Johmatra is comprised of almost one hundred city-states?"

"One hundred is an exaggeration," N'hahseen explained. "There are about thirty city-states east of the mountains that wield any kind of real power. The rest are… I'm not sure of the word in your language. They move like moons around the city-states they serve. They are tied to them. So when I say I can give you seven city-states, that means more like forty."

"I have conditions." N'hahseen could see that the wall holding Yarrow's anger and outrage back was cracking; he could sense the eerie blue light spilling through the gaps. "I won't work with slavers."

"When I assume power, I can work to advance the cause of the sl—of the Emiri," N'hahseen said, holding his arms out from his body. "I want very much to forge a friendship with you, Yarroway L'Estrella. I feel Fane would approve. But change will take time. You must understand that if I demand my sister cities free their slaves, we will lose their fealty, and thus their soldiers."

"I don't know if I can fight alongside slavers," Yarrow said. "I might rather be defeated."

"I tend to agree," Octavian said. "I'm giving up a great deal to be on the right side of history. I don't want to trade one set of chains for another."

"Then perhaps we're not doing the right thing at all." D'Aurelian seemed a counterbalance to his ruthless lover, but N'hahseen also knew better than to discount his devotion to Rosecairn and his homeland. "How will we be remembered if we're defeated and the kingdoms fall under the rule of the temples?"

"I like to imagine we'll be remembered as striving toward freedom even if we fell short." Octavian curled and uncurled his fingers like he wished he had something in his hand. "I don't want my name on the side of those who sat back while our liberties were taken away one by one. I want to at least be one of the people who did something."

N'hahseen nodded; it was something the westerners did to show agreement, and he wanted to be viewed as one of them. "I also want to be remembered as one who did something. I want to try for peace, and I want to see everyone shares in the prosperity when Fane returns. I wish to help in your plan to put the young prince on the throne."

Sasha was watching him closely and N'hahseen felt gooseflesh rise along his arms. He felt sure Sasha knew everything: his desire to reclaim Kahladryia, his indifference at Garith's kingdoms falling to ruin, even his ultimate goal of manipulating Thane to his own ends. But how could he? N'hahseen waited for Sasha's accusation, but it never came, and that worried him more than if it had.

"I wonder," Courtenay said, "how the mages here will be received by your countrymen. Will our assistance earn us the right to exist and practice magic?"

"Will Kahladryia's knowledge be made available to us?" Octavian lusted after learning more than anything else. N'hahseen respected that. He could also use it.

"In my family's palace are a great many magical texts and scrolls," N'hahseen said. "When I reclaim it, they will belong to me alone. I would be glad to give you access to them. They could be instrumental in helping our cause."

Octavian leaned in, ready to agree, N'hahseen was sure.

Yarrow cut off anything he might have said. "Our cause is not our cause! You are not on my side. You have no idea what I want or what I'm trying to do. You're the same as all the rest. You want to use me to get what you want. And I'm supposed to let you? Thank you for the fucking privilege?"

"We need an army," Octavian argued gently. "Your ideals are admirable, but… but I have seen what happens to idealists in this world, Yarrow. What choice do we have but to take assistance when it is offered?"

"I have a choice! I'll roust those bitches from their temples, and then I'll burn that cursed land to the ground. I do not have to take what others think I deserve, let them do to me as they like. Not anymore. I have a choice!"

Sasha stood. "You don't. Or rather, you have the choice between a chance of success and none. How badly do you want this? That is what you must decide. You must choose whether this is important enough to make exceptions, or you must concede to your cousin's demands and leave this place."

"How can I?" With his eyes wide and glistening, Yarrow looked impossibly young and vulnerable. No one would ever suspect him of holding so much power inside.

"I did not say it would be easy," Sasha said.

"What would you do?" Duncan asked. Everyone turned to Sasha, and it occurred to N'hahseen that he didn't know what position Sasha held, what title. Everyone seemed to defer to him, though.

"Simple. I would assemble a small team of highly skilled individuals. We will never sneak an army—even a small one—beyond the borders of Kahladryia. I would infiltrate the palace under the cover of darkness and kill every person who might oppose N'hahseen's rightful rule. Then I would offer the soldiers and citizens a choice. Soldiers and citizens like stability, security. I believe, if the right words are said, it will not take much to gain their loyalty. Provided they are left with no other alternative. And left to wonder if their opposition will earn them a similar fate."

N'hahseen couldn't conceal his excitement. "You can find people capable of something like this? It will not be easy."

"I can," Sasha said. "However, they will expect to be compensated."

"Kahladryia is very wealthy."

"I may ask for more than material wealth." Sasha looked at him, and N'hahseen struggled not to flinch from his dark eyes.

"Should *your people* become involved in this?" Corbin asked.

"Unless I hear from a higher authority, it is a job. Death bought and paid for. If you wish to remain behind, I'll honor it."

"No, I want to be there." Corbin's almond eyes slid from Sasha to Yarrow.

"And me," Octavian said.

"We will return to Eirion-Vale," the queen said, her expression strong and set despite the grief it thinly concealed. "I'll speak to Garith. Perhaps all of this can still be avoided. Still, it will be a good thing for Yarrow to have Kahladryia in his corner. It might sway the king's decision."

N'hahseen wondered if he should seize the opportunity to offer the queen an heir of Fane's bloodline. His gaze shifted to Courtenay, and he decided it wasn't worth the risk. Perhaps later.

"Someone will need to stay here to defend the islands," Duncan said. "If the priestesses think they are vulnerable, they're likely to strike. I have led men before, and the Emiri trust me. Besides, someone should be here in case Marly…. In case they make it back."

"Won't Yarrow be here?" N'hahseen hoped he would stay. The other mage was too unpredictable; he could ruin everything with an ill-timed diatribe against N'hahseen's people and their traditions, and he didn't have the sense to hold his tongue even when it benefitted him.

"No." Yarrow now seemed calm, his arms wrapped around himself as he gazed out toward the sea. "No, I need to go that way anyhow."

Everyone looked at him, but no one wanted to point out that he was mad or that his words made no sense. Normally N'hahseen would have thought Yarrow deserved a quick death—his magic was clearly a burden to him—but for Kahladryia, he would, as Sasha had said, make an exception.

"I must contact some people." Sasha nodded to Corbin.

"We should also plan for our journey," the queen said, smoothing her gowns in an obvious attempt to regain some control over her situation.

"I can arrange for escorts," Sasha offered.

"No," Denna Corina snapped. "We will be fine. You cost too much, and I do not wish to add to my debt."

"I'd like to find Zura and Toumo," Duncan said. "Discuss the best ways to fortify the islands."

"I need to get word to my people in Rosecairn," Octavian said.

Soon N'hahseen was left alone with Jorian and Courtenay. The wind rattled the dry grasses growing in clumps around the courtyard, the fountain tinkled, and the waves crashed rhythmically in the distance. N'hahseen liked the way the lanterns cast squares of colored light across the sand, and he could hardly believe the slaves had conceived of something so enchanting. But then, he'd been wrong about many things, so secure in his beliefs as to be blinded. He couldn't conceive of Jorian, a servant, possessing needs and wishes beyond N'hahseen's comfort. He couldn't conceive of Courtenay, an Esperon mage, being anything but a backward monster who put her own desires ahead of the good of the world.

Looking at them now and knowing he would soon lose them, he found it hard to feel like he'd won a victory.

Courtenay sat down next to him and drank from a forgotten bottle of wine.

N'hahseen watched her, waiting until it hurt too much to hold the words in. "What will you do? Return to Espero to inform them of these recent developments?"

She turned to him, her fair eyebrows bunched together. Then she smacked him in the shoulder, and not playfully. It stung. "No, you idiot. I'm coming with you. Do you think I'm sending you off on a ship full of the world's most dangerous assassins by yourself? You wouldn't stand a chance."

"Are you trying to imply I need your help?" He tried to sound cross, but it was hard through the smile he couldn't seem to suppress.

"Yes," Jorian answered. "That's why I'm coming too."

N'hahseen's eyes stung; it must've been the salt in the air. "Both of you will be in much more danger than I will. You're heathen mages. Jori, you're a wanted criminal! And, and Court, you have bright yellow hair! You'll stand out like a waterfall in the desert. Why would you do this? You… you hate me, don't you?"

"Less than I used to." Courtenay slid closer to him, her thigh pressed flush against his leg. She put her hand on the small of his back. "I would feel a little bit bad if you perished when it was my task to watch over you. Professional integrity."

Jorian reached across N'hahseen's chest and cupped his chin, urging N'hahseen to face him. "I can help you. You have no idea how many Emiri resistance fighters are in your household. I speak their language, and I have some credibility with them. I can be useful."

"And that's all?"

"No," Jorian said.

"Then…?"

"Pherara, N'hahseen! I want to be with you, to help you if I can. I think you'll do the right thing."

Courtenay reached across N'hahseen's lap and grasped Jorian's wrist. Their eyes met, sharing something, but N'hahseen didn't feel excluded. He felt… strange. Unused to people wanting to do things for him without hope of reward. Unused to people liking him without being obligated. It was hard to believe. "You… you want something from me."

Courtenay's tongue slipped between her lips, and she rubbed them together. "I do. I've been curious. Since you got into the bath the first day we met, actually."

Jorian's breath was warm against N'hahseen's face, but he spoke into N'hahseen's deaf ear. When N'hahseen turned to hear him better, Jorian's pupils were wide, only a thin ring of brown surrounding them. Strips of red stretched across his cheekbones, and his skin was hot when N'hahseen pressed his thumb against it. "What did you say?"

"I said I've imagined being with you. I've thought of it often. At first I hated myself for wanting you… the enemy. But you're not. You want to do the right thing."

"You're adjusting." Courtenay's voice was crisp and clear, her breath scented with wine.

N'hahseen found himself breathing hard, pressed between the warmth of their bodies, surrounded by their smells, their magic. It all mingled in a very agreeable way. "What will this mean?"

Courtenay's laugh vibrated through him, filling his belly and reaching down through his groin to his thighs, tightening his skin. "It doesn't have to mean anything, other than that we're here, we're alive, and all of us are lonely."

Jorian's hand, with Courtenay's still twined around his wrist, moved slowly up N'hahseen's inner thigh. A jolt shot through N'hahseen when their fingers grazed his hard shaft. A shudder ran up his arms, and his lips fell open around a moan he couldn't contain. He still had so many questions, but they drifted away like the clouds pushed by the ocean breeze as their hands roamed over his body. This sensation was completely new to him, so different from being with his kahlka.

"We should go inside," Jorian said. "I know the Emiri make love out in the open, but I'm not that enlightened. Yet."

Chapter Twenty-Three

THE ROOM Yarrow had provided for N'hahseen didn't contain much: a mat for sleeping on the floor, a battered chest in one corner, a pitcher for water, and a chamber pot for his other needs. It was far from what he was used to, but unlike his chambers in Garith's castle, it granted him space, light, and air. There wasn't really a wall on the south side, just a series of wooden pillars with thin fabric curtains between them, cloth printed with sea stars and ocean flora. Tonight, the wind parted them gently, showing a dark sky smudged with wispy lavender clouds when they fluttered open.

N'hahseen moved his hand in a figure eight pattern, and all the candles and lanterns in the room sprung alight. Most of them surrounded the bed, clustered near the pillows so N'hahseen could read in the evenings. The flames flickered in the sea-scented wind and stained Courtenay and Jorian with mutable shadows.

Courtenay's neck was long and slender. Despite her tan, her skin looked like pale silk in the firelight, markedly lighter than Jorian's, much lighter than N'hahseen's own. The contrast was stark and beautiful when he pressed his spread fingers against the sides of her throat, moving them up the delicate cords of muscle and into her wild tendrils of hair. He cupped the back of her head and moved closer, her body lithe and taut against his, with the exception of the softness of her small breasts. She put her hands on his hips, fingertips digging into the flesh of his ass. Her tongue darted out, sweeping across her bottom lip, and then she kissed him.

Fane, it felt like it had been so long. Her mouth was like a drink of citrus water after riding across the desert, washing away all the accumulated dust. Like the precious rains that let the dry ground take a breath and let it out in a carpet of flowers that bloomed before the clouds even dispersed. But it was more than that—something he'd never tasted or felt. She was kissing him, sliding her tongue against his because she wanted to. Only because she wanted to. Wanted him. He'd never been with a person who wasn't obligated to please him. That thought, more than anything, made him harder, and he pressed against her belly, groaning into her mouth when she returned the pressure.

There was warmth against his back, a hard and supportive plain of muscle. Jorian swept N'hahseen's long hair out of the way, and his lips grazed the side of N'hahseen's neck. A shudder racked N'hahseen's body, and he tightened his fingers in Courtenay's hair. She gasped and bit his lip as Jorian nibbled at his earlobe. Jorian moved his hands beneath N'hahseen's arms and up his chest until he reached the clasps on the gauzy, sleeveless tunic N'hahseen wore. Jorian undid them with expert fingers, and the garment dropped open, allowing Jorian to skim his roughened palms over N'hahseen's nipples.

Fane, he was hard. He was wet, dripping, his loose trousers glued to his cock. He was shaking, and not completely from arousal. He'd always liked to think his kahlka enjoyed the time they spent with him— he didn't have the cruel appetites or strange quirks of some of the other descendants—but he'd never troubled himself. Not like now. He wanted to bring them pleasure. He wanted to see another person happy because of him, and now he worried he couldn't accomplish it. No one had ever expected much from him; he'd been told he was perfect in every way, and he'd only recently seen that wasn't entirely true. His kahlka certainly wouldn't have told him if he was no good at sex.

"What's wrong?" Courtenay stepped back from him until the wall stopped her, her arms extended straight and her gem-like eyes searching his face. Jorian moved to stand beside her, his gaze cast down and a shy blush painted across his sharp cheekbones.

N'hahseen moved away and brushed his tunic off his shoulders. It wasn't something he could explain, not without dampening the heat they were stoking. There was no time to explain how he'd never been able to share much of himself with another, how it had been lonely on the pedestal where he'd been placed, and he hadn't even realized it until he had been knocked down. This was no time for a philosophical debate, and more than that, he didn't want to be the center of attention for once. He'd adapted to a great deal recently, and here was something else he'd never imagined doing: putting others before himself. But he knew he could. He wanted to. In fact, he'd never wanted anything more. The idea of it sent a weird thrill through him.

He smiled. "Nothing. I'm… overwhelmed. At the favor Fane shows me to have both of you here." Their bodies seemed to reach for him; Courtenay's nipples darkened and poking against her flimsy shirt, Jorian's ample cock tenting his trousers. "Can we undress? Move to the bed?"

He wondered if they'd kiss, help each other out of their clothes. He wanted to see that, see their hands and mouths on each other, them kindling each other's desire, but he didn't feel it his place to ask. So, without taking his eyes off them, he stepped backward toward the mat. When he reached its edge, he toed off his shoes and pulled his trousers down, exposing his darkened cock head poking out of his hood and his balls knotted up tight against his body. Here in the dark, he swore he saw magic flowing in golden rivulets through the furrows of his scars. He'd never noticed it before, but then he'd never been this aroused.

Courtenay was confident, secure in what she wanted. She shed her clothing and stepped up to N'hahseen, her toothy smile almost predatory. She traced her fingertips over his scars, making them spark and tingle in the wake of her touch. A burnt mineral scent mingled with the aroma of the sea as she scratched lightly down his sides, leaving faint pink lines. She cupped his balls and rolled them over her fingers. "So you've never been with another mage."

He shook his head. Of course he hadn't.

Her hand heated and crackled with energy as she moved it up his shaft, the warmth just at the cusp of being too much. N'hahseen's belly clenched and his lips quivered as Courtenay spoke next to his good ear. "I think you'll like it. Do you want my mouth on you?"

He did, and his dick bucked under her hand. Her lips were glistening and swollen. Over her shoulder, Jorian watched with wide eyes, like a young deer pursued by a pack of hungry lizards. He removed his clothes, but stood with his hands crossed over his groin.

"I have a better idea." N'hahseen led Courtenay to the bed and urged her to lie down on her back. Then he approached Jorian and ran his hands down Jorian's arms, pecking lightly across his lips, with slow, careful movements so as not to startle him. When some of the tension dropped from Jorian's body, N'hahseen wove their fingers together and directed him to lie down next to Courtenay. Jorian seemed to like the guidance, the surety of being told what to do. When N'hahseen moved his hands away, Jorian was pulsing hard, clearish white precome winding down his shaft and into the dark curls beneath it. N'hahseen leaned down and scooped that trickle of seed up on his tongue before moving up to suckle at Jorian's crown and harvest the rest. Jorian must've expected something very different, because his head lolled back on the pillows, and his muscles lengthened and relaxed as N'hahseen sat up on his heels, licking his lips.

He put a hand on Jorian's belly. Jorian had filled out, gained muscle since they'd last seen each other. His body, his magic, was powerful and controlled, but he was clearly nervous. "What's wrong?" N'hahseen asked.

Jorian's breath ghosted over N'hahseen's sweat-damp forehead. "I'm… thinking too much. Trying to decide how to react. It's a habit I got into while…. That isn't what I want. I just want to feel, to react."

"Then react." Courtenay propped herself up on her elbow, leaned over Jorian, and brushed her lips over his. His eyes fluttered shut as she whispered, "Just concentrate on the sensations."

N'hahseen moved his hand up Courtenay's thigh, toward the red flesh peeking out beneath her dark blonde curls. Fane, her skin was soft. In contrast, Jorian's firm thigh was dusted with hair, springy and coarse under N'hahseen's opposite hand.

Courtenay's words seemed to reassure Jorian, and he relaxed, leaning back and giving his cock a few languid strokes. He ran his fingers along Courtenay's collarbone. "I need this. I need to find myself again."

N'hahseen tapped his forehead. "You're both so beautiful. I'm… I'm going to make you both come, bring you to ecstasy. Have you screaming my name."

"That's what you want?" Jorian asked in a whisper.

Instead of answering, N'hahseen bent at the waist and wrapped his lips around Jorian's cock. He groaned as he lowered himself, feeling Jorian slip into his throat, tasting the nectar Jorian leaked. Soon Jorian relaxed enough to rest his hand on the back of N'hahseen's head, and before long, his body tensed with imminent release.

"Not yet," N'hahseen panted against Jorian's sac. He grasped Jorian, stroking, as he pushed Courtenay's knee up with his other hand. Though she was pliant and accommodating where Jorian was hard and unrelenting, they tasted remarkably similar: salt and sweetness finished with a meaty tang. He sucked her little nub between her lips into his mouth as he reached up to knead her breast. Her back arched off the mat and she grabbed his hair, pushing his face deeper into her folds. He was happy to comply. "Come for me, River Whiskers," he said.

Her laugh shook her belly, but it ended on a squeal when N'hahseen pushed two fingers inside her and flicked his tongue against her swollen root. Her head thrashed from side to side and her hips bucked as her body contacted rhythmically around his fingers, beneath his lips. Fane, it was alluring to see her lose control to her bliss. He loved that he'd done that to her—*for* her. He kept going until she pulled him away by his hair.

N'hahseen sat up and turned his attention to Jorian. "Tell me what you want. I would like very much to repay you for taking such good care of me all those years."

"But I did that because—"

N'hahseen dragged his thumb across Jorian's lips, then back along the edges of his teeth. He groaned as Jorian's tongue flicked against it. "It doesn't matter why. You lied to me and used me, but I used you. I treated you… I'm ashamed. I know an evening won't make up for it, but I want… I want to serve you. It's not something I expected to enjoy so much."

"You don't have to explain, and I don't expect you to trust me. But I trust you… at least in this." Jorian's legs fell open, one heel hooked around Courtenay's knee. His spill smeared across his belly, matting the black hairs there, and his lips were dark and swollen, his pupils wide. The dark cleft under his balls filled N'hahseen's imagination. "Fuck me. I want you inside me, N'hahseen."

N'hahseen had done that before, but never without oil. "I don't want to hurt you."

Jorian squeezed N'hahseen's cock at the base, making N'hahseen's seed well up at the tip. "You're wet," Jorian breathed. "I'll be fine. Please."

"You don't have to beg." N'hahseen positioned Jorian's ankles on his shoulders and aligned himself with Jorian's opening. "But tell me if it hurts."

"I like it to hurt… a little. Please. N'hahseen, put it in me. I have wanted to feel it for so long. I can't stand waiting anymore."

His name on Jorian's lips, that pleading tone…. N'hahseen pushed forward, burying himself in tight flesh. Jorian grunted, but he curled his hips up at the same time, meeting N'hahseen thrust for thrust. His eyes screwed shut and his mouth contorted.

"This is how you like it?" N'hahseen panted, pumping hard into Jorian, sweat breaking from his pores. "You like it hard?"

"Yes." Jorian reached for him, but N'hahseen caught his wrists and pinned his arms over his head. He'd heard it said that the best servants anticipated the needs of their charges, knew without being told.

Next to them, Courtenay's fingers fluttered among her blonde curls. She reached over and rested her hand on N'hahseen's lower back, right above where his hips snapped forward and back. N'hahseen met her eyes before looking back at Jorian's flushed face. "Tell me you like it. Fane… tell me you want me."

"Yes… oh, Pherara! Yes! Fuck me, N'hahseen!"

N'hahseen slammed against him, burying himself in Jorian's body. Jorian pushed back, and his arms strained against N'hahseen's hold. He wanted to touch himself, stroke his cock, N'hahseen knew. But he also knew being denied aroused Jorian; his cock had grown even thicker, and it bounced against his belly in response to N'hahseen's movements. When his moans edged toward desperation, Courtenay reached for him. "Can I?"

Jorian's eye opened to slits, and his tongue scraped along the edge of his teeth as he muttered for Courtenay to continue.

The three of them moved together, and the brush of Courtenay's fingers below his navel made N'hahseen shudder. He reached over to touch her, but it was difficult to concentrate on so much at once, especially as the waves of tension and pleasure broke hard against his body. But he must have managed, because Courtenay's breath came in little gulps, and her belly trembled. "Come for me. You… I… Fane."

"I… ah! Ah!" Jorian's whole body coiled tight and then broke apart with his release. Come shot all the way to his chest, soaking the sparse hair between his pectoral muscles. Beneath N'hahseen, he shook like the world was tearing itself apart, and his anus clenched around N'hahseen, pulling N'hahseen into the ether with him. N'hahseen howled as he came harder than he had known it was possible to come. It was like his flesh converting to magic, to energy. For a few heartbeats, gold sparkles filled his vision, stars exploding behind his eyes, and then he collapsed off Jorian, onto Courtenay's soft bosom and into her waiting arms.

She leaned down to kiss him, using the heel of her hand to stroke away moisture from his cheek. He wasn't sure if it was sweat or tears.

He lay there trying to recover, trying to will the particles that comprised him to hold together. He felt like he'd exploded and been spread across the sky. Slowly he came back to himself, and his limbs felt more solid. So did his belly and his throat. He was hungry and thirsty, but not so much he wanted to rise from his humble mat, not when both Courtenay and Jorian lay on their sides next to him, their arms crossed over his chest and their legs wrapped around his thighs.

A threesome. He'd done it before with his kahlka, and he'd read about it in the smutty little book Courtenay had given him, but it had never been like this. This had been real, messy, unchoreographed. They hadn't moved together with perfect precision. If anyone had been watching, their tryst wouldn't have looked practiced or graceful. And so much better for it. Courtenay was flushed, breathing slowly through parted lips, and Jorian's eyes were glazed as he absently toyed with the fine hair above N'hahseen's groin. Their fluids mingled on N'hahseen's chin and cheeks, and the smell of the three of them filled the room.

"I was afraid of doing this," N'hahseen admitted.

"Why?" Courtenay stroked along his jawline, his stubble catching against her fingers.

"I worried I wouldn't satisfy you. I've never been expected to do so before, but… but I wanted to."

"Wanting to goes a long way. I'm satisfied," she sighed out.

"Me too," Jorian said, kissing N'hahseen's cheek. "And tired. And hungry! Do you think we might find something to eat?"

"I'll go." N'hahseen sat up and raked his fingers through his hair before reaching for his trousers. Never once had he needed to find his own meal, but he found he liked doing things for others. He craved the satisfied smiles he'd see if he returned with a tray of food, and so he dressed and left the room.

Being alone on the beach allowed him to gather his thoughts and consider the implications of what had happened. Not the sex—he did that all the time—but his reaction to….

It was odd to even let the word form in his head. He stopped at the edge of the water and curled his toes around the small stones and bits of broken shells.

Serving. He'd enjoyed serving far more than he'd ever enjoyed being fawned over by his kahlka. Being there on his knees between their legs, working for their pleasure, had made him feel… real. What would his mother say? He tapped his forehead. She would berate him. Fane, she'd be delighted to have an excuse to tear him to shreds for being weak, for lowering himself, for behaving like a slave. She'd say he had no self-respect, that he was a disgrace to Fane's memory and blood.

Except she wouldn't. She was dead, and he only regretted she would never get to see Kahladryia firmly in his hands.

Feeling light, he moved toward a small fire in the distance. His contentment lasted until he saw the dozen or so people around that fire.

The slaves.

N'hahseen retreated a few steps, but it was too late. They'd seen him. Their large, strange eyes reflected the flames, all pointed in his direction. He tensed, waiting to see if they would attack him or let him apologize and go on his way. Would Yarrow's tolerance of his presence extend to them? He never imagined he'd be afraid of a group of slaves, that he'd find himself needing to explain his presence, but many things had changed since he'd left his crystal palace.

"I'm sorry for intruding," he said, holding his arms out to his sides. "I did not mean to intrude."

"What are you doing out here all by yourself?" asked an Emiri man with long orange hair. His tone was suspicious, but it lacked the threat N'hahseen anticipated.

"I was…. My companions, Courtenay and Jorian, were hungry. I should go. Check the kitchen, I suppose."

An Emiri woman canted her head at him. "You? *You* were fetching morsels for the Esperon mages?"

"Yes? I am not lying."

"I did not say you were," she answered.

For what felt like forever, they all stared at him. When he couldn't stand it, he broke the silence. "I'll go."

"Wait," said the redheaded man.

N'hahseen flinched.

The Emiri pointed to an iron pot. "Go on, then."

"T-take some?" He expected them to at least make him beg, humiliate him by making him admit he needed charity from slaves.

The Emiri just laughed. "You did say you were hungry."

"Yes." N'hahseen smiled. "Yes… thank you." He scooped some of the shellfish from the pot into a ceramic, fish-shaped platter someone handed him.

Back in his room, the three of them had to eat with their fingers, plucking up the shiny black shells and sucking the meat from between them. The broth was delicious, and even better when lapped up from Courtenay or Jorian's lips or fingers. They giggled and poked each other's ribs, teasing each other when the juice ran down their chins and dripped onto their chests. That led to more licking and kissing, and it took them a long time before they set the dish aside.

"Did you know there are creatures in the desert?" Jorian lay on his side, his head tucked under N'hahseen's arm and his cheek on N'hahseen's chest. His short hair was thick with perspiration and a film of salt. When N'hahseen carded his fingers through it, it stood straight up.

"Course I did. I've been hunting." In protected little parks, where the animals were drugged and docile and he was never in any danger, but N'hahseen left that off.

"No. Not beasts. They're like men, but bigger. They have magic, and they have wings made of light, and horns. Like…."

"Like Yarrow does sometimes," Courtenay said.

Jorian nodded against N'hahseen's chest. "I hadn't considered that, but yes. I met one of them. The Arbek nomads said I had to get his permission before leaving. He told me he was a descendant of a race of beings who lived long before Fane. He said the world was out of balance and that I had to find the solution. That was why he let me live."

N'hahseen stretched out one of Courtenay's curls, released it, and watched it spring back into shape. "I feel it. I felt it very strongly when I came to the west—magic clogged up, muddy and thick when it should be clear and flowing fast. I thought…."

"You thought it was because so many of us unworthy mages are taking more than our share," Courtenay said.

"I admit it. But I've reconsidered. There's more going on, and Yarrow knows what it is."

"Yes," Jorian said. "It's something to do with the goddesses. Ph— he killed one of them. Killed a goddess. How is that even possible?"

N'hahseen watched the shadows flitting across the ceiling. His philosophy hadn't accounted for goddesses any more than it had accounted for the creatures Jorian had described, but something told him they were connected and that Yarrow stood at the center. "We need more information. We need to persuade Yarrow to tell us what he knows."

"Good luck." Courtenay snorted. "He despises you and all of your people."

N'hahseen caught her hand and kissed the back. "But not you. He respects the Esperons. If you learn anything, will you share it with me?"

She stiffened and remained silent.

N'hahseen sighed. So some mutual pleasure hadn't made them allies. What had he expected? Sex had only ever been a pastime for him. Why should this be different? Suddenly the shellfish didn't agree with him, and he grimaced at the sour taste in the back of his throat. Jorian, half-asleep and absently tracing the markings on N'hahseen's chest, wouldn't tell him either. Their loyalties lay elsewhere.

So did his: with Fane, Kahladryia, and the world's magic. He needed to remember that.

Courtenay shifted and sat up. "I should go back to my room."

"Stay."

"Why?"

"Does there have to be a reason?"

She stretched out with her back to him, and N'hahseen pulled a blanket over her hips. Soon her deep and even breathing told him she'd fallen asleep.

He'd never slept in bed with another person. He supposed he could have requested it, but he'd never wanted to. Now, he tried to enjoy it, to feel the comfort of physical closeness even if barriers still existed between all of their minds. But he remained awake, trying to put together a puzzle when he was missing half the pieces.

Chapter Twenty-Four

THERE ARE people here to protect. Duncan looked out at the mist blanketing the islands and refracting the light into a soft, blue-gray glow. In the wake of discovering almost everything he ever believed had been a lie, he needed something to hold on to, something he could get behind without a stirring of doubt, and in the storm of confusion, he'd found a single, solid thing. *There are people here who only want to live their lives. They don't want to die, and I can keep some of them alive. I can fight for those who cannot fight for themselves.*

If he focused on that and ignored the rest, it was almost bearable. Fight. Kill enemies. It had never been what he'd wanted, but he was good at it, and he didn't have much left.

The king had been busy in the week it had taken Sasha to organize his excursion to Johmatra. Garith had stripped Duncan's title, annulled his marriage, and sold Arauna off to some Defender. His assault on Rosecairn had been a disaster, and he'd backed off, moving his forces south along the river. Consolidating them. Preparing to move against the Twenty-Nine. Duncan tried to be generous, tried to believe Garith thought he was doing the right thing. After all, Duncan had once thought the same thing.

"Many of your soldiers deserted when Garith reclaimed Windwake." Sasha appeared perched on a rock. Duncan hadn't seen or heard him approach through the thick fog, but it didn't startle him anymore. "I sent some of my people to see that they get out of the bairny safely and without detection. They'll be brought here, if they wish, or snuck into Rosecairn to help Octavian's people."

"Thank you, Sasha."

"Do you want your son brought here?"

Duncan closed his eyes. Though raw, they held no more tears to spill. "No. There's nothing for him. I can offer him nothing."

"Well, I have people in the castle. Your wife's new husband won't be able to get him out of the way."

"Thank you. I know this is not your fight. Yours or your people's."

"Your fight is my fight."

"And Yarrow's? Is Yarrow's quest to tear the world in half and stitch it back together into something he thinks more pleasing yours as well?"

Sasha's silence was unusual, as was the confusion on his face when Duncan turned toward him. "Yarrow was right about the goddesses."

"But?"

"I love him." Sasha shook his head. "I almost wish I didn't, but it's here." He pressed his clenched fist against his belly. "Twisted up in my flesh and my bones. I couldn't excise it without tearing myself into ribbons."

Sasha's uncertainty was possibly the most frightening thing Duncan had ever witnessed. He felt so nauseated he had to sit down. "Why would you excise it? Sasha?"

Their eyes met. Sasha's were dark voids that sucked in the light but reflected none of it back. Duncan had never gotten used to it, but he could still see the man behind them. He had to believe he could. And right now, he could see Sasha wrestling with something—and Sasha didn't wrestle with things. He snuck up on them and killed them while they slept. "It's not my purpose to save the world. It never has been. I'm called to serve Thalil, and he cannot order me to harm either of you."

Duncan didn't know what to say. Once, he would've reminded Sasha of the good he'd done, but now, he wondered if any of it had mattered. "If you want me to reassure you, I don't know if I can. I don't know what's right anymore. All I know is I will try to save people where I am able."

"And what would you sacrifice to save them?"

"What do I have left?"

"Yarrow. Me. How many people would you trade—"

"Stop. There's no sense in this talk."

"I suppose not. That eases my mind, actually. If there's no point, then I can be selfish. It comes easily to me."

"Stop."

"You misunderstand. I don't say it in the hopes that you'll convince me that it isn't true. I can look on the world without that gauze over my eyes. I have no responsibility to anyone but you, Yarrow, myself, and Thalil."

"If there are no goddesses, then I suppose there's no reward for righteousness anyway," Duncan said.

"Do you believe that?"

"No."

"Good." Sasha smiled. "The world will need people like you when this is over. If there's anything left."

"You're more likely to outlast this than I am."

Sasha arched a brow. "You're in remarkably good health."

Yarrow arrived, preventing Duncan from voicing the suspicions he'd been ignoring for… years now. Dew beaded on his white hair, and his eyes were bright in the gloom. Now, they glowed almost all the time and not just when he was excited or working magic. His wings hadn't formed, but the mist parted where they would've been. He held something wrapped in printed cloth against his chest. Without a word, he sat down in the sand and unwrapped it.

Duncan gasped. The goddess's breastplate. It was a simple thing, unadorned, though Duncan didn't recognize the metal it was made from. Something striped with shifting bands of color like the inside of a seashell.

Yarrow ran his fingers along the dip at the neck. "I tried to destroy it. I tried everything I knew. Then I sat with it. I didn't study it, not really. I don't know how to study things the way they do in Espero. There's a method to that that doesn't make much sense to me. But I did think about it. After a while, I heard it. Echoes, anyway. Like a song I recognized, but I couldn't remember where I heard it. But then I did remember… the… the other part of me remembered.

"It's his magic. My…. Fane's. He made it, not Myint. He made it for her." Yarrow looked up. "I want you to wear it, Duncan."

"I don't want it." Duncan spoke without thinking. "Throw it in the sea."

"I can't," Yarrow said. "It's too powerful. I can't risk anyone else getting it or using it. I have to give it to the only person I can think of who won't use it for his own gain… use it to hurt people or gather strength…. You have to take it."

"It's just a piece of armor." Duncan watched the little prisms the breastplate threw off where the sun hit its edges. "Even if you give it to me, there's no guarantee I won't lose it. I'll have to take it off sometimes."

"I know," Yarrow said. "I thought about that, and I listened. I can do a spell, the same spell Fane did when he gave it to her. I can tie it to you, and no one else will be able to use it while you're alive. You… you'd be guarding it, really. Keeping it from our enemies."

"And what else will it do?" Sasha asked.

After a tense silence, Duncan prompted, "Yarrow?"

Yarrow shook his head. "I don't know all of it. The magic is very complex, and it changes. It draws in ambient arcane energy—that's the term D'Aurelian used—and adapts it to the situation. If you're struck, it forms a shield. If there's fire, it can douse it. If you fall, it will cushion it. It has… almost an awareness."

"I don't like this." Duncan still didn't trust the sources of Yarrow's information. Then Sasha's words returned to him. *What would you sacrifice?* "Can't you give it to Sasha?"

"No."

"Why?"

Sasha answered. "Isn't it obvious? I'm not good. I would use it to my advantage."

"You also do not need it," Yarrow said.

"And I do?" Duncan asked. "Why?"

"To… to protect people. You have to live! I—people need someone like you, someone to give them hope that people are moved to be decent without the chance of reward or threat of punishment."

"And how will it help me live? Beyond what you've already said?"

Yarrow spoke quickly, eyes on the ground and fingers clawing patterns into the sand. "It pulls in magic—that ambient stuff D'Aurelian talked about—and it… it uses it to renew muscle and skin, bones. It makes them regenerate constantly, keeping them young. You young."

"I don't want to be immortal," Duncan said.

Yarrow's eyes widened until he looked completely deranged. "I need you to! I need to know you'll be with me, that you won't be taken away like everyone else. I can't keep losing and losing and losing. It's going to drive me mad. I… I could be terrible. I feel it behind my eyes, itching under my skin like it wants to break out. The desire to tear things down. Just for no reason. Sometimes the only reason I stop is because I don't want you to stop loving me, to be disappointed. I need you to help me hold it in. I can't…. Just… just please."

"I don't want to be immortal," Duncan repeated dumbly. He was already so tired, feeling like a piece of metal hammered too thin, brittle from too many reheatings.

"Would you rather someone else is?" Sasha asked. "One of the Defenders? *Baska*, one of the priestesses? Someone worse?"

"Give me a moment." Duncan stood. Sand and sea grass clung to his trousers, but he didn't bother brushing them off as he walked to the edge of the water and let the tides soak his boots to the ankles. He looked up at the sky, striated with dark clouds and trimmings of diffuse light. He wanted to pray, to ask for advice, but no one would be listening. No one had ever been listening, and he had to decide for himself, and that was much, much harder. In the end, by doing this, he could stop people from being hurt. If he refused, he might have to watch others suffer because of his fear, and he didn't need a goddess to tell him that was wrong. He returned to Yarrow and Sasha, feeling tired to his core. "All right. Do the magic."

Pherara touched her belly. It might've been instinctive, might've been a calculated gesture to evoke vulnerability and elicit sympathy. Thalil wasn't sure.

"He did it," she said in a near whisper. "He killed Myint."

"Worse than killed," Thalil said. "You know exactly what happened to her."

"And now the others know as well. Word is spreading amongst the people, and it's breeding doubt in the goddesses. The temples cannot keep it quiet. The others are scared."

"What a delicious image." Thalil licked his lips as he imagined his father's wives cowering, huddled together. One thing he never grew tired of was watching his assassins appear to someone who thought he was untouchable, like a noble or a king. That moment of realization, the sudden knowledge that wealth and power could not save them, was the final act in a beautiful play for him. That delightful little twist that everyone else saw coming. It was like a sip of sweet wine after an especially fine meal. They usually resorted to bargaining, then begging. Would the goddesses do the same?

"But what does it mean for us?"

"It means we need to choose very carefully," he said. "We need to side with the victor. We have a great deal at stake, now." He draped his hand over hers.

She swatted him away. "Remember our bargain. This child is mine. Your role ended when your seed left your body."

He pouted. "You make it all sound so vulgar. It seemed to me that you enjoyed the time we shared."

Her eyes narrowed. "A means to an end, the same for me as it was for you. Your… performance was adequate, but I know you. You have never loved anyone but yourself. There's no need to pretend now. Tell me. Do you think Yarrow can prevail?"

"I'm liking his chances, but it might be time for us to help him along."

"Openly?" she asked. "I thought you didn't want the others to know."

"I don't want them to know my father has found a way around the spell to destroy him."

"Then you think the boy…?"

"I'm sure of it."

"But he is lost," Pherara said.

"Not lost," Thalil said. "Hidden. Safe, for now. I am about to deliver him into just the right hands." It had been a stroke of particular genius, that idea, and he could scarcely contain himself waiting to see how it would play out.

"And then what?"

"Then you must find a way to convince Yarrow to spare you when he culls the others."

"Me?" Her downy eyebrows lifted. "Why not you?"

Thalil looked at Sasha, who watched over Yarrow's shoulder as the mage executed his complex spell amid a funnel cloud of blue and silver sparks. "He not only owes me, he needs me. I hold something precious to him in my hands, and he knows I can snatch it away."

"And he is who we want in charge of the world?" Pherara asked. "You said yourself he's mad."

"He doesn't want power," Thalil said. "He hates the thought of telling others what to do almost as much as he hates them trying to tell him what to do."

"So the champion of the people is a man who hates the people and thinks they are savage, stupid sheep."

Thalil tipped his head and looked up at her through his eyelashes. "An accurate assessment."

"Then… what? Why do all of this?"

"Honestly? Part of it is vengeance, I'm sure," Thalil said. "But I think Yarrow just hates rules. He hates authority and people who feel entitled to wield it. He wants to remind them they can be knocked down, that the order they've so meticulously built is all an illusion. Maybe he thinks even savage, stupid sheep should be allowed to see beyond the borders of their pens."

"Illusion can be useful," Pherara said.

"Perhaps, but they've all been torn away from his eyes. Burned off. And there's the truth. If I had to guess, I would say he finds it terrifying and beautiful, a sharp blade in the moonlight. He thinks if he can bear it, then others should as well. He thinks it's weakness to hide behind comforting lies."

Pherara walked to the edge of the sea and lifted her hand to summon a refreshing wind. It made her hair and the gauzy layers of her gown flutter out behind her. "I have watched people for a long time. I fear that, even if he tears down all their illusions, they will build up new ones in time. I don't know if most of them can stand staring into that naked flame without a screen to dull it."

Thalil canted his head as something in the spume caught his eye. He knelt and picked up a fascinating piece of reddish sea glass. "It will be interesting, that's for sure. It'll probably be the most fun we've had in a few thousand years. And I intend to have enough life and power to watch every moment of it."

Chapter Twenty-Five

Sasha wrapped a length of dark cloth around his head to hide his hair, and twisted the end around the lower half of his face. He covered his bloodred-and-black leather armor beneath a long cloak. In the cold of the Kahladryian desert, neither would attract attention. He checked his weapons and equipment, and then he put a foot on the railing surrounding his second-floor balcony.

Finding lodging for the two dozen Crimson Scythe assassins and the others who'd come on this mission had presented a unique difficulty. The city-state lay far enough inland that travelers and traders were uncommon. A large group of them seeking a place to stay for an extended period would've raised suspicions, and so Sasha was forced to split them up, devise separate cover stories and the evidence to support them, and scatter his people throughout the city and the towns surrounding it.

"Where are you going?"

Sasha turned to Octavian. The two of them, along with D'Aurelian and a few agents, were hiding out in a brothel. Upon arriving, Sasha had killed the owner and struck a bargain with the whores: keep quiet and keep business going, and they got to keep all the coin they earned, instead of giving half to the whoremaster. When they left, they would leave the whores ownership of the establishment. With Jorian's help, he had even drawn up documentation so everything would appear legal— along with the timely discovery of the whoremaster's corpse and a teary letter detailing how he'd fallen in love with a married noblewoman before taking his own life. In days, they'd grown so popular many of the whores were offering their services free of charge.

"I'm going to observe the palace," Sasha said. "I've discovered five ways we can enter undetected, and I've memorized the guard rotation and the locations of the barracks."

Octavian leaned a shoulder against the jamb of the door leading in to their quarters and crossed his ankles. "That sounds like excellent progress. What's the problem?"

"This is more than a murder," Sasha said. "We need to take the palace, yes, but it won't mean anything if we don't win the loyalty of the guards there and throughout the city. The conundrum here is to murder their divinely chosen sovereign and make them think we've done them a favor."

Octavian rubbed the fingertips of his right hand against his thumb, almost like he was writing. Sasha had noticed he did it when he was thinking. "What we need is a show. We need to set it up so N'hahseen heroically kills his stepfather, and we need to make sure it happens in front of as many people as we can manage. He needs to be portrayed as a savior rather than a conqueror."

"You're very sharp," Sasha said with a small bow of his head. "I'm glad I let you live all those years ago."

Octavian smiled and returned Sasha's bow. He had been beautiful at eighteen, all long limbs, creamy beige skin, big eyes and lips that showed his every emotion through their twists and dips. The face of the man regarding Sasha now was guarded, eyes calculating, skin lined and scarred. Silver sparkled among his glossy brown hair, but he was still very appealing. Maybe even more so. "I'm glad you let me live too. Sometimes I even wonder what might've happened if I had come with you, how things might've been different."

Sasha had thought about it once or twice since meeting Octavian again. "When we met the first time, the past and the future held no value for me. Neither did other people. Lately, though… it's an interesting diversion to imagine various scenarios."

"Old age leads to reflection. I've found regret, as useless as it is, creeps in like the ache in my joints when the weather is on the change. Not that you are probably troubled by such things."

"Which of the two are you referring to?"

Octavian pushed off the doorjamb and stepped close to Sasha, his eyes searching Sasha's face—probably trying to dissect and identify the magic working in Sasha. "You look exactly the same as you did when I first saw you. Everything except for your eyes."

For a few quiet moments, they stood looking at each other, the cool, quiet air swelling with old tensions. Octavian cleared his throat into his fist. "I suppose I should let you get on with it."

"Why don't you come with me?"

"Why?"

"I could use the skills of a mage. Parts of the palace are warded, inaccessible to me. I believe they include the lord's chambers."

"Wouldn't you rather take Yarrow?"

"Yarrow is not cut out for this type of work. His convictions are too strong."

Octavian pushed his lip out, feigning a frown. "You choose me for my lack of conviction, then? I'm not sure if I should be flattered."

"I choose you because you understand that sometimes the best way to realize your goals is to smile at your enemy so he doesn't see the dagger in your hand. You know that just because you believe something, you don't have to shout it to the heavens. Do you not want to go?"

"I love D'Aurelian," Octavian said. "But you will always have a special place in my memories. Over the years, I thought I'd idealized you—you did me a great service after all—but now I find my recollections were rather accurate. You're impressive, and you tempt me."

The warmth on his face surprised Sasha. "I could allow myself to be tempted as well. But we are not the kind of men held prisoner to our emotions. Besides, we'll be busy. We'll hardly have time to stop off for a tryst while sneaking through the palace, unraveling magical wards, and eluding guards. We're not characters in a smutty little book from an Elvaran brothel."

Octavian chuckled. "I suppose that's true." He was already wearing simple, dark clothing—snug trousers and a shirt with a leather tunic over top—so when he covered his hair and face like Sasha, he blended nicely into the shadows. One after another, they leapt to the ground, their boots landing softly at the back of the brothel. Two of the whores sat on the stone stoop. One washed her feet in the basin by the pump, while the other raised the pipe he'd been smoking in greeting. Sasha acknowledged them with a nod.

It was late, but the brothels and drinking establishments in the area were still doing a brisk business, and Sasha and Octavian easily mingled with the people on the streets. They didn't speak, both of them knowing their foreign tongue would incite curiosity.

When the streets emptied out and the sandstone houses, with their crystal windows and lacy golden screens, stood dark and quiet except for the cobalt glass lamps hanging from their eaves, Octavian leaned close and spoke softly. "Tell me what you've discovered so far."

"Most of the guards are new. The master of the city is paranoid, and so he dismissed everyone who he thought might've been loyal to his wife. That means an untrained force."

"And one without time to feel much devotion to him. He'll be unproven in their eyes."

Sasha nodded. "It's also to our advantage that none of them know each other well. I already have eight of my people posing as palace guards."

"I bet some of the men who were fired had been serving for years," Octavian mused. "Maybe for most of their lives. They'll feel slighted. We should reach out to them. I have a feeling they'll like the idea of assuming their former posts under a ruler who will appreciate them. We could send N'hahseen."

"N'hahseen. I understand he's a rather mythic figure to these people, some sort of an omen." Briefly, Sasha wondered how far he could trust Octavian. "I'd feel more comfortable if I had something on him. Something I could use to force his hand if he decides he doesn't need us any longer."

"I've been thinking the same thing," Octavian said. "Maybe we'll get lucky in the palace."

Sasha ignored the double entendre. "Your idea is a good one, though. We should find those soldiers and reach out to them. If they back N'hahseen, the greener recruits are likely to follow their lead.

"I'll have my people feel them out if possible. If most of them can be convinced to stand down while N'hahseen walks through the front gate with an army at his back, we'll have both the spectacle we need and an easy victory. This night has already yielded fruit."

Octavian shrugged. "I've always been good at this type of thing."

Sasha had seen much in life—even beyond it—but the crystal palace of Kahladryia warranted a few moments of appreciation. It dwarfed any fortress in Selindria or Gaeltheon, dozens of domes and minarets stretched over a hillside at the northern corner of the city.

Between the towering main buildings and the labyrinthine covered walkways connecting them lay gardens the size of farmer's fields, full of flowers and herbs that scented the night air. Some were small forests complete with ponds and streams. All of it looked made from the clearest glass held together by golden seams. Tonight, lit from the fires within, it glowed and sparkled like a beacon.

And that worked to their advantage. No one inside would see Sasha and Octavian flitting along the perimeter or vaulting over the inner wall. Crouching in a copse of trees while the patrol went by was easy enough, and Octavian followed Sasha's lead as if Sasha had trained him himself. Soon they reached a small grill, and Sasha picked its simple lock and flipped it open. Octavian didn't need to be told to follow him inside.

"The warded wing is this way." Sasha tilted his head, and they moved through the hallway and up a set of winding stairs. Another long corridor overlooking a waterfall and aquatic garden led to a large archway flanked with golden lizards three times the size of a person. The filigree doors beneath looked flimsy, woven from gold thread, but Octavian skidded to a halt and pressed a hand against his temple.

"The magic is strong and complex."

"Can you break through it?"

Octavian shook his head. "I could tear it down, but it would do a lot of damage. The force I would need to use isn't something I'm accustomed to controlling. This might surprise you, but I'm a better healer than anything."

"That actually doesn't surprise me," Sasha said. "But where does that leave us? If we destroy these wards, they'll know we're here and put up stronger ones. Is this something that can be erected and dissolved easily? I doubt the master of the house confines himself to his rooms."

"No." Octavian took a deep breath and pushed his shoulders back. Arms extended and palms flat, he approached the gates, stopping with about a foot of space between them and his hands. As he inched closer, veins of pale green light and a vegetal smell emanated from his hands. The slender spirals popped and crackled when they touched the magic surrounding the gates, and Sasha could see the ebb and flow of energy between them and Octavian, could see a chartreuse glow that made Octavian's bones and blood vessels stand out against it. Octavian scrunched his eyes shut. Deep lines marred his forehead, and the rose color drained from his lips. By the time he withdrew his hands, Octavian listed to the side and would have collapsed if Sasha hadn't caught him.

Sasha dragged him to a darkened corner to the left of the gates and helped him to sit down behind an enormous gilded pot full of some kind of cacti.

"Are we safe here?" Octavian rasped.

Sasha nodded. "I've never encountered many servants in this part of the palace, and even fewer guards. Were you able to learn anything?"

"It's… hard to explain. The magic is strong, but it lacks artistry. It's heavy-handed. The best way I can describe it is as some kind of a lock. It felt incomplete, like it was missing an element."

"The key," Sasha guessed.

"I think so. I bet it's something simple, maybe a few words, or… or an object. Something about it held the same vibrations as the crystal of the walls. Think…. Who would need access to these rooms? Someone has to bring food." Octavian clutched Sasha's arm. "Do you know the way to the kitchens?"

Sasha bowed his head. "There are fourteen of them."

"Damn. Well, let's try to remember. What has N'hahseen told us about his stepfather? He despises the man, says he's weak, unworthy of ruling Kahladryia. I guess it's not surprising that he isn't familiar with the man's favorite foods."

Sasha watched the way the firelight summoned strands of red and gold in the crystal walls, almost like the veins and arteries in a living being. "I bet he drinks. Mages always drink."

Octavian's laugh was dry and strained. "We do. It can enhance the magic or help us damper it down when we don't want it niggling…. How many wine cellars in the palace?"

"Three. One is close."

Grasping Sasha's shoulder, Octavian hauled himself to his feet. "Let's check. If nothing else, I'll make off with something to help me get to sleep later."

"The whores' wine not to your taste?"

Octavian gripped the gilded banister as he made his way down the staircase. "People don't go to whorehouses to drink. I have a friend who quit the mercenary life to live on a vineyard. The wine he sometimes sends me… I wonder if they will be all right, Breeze and Alain. If it comes to war."

"The best thing we can do is secure this alliance," Sasha said. "With power at our backs, we can force Garith to negotiate."

"Should I be surprised that you don't want war?"

"No," Sasha said. "War is too straightforward for me. Battles are too honorable. I don't like facing my enemies on even ground. I like to have all the advantages I can gather. Their not knowing I'm coming is not something I like to relinquish. Here. This door leads to the cellar."

They descended the steps into a dark space surrounded by brown stone walls instead of crystal. Casks stood in columns, and bottles rested in niches between them. Sasha heard scuffling behind him, and he remembered Octavian couldn't see in the dark. "Cast some light," he whispered.

The green glow made everything look two-dimensional and grainy, as if drawn by ink and a brush. Sasha blinked, trying to acclimate, as he crept carefully along the stone path between the barrels and racks. But it was too bright, erasing everything beyond the verdant bubble surrounding them, negating the nuances Sasha would have normally noticed in the shadows.

He never even saw movement before he felt the blade pressed to his throat.

The body behind him was small, but the posture expressed confidence and experience. He smelled charcoal and something that reminded him of the sea. As a test, he moved as if to break away. His captor pressed the knife against his neck, breaking the skin, and twisted an arm behind his back. A female voice hissed out something in Johmatran.

Sasha answered with one of the few phrases he knew in that language: "I don't understand."

"You do what here, shagiri?" Broken Selindrian with a touch of Emiri.

"I have come to kill the man who rules the city."

The pressure on his wrist loosened a little, and the blade stopped excavating the meat of his neck.

"You have mage." She was surprised but not afraid. "Not mage who enslaves."

"No," Octavian said. "I… I hate slavery. I fight for freedom. Please, can we speak? Talk?" He pointed to his lips.

The woman released Sasha, stepped into the light, and held her arms out to her sides. "Talk, mage and shagiri?"

Octavian was a quick study. He mimicked the Emiri woman's gesture, holding his arms out from his body. "Talk, please. You're a servant here?"

"Slave, but… not."

"Are you with the resistance?" Sasha asked. "Yu-me?"

Her fire-colored eyes narrowed. "Yu-me. You know?"

"I do," Sasha said. "I knew Sai Yu-me. I know Yarrow. Yarrow is my syrai."

"Syrai, then. Us." She pointed to herself and then back at them. "What is needed?"

"A way through the doors," Sasha said. "A way to get to the ruler of the city."

"Bring to him… shagiri?"

"Oh yes." Sasha indulged in a small smile.

She tapped her forehead. "Killed… slaves. Hundreds. Thought slaves would… would… betray."

"I'm sorry." Octavian's hair fell across his face when he lowered his head. "We will make him pay for it. We just need a way through those doors."

"Can help," she said. She reached beneath the ratty shift she wore and withdrew a crystal, wrapped with wire and suspended from a leather cord. "Get in." She pressed it into Sasha's hand. "Give to him shagiri."

"I promise," Sasha said.

"When?"

"Soon. Keep alert. Keep your eyes open. When it happens, keep your people safe. Find us after. We will take all of you back to the Twenty-Nine. As many as we can fit on our ships."

"Take my people. I stay," she said. "Stay until all… all have yu-me."

"We'll do what we can to help," Octavian said. "What… what are you called by your mother and her syrai?"

"Called Kori. You go now. Mages leave… a path behind."

"Yes, we will." Octavian clasped her hands. "Thank you. We won't waste this."

Kori pointed them to a door that led from the cellar to a small garden: succulents surrounded by piles of glossy stones. From there, they easily made their way beyond the palace walls and back to the city streets. Before long, the music and drunken voices of the pleasure district welcomed them.

"Can I see the pendant?" Octavian asked.

Sasha handed it over.

"I'll examine this, but I'm already confident it will get us past those gates. By the way, what does shagiri mean?"

"Death."

"That's what we're bringing, then?" Octavian asked.

"It's all I have to give," Sasha said.

Chapter Twenty-Six

Courtenay was proud of N'hahseen—not something she ever thought she'd feel when she'd first met him. Then, she'd never imagined being able to stand his presence. But he had impressed her when Sasha had suggested they seek out the soldiers his stepfather had dismissed. He'd accepted the danger of the mission without either cowardice or arrogance, and he'd listened to the advice of the others without letting the more opinionated among them—Yarrow—push him around.

They'd found the group of several hundred soldiers, led by an older man named Saleesh Abdarji, heading east in search of mercenary work. Many of the city guards had joined them, bolstering their numbers to almost a thousand. Most of them were milling about the tent city they'd erected along the road while N'hahseen spoke to their leader.

Courtenay sat outside her own small tent with Jorian. She poked the embers of their fire with a stick, stirring up sparks.

"Are you feeling better today?" Jorian asked.

She shrugged. "It's just anxiety, I'm sure. I always lose my appetite when I'm worried. The smell of roasting lizard doesn't help, though."

He chuckled. "I know. I was stuck eating it for years. The Emiri food was a nice change…. At least it was fresh."

She nodded as another wave of nausea hit her. What she really wanted was a roll Alain had made when she was growing up, the dough spongy and light, the filling made of nuts and raisins, and the whole thing smothered in butter and honey. She didn't really feel like talking about it, though, didn't feel much like talking at all. Jorian seemed to take the hint because he took out a small book and began writing in it with a quill. Courtenay wanted to retreat to her bedroll in the tent, but she knew she wouldn't be able to sleep until she heard news from N'hahseen. He'd been negotiating with Saleesh for three days, and she was getting impatient. Yarrow was like one of the Emiri boulders ready to explode. Only Sasha was keeping him from singlehandedly razing the palace to the ground—for now. Jorian, though quiet, at least made pleasant company. It was better than being alone.

Hours passed before N'hahseen appeared, escorted by six soldiers. With their armor and shaved heads, it was hard to tell if they were men or women, harder because Courtenay had been dozing on her side on her rug by the fire. She sat up and rubbed the sleep from her eyes as N'hahseen spoke to his guards in Johmatran.

"Thank you for your service."

"Do you need us to remain, First Son?" A woman. The suspicion on her face as she regarded Courtenay and Jorian was plain.

"I will be fine. It has been a long few days, and I would like to retire."

"We would be happy to remain and ensure your safety."

"No," he said more firmly. "You're dismissed."

When they departed, N'hahseen turned to Courtenay and motioned toward the entrance to their conical tent. The three of them went inside, and a wash of diluted gold light covered the floor as N'hahseen cast a ward so they wouldn't be overheard talking.

"I suppose there are advantages to being around people who have no understanding of magic." Courtenay waved her hand to light the lanterns, arranged some square cushions, and sat down. She was exhausted and feeling a little sick again. "That spell would never work in Espero. It would be like erecting a sign that said 'secret meeting going on.'" She realized too late how unnecessarily combative she was being, but she was irritable, hungry, and tired of sleeping on the ground.

"Do you have any news?" Jorian asked.

N'hahseen sat down and extended his arm. Jorian got underneath it and nestled against his side. "Saleesh will help us. It cost."

"Cost what?" Jorian asked.

"The usual," N'hahseen said. "Reinstatement of his position. A promotion. Jobs for his men. Property. Money, of course. But that was the easy part. I had to convince him we could win, that him and his people wouldn't be put to death as traitors alongside us. That would have been much simpler if Sasha and Octavian had shared their plans with me."

"But you did convince him," Courtenay said.

"Yes. He wishes to make plans. He wanted to do so tonight. It made me look like a weak fool to tell him I had to consult with a western criminal first, but I managed to persuade him to accept it."

Courtenay nodded, reached for the small pack she'd brought, and found the small mirror Octavian had spelled so they could communicate. As she drew the symbols on its surface, she relayed the information to Jorian and N'hahseen.

"Octavian says to have Saleesh send a messenger to your stepfather. The messenger should ask to arrange a meeting. He should tell them that you will arrive at the palace in three days, at dawn."

"That's the stupidest—"

Courtenay held up a hand to stop N'hahseen's impending tirade. "Sasha wants me to tell you he is aware your stepfather will lay a trap for you. He says it is taken care of."

"Taken care of how?" N'hahseen demanded.

"He… will not elaborate. We are to go to the palace's front gates in three days' time, accompanied by no more than a few dozen men. The rest of the soldiers should be stationed outside the walls."

N'hahseen snorted. "Tell that thug this: he knows nothing of my stepfather. The man will not even appear to meet with me. He'll hide in his chambers and send his people to kill all of us."

Courtenay relayed the message. "Sasha says he knows. He says he has taken care of it."

"Do you think we should trust him?" Jorian asked.

"Do we have any choice?" As silly as it was, Courtenay lowered her voice as if they could be overheard through the mirror.

"Yes!" N'hahseen had no qualms with shouting. "We do now. We have a thousand trained warriors. We could cut our ties with these… people."

"We made them a promise," Jorian said. "It wouldn't be honorable."

"At this point, my life and Kahladryia's future matter more," N'hahseen argued.

Courtenay shook her head. "Sasha says: You are likely debating on whether to proceed without us. You think that now that you have a small force, you no longer need our assistance. You are mistaken.

There are many things you do not know, and without us, you will fail. He wants to know if we wish to proceed. He—Pherara! That twisted son of a bitch!—he wants to remind us that Yarrow can always pursue an alliance with your stepfather. He also says that you need to not only win, but hold Kahladryia. For that you will need the alliance with Yarrow."

"We must make a decision, it seems," Jorian said.

"I don't trust Sasha," N'hahseen said. "There's a very dark magic working in him, and yet he is not a mage."

"We have to proceed with this plan." Courtenay knew they had no choice. "He's bluffing about an alliance with your stepfather. Yarrow would never agree, and I think Yarrow is one of very few things that mean anything at all to Sasha. If Yarrow wants us to prevail in this, I believe Sasha will see that it happens. I do not disagree with your needing help from them in the future, either. You are young, and those with their sights on your city might see you as an easy target."

"I… very well. Tell him we will be there. But in the meantime, we should be ready for betrayal and have plans in place to protect ourselves. Or…." N'hahseen looked at Jorian, then at Courtenay.

She knew what he had left unsaid as she sent the message. He needed to plan to protect himself in case they also had their own agenda. He couldn't trust them.

And he wasn't entirely wrong.

"There." Courtenay wrapped the mirror in one of her shirts and stuffed it back in her pack. She rubbed the cramps forming at the back of her neck.

"Are you all right?" N'hahseen asked. "You're pale. Your face looks a little swollen."

"I could use some water," she said. "Isn't there a stream nearby? Something cold and fresh would be nice. Something that doesn't taste stagnant from the canteens." Guilt poked at her for taking advantage of N'hahseen's desire to serve and please, something she'd discovered when he'd been at his most vulnerable, but she needed to talk to Jorian alone.

"Yes, of course." N'hahseen stood, found a ceramic pitcher, and bent to kiss her on the forehead. "When I come back, I'll see what I can do about your sore muscles. I learned more than a few tricks from my kahlka."

As soon as he left the tent, Courtenay leaned close to Jorian and whispered, "We need to get word to the council."

"I already have," he said. "I gave a message to an Emiri agent when we made port. The council will know not to make any deals with Garith. They'll know he might not be the strongest player after we're done here. They'll stall, bide their time if nothing else."

Courtenay stiffened. She'd underestimated the sweet, scholarly mage. "You didn't tell me."

"Should I have?"

"We're on the same side."

He met her gaze with narrowed eyes. "Everyone seems on his or her own side. I… that was unfair. I do trust you. My years here left me suspicious. I can't quite shake it off. I only hope we're doing the right thing. When we go to the palace, we'll be defenseless. N'hahseen has told the others we're ambassadors from Espero, but we can't reveal that we're mages. That will destroy his people's trust in him and likely forfeit our lives."

"We have to put our faith in the others."

"Right." Jorian rubbed his temples with his thumbs. "Put our faith in a ruthless assassin, a mercenary so calculating he managed to con a title out of the king, and Yarrow…. He's so mad I don't know if he even sees the same world as we do. I look at his eyes, and I cannot imagine what's going on behind them."

"Here." Courtenay moved behind Jorian and began kneading the back of his neck with her thumbs and fingers, working out the knots she found before moving up to rub the scalp beneath his short hair. She summoned her magic to heat her hands, and he sighed with relief as she placed them over his forehead and eyes. "We'll look out for each other. You watch my back and I'll watch yours."

"And N'hahseen?"

"N'hahseen. I thought he would be a monster. I don't think he is, but if it comes down to him and Espero…. Jorian, so many of our people have died because of the Johmatrans. I know you have a history with him…."

"If you're asking if I like coupling with him so much I would betray my homeland, the answer is no."

"I didn't mean—"

He reached up and stroked the back of her hand. "I don't blame you for asking. The man I was, before all of this happened…. I was there when the Johmatrans attacked the university at Pala Reapaza. I was working in the library. I-I was so scared I pissed myself. Do you know what I did?"

Courtenay curled around him and laid her cheek against the top of his head, wishing she could use her magic to rid him of this pain as easily as she could cure his headache. "No."

"I ran and hid in a secret room where we kept rare books, spelled the door, and hid. I stayed there for probably a day and a half. I just didn't want to die, but when I finally came out, I realized there are worse things.

"Almost everyone I'd ever known—teachers, students, friends, even the servants who dusted the shelves—were dead. Heads cut off, bodies bloated and stuck to the ground with their own blood. The smell. I'll never forget it. I can still taste the death on the air. That was when I swore to myself I would never be a coward again. I would do anything in my power to make sure nothing like that ever happened again. Seeing that… it made me strong. I kept it in my mind while I posed as N'hahseen's servant. It forced me to face every new day, but…."

"But you couldn't hate him."

"He's spoiled and deluded, but he isn't cruel. It's hard to stand against everything you've been taught to believe. His rule could benefit Espero. But if it doesn't…. If it doesn't, Espero comes first. I swear it."

She shushed him as she continued massaging his head and face, and he leaned back against her, succumbing to the sedative spell she wove. "I believe you. I don't like going in blind, but at this point, all we can do is hope for the best. I'll look out for you as best I can, and I know you'll look out for me."

THE PALACE guards readily opened the front gates, and Courtenay marched into the courtyard beside N'hahseen and Jorian. There was a huge fountain at the center—Fane, she assumed—of a man holding a boulder-sized sphere above his head. Water cascaded over it, catching the pink light of the sunrise. Beyond the statue, two wide staircases wound up to a platform. On either side, soldiers and archers lined the walls. Despite the three dozen warriors behind them, Courtenay, N'hahseen, and Jorian would be helpless when they stepped into that space.

But N'hahseen pranced forward anyway. He'd prepared for the occasion and decked himself out in the finery worthy of the god his people considered him: a sleeveless black vest that trailed behind him over a snug golden shirt and trousers, pauldrons that resembled gilded wings with red gems dangling from the feathers, square-heeled red boots that reached his knees, with more gold panels at the shins, a single glove made from orange-and-black lizard skin, chains curving over his opposite shoulder. Jorian had braided his hair along the crown of his head and teased it into spikes at the back, then dusted them with metallic powder. A circlet, adorned with spikes and gems, covered his forehead, intricate beading hanging in front of his ears. They'd lined his eyes with red and black, stained his lips ebony, and tinted his cheekbones with golden powder. Jewelry covered his wrists and the shells of his ears, a ruby the size of an apple hanging from his neck. Courtenay couldn't believe he'd brought all of it to Gaeltheon, and then on the sea voyage back here, but she had to admit he commanded everyone's attention as he strode to the foot of the stairs. He reflected the light like the precious jewel his people thought he was.

"Bring out the usurper." N'hahseen's clear voice carried across the courtyard. "Let him face me, the rightful ruler of Kahladryia, unless he is a liar and a coward."

In the eerie quiet that followed, Courtenay heard the creak of bowstrings pulled taut. She saw spears hoisted, the points aimed at them. It took all her concentration to wrestle down the magic that rose to defend her. If she showed herself as a mage, N'hahseen's claim on the city-state would be sacrificed. But she wouldn't die here. She wouldn't let Jorian, who stood clutching his hooded cloak at the chest, perish in what they had known was a trap. Not after all he had relinquished for his duty to Espero and his people. Flames danced under her skin as she prepared to conjure a shield that would incinerate anything aimed their way.

Before she could complete the spell, some of the guards turned on the others, slitting their throats from behind, each of them eliminating three or more loyal soldiers before the rest could react. Bodies fell from the walls, raising clouds of dust when they hit the ground. Blood branched out over the sand, glossy under the brightening light. The remaining guards lowered their weapons.

Everyone waited. The grunts of the guards behind Courtenay, the chink of their weapons against their armor, resounded in the silence. She was vaguely aware of the city's people gathering outside the palace's gates to watch the spectacle.

N'hahseen stood a dozen feet in front of her, his chin held high and his hands open to the sky. "I am waiting. I will not be patient much longer."

A set of double doors on the balcony overlooking the courtyard burst open. Sasha and Octavian stepped through, hauling a twisted little man by his bony, misshapen arms. Yarrow and D'Aurelian stood behind them.

"If you want Kahladryia, then face her rightful ruler," Octavian said. "The son of the woman you murdered. The one who is so clearly descended from Fane in both appearance and power."

The murmurs of the people behind the gate rose as Sasha and Octavian tossed N'hahseen's stepfather down on his chest. His deformed, stubby legs didn't seem capable of helping him to stand, so he dragged himself forward until he could use the railing to pull himself up. "Guards! Kill these invaders."

None of the soldiers responded.

N'hahseen gestured to the man clinging to the banister. "Look at him, and then look at me. Which one of us do you suppose Fane intended to rule this beautiful city? I have returned to ensure prosperity for my people and gratitude for the brave men and women who defend them. Kahladryia is mine by the right of Fane's blood! Does anyone dispute this? Can anyone here claim my words do not ring true?"

The crowd at the gate cheered, and people banged their fists against the gold filigree. Courtenay allowed herself to relax a little, the flames of her magic dying down to embers.

Wisam turned to his guards. "I will give all of you one last chance. Those who stand next to me will be rewarded, while those who do nothing will suffer every torment I can imagine. As many of you know, my imagination is a very fertile place."

"I won't make threats," N'hahseen countered. "I do not need to. I trust my people to see what is right and follow the will of Fane. May he return and bless us all." He gestured to his stepfather. "Apprehend the traitor."

Sasha, Yarrow, Octavian, and D'Aurelian stood aside. This needed to be finished by Kahladryians, without foreign interference. The guards on either side of them moved forward to carry out their First Son's orders.

Just before they could seize his arms, Wisam made a motion with his hand, and a jaundiced light burst around him. Surrounded by an egg of power with wormy green coils crackling over the surface, he floated over the balcony's railing and down into the courtyard, where he hovered above N'hahseen.

They would face each other after all. Courtenay's fists clenched around the fabric of her trousers. She hadn't witnessed much of N'hahseen's magic, and she knew too well that knowledge and study did not always translate to prowess in battle.

One of the archers fired on Wisam, but the arrow bounced off his shell and fell to the ground, where it rapidly rotted into olive-colored ooze. A force like a storm struck Courtenay's magical perception, barely controlled power swirling and building, carrying a scent of ice and ozone and ready to level everything for miles. She looked up at Yarrow, and so did N'hahseen.

They coordinated their attack. Though Yarrow neither moved nor spoke, a fine bluish mist surrounded Wisam's egg. Frost sparkled across its surface, weighing it down and dragging it toward the ground. As Wisam fought against the enchantment, using his fetid magic to melt through the encasement, N'hahseen struck. He raised his hand, holding a shaft of blinding golden light, and threw it like a spear at his stepfather. Brittle, Wisam's shield cracked up the center. Pieces of it fell on the sand and decayed into stinking puddles.

Courtenay could feel Yarrow's impatience—or rather, his magic's. It wanted to grab Wisam in a sapphire claw and pop him like an insect, but Sasha held an arm across Yarrow's chest, calming him. For now.

N'hahseen didn't need his help. Spheres like sunlight orbited his outstretched arm, and one by one, he hurled them at Wisam. Between trying to block them and working to repair his barrier, the other mage was rapidly running out of energy. His egg's shell grew thinner and thinner, peeling away like sunburned skin to rot on the ground.

"We can end this now," N'hahseen said. "Fane's will has clearly been demonstrated. Stand down."

Wisam laughed even as his power sputtered like a fire running out of fuel. "I don't think so, my beautiful boy. You think you are so special, so pretty and so powerful. You think everyone loves you so much. But they don't. Even your own mother feared and despised you. In fact, she made sure you'd be kept under control."

Wisam chanted in a flat tone, saying words so old Courtenay would have to look them up to understand his spell. All she knew was that they were negative—words of undoing with sharp edges like a serpent's teeth. And just as venomous. Hearing them, feeling them echo inside her, made her fight to keep from emptying her stomach.

N'hahseen glowed, and a wave of dry heat swept out from him. At first Courtenay assumed the magic was his, but then he started to scream. His markings flared, burning through his clothing and armor until it fell away, smoking, leaving him bare above the waist. Light spilled from the mystical patterns carved into N'hahseen's flesh. He fell to his knees and pressed his hands to them, his voice failing as he cried out in agony.

If she squinted, Courtenay could see what was happening. Somehow, Wisam was manipulating the markings, triggering something in them to rip the magic out of N'hahseen. Flickering golden trails flowed to Wisam, feeding his own spell—and tearing N'hahseen apart on their way out.

Within a few heartbeats, several things happened. Sasha yelled, "Enough," climbed atop the balcony railing, leapt down, and landed atop Wisam's barrier with a dagger drawn. Unlike the arrow, his blade penetrated the shell, leaving a charred, black cut Wisam couldn't seem to seal. Instead, his infected magic pulsed, throwing Sasha off and sending him skidding across the sand on his back.

Yarrow screamed, "Sasha!" and jumped from the parapets, his luminous wings springing from his back to slow his descent. As he ran toward his friend, Wisam spread his palms, pulling the two decorations on N'hahseen's chest away from each other, slowly ripping N'hahseen in half.

Courtenay knew she had to act. She summoned her power and stepped forward, but Jorian raced around her and lifted his arms with a cry of pure pain and outrage. The ground rumbled and shook. A spear of crystal broke through the sand, wobbling and wavering as if molten. It rose beneath Wisam and then surrounded him, sheathing him in clear stone. He twisted and struggled for a brief moment, and then he went rigid, still surrounded in his greenish egg. Even the spell was frozen in place. Courtenay had never seen magic like it—time stilled with the crystal encasement. The whole thing looked like a pillar with a green eye suspended near the top. At the center, Wisam would be perfectly preserved in a fetal position, a look of surprise on his twisted lips. Horrified, Courtenay realized he wasn't dead—wasn't even unconscious—just frozen in the moment he was sure would mark his triumph.

Jorian slid to a halt at N'hahseen's side and dropped to his knees, his hands shaking hard as he moved them back and forth over N'hahseen's chest, an inch from his skin but not touching. Courtenay ran to join him. N'hahseen's markings bled bright and freely, probably as they'd done when they'd first been cut into him. His skin had split above his sternum, but the wound wasn't deep. Jorian had been too quick for it to do much damage.

N'hahseen coughed and his eyes fluttered open. "Do not… don't heal me. You… cannot be seen using magic."

"Fuck that," Jorian said, continuing his ministrations.

Courtenay looked up at the macabre monument that would mark this battle. "I am afraid the damage is done." She shook her head. "Pherara, Jorian. Later I want to talk about how you managed to accomplish that."

"Later, I might even figure it out myself." Jorian draped a hand over N'hahseen's forehead. "There. That should be enough to get you back on your feet. If I'm not mistaken, there are hundreds of people here who will be expecting you to say something. I… I cannot stand beside you while you do, but…." Jorian brushed off the circlet N'hahseen was wearing, reached beneath his cloak, took out a delicate headdress with a black stone at the center, and placed it on his head.

N'hahseen reached up and touched it. "You kept this?"

With a shy smile, Jorian rubbed the back of his neck. "Not sure why. I could've traded it away loads of times."

Together, Courtenay and Jorian helped N'hahseen to stand, and when he was steady, they moved away from him. Smeared with blood, his fancy clothes hanging in tatters, he somehow looked even more regal. Though banked, his power was palpable, and his steps were steady as he walked to the stairs and ascended them to the balcony. When he placed his hands on the railing, his head just rose above the pinnacle of the spire Jorian had conjured. His voice was as clear as the crystal.

"Fane's will has been carried out here today. I. Am. Kahladryia!"

In the few moments of silence that followed, Courtenay wondered if N'hahseen's people would turn on him because of the magic Jorian had used. But Saleesh stepped forward and banged his weapon against his shield. The dozens of soldiers standing in two straight lines behind him followed his example. "For Kahladryia and Fane!"

"Kahladryia and Fane!" the soldiers echoed.

"Kahladryia and Fane!" The people outside the gates clapped, stamped, and shouted.

Since she could do it without anyone's notice, Courtenay pried the cloud cover apart a bit so a shaft of light fell directly on N'hahseen. Then she turned to Jorian as some of the palace guards encircled him. "We'll have to take this heathen mage into custody," one of them said.

Courtenay shouldered through them to stand in front of Jorian. "This man is an ambassador of Espero and a valued ally of the First Son. N'hahseen would not want him violated. And I will not stand for it."

The soldiers looked surprised at hearing their language from her tongue, and many of them looked dubious, but they stepped back. Courtenay hurried to take Jorian's hand and lead him toward the steps. The safest place for them was with N'hahseen and the others. Yarrow and Sasha followed them up the stairs, Sasha moving as he always did— like ink sliding down clean paper—with no indication that he'd been injured in his fall.

Saleesh and some of his soldiers joined them on the balcony. "We'll secure the palace, First Son," the big man said.

"Thank you, Guard Captain," N'hahseen answered with a dip of his head.

A shiver moved up Courtenay's spine as Corbin appeared from behind a pillar. She hadn't noticed him during the battle. "Some of the palace soldiers disappeared as soon as the fighting started," Corbin said. "We wouldn't want them to have the opportunity to regroup and trouble us at a later time."

"We wouldn't," Sasha agreed. "Go. Have fun, but be mindful of eyes on you if you use your skills."

With a somewhat mocking bow to Sasha, Corbin vaulted over the edge of the railing.

The rest of them went inside. A staircase led down to a long hall with a lily-dotted pool in the center. Courtenay didn't realize how exhausted she was, how tense, until she sunk down onto an upholstered bench. "I suppose we were victorious."

N'hahseen smiled. "There will be fallback from what happened, but we'll handle it."

"I caused trouble for you," Jorian said. "I'm sorry."

N'hahseen reached out his hand. Jorian took it and sat down on the bench where N'hahseen reclined on his side, next to his belly. N'hahseen stroked his knuckles down Jorian's face. "You… you acted to my benefit with no thought of your own safety or future. What more could I ask or expect? I… was not aware I… that Kahladryia's fate meant so much to you."

"I wasn't aware either," Jorian said, his voice rough. "My magic knew what was important."

"The magic always knows." Courtenay hadn't meant to say it out loud, and her cheeks warmed. Still, she trusted her revelation. "I wonder if—when—we heal the world's magic, will we be able to understand each other better? When mages are together, it's… intimate. If everyone has some magic running through them, won't it be harder to hate? Harder to kill someone whose experiences you can feel as your own?"

"It would be something to leave the world changed in such a profound manner," Octavian said. "But I think we still have a long way to go."

"I'll begin that journey now," Yarrow said. "I believe a large piece of this puzzle lies in the desert to the north of here."

"It does." Blue-black feathers landed on the polished tiles, followed by bare feet with toes tipped in long, black talons. Courtenay flinched from the large, nearly naked creature with the curved ebony horns.

"Bensali," Jorian whispered.

"My friend." The creature bowed. "Have you figured out the puzzle I gave you?"

"No, not yet," Jorian said. "Though it has made me think."

"Always a good thing." Bensali's smile revealed long, sharp fangs. "And I have the utmost faith in you."

"You could just tell me." Jorian stood without flinching, looking up at the creature.

"What fun would that be?"

Yarrow stepped close to Bensali, the blue light in their eyes seeming to volley back and forth. "You know of what I seek?"

"I think I do. I think I know a great deal about you, and I think we can assist each other. And if we can't, we can certainly entertain each other."

"Let's go," Yarrow said, his hand closing around a suede pouch hanging from his neck.

"I'm coming with you." Sasha came to stand behind Yarrow.

"And what if I don't agree?" Bensali asked.

"Then I'll kill you."

The creature grinned as if certain Sasha was joking, but the smile slowly slipped from his face, replaced by some mélange of caution and temptation. "Then I suppose I should agree. But just the two of you. I am not heading a caravan."

"The rest of us will stay here," Octavian said. "We don't know what might happen in the next few weeks. The situation is still volatile, and we must handle it carefully."

"The next few weeks will be filled with dinners and meetings," N'hahseen said, "as I endeavor to convince our old allies to side with me and the Twenty-Nine against the blessed sovereign of Selindria and Gaeltheon. It will be as complex and delicate as any spell any of us has ever cast."

For Courtenay, it was like staring out across a plain covered in mist. They'd sent out their voices, their intentions, and now they could only wait for the echoes to come back, for the call to be answered or ignored. Until then, they were stumbling blindly through uncharted lands. She walked around the pool and sat next to Jorian and N'hahseen, because it wasn't as frightening if she had a hand to hold, if she knew she wouldn't get swallowed up by the fog and cut off. If they got lost, at least they would be lost together. "I'll do what I can."

Jorian stood quickly. "I almost forgot." He hurried to give Yarrow a strange, clear dagger he'd had sheathed on his belt. "I was supposed to give this to you."

When Yarrow looked at the knife, his eyes reflected its light—or it reflected the light from his eyes. "Keep it. I don't need it now that I can remember."

"Remember what?" Courtenay couldn't help asking.

"Ash and echoes, the things that were, that can be again. They *want* to be. They're calling. I… I have to go." Yarrow opened his wings, clutched Sasha to his chest, and ascended toward the open doors of the balcony above. Bensali followed, and soon they both became specks on the horizon, and then they were gone.

"I almost envy them," Octavian said. "I cannot even imagine what they will see, what they'll learn. I wonder if we'll see them again."

"We will," Courtenay said with certainty. "Do you know what we should do while we wait?"

N'hahseen raised an eyebrow and everyone else stared at her.

"We should have some fun. I miss having fun. We should find some food, some wine, some musicians…. The world tearing apart can wait a little longer, yes? If we can't be happy for one night, what are we saving, anyway?"

Book One of the Blessed Epoch

For the past few years Yarroway L'Estrella has lived in exile, gathering arcane power. But that power came at a price, and he carries the scars to prove it. Now he must do his duty: his uncle, the king, needs him to escort Prince Garith to his wedding, a union that will create an alliance between the two strongest countries in the known world. But Yarrow isn't the prince's only guard. A whole company of knights is assigned to the mission, and Yarrow's not sure he trusts their leader.

Knight Duncan Purefroy isn't sure he trusts Yarrow either, but after a bizarre occurrence during their travels, they have no choice but to work together—especially since the incident also reveals a disturbing secret, one that might threaten the entire kingdom.

The precarious alliance is strained further when a third member joins the cause for reasons of his own—reasons that may not be in the best interests of the prince or the kingdom. With enemies at every turn, no one left to trust, and the dark power within Yarrow pulling dangerously away from his control, the fragile bond the three of them have built may be all that stands between them and destruction.

www.dsppublications.com

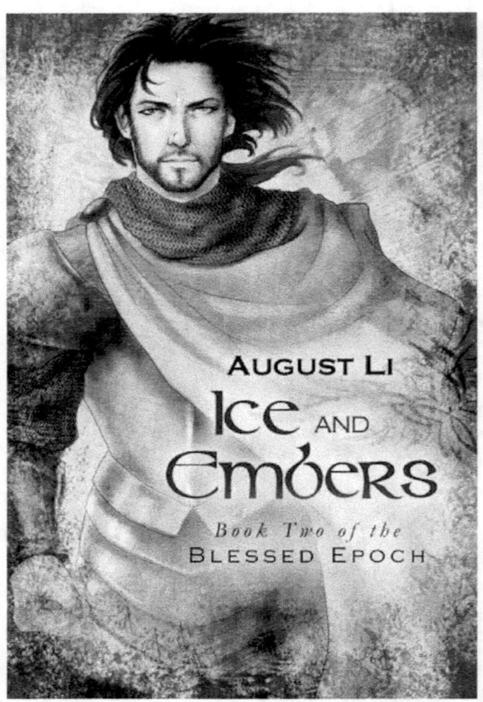

Book Two of the Blessed Epoch

Despite their disparate natures, Yarrow, Duncan, and Sasha united against overwhelming odds to save Prince Garith's life. Now Garith is king and the three friends may be facing their undoing.

Distraught over Yarrow's departure to find the cure to his magical affliction, Duncan struggles with his new role as Bairn of Windwake, a realm left bankrupt and in turmoil by his predecessor. Many of Duncan's vassals conspire against him, and Sasha's unorthodox solutions to Duncan's problem have earned them the contempt of Garith's nobles.

When word reaches Duncan and Sasha that Yarrow is in danger, they want nothing more than to rush to his aid. But Duncan's absence could tip Windwake into the hands of his enemies. In addition, a near-mythic order of assassins wants Sasha dead. Without Yarrow, Duncan and Sasha can't take the fight to the assassins. They are stuck, entangled in a political world they don't understand. But finding Yarrow may cause more problems, and with his court divided, King Garith must strike a balance between supporting his friends and assuaging the nobles who want Duncan punished—and Sasha executed.

www.dsppublications.com

Book Three of the Blessed Epoch

Sasha was born to, and has always defined himself by, the secret assassins' Order of the Crimson Scythe. He chose the love of Yarrow L'Estrella and Duncan Purefroy over his duty to his clan, forfeiting his last mission and allowing Prince Garith to live. Now, the order—previously Sasha's family—has branded him a traitor. He's marked, and that means the brethren of the Crimson Scythe won't stop until Sasha is dead.

Garith's twin kingdoms balance on the brink of war, and all three men have reasons to help the king, whether loyalty, duty, the interests of their own lands, or gold in their pockets. Still, Yarrow and Duncan are willing to abandon their reasons to seek out and destroy the assassins' order to keep Sasha safe. But Sasha isn't sure that's what he wants. Loyalties are strained by both foreign invaders and conspirators in their midst. It's hard to know which side to choose with threats piling up from every direction and war looming, inevitable, on the horizon. Their world teeters on the precipice of change, and Sasha, Duncan, and Yarrow can only hope the links they've forged will hold if Garith's kingdom is torn apart.

www.dsppublications.com

Book Four of the Blessed Epoch

An assassin's unexpected mercy granted Octavian Rose his life and freed him from his father's control, but it left him with little more than the clothes on his back and the determination not to waste his chance at a life of his choosing.

As Octavian sets out to make a name for himself, he refuses to compromise his ideals for money or status—a decision tested as he works his way up the ranks as a mercenary fighter and novice mage. Along the way he forges friendships, takes lovers, and makes bitter enemies, all while striving for the power he feels he deserves and can wield fairly.

With the advent of the Blessed Epoch and the discovery of new cultures, the world is changing. Octavian's decisions will affect not only those closest to him but will have profound worldwide consequences that he cannot begin to imagine. For twenty years, Octavian does what he must, and his choices bring him brilliant victories alongside crushing losses. Time and again, he must choose between what is right for all and what is beneficial to him, while hoping for the wisdom to tell the difference.

www.dsppublications.com

AUGUST LI is an author and artist. He's a lover of cats, foxes, books, video games, Asian ball-joint dolls, and all forms of creative expression. All of his extra time and money go toward traveling and exploring as much of the world as possible. Born in Hong Kong, he lives in Philadelphia, Pennsylvania, with two cats and many imaginary friends.

Blog: foxhatandfriends.wordpress.com

Also from DSP Publications

www.dsppublications.com

For more
great fiction
from

DSP PUBLICATIONS

visit us online.
WWW.DSPPUBLICATIONS.COM